"Beth O'Leary can do no wro books, and *The Wake-Up Cal* ___ gorgeous, evocative romance. Beth has a gift for creating complicated, tenderhearted characters and dreamy, whimsical settings that you never want to leave behind. Put this on your TBR immediately."

—Carley Fortune, *New York Times* bestselling author of
Meet Me at the Lake

"This delicious rom-com will please even the most jaded readers."

—Good Morning America

"This is Beth O'Leary at the height of her powers. Hypnotically good, fresh, fun, and moving, with one-liners that made my sides hurt, characters I want to take out to dinner, and one of the best endings I've read in some time. This is not just a great rom-com, this is a Beth O'Leary rom-com, and in my opinion there is no better writer out there."

—Gillian McAllister, *New York Times* bestselling author of
Wrong Place Wrong Time

"Beth O'Leary never misses. *The Wake-Up Call* bursts with Beth's signature heart, wit, and charm, topped with sizzling enemies-to-lovers banter. Brimming with palpable warmth and depth of character, this one is for the hopeless romantics in all of us."

—Amy Lea, internationally bestselling author of *Exes and O's*

PRAISE FOR
The No-Show

"Beth O'Leary is that rare, one-in-a-million talent who can make you laugh, swoon, cry, and ache all in the same book, and *The No-Show* is her most moving yet. O'Leary's wit, charm, and heart are on full, fantastic display in this cozy, surprising, and deeply satisfying novel. I couldn't possibly love it more."

—Emily Henry, *New York Times* bestselling author of *Book Lovers*

"Achingly clever."

—Sophie Cousens, *New York Times* bestselling author of *Before I Do*

"It's the kind of book that leaves an impression on your heart. A truly special read." —Holly Miller, author of *What Might Have Been*

"There are few authors who are able to capture the realities of romance and the deep impacts of trauma, let alone in the same book. . . . As O'Leary's layered and enthralling story unfolds over the course of the book, she reveals her characters to be so unavoidably human it's hard not to relate to them, even if you've never climbed a tree." —*USA Today*

PRAISE FOR

The Road Trip

"This book is perfect." —Rosie Walsh, bestselling author of *Ghosted*

"As with her surprise hit *The Flatshare*, O'Leary expertly balances humor and heart while introducing a zany cast of twentysomethings. . . . Readers won't want this crazy road trip to end."

—*Publishers Weekly*

"*The Road Trip* is a humorous yet deeply moving journey toward confronting the past, forgiveness, and reconciliation, with a poignant detour to a summer of young love in Provence. I loved the vivid cast and the depth and intimacy in O'Leary's writing."

—Helen Hoang, *New York Times* bestselling author of
The Heart Principle

"Read this! Absolutely loved it!"

—Christina Lauren, *New York Times* bestselling author of
The Soulmate Equation

TITLES BY BETH O'LEARY

The Flatshare
The Switch
The Road Trip
The No-Show
The Wake-Up Call
Swept Away

Swept Away

Beth O'Leary

Berkley Romance
New York

BERKLEY ROMANCE
Published by Berkley
An imprint of Penguin Random House LLC
1745 Broadway, New York, NY 10019
penguinrandomhouse.com

Book design by Daniel Brount

Library of Congress Cataloging-in-Publication Data
Names: O'Leary, Beth, author.
Title: Swept away / Beth O'Leary.
Description: First edition. | New York: Berkley Romance, 2025.
Identifiers: LCCN 2024029839 (print) | LCCN 2024029840 (ebook) |
ISBN 9780593640142 (trade paperback) | ISBN 9780593640159 (ebook)
Subjects: LCGFT: Romance fiction. | Novels.
Classification: LCC PR6115.L424 S94 2025 (print) | LCC PR6115.L424 (ebook) |
DDC 823/.92—dc23/eng/20240712
LC record available at https://lccn.loc.gov/2024029839
LC ebook record available at https://lccn.loc.gov/2024029840

First Edition: April 2025

Printed in the United States of America
1st Printing

The authorized representative in the EU for product safety and compliance is
Penguin Random House Ireland, Morrison Chambers, 32 Nassau Street,
Dublin D02 YH68, Ireland. https://eu-contact.penguin.ie

*For my parents, who have always been there for me,
no matter how choppy the waves*

Swept Away

DAY ONE

Zeke

I WAKE UP on the houseboat wearing a trilby.

. . . huh.

I look around, moving gingerly. You've got to approach a hangover like this carefully in case it's a feral one. The boat's not changed much in the last five years: same wonky rectangular skylight, same wooden cupboards built into the sloping walls. One thing should be different, though—there should be a Lexi in this bed with me. A gorgeous, surprising, complicated Lexi.

I frown up at the skylight, pushing the hat back off my forehead. Has she . . . already left? I thought we'd have coffee first, at least, but I guess this is karma doing her thing. You can change your ways, but the past'll always catch up to you, and I've snuck out of enough morning afters to earn a stint as the one left behind.

The houseboat sways beneath me. I grip the side table. Must be one of the larger boats from the marina passing too quickly. There was a surprising amount of that last night, and some drunk idiot threw something at the hull, too. The sound had been loud enough to make Lexi pause beneath me for a few gasping breaths before she said, *Do we need to go check that out?* We'd started to get up, then kissed again, then forgotten all about it. It was an amazing night—worth breaking all my rules for. The sort of sex that makes you wonder why you ever do anything but that.

I close my eyes again. God, she was beautiful. Is beautiful. I guess she's still beautiful, she's just doing it somewhere else.

There's a new cold twinge in my stomach, a kind of wistful sad feeling, and I stay still for another moment to figure it out. I think I'm almost . . . missing her. Which is ridiculous. We met *yesterday*. Maybe this is the thing everyone says happens once you "open yourself up to finding something meaningful"—the bit where suddenly everything seems to hurt. Not sure how I feel about it, so far.

I slide out from under the duvet, shedding my trilby and reaching for my boxers. When I open the bedroom door, I find Lexi standing at the sink in the tiny galley kitchen, wearing the same massive bun and irritated scowl she had when we first met. I smile when I see her, and it feels sort of like a reflex, like jumping at a loud noise. I'm glad she's still here. She doesn't smile back.

"Oh," she says. "You're up. I'm just figuring out coffee."

"Hey. Yeah, sorry, I should be doing that," I say, immediately getting distracted by the sight of myself in the bathroom mirror.

The door to the bathroom is just behind Lexi, a concertina one that my dad made himself. It's folded back into the frame right now, giving me a full view of my embarrassing bed hair. I pat sleepily at my head, despite having been cursed with this hair for twenty-three years and knowing full well that without mousse there's absolutely no way to sort out the situation. One curl's sticking up at the front, like a question mark hovering above my forehead. Should've kept the trilby on.

"There's no kettle," Lexi mumbles, pulling open all the cupboard doors in turn. This shouldn't take long—there're only four—but she does each of them twice, in a different order, as if she's not sure which one she looked in last.

Guessing Lexi's not a morning person, either.

"Yeah, no," I say, having another go at my hair. "I don't think the boat's hooked up to shore power anyway right now, and . . ." I lean to open the fridge beneath the countertop, then wince. It smells of gone-off cheese. "Yeah—the battery's flat."

I pause midway through closing the fridge. That's weird. It's fully stocked with food. I asked to buy all fixtures, fittings and furnishings, and the seller agreed to leave basic bedding and kitchen essentials, since it was a rental and she wasn't attached to any of that stuff anyway. But do fixtures and fittings include, like, groceries?

"The fridge isn't working?" Lexi says, ducking down to stick her hand inside. "Shit. I didn't notice."

She rubs her forehead. She's got a thin gold ring on her pinkie finger and it catches in a sunbeam edging through the kitchen window's curtains. The kitchen on this boat leads straight into a living space that's maybe three meters by two: it's got a wood burner, two fixed chairs and a corner sofa. The fixed chairs are new. I don't love them—there's not really room. I frown, noticing that the cushions from the sofa seem to have ended up on the opposite side of the boat sometime during the night. Which is . . . also weird. Was that us, last night?

"I'm not totally on top of everything right now," Lexi says, testing how cold the milk is with the back of her hand. "Seems I can't offer you a coffee."

"You don't need to make me a coffee. Why don't I go out for them? Bring us back some pastries and flat whites."

She looks up at me, suddenly focused. I wonder if it was the term *pastries* or *flat whites* that got through to her.

She takes me in. Her eyes scan across my bare chest and flick up to my bad hair. Lexi's eyes are round and icy blue. Sharkish, in a gorgeous kind of way. They're what snagged me at the bar—well, not first, first was her line about how *suffragettes died for this shit,* then second was the curves, *then* it was the eyes. They're what made me break my rules.

"I've actually got quite a bit to do today, so . . ." She looks away.

No coffee, then. All right. That's fine. Better, probably.

"Can I walk you to your boat?"

Her eyes snap back to mine. "What?"

"Uh . . . I just . . . was thinking I could walk you back . . . ? Or not?"

She's looking at me as though maybe I'm really stupid, even though last night she'd said, *You're smart, aren't you? Not school-smart, but actually clever.* It'd made me embarrassingly happy—I've never been called clever before, except in a sentence like, *You think you're so clever, don't you, Ezekiel?*

"You don't need to walk me anywhere," she says. "This is where I'm staying. I'm staying on this boat."

"Umm . . . hey? What do you mean?"

"I'm staying on this boat," she repeats slowly. "As in, this is my friend Penny's houseboat. And I'm staying here for a bit."

"Uh? No? This is my houseboat," I say, leaning a hand on the counter as the floor shifts beneath me. "I bought it on Wednesday."

Lexi's eyes grow even wider. "Are you fucking with me or something?" she asks, straightening up to her full five foot one—five foot three if you count the bun, she'd said at the pub.

"No," I say, trying to focus. I need water, fried food and one of those coffees that's so strong it erodes the roof of your mouth as you drink. "It used to be my dad's. He lived here when I was a kid. When he passed away a few years ago, I sold it, but then I decided . . . Yeah. You know. I came up here to buy it back. Didn't we talk about this last night?"

More deadpan staring.

"We talked about you buying a houseboat last night, yes," she says. "But it wasn't this houseboat. Because this is Penny's houseboat."

I guess I'm . . . missing something here?

"Is this a joke?" I ask.

Lexi reaches into the back pocket of her jeans and tugs out her mobile phone, frowning for a moment before shoving it back in again. "OK, I have no signal, but if I did, I'd show you—it's on Houseboat Getaway Rentals."

"It was on Houseboat Getaway Rentals," I acknowledge. "Before I bought it. Is your Penny called Penelope Manley?"

Lexi freezes. "Yes," she says, voice low with suspicion.

"Right," I say, relieved. "Then she just sold me this boat."

"No, she didn't," Lexi says, after a moment's pause. "No, she didn't. She would have told me if she was selling this boat. It wouldn't be online anymore, either—it wouldn't be showing up on Houseboat Getaway whatever-it-is, would it? That's . . . No." She scowls, shoulders tense now. She's getting upset. "Is that why you came home with me from the pub? So you could get on this boat and claim squatters' rights, or something?"

"No! What? I didn't even . . ." I rub my eyes hard. "Last night . . ." I try to piece it back together. "I fobbed us into the marina. We chatted to Paige, you helped her sort the rope, then . . . we headed in. How did you not realize this was my houseboat?"

"*You* helped her sort the rope. And *I* fobbed us into the marina."

This kind of feels like pointless semantics, as my sister, Lyra, would say.

"Didn't it seem weird to you that Paige said it was my boat?"

"She didn't," Lexi says, staring at me. "She said . . ." She presses her hand to her forehead. "I can't remember exactly, but I'd remember if she'd said that. This is ridiculous. Penny wouldn't sell the houseboat without telling me. The key was still in the key safe, everything is the same as always . . ."

"I picked up the keys from the company that manages the boat rental yesterday," I say. Though I haven't actually checked there aren't extras in the key safe, so I guess she could be telling the truth.

"This doesn't make any sense."

Lexi looks around, staring at the mustard-colored curtains pulled across the windows, the bland seaside paintings, the kitschy corgi-themed clock screwed to the wall in the narrow sliver of space between the bedroom doorframe and the kitchen cabinets. I follow her gaze and notice the time. Half twelve. I'm always a fan of a long lie-in, but that's late even for me. When I turn back to Lexi, she looks kind of crumpled, as if someone's just given her some really bad news, and I feel shitty all of a sudden, because I think that someone might be me.

"Shall we go out for coffee?" I say. "Talk this over properly?"

She's frowning down at her phone again.

"Lexi?"

"No," she says, looking up at last. "I'm not going to leave the houseboat. It doesn't seem sensible. In the circumstances." She gives me a rare smile. It looks totally insincere. "You are welcome to leave the boat, though."

. . . hmm.

"Shall we at least sit down?"

"Maybe you could put some trousers on," she says, "if you're going to sit on Penny's sofa."

"It's not . . ."

I deliberate. Best not. Caffeine first.

"I'll get dressed," I say, turning on my heel and stepping back into the bedroom.

My bag is jammed by the bed, sitting in a pool of sunlight. It looks like a perfect July day outside—the skylight shows a rectangle of rich blue sky.

As I yank on last night's trousers and the one clean T-shirt I packed, I try to sort my head out. Being back on Dad's old house-boat is weird enough without adding in a beautiful woman who won't let me sit on the sofa.

I emerge from the bedroom to find Lexi staring at the little wood burner as if she's lost in thought. She looks a bit intimidating: the leather jacket, the frown, the way she plants her feet like she's waiting for you to try to throw her off balance. She makes me want to figure her out, which I have no right to do. This was a one-night thing, even if it's dragged on a bit. She was very clear about that, and . . .

"I'd like you to go," she says.

. . . she's definitely not changed her mind.

"Last night was . . . Well. You know, you were there," she says. "But we had an agreement, so yeah. Thanks. Good-bye."

I'm the one who's staring now. She might play tough, but she's not meeting my eyes. I'm hit with a memory of the two of us kissing against the marina fence last night. *What the fuck are you doing to me, Zeke?* she'd said. *I'm literally shaking.*

"I'm not leaving. This is my boat."

I pull out my phone. I've not got any signal. I know Gilmouth's not exactly the metropolis of Northumberland, but how have they not sorted out their rubbish phone coverage yet?

"I'm sure I can find something in my emails that proves I bought it."

I scroll through the downloaded messages, trying not to get pissed off. People often take me for a pushover—it's the clothes, maybe, or the "propensity to daydream," as my mum always puts it. But I'll stand up for myself when I have to.

"Let's just go somewhere where we've got some signal," I say, giving up on my email. All my downloaded ones seem to be news-letters from brands telling me how eco they are.

"OK. You first," she says, tipping her head toward the door.

"Seriously?"

She just blinks at me.

"You want me to walk out first? What, so you can . . . shut me out? Of my own boat?"

"I have no reason to think you own this boat."

"What about my *key*," I say, but I'm already patting my pockets and realizing I don't know where it is. Bedside table? In my bag? "Look," I say, "if you want, we can walk through the door together."

We both turn to look at the short, narrow door to the deck.

"This is ridiculous," Lexi says.

"No, yeah, I'm with you on that."

We wait in silence, contemplating the door. She glances at me. Checking to see if I'm budging. I look back at her, perfectly polite, not going anywhere.

"Oh, fine," Lexi snaps. "I'll go first."

She wrenches the door open, and then pauses there, framed against the sky.

I let myself look at her. Hourglass figure, bun shifting on the top of her head as the water tips us back and forth, her big black boots braced on the bottom step. I've never met anyone like Lexi before. Suddenly that new cold twinge starts up in my stomach again and I don't want her to walk out of that door.

"Wait," I say, just as she turns to look at me.

I inhale. Her expression's completely changed. She looks . . . horrified.

"Zeke," she says, staggering up the steps onto the tiny deck.

I'm right behind her. I duck through the door. The first thing that gets through to me is the smell, not what I'm looking at—it smells fresh, like sun and salt.

I straighten up and stare out at the water.

Water. Just water. Sea and sky and sea and sky and sea and sky. No boats. No marina.

No *land*.

"Fuck," Lexi says, clinging to the railing. "Zeke—are we out at sea?"

THE DAY BEFORE

Lexi

I SLUMP OVER the bar of The Anchor, reaching one hand out for the glass of red wine that Marissa is pouring me. She holds it slightly out of reach, so I have to grope around and eventually lift my head to locate it. I glower; she smiles.

"All set on the houseboat?"

"Well, I've stocked it with carbs, cheese and booze, if that's what you mean."

"That'll do. I really am sorry about the room," Marissa says.

I take a slug of wine and then fold over again, resting my cheek on the sticky surface of the bar top. The smell of the pub is so familiar to me: hops, frying oil, the fuzzy tang of a Hoover run over dirty carpet. It's the smell of my childhood—my life, really. I was raised here, and here is where I've stayed.

"It's all right. Not your fault that I picked this week to try out being overdramatic," I say, flashing a tooth-baring smile at the fisherman staring at me from the other end of the bar.

You can tell the fishermen by their waterproof trousers and wrinkles. When I was a kid, they were always the worst for the hair-ruffling. *Sweet little thing!* they'd say to five-year-old Penny, when she started spending time here in the pub. *Cute as a button!* With my bowl cut, square shoulders and blockish face, I always got, *Hello, little lad!* This particular fisherman looks startled by my humorless grin and goes back to staring into his pint.

"Well, still, I'm sorry I scheduled my building work for the week you decided to lose your shit," Marissa says, patting my hand.

Marissa owns The Anchor now—we sold it to her once we finally teetered close enough to bankruptcy to allow ourselves the luxury of giving up on Mum's dream for good. I am still co-manager, but Marissa employs me these days instead of the other way around. Everyone felt sorry for me and Penny when we had to sell up and move to one of the new flats around the corner, but all I felt was relief.

Marissa is redecorating the bedrooms upstairs, which means I can't crash here. This is unfortunate, given that I just marched out of my home with half my belongings in a duffel bag and have nowhere else to go.

Thank God the houseboat is unoccupied this week. It took me five attempts to get the combination of the key safe right, but I got there eventually.

"You need more friends," Marissa says.

This is probably true. I'm not the loads-of-friends type, though. I have my people, all fiercely precious to me, their spots in my life hard-won. I have my family. And that's it. I should try to make new friends, really, but that requires *putting yourself out there*, and—worst of all—waiting around to see if people still like you once you have.

"And a boyfriend," Marissa says.

"What is this, the 1950s? I don't need a boyfriend. Suffragettes died for that shit, Marissa."

"You need *something*," Marissa counters, wiping down the Stella tap. "Other than your job. Which you don't even like."

"I like my job!" I protest, still face down on the bar at which I work.

"You're only saying that because I pay you."

"I had Mae," I say, and I'm embarrassed to hear my voice catch on her name. "I didn't need anything else."

"You still have Mae, Lexi," Marissa says softly. "Just maybe not for every minute of the day anymore."

I lift my head and twist in my seat, my heart clenching tightly. I can't think about this. Not seeing Mae wake up with wonky plaits every morning. Not seeing Mae padding downstairs with Harvey the bunny tucked in the crook of her elbow when she can't sleep. Not seeing Mae for all those thoughtless little Mae moments of the day, the ones that make my life into something meaningful.

I down a few more mouthfuls of wine. Marissa watches me critically, then shoves her glasses back up on her head, catching a loop of her mousey hair so it sticks up behind them. I don't bother telling her—she won't care.

"I think what you *really* need is a distraction," she says, then turns to scan around the pub. "There," she says. "The man by the window with the book."

"He sounds pretentious," I say, without looking around.

"That was impressively judgmental, even by my standards," Marissa says, pulling her glasses back down onto her nose again. "Though you may not be totally wrong. He's dressed like he's in a magazine shoot. But he's reading a self-help book. And he's drinking a pint of bitter. I don't know how to add these things up. Are those trousers made of *velvet*?"

Fine: I'm curious. I turn on my bar stool to look at the man sitting in the paisley armchair in the window, the one with the best view over the marina.

His outfit is what draws the eye first. He's wearing a suit waistcoat, silky and gray, with no shirt underneath, and three fine silver necklaces lie against the triangle of his bare chest. His black velvet trousers are tucked into his boots, which are stretched out lazily under the table. Generally speaking, the only men you see in The Anchor with their trousers tucked into their boots are ramblers, and they do not look like this.

Above it all is a mop of dark brown ringlets, parted in the center. He's a lot younger than I expected when Marissa said *man with book*—twenty, maybe. But there's an old-soul vibe to him. I can picture him sitting in a bar in the 1920s, wearing braces, or maybe further back still—maybe he should be leaning lackadaisically against a ballroom fireplace in *Bridgerton*.

I swallow. I don't want a guy who looks like that. If I'm going to distract myself, I want someone I feel comfortable with. Someone average.

"He's basically a teenager," I say, turning back to Marissa.

Marissa squints at him. "Oh yeah, he is kind of young. The biceps threw me off."

Despite myself, I glance back over my shoulder. He's shifted, and now I can see the front cover of his book. I almost laugh. *Surviving Modern Love*. It's a dating guide that's everywhere at the moment—Penny's been trying to get me to read it for weeks. It's aimed at desperate women who suddenly feel their biological clock has started ticking, aka me—not at twenty-year-old boys who look as if they might front a reasonably successful pop-rock band. If pop-rock is still a thing.

He looks up and meets my eyes. A shiver runs over me like a bird skimming the water. The corner of his lip lifts in a curious smile, drawing a faint dip in his cheek.

I snap back to Marissa. My heart is suddenly thrumming.

"I believe I just witnessed a *moment*," Marissa drawls. "Eyes meeting, sparks flying, et cetera."

"You witnessed a man wondering why the two women at the bar are openly staring at his trousers."

"That boy is not unaccustomed to being stared at," Marissa says, examining him again over her glasses. "You don't dress like that to fit in. Hang on, Penny's calling me," she says, checking her phone.

"Don't answer."

Marissa cuts me a look.

"You'll have to lie when she asks whether I'm OK," I say. "You hate lying."

She rolls her eyes, but lets the call ring out, then frowns at her phone.

"*Gack*," she says. Marissa's favorite non–swear word—she used to swear like a sailor, but with Mae around all the time, she had to adapt. "Take the bar, would you? I need to call a supplier."

I assess how drunk I am. Medium drunk. Perfectly acceptable here at The Anchor.

"Sure," I say, already sliding off the stool.

By the time I'm behind the bar, grabbing my apron and securing it at my waist, the book-reading velvet-wearing twenty-something is walking over. I shoot a venomous look at Marissa, who smiles smugly at me over her shoulder as she heads to the door. She has coordinated this beautifully. Call a supplier, my arse. She just saw he'd need a new drink and wanted me behind the taps before he got to the bar.

"I thought you hated lying!" I shout at her as she opens the door.

"Doesn't mean I'm bad at it!" she yells back.

And just like that, he's right there in front of me.

"Hey, can I get you a drink?" he says, tilting his head.

He's taller than I thought he might be when I was checking him out at his table, and he speaks quietly, leaning his forearms on the bar as he looks at me. He's got heavy eyebrows, almost too heavy for the delicate lines of his face; he's the sort of handsome that only works in certain lights, but when it works, it's stunning.

"I think that's my line," I say.

He pauses, thinking. "Huh," he says, glancing back at the paisley armchair. "When I was sitting there thinking about what to say . . . you were not the bartender."

I press my lips together to hold back a smile. I hope he can't tell how much he's surprised me. I know I should have the confidence to think a man like this would fall over himself to buy me a drink, but I don't, not anymore. I am painfully conscious of my roots showing, and the fact that I've probably owned the leather jacket I'm wearing since he was in primary school.

Then there's the dogged misery in my chest. The sense of loss. Maybe the issue isn't that I'm thirty-one, it's that I feel about one hundred.

"Well, things change," I say. "What can I get you?"

"Uh," he says, "a large gin and tonic?"

I reach for a clean glass. He watches me, a slight frown gathering between his eyebrows. Marissa's right: he doesn't quite add up. I'd say he's the artistic loner type, a bit brooding, a bit lost. A hot emo kid born in the wrong decade. But that *really* doesn't mesh with the shiny self-help book in his hand.

He catches where I'm looking. "You read it?" he asks.

"Nope. Any good?"

"A lot of people seem to think so," he says, turning it to look over the back cover. "Says here it's 'the answer to our prayers: a guide to finding authentic connection within the confining artifices of modernity.'"

I raise my eyebrows. "And what do you think?"

He pauses at the question, tilting his head the other way. There's something a little dreamy about his eyes, almost a sleepiness; it's strangely sexy, as if I'm seeing him just after he's woken up.

"I think it's a big pile of bollocks," he says lightly.

I have to bite back another smile. "Nine fifty," I say, pushing the gin and tonic with lime toward him.

If I hadn't already known he lived down south from his accent, I'd have got it from his face now—he looks briefly staggered to have got a double for less than a tenner. He taps his phone to the card reader and then pushes the drink back toward me.

"It's for you," he says. "How'd I do?"

I consider it. I do like a gin and tonic. "Not bad," I say, reaching for it.

His face melts into its first proper smile. His front teeth are slightly crooked, touching each other like crossed fingers; he bites down on his smile before it's fully grown.

"Can I ask your name?" he says.

I force my gaze away, across the pub, noting the regulars— Barney, Hazzer, the woman who always orders double shots of whisky. I can't decide if I want them to come over and save me from this conversation or stay where they are.

"It's Lexi," I say eventually, because I can't think of a good reason not to answer.

"I'm Zeke. Ezekiel Ravenhill. Full name in case you want to stalk me." He taps *Surviving Modern Love*. "It says here that before 'progressing with an individual,' you should have researched each other on every available social media platform. It's in the section on the advantages of modernity."

I stare at the book in horror. "Fucking hell, really?" I look up at him. "Is that what people do?" I just about swallow back the *nowadays*, narrowly avoiding sounding eighty-five.

"Well, not me," he says. "I'm not online."

"Really? No social media at all?"

I find this unfathomable—I'm absolutely addicted to Instagram. Sometimes I don't even notice myself opening the app, I'm just there, scrolling through everyone else's lives, getting progressively, predictably sadder.

"It's just not for me." He shrugs, settling on a stool. "This book says you've got to embrace that stuff if you want to survive, so . . . I guess I'm a dying breed."

He looks genuinely sad as he says this, which strikes me as odd—I am finding it hard to believe that a man like this needs advice from a self-help book. He is very assured in how he watches me, for instance, very smooth. Even when I'm not looking at him, I can feel his light, warm gaze taking me in.

I don't like being looked at, generally. It's easy when I'm with Mae—nobody looks at you twice if you've got a kid with you, as if you've entered some other category of personhood where you're always the supporting act. The same thing happens when you're the bartender, actually: you're part of the background. It suits me perfectly.

Then Zeke's eyes shift away from me as he looks around the pub. And to my surprise, I find I want his gaze back again.

"Sorry," he says. "I'm getting a weird case of déjà vu. Did this place use to have blue carpet?"

"Yeah, actually." We changed it after Mum died. A big revamp that we didn't yet realize we couldn't afford. "Have you been here before?"

"A while back, yeah. My dad used to live on a houseboat in the marina, so I was in Gilmouth a lot as a little kid. I've only been back once since I was thirteen, though—to sell his boat when he died."

"Oh," I say, a little startled. "I'm sorry."

"It's OK. I bought it back again yesterday."

"Oh, right," I say, trying to keep up.

"That's why I'm here. Buying back my dead dad's old boat, five years on. I've got two days off work and a whole big plan to put the past to rest and, like . . . sort my head out." He shakes his curls, as if he's trying to get water out of his ears, and gives me a rueful smile. "It's all part of my quarter-life crisis, according to my brother."

I think about the fact that I have just moved into my best friend's houseboat on the sly, with one holdall and two bags of food from Tesco, and I wonder if Zeke and I have more in common than I thought.

"So you know The Anchor?" I ask.

Those hazy eyes resettle on mine. They're light brown, almost amber.

"Dad never brought me here as a kid," he says. "But I might've been in when I came up to sell the boat. This bar feels familiar. You don't, though, and I feel like . . . I'd remember you. Were you working here in . . ." He glances aside as he tries to figure out the date. "Summer 2019?"

I think about it. I wasn't, actually. I spent that summer staying in a caravan in Devon with a baby-faced man named Theo, who I'd hoped was the love of my life. He got *Lexi forever* tattooed on his pasty upper arm, a rare act of rebelliousness that didn't suit him at all; I think it was because his ex had told him she liked men with tattoos. Even then, I'd had the sense not to get *Theo forever*—he'd accused me of commitment-phobia, but turns out I was just right. When I informed Theo that I planned to stay home and help my best friend raise her child, he left so fast he didn't even take his beloved Nintendo Switch.

"Nope," I say. "That was a rare summer off." My only summer off, actually.

"Knew it," Zeke says. "You're too beautiful to forget."

That makes me snort a laugh.

"You think I'm joking?"

"I think you've used that very cheesy line before."

"I mean it. You're really beautiful."

"I'm not. But thanks."

He pauses; I get the sense I've thrown him slightly.

"Sorry, what do you mean, *I'm not but thanks*?"

My head is a bit fuzzy from the wine, and my body wants to twist away from his compliments—I can't bear the way they make me feel. I shovel through the tub of ice to loosen it up.

"So, Zeke Ravenhill, who has all the smooth lines," I say, taking a savage stab at a particularly large lump of ice, "how am I meant to know you're not a total arsehole if you're not stalkable on social media?"

He looks back to *Surviving Modern Love*; I think he's weighing up whether to allow me the change of subject.

"Not sure my Instagram would be advertising the red flags, if I had it," he says eventually, running his hand across the front cover. "But it's a good question. If you want, we could, like, ring my mum?"

I chuck the shovel back into the tub and try to stand still, folding my arms. I'm a bit jittery. I've not felt this way around a man for so long; I'd forgotten the electric, zingy excitement of just *flirting* with someone.

"What would she say?" I ask.

He smiles slightly. "She'd probably say I'm a puzzle. That's what she usually says. 'You know, Ezekiel is a bit of an odd one out. But he means well, and when he realizes his potential he could really make something of himself,' et cetera. The sorts of things you say about your least successful child."

I lean back against the counter behind me. I wonder if he realizes how revealing that was, and how much more attractive it is than the chat-up lines—I have always had a soft spot for slightly broken people. I think again about Marissa's suggestion, that I just need a distraction, and I feel a whisper of the woman I was before: the woman who would never look at any guy and think he was too good for her.

"Is she right? Do you mean well?" I ask him.

"I do lots of things well," he says, poker-faced, but teasing.

Normally, when a guy chats me up, there's a pressure to the conversation, as though every word exchanged ups the expectation, but Zeke just seems as if he's . . . playing. It's confusing.

"Are you flirting with me because you want to have sex with me?" I ask, looking him right in the face.

I can't read Zeke's reaction. I expected him to seem startled, but he just looks down for a moment, as if he's gathering himself, or perhaps deliberating.

"I'm flirting with you because I think you seem interesting, and beautiful," he says lightly, looking up at me again. "And maybe kind of . . ."

Don't say sad. *Don't say* lonely.

"Bored?"

I blink.

"But is that what you want, Lexi?" His voice drops slightly, and my stomach turns over. "Is that what you're looking for?"

I open my mouth to say yes, but at the last moment I find myself blurting, "I'm thirty-one."

"OK," Zeke says, unperturbed. "I'm a Pisces." And then, at my unimpressed expression: "Are we not sharing facts about ourselves? Is that not the game?"

I snort. "You look about twenty. It would be weird. You're too young."

"I'm twenty-three. Not too young. Just right," he says, with a new, cheeky smile that draws a dimple in his left cheek.

The very thought of a night with this stranger who is eight years younger than me feels decadent and forbidden, but I don't have an early-morning wake-up to think of now. I don't have a little person to get home for—Mae is with Penny and Ryan. She's got everyone she needs.

"I want one night," I find myself saying. "One night of stupid, reckless fun. I want to get drunk and enjoy myself."

He tilts his head to the side. "I can give you that."

Heat unfurls in my belly like a rope snaking loose.

"When do you get off?" he asks, his voice steady. "Have a drink with me. Properly," he says, eyes flicking to the gin and tonic I've barely sipped while I've been busying myself behind the bar.

"I'm not actually working, officially. So . . . I'm free as soon as Marissa walks back through that door."

My gaze shifts toward the pub entrance. He turns slowly, exaggeratedly, and watches the door, too, shooting the occasional hot, amused glance over his shoulder at me. We wait. There's a low pulse beating through me now. I can't remember the last time I did something like this. Something irresponsible. Something spontaneous.

The door opens. My hand is already on my apron, fingers shaking a little as I untie its ribbons.

"Where are we going?" Zeke says, as I move around the bar toward him.

"Nowhere," I tell him. "This is Gilmouth. You want a drink, there's nowhere else to go."

Zeke

THERE GOES "COMMITTING to the long-term in both thought and action." There goes "dedicating oneself to the pursuit of authentic connection." I leave *Surviving Modern Love* on the bar as Lexi and I move to the armchairs by the window—looking at it just makes me feel guilty. It's the dumbest one of these books I've read so far anyway. What the hell are the "artifices of modernity"?

Truth is, it's been so long now, and I missed it, I guess. This easy back-and-forth with someone who really only wants one thing from me, something I know I can give. It means breaking all my rules, but . . . what's one more one-night stand, really? What's the harm?

Outside, the streetlights have come on, bright gold against the silhouetted masts of the marina. Lexi puts her feet up to rest on the old-fashioned radiator underneath the window, and I do the same, my black boots beside hers. Almost-but-not-quite touching.

There's a quiet promise of where the night's going in the air between us. I feel myself slipping into the rhythm of it all. The way our gazes meet, flit away, then join again, and how our bodies lean toward each other. Her saying *I want one night* keeps going around my head, and the way she looked as she said it, like even speaking it out loud was enough to turn her on.

"Are we wearing the same shoes?" Lexi asks, looking at them over her glass.

I knock her foot gently with mine. "That a problem?"

"Only because you wear them better."

I laugh. She stays deadpan—she's hardly cracked a smile since we started talking. Even sprawled out with her feet up, she still has one arm drawn across her body like a shield. Everything about Lexi's like this—kind of hemmed-in, muted, like someone's dialed her down. You can tell she's complicated.

I am *such* a sucker for complicated.

"I can't believe we've agreed to spend the night together before we've even kissed," she says, eyeing me. "This is extremely out of character for me, just so you know."

"Is that what kissing is, for you?" I say, amused. "Like an audition?"

The look she gives me says, *Yeah, duh. What else could it be?* And I think, OK, so someone's never kissed you like you deserve to be kissed, then.

"Come here," I say, tipping my chin.

She raises her eyebrows. "You come here."

I smile. She's actually making me a bit nervous, in that butterflies-in-the-stomach kind of way—something about this night feels different from the nights I've had before. Maybe it's me, changing. I hope so.

I drag my chair right up to Lexi's, arm to arm, then twist in my seat so I'm facing her. She looks back, tense and kind of defiant, almost as if she's daring me to do it. I don't say anything; I just wait and watch her from a few breaths away. I want to see her relax before I move to touch her.

She takes a swig of wine, holding my gaze. She's breathing a bit unsteadily now, and I feel my body tighten in response.

"Go on, then," she prompts.

I just tilt my head. Keep looking. Trace over her features, those extraordinary, icy blue eyes, the strong set to her jaw. I watch her lips part, feel her gaze touch my mouth, and I keep waiting.

She huffs. "Fine," she says, and leans over to kiss me.

I can tell from the way she kisses that Lexi thinks I'm a kid who doesn't really know what to do—she thinks she's going to have to show me how. It doesn't take long to fix that. I slant her mouth to mine, ease back, feel for what she likes. She lets out a surprised hot breath when I brush my tongue lightly against hers, so I do it again, and smile against her mouth when her fingertips tighten on my forearm.

"Huh," she says, breathless, as I pull back a little.

She's looking at me differently. I swallow, glancing away toward the bar.

"Do that again," she says, reaching up to turn my face back toward her.

I pull her in. After a few minutes of kissing her, I can feel the impatience in her body, that buzz she's holding in.

"Let's go," she breathes.

I shake my head.

"We've got all night," I say, smoothing back a loose strand of her hair. "I promised you stupid and reckless and fun. So . . ."

I raise my eyebrows at her, like, *What does stupid and reckless and fun look like to you?*

Lexi's eyes dial a little brighter. "All right," she says. "Let's do shots."

~~~~~~

We finally leave The Anchor when a crowd of pub-crawlers arrive on a coach from Newcastle just before closing. I nick a brown trilby off the table as we go, and Lexi looks disapproving, even though it's a tacky dress-up one and all the kids in costume are too plastered to care.

"It's wrong to steal," she says, leaning into me.

"Not stealing—rehoming," I say. "Probably only cost him about two quid anyway."

She narrows those round eyes, looking up at me. "Am I being led astray right now, young man? Are you what astray looks like?"

I ignore the twinge in my chest and smile, kissing her again, my hands finding the dip where her leather jacket nips in. We stumble away from the bar, not wanting to break apart, until we reach the marina fence and press against it, first my back to the wire, then hers. Every centimeter of us is touching. Just the feel of her is enough to make me want her so much I'm aching, especially after making out in the pub like teenagers all evening. It's been a while, and I like this woman. A *lot*.

When we finally step apart, we're standing in a cloud.

A sea fret. A sudden fog coming off the water. I remember there was one when I visited my dad here as a kid. Like someone's taken an eraser to the world and left nothing but us.

Lexi pulls back, the fence bouncing a little against our weight, and says, "Am I drunker than I thought, or . . ."

"It's not just you. The world's gone."

"Oh. Well. I won't miss it," she says, and fists my waistcoat, pulling me in for another kiss as the fog smokes around us.

My lips feel burned and my chest's tight, as though something's winded me and I'm only just getting my breath back. Everything else that matters to me—work, those books, all the shit with my family . . . it's as though it's drifted away and tonight there's just Lexi.

I love this feeling. Nothing clears your mind like this kind of wanting.

"What the fuck are you doing to me, Zeke?" she whispers. "I'm literally shaking."

"Shall we go to my boat?" I ask, glancing in the direction of the marina gate and already fumbling in my pocket for my fob. It's the first time I've ever called it *my boat*. It feels kind of weird. I'm not a boat person. My dad was the boat person, and I was the person trying not to be my dad.

Lexi is leaning into me. "Let's go to mine."

"Sure, OK."

The moment I press my lips to hers again, she lets out a moan that sears right through me, turns me hard in an instant. We break apart when we reach the gate. She stumbles into the fence just as I reach to fob us in, and I think I've missed the sensor, but then the gate swings open and we're falling through the fog, already grasping each other again.

"Hang on," she says, pausing for a moment to squint into the darkness.

We've ended up right by Dad's—my—houseboat, its blue paint dim in the fog. You can't see much: the shape of an old-fashioned bicycle strapped to the roof, the thin metal chimney for the wood burner, *The Merry Dormouse* painted in white on the bow. I remember Mum carefully touching up those letters with a paintbrush, back when the boat was the family holiday spot, before the divorce—before it became Dad's home, and somewhere Mum was never welcome. In retrospect, it surprises me that he didn't rename it.

"Let's just . . ." Lexi begins, stepping toward the boat.

I do the same, then remember she wanted to go to her place, so I say, "Are you sure?"

She frowns at me. "Yeah. I'm sure."

"Your stern rope's snapped!" a voice calls down the pontoon.

Paige Something-or-other. I can't believe she's still kicking around this marina—her houseboat was always moored next to *The Merry Dormouse*. She's a bit . . . annoying. She would wander into our family evenings on the deck, "popping by" with a mug of herbal tea in her hand, hanging around until it was borderline uncomfortable. The kind of person who can't read a room. Her brother died, and after that she was *never the same again*, that's what Dad used to say—one of those meaningless phrases he trotted out all the time, like his favorite one about the split from my mum: *Some things are too broken to be fixed*.

"A snapped rope sounds bad?" Lexi says, pulling away from me to look.

"This boat always was too long for this pontoon. Here, it'll be all right, you can reconfigure your head line into two springs," Paige says, appearing suddenly through the fog. "That'll be fine for the night. If your friend gets the center of the rope looped around the cleat on the pontoon, I can make fast at the bow and stern if you just hold on to the boat for me. Tide's completely slack right now, so should be a super quick job."

"Thanks," Lexi and I say in unison.

I'm lost, to be honest. Dad wasn't particularly good on nautical lingo, and he never taught us this sort of stuff.

"I'll check in on you again in the morning with some spare rope, so we can get you properly moored," Paige says. "But this should do you for now, all right?"

She beams at us. She's probably quite nice, really. I bet she was just lonely, all those times she crashed our evenings. I can see it now that I'm not ten.

"That's really kind. Thank you for your help," Lexi says.

I grip the side of the boat as Lexi heads off to follow the instructions she's been given, and Paige works around us. This, I've done plenty of times—holding the boat steady for Dad was my and Jeremy's specialty, as kids. Lyra less so. It's always been hard to get my sister to do anything as obliging as helping out.

Things are spinning—I've had a shot or two too many, maybe. I take a breath, tasting the fog on my tongue, my body aching with

heat and desire. I can't even see Lexi—can't see further than a meter or so now, the fog's so thick—and the weird lost feeling freaks
me out a bit.

"Nearly there!" Paige shouts cheerfully from somewhere in
the fog.

Almost everything I recall about *The Merry Dormouse* is from
the time after my parents' divorce—I was only four when Dad came
to live here permanently. For a moment I feel as though I can hear
him playing his crappy homemade ukulele, or humming his way
around the kitchen, or puzzling over a sudoku with Lyra and Jeremy. I remember sitting on the deck with the two of them, Dad
hovering behind us as he taught us to fish. Even at that age I could
sense how desperately he wanted us to enjoy it, and the pressure of
it all had made me sweat, because of course I was shit at fishing, and
the others caught so many we had to freeze some.

"Paige's done, apparently," says a warm, throaty voice behind me.

I turn to see Lexi appearing from the mist, lips bee-stung,
cheeks flushed. She stumbles slightly and her body collides with
mine, and just like that we're kissing again. Within seconds, my
mind is one hundred percent her. There's . . . I don't know, there's
something about this woman. She's different, I think, and then I
tell myself she can't be. She just wants one night.

"Sleep well, you two!" Paige calls, distant in the darkness. The
fog whirls and steams, quieting the other sounds of the marina.

"Thank you so much for helping us out," I call, my hands still
resting on Lexi's waist.

I make a mental note to take Paige a bottle of wine tomorrow as
a thank-you, knowing already that I'll forget. I'm not good at that
kind of stuff even when I'm sober. Mental notes just drift out of my
head—I've always been that way.

"So," Lexi breathes, pulling back a little. "Bedroom?"

She cranes her head to look through the boat's windows.

"Yes. Definitely."

I help her up onto the deck. She tries the handle as I'm patting my pocket for the key, but it's open. I must've left the door unlocked earlier—habit, I guess, as Dad never used to lock it. We tumble down the steps into the living area. First time I walked back in here earlier today, it shocked me with its smallness, maybe because I was a lot littler when I used to stay here, or maybe because it *is* small—twelve meters long, low-ceilinged and cramped. The sensation of the floor shifting underneath my feet makes me feel sick, and I have to grip the wall as I step through into the bedroom. I'm getting déjà vu again. I turn to Lexi and shut the old thoughts away.

Once we're in bed, there's no danger of anything tugging me away from her. She's so fucking beautiful. I feel her hesitation as I pull back to look at her body under the covers, even in the near-blackness—we hit the light switch, but it didn't work, so all we've got are the foggy lights of the marina and the full moon in the center of the skylight above us.

"You're incredible," I tell her, my hand tracing a gorgeous rolling line from breast to waist to hip to thigh. "Do you know that?"

She's keen to press herself against me and I'd bet half of that is to stop me looking. She meets my gaze squarely, hot and fierce, but I've not forgotten that she said, *I'm not but thanks* when I told her she was beautiful. One night's not enough to undo whatever's made her feel that way. I can give her what she asked for, though: reckless fun. A night to escape the real world.

As I kiss my way across her collarbone, I settle in. Let my mind clear. She moans, and my body heats in response. I taste her skin, touch her, try to show her what I mean when I say she's incredible. Our bodies seek a rhythm together, and I already know how to please her, how to take the slow, teasing, meandering path to where we want to go. I press hot kisses to her stomach and feel her writhe.

But then I look up. Her unraveled hair, open mouth. Those smart wide ice-blue eyes. Our gazes meet, and it sends this *jolt* through me. Like I've burned myself. It knocks me out of rhythm. I hear my own breath catch.

I can't seem to switch off.

It doesn't usually feel like this, says my head, but I duck down, kiss the fine skin of her upper thigh, ignore it. One night, one night, one night. Surely if I know how to do anything right, it's that.

DAY ONE AGAIN

Lexi

WE BEGIN BY panicking.

"We can't be in the sea," Zeke keeps saying, which is infuriating, because, look, there's the sea, and *look*, here we are, bloody well definitely in it. The sun slashes bright across the water and the boat creaks beneath us.

I don't want to think about the creaking. I've never been particularly involved with the houseboat—Mum had it for less than a year before she died, and she left it to Penny, so she's always handled the upkeep and rentals. But I do know it's a "refurbished" Dutch barge, designed to be more house than boat. Mum bought it to rent out—her "savvy business decision," she always called it, a tongue-in-cheek reference to the fact that she basically just fell in love with the cute little windows and the idea of it all. This boat is supposed to sit in a marina with plant pots on its roof. It's called *The Merry Dormouse*, for fuck's sake. The chances of it being seaworthy seem extremely slim.

"Did someone—did someone untie my boat?" Zeke asks.

He spins to the other side of the deck, leaning so far over the railing I have to resist the impulse to step forward and grab him.

"*Penny's* boat," I snap.

Zeke stays unnaturally still, leaning over, ringlets falling forward as he stares into the water. The railing out here on the deck is a thin, rickety thing—just a few poles, really, more a boundary line than anything protective. For a split second I imagine Zeke slipping and sliding out under the bottom rail. My gut seizes. If one of us falls into the sea, can we even get back up here?

"Lexi," Zeke says, "what did you actually do when we retied the rope last night?"

"What? I did what the busybody neighbor told me to do, I held on to the boat while you got the center of the rope around that thingy and she did the knots. Zeke. Zeke?"

He is terrifyingly quiet. Eventually, at last, he turns. His hair is wild, and his eyes are so wide I can see the whites all around his irises. Fear congeals in the back of my throat.

"Paige told *you* to loop the center of the rope around the cleat on the pontoon," Zeke says. His voice is so quiet I can barely hear him.

"No, she didn't. She told you to do that. She said . . ." I trail off. "Fuck. Fuck, fuck, fuck."

I watch Zeke figure it out. How we both took that sentence. How we both thought Paige was talking to us when she said *your boat.* How we both thought the other person was the *friend* who would secure it at the pontoon, and how easily that went wrong in the fog and the darkness.

I feel sick. Not just nauseous, but as if quite suddenly I am going to vomit. I press my palm to my mouth and run to stand beside Zeke, leaning over—not as far as him, but far enough.

The boat is tied to itself.

"Are you fucking joking?" I say, clinging to the rail. "You didn't loop it around the thingy on the . . ."

"The cleat," he says. His voice is still quiet, but there's an edge to it now. "On the pontoon. And no, I didn't. Because you were supposed to do that."

"You think this is my fault?" I say, voice rising.

"Well, I don't think it's mine."

With his jaw clenched and fear all over his face, he looks about eighteen. Which isn't that far off, really. He is just a kid. Which means I have to be the adult here, when all I want to do is panic.

"We need to stay calm," I say, looking back at the rope with another lurch of nausea. It's just looped there, lying against the round punchbag-type things that hang on the side of the houseboat to stop it getting damaged if the water jostles it into the dock. Or the pontoon. Or the . . . whatever-it's-called.

Zeke breathes out slowly through his nose. "You're right. It doesn't matter how we got here. Just how we get home."

"Our phones," I say, scrabbling in the back pocket of my trousers. Never have I felt so grateful to hold my mobile in my hand. It lights up, showing my screen lock image: Mae beaming and bright-eyed on the beach, trousers rolled up to her knees, arms upstretched to the sky.

There are a few WhatsApps waiting from Marissa, and one from Penny—*Lexi, please, just call me.* On the top right of the screen there's an empty triangle and an exclamation mark. No signal.

If I was scared before, now I'm terrified. Horrified.

No signal? At all? Not even one of those random letters that comes up sometimes, an E, an H?

"Is your phone . . ."

"No signal. I can't even call 999." His voice is heavy with horror. "I thought you could always call 999."

"I think phone signal goes if you're far enough out to sea," I say. I'm flicking through my phone settings. My battery is at thirty-six percent. "Shit. I'm going to turn mine off, save battery."

"We might just be in a signal black spot. How far could we get in, what, ten hours?" Zeke asks, swiping his hair out of his face with both hands, one still clutching his phone. He blows out between his lips. "Maybe twenty kilometers?"

"*Twenty kilometers?*"

"Yeah, now you say it like that, it sounds quite far," Zeke says, voice weak.

I have to get back before anyone finds out what's happened to us—I can't have Mae knowing I'm in danger. I lean against the large wheel fixed to the body of the boat. My hangover loiters at the edge of my consciousness: slick, sweaty hands, dry throat, pounding head.

"That bang we heard last night," Zeke says, staring at me. I see myself reflected in his pupils, a tiny person, small and lost. "I bet that was us hitting something as we floated out of the marina. The seawall, maybe."

"Can we steer this thing? Get the motor going?" I say, realizing the significance of the wheel I'm currently propped against. It looks ridiculously oversized, as if it belongs in a *Pirates of the Caribbean* film, but presumably it isn't just ornamental. There's a white tarpaulin here, retracted so this section of the boat is exposed to the sun and connects seamlessly to the deck, but it's definitely some sort of steering . . . space. There are dials and handles and a lever that looks like it's from the TARDIS.

"I don't think so," Zeke says, swallowing. "Battery's flat. When I bought it, your friend said the houseboat needed refueling."

I flinch at the reference to Penny. She really did sell it without telling me, then. Penny, *my* Penny, who always cuts herself shaving (*Lex, it's happened again! Bloodbath! Bring chocolate!*) and who once described talking to me as *having an inner monologue*. Thinking of her makes me want to turn my phone back on; my phone is never off. But if the battery dies . . .

"Would a houseboat like this have a radio, or a sea . . . phone, do you think?" I say, trying to remember the few times I dropped in to check on the boat for Penny.

"Dad never had that sort of stuff. Would your friend have installed anything?"

I make a face. Penny outsourced general upkeep of the houseboat to a local agency, but I think they were just responsible for plugging holes and varnishing things, not installing radios. And there's no way Penny would have sorted that herself. She's really not a details person.

"I'll go look," Zeke says.

He ducks back inside. I let out a slow, shaky breath and try experimentally turning the wheel. Nothing happens. I've never had a panic attack before, but I've seen people have them on the telly. Maybe I could give it a go. I have the vague sense that it would make me feel better, like the thought of throwing up when you're nauseous.

"No sea phone," Zeke says shakily, reemerging up the steps. His pupils are so dilated his eyes look black. "Not that I can see anyway."

The fact that he has taken my "sea phone" term and run with it is not encouraging. One of us, ideally, should know what that device is called.

"I have to get back," Zeke says, his voice a little strange. "I have to work tomorrow. I'm booked on the three-fifteen train home."

There is a pause as we dip gently back and forth on the ocean and contemplate how surreal concepts like trains and homes and jobs feel right now.

"That's fine. That'll be fine." My voice sounds strange, too. "That's hours. We'll be rescued any minute now, definitely."

~~~~~

Three hours pass in a bizarre, unfathomable blur. We search for flares. There aren't any. We've got most of the basic stuff Penny kept for guests on the boat—the IKEA plates and mugs, the two sauce-pans, the white bedding that fits on the awkwardly sized bed—but either she never had life jackets and flares on here, or she's taken them off. She left a little first aid kit tucked in a cubbyhole in the bathroom, though, so that's something. And though the battery is flat, we do have water—there's a tank set into the frame beneath the bed, labeled "white water (fresh)."

Zeke is in the living space, staring at the battery banks under the trapdoor in the sofa; I'm in the bedroom. I needed to get away. He's so . . . I don't know. So *here*. Everywhere. This houseboat is *very* small, and he's always so close to me, this wide-eyed, broad-shouldered guy somewhere between a sleepy teenager and a confi-dent man.

I press my back to the wardrobe and close my eyes. *Breathe. Breathe.* I'm sticky with sweat and fear, but of course I can't use the shower: no power. Earlier I changed into a white T-shirt and gray jogging bottoms, but I'm boiling now—the sun is fierce, and the boat is becoming stifling.

"Lexi?" Zeke calls.

I keep my eyes closed. A hot shiver passes over me. It's not like I can ignore him; he knows exactly where I am. There's nowhere I can go, no way to walk away from him.

I'd be the first to admit that I have a pretty low opinion of men, generally speaking. Experience has taught me that they're useless at best and dangerous at worst. I know that good ones must exist, but I've met very few. Instead, I've been walked out on, betrayed, let down. I've been groped in bars, harassed at work—nothing *terrible*, nothing that would beat any other thirty-one-year-old woman's sto-ries, but all that bog-standard awfulness has meant that right now I can feel myself looking at Zeke a little differently as the day wears on.

This morning I saw him as a frightened kid, but just now while he was looking at the battery banks, crouched down on the floor, T-shirt pulled against the muscles of his back, he had looked so *male*, and like such a stranger. He's not actually a kid: he's twenty-three. That's young, but not that young. A man can do a lot of harm by the age of twenty-three.

We're stranded here together, and we're strangers, and all of a sudden I'm feeling so aware of what it means to be trapped somewhere with a man I don't know.

"Lexi?" he calls again.

"I just need a minute," I shout back, and I wince as my voice breaks slightly.

"Oh. OK. Sure."

He sounds surprised.

I know nothing about this man. I have the things he said to me in the pub—which could all be lies—and his own assertion that his father once owned this houseboat, and that now it belongs to him, even though *surely* Penny would never have sold it without telling me first. What if he did this on purpose? What if he's faking the shock? What if this isn't a stupid accident—what if he's stealing Penny's houseboat? What if he's kidnapping me?

I lift my hands to my forehead and look around, trying to calm my breathing. I need to get a handle on this situation. I need to get back in control. My gaze lands on Zeke's bag, open on the floor by the bed, his waistcoat from last night stuffed into the top. I barely hesitate before dropping to my knees to rummage through it.

Clothes, basic toiletries, his wallet. His driving license says *Ezekiel Ravenhill* and shows a picture of a man with short hair and a beard; at first glance my stomach lurches, because it looks nothing like him, but actually, once I look at the eyes, I realize this is Zeke with his curls cut off. They're such a defining feature, he looks totally different without them.

My heart does a little hiccup as I find his phone charger, curled in a neat nest of wire. My phone is still switched off; it looks so sad on the side table, black and dumb. There's a spare pair of boxers in here, some tissues, gum, plus a pack of condoms I recognize, and another one—flavored. I tend to associate flavored condoms with teenagers, or, occasionally, with men who really want a blow job and have seriously misunderstood the reason they're not getting one. I'm not sure what to make of this except that it's surprising.

My hand stills on the last object in the bag.

It's a soft leather sheath, about thirty centimeters long. I pull it out and unfasten the clasp. I expect it to open like a regular bag, but instead it unfolds, like a wallet.

Inside are six knives.

I breathe in sharply, almost dropping the whole thing. Why the hell would this man have a set of knives in his duffel bag? I put them down on the floor and sit back on my heels, breathing fast. My back scrapes against the side of the bedframe.

This boat. It is too small. I close my eyes tightly and imagine myself safe at home, standing in the middle of the rug, Mae's pens and coloring books scattered everywhere. I can almost smell the gravy from dinner the night before, a meal eaten on the sofa in front of *EastEnders*; I can almost hear the cars shooting by on the road outside, making the window rattle in its frame. Then I open my eyes, and here I am, stuck in the North Sea on a houseboat with a man who might well be planning to kill me in my sleep.

I hitch myself up to sit on the edge of the bed and drop my head into my hands. Zeke seems so harmless. I remember how he was last night, how he made my body light up, how *good* I'd felt in his arms. But then there's the aftertaste, the next thought: he's still a stranger, and he's a man, which means he's strong and capable of cruelty.

And then there's that professional-looking set of murder weapons in his duffel bag. Which is *really* saying *serial killer* to me right now.

I hear Zeke moving around in the kitchen, just on the other side of the door, and I flinch, pulling my arms tightly around myself. My heart is thundering in my chest as I wait for him to come in, but he doesn't—his footsteps move away.

I can't stay in this room forever. Right now I have the advantage—I have the knives, and he doesn't know I have them. I shake out my arms, irritated to find myself curled in a ball like this. This isn't me. I reach down to pull the smallest knife from its sheath, testing the point with one finger and then wincing in surprise as it draws a tiny drop of blood. They're *sharp*.

I crack open the door. Zeke is nowhere to be seen, which means he's on the deck, or possibly in the sea, which right now I am feeling pretty fine about.

The first thing to do, surely, is make sure there are no other potential weapons available to him. I turn to the kitchen, glancing toward the deck before I check the drawer where the knives live.

There are no kitchen knives.

I check in the tiny sink, and the even tinier drying area beside it—no knives. I check the cupboards, my movements becoming increasingly frantic, my grip on that little knife tightening. There aren't even any scissors. I know there were scissors before—I saw them when I was rummaging around for coffee this morning.

"What are you doing?" comes Zeke's voice from the doorway to the deck.

I spin, Zeke's knife in my hand. He pauses on his way down the steps as he clocks my raised weapon. With his ripped-knee jeans, beanie hat and bare feet, he looks more hipster than murderer, but the blood is pounding in my ears and I can't think straight anymore. I'm in a fighting stance, crouching low, knees bent and feet set.

"Stay there," I bark.

He frowns with a slow head tilt, as though he's just taking me in, knife and all.

"Lexi? What's . . . going on?"

He looks sleepy from the sun, his eyes still adjusting to being indoors, his face already kissed with the start of a tan.

"Where are all the kitchen knives?" I ask, my voice raised.

"I've got them," he says, nonplussed.

I raise the small knife a little higher. This isn't feeling quite right, but he's just told me he's got all the pointy things, so a raised knife feels wise.

"Why have you got my knife?" he asks.

"I have your knife because you've got *all* the knives. Why do you have all the knives? Why do you have a bag *full* of fucking knives?"

Realization dawns on Zeke's face. "Oh. Oh. Lexi. Really?"

My blood pressure is slowly dropping. It is very hard to imagine this man murdering me right now. But his surprise is irritating, too—is it that difficult to believe that I might feel at risk?

"You didn't answer my question." I lean my hip against the counter, arm dropping to my side. The ready-to-fight pose is starting to feel a bit ridiculous in the face of his open bewilderment.

He pulls the beanie off and pushes his ringlets out of his eyes.

"I'm making us lunch," he says, gaze steady on my face. "There was a disposable barbecue in the cupboard, so I'm cooking on the deck. My knives are in my bag, but you were having a moment to yourself in there, so I thought I'd just use the houseboat ones."

I swivel to look at the kitchen counter, noticing what else is missing besides the knives: the chopping board, the net of onions.

"What do you mean, your knives?" I say, my voice hoarse.

"I'm a junior chef," he says. "My boss got me my own set of knives at the end of last year, and they always come home with me after a shift, so . . . they were in my bag. I came straight from London to Gilmouth yesterday."

I absorb this, my breath still coming fast. I hope he can't see how much my chest is heaving.

"Why would you— Did you really think I'd hurt you?" Zeke asks, his voice raw now.

My hand is shaking and sweaty on the knife.

"You're a man, Zeke," I snap. "A man I don't really know."

His hand flies to the back of his head, staying there, braced.

"God," he says, after a moment. "I didn't think about it like that."

"No. Such is the joy of being a man, I guess."

"But . . . you've . . . We . . ." He rubs a hand across his mouth, frustrated with himself, I think. He stays on the steps, that beanie resting against his knee as if he's just doffed his cap. "You're older than me."

It's interesting how uncomfortable it makes me to hear that out loud.

"And you're so . . . tough. And—I don't know." He pauses for a long moment, eyes down, thinking, then he looks back to me. "Have you felt safe? Please tell me you've not felt unsafe today."

"On this boat in the middle of the sea?" I hedge, rubbing my thumb along the handle of the knife.

"On this boat with *me*," he says softly. His hair is falling forward again, one dark ringlet across his eye. "Did you think I was going to, like . . ."

He can't seem to bring himself to finish the sentence; he's looking at me with horror, and I feel another flash of irritation at the incredulity in his face.

"I'm going to hazard a guess that when we left The Anchor, you didn't think twice about how nobody knew who you'd gone home with," I say.

He shakes his head slowly. "Yeah, no. That didn't cross my mind."

"I did. I weighed up that risk. I made sure Marissa knew we were going to the marina. If I'm out late, I walk home with my keys in my hand, because you can do real damage with keys if a man attacks you. I cross the street if there's a guy coming the other way after dark. And when I'm stuck in a small space with a man I don't know, part of me will always ask the question, *Am I safe?*"

"I didn't . . ." Zeke swallows. He looks pained, as if he's bleeding from somewhere, as though he should be clutching a wound at his side. "I would never hurt you. I would never hurt anyone."

He comes down the steps then, arms out to me. I raise my hand, like *uh-uh, no further*. He stops stock-still immediately, eyes getting a little wider.

"You can have my knives," he says, voice soft. "You can have all the knives. Keep them under your pillow. In your shoes. Wherever you like. I can be on a knife ban. I'll come get you if anything needs chopping."

I narrow my eyes. "I'm not being crazy. Do not act like I'm being crazy."

"No, I don't think that at all. This . . ." He pauses, trying to find the words. "This situation is crazy. I get why you wouldn't trust me, especially after finding . . ." He nods at the knife.

My shoulders relax slightly at the acknowledgment. I watch him for a while, my eyes running over him—the soft curls, the handsome, youthful lines of his face.

"Did it occur to you, too? That I might have kidnapped you, or something?"

The corner of his lip quirks up. "No. Sorry. When you were waving a knife at me, I did start to feel a *bit* like I might have misread you, but no." He lifts one shoulder in a shrug, and says, "I got your vibe last night. I know we don't know each other well, but I feel like . . . I kind of do know you. In a way."

My cheeks start to heat. "Let's just . . . The knives can go back to living in the kitchen drawer," I say.

"Sure. Yeah. Whatever you're comfortable with."

I frown, lifting my chin slightly. "Is something burning?"

"Caramelizing," he says automatically, then he tilts his head, smelling. "But maybe burning in about four seconds," he adds, spinning toward the steps to the deck.

I watch him go, and take a quiet, shaky breath.

"I'm going to get changed," I call after him as the door swings shut. "All right? Just give me some space."

"Of course," he calls back.

I stand there for a moment. I feel a little calmer. One problem at a time: I may be lost at sea, but I no longer think the man I'm with is a murderer. I'll take that win right now. I turn back to the bedroom, pushing the door shut behind me.

The room looks different after that interaction. The sheath of knives on the floor is clearly a set of chef's knives; the bed is back to being the one we spent our night in, disheveled and warm. My breath slowly steadying, I drag my bag out from the bottom of the wardrobe and rifle through it. I'm so sticky and hot now, I need shorts, but . . . Ugh. Why is it that when you're packing a suitcase, you suddenly think you'll wear things you haven't worn in years? The only ones I've put in are denim shorts, too tight, but it's that or staying in these thick jogging bottoms, so I wriggle on the shorts.

I brace myself before walking out onto the deck. Zeke smiles at me slightly warily. The episode with the knives has changed things. We were strangers, then lovers, and now we're back to strangers again. He's pulled the beanie back on, despite the sun's heat, and is untangling the necklaces against his chest with one hand while he turns the vegetables on the barbecue. I remember feeling those necklaces trailing against my bare skin last night as he moved up my body to kiss me, and I look away sharply at the thought, staring out at the open sea.

Still no boats. I can't believe there are still no other boats. The water seems even smoother than earlier, an endless, shining lake.

"Thank you," I say abruptly. "For having that conversation with me."

"Of course. I'm so sorry I didn't . . . I should have made you feel safe," he says quietly, looking at the barbecue.

"Well. Yes. But maybe that was a bit of a tall order right now," I say, raising my eyebrows at the big, blue, yawning emptiness on all sides. I don't want to undermine what I've said to him, but also, I suspect I might not have freaked out to that extent if we hadn't been drifting helplessly in the middle of the ocean.

"We'll be OK," Zeke says after a moment. "People survive at sea for ages just holding on to a plank or a floaty coconut or something."

Clearly he's on a being-brave kick right now. Good for him. When I don't answer, he sets his barbecue tongs down and unfolds one of the striped blue-and-white deck chairs jammed beside the steering wheel. I noticed those earlier, but left them where they were, because sitting down feels like settling in. The sea glimmers in grays and greens, sunlight catching in its surface like silver glitter. Against its depth, the deep blue of the sky is oddly two-dimensional, like a wall painted in one shade of cobalt.

"Sit down. Rest. Someone will rescue us soon," Zeke says. "A ship will come by."

I ignore the deck chair. I'm not nearly as confident about being rescued as I was three hours ago. We've not seen a single boat yet. We got on the houseboat at about midnight last night, and it's three thirty now—that's more than fifteen hours of floating around without seeing another soul.

Wherever we've ended up . . . I'm starting to worry it's somewhere no one else goes.

Zeke

WE'RE INSIDE THE boat now, me on the sofa, her on one of those new chairs—it's just too hot out on the deck. I lean over to top up Lexi's cup of milk. We decided to drink that first, though really we should probably have chucked it already—it's been in a warm fridge all night. Food hygiene's drilled into me, but there's no five-star rating to hit here, and throwing food away feels so stupid. All the options feel stupid. *I* feel stupid.

I can't believe I made her feel afraid.

"Thanks," Lexi says, without looking at me.

I fidget, pulling one foot up underneath me, trying to get comfortable on the thin cushions of the crappy wooden "sofa." I'm already feeling cooped up. I remember this sensation too well. Dad, Lyra and Jeremy would sit on this sofa hunched over their wooden puzzles for hours, and I'd be fizzing up like a bottle of Coke when you shake it—like I was going to explode. *There's plenty of puzzles to do*, Dad would say. I hated those puzzles. I tried to sit down and figure them out, but it'd take less than a minute before I'd feel my fingers flexing with the urge to chuck the little wooden cubes against the wall.

I miss my mum. I should probably be thinking of my dad right now—that's why I bought this boat, isn't it?—but when it comes to crisis situations, it's always Mum I want. Call my dad for advice and he'd give you a weird hack he saw on Reddit, or something some bloke told him in a pub garden in 1998. My mum can be overbearing, and my relationship with her is all kinds of complicated, but right now I'd kill to hear her pick up the phone with a brisk *How are you, Ezekiel? What do you need?*

"I think I'll just . . . get back to making the inventory," Lexi says, standing up to take her plate to the kitchen.

Things are feeling awkward. No surprise, probably, since in the last twelve hours she's accused me of boat theft and held me at knifepoint. Meanwhile I've barbecued, been emotionally illiterate, and poked at some boat mechanics I'm totally unqualified to understand. I grit my teeth, so pissed off with myself. I know I'm no saint, but I am *not* that sort of man.

"I'll get back to watching for boats," I say, since that's actually useful.

"Right." She doesn't even turn around.

As I stand up, I'm suddenly hit with the weirdest feeling that none of this is real. As if I'm standing in the middle of a set. As if someone is going to remove a panel of sky and I'll find it's just plywood.

I stop and stare at it all. The mini oil paintings of animals and seasides in their tatty frames. The chairs opposite me, fixed to the spots where Dad used to keep three mini beanbags, one for each of us kids. The paisley-patterned standing lamp that was definitely Dad's, but that I can't imagine him ever going out and buying, because I can't really imagine my dad doing anything that normal. And the dark wood everywhere—the walls, the floor.

"You OK?" Lexi asks. She's turned around now, leaning back against the kitchen countertop, watching me.

"Yeah. Just feeling sort of . . ."

I can't find a way to say it. I chew at my cheek, embarrassed—
I'm often slow to find the right words. But Lexi doesn't act like it's
strange that I've run the sentence out before it's done. She just waits.

"I, uh, I felt for a second like everything wasn't really here."

Lexi nods, and for a moment her eyes soften. "That'll be the
shock," she says.

"Right. I guess I'll . . . adjust."

Her eyes sharpen again. "You won't need to adjust," she says,
turning her back to me again. "Because any minute now, we're getting off this boat."

~~~~~~

Six hours later, and we're still here.

It's getting . . . I don't know. Both more and less surreal. We've
ended up having to do normal stuff, like making dinner—three-
cheese pasta, on the tiny gas hob—and saying *excuse me* as we
squeeze past each other in the narrow gap between the kitchen and
the bathroom. But with every minute that passes, it becomes more
obvious that we're in a properly horrifying situation.

I've not spent a lot of time imagining how I'd do in a survival-
type scenario, but I'd have backed myself to be one of the ones
building a life-float out of tree branches or swimming out to search
the fallen plane. No planes or trees here, though. We've got flea-
market wall art, dead batteries and Tesco Value salad. I kind of wish
this was a desert island—I wish I was writing *HELP* in the sand
and collecting wood for a signal fire. Instead, I'm wondering how
long Red Leicester takes to go bad, already itchy with cabin fever.

"So," Lexi says, clearing her throat as I pass her a bowl of pasta
on the deck. "We should probably . . . talk."

"Sure," I say, pulling out both of the deck chairs with my free
hand. "What do you want to talk about?"

"Well, I hardly know you. And right now you're the only person who can help if I fall into the sea and a bunch of sharks try to eat me. So we should probably build on the trust."

Her eyes tighten slightly as she says this—embarrassment, maybe, about the whole thing with the knives. I don't want her to feel embarrassed. *I'm* the one that's been a total idiot.

"Tell me about why you bought this houseboat," she says.

I appreciate the gesture. It's the first time she's actually said she believes it belongs to me, not Penny. It's an olive branch, maybe.

"It was my dad's, like I said at the pub," I say, sitting down beside her. "We have some unfinished business."

The deck chairs just about fit side by side. The sun's off to our right, low in the sky. It makes me think of a lemon fruit pastille: it has a kind of sugarcoated haze to it. I look away from the empty horizon.

"Didn't you say your dad's dead?" Lexi says, wincing as the deck chair sags beneath her.

I nod. "Heart attack, five and a half years ago."

"OK, so, is this houseboat haunted by his unsatisfied ghost or something?" she asks, without particular alarm.

I laugh. It's the sort of thing Dad would've joked about doing—haunting us all after he's gone. Lexi looks surprised for a moment, and then smooths her face clear.

"Most people tiptoe around dead people," I say, trying a forkful of the pasta. It's good: just the right amount of nuttiness from the Red Leicester, smooth texture from the milk. Wish we'd had cream, though. "You're very chill. Talking about it."

"I'm not very sentimental." She points at her chest with her fork. "Hard bastard, I'm afraid."

Hmm. She's definitely tough, but I wouldn't say *hard*.

"I didn't even cry when my mum died," she says. Kind of defensive, like she's annoyed I didn't believe her.

"I'm sorry you lost your mum," I say.

"Yeah," she says. "It's been four years, so I think I'm supposed to say I'm over it, but I'm not sure I am, actually. Is it the shock, or is this really bloody delicious?" She stares down at the pasta as if she's just noticed it, even though she's four forkfuls in.

I smile. "You can't go wrong with that much cheese."

This actually isn't true. I'm kind of proud that this dinner isn't just a big sticky beige lump.

"And you don't have to be over it," I say. "My dad died in 2018, and, like . . ."

I try to find the words for the total mess that's been my grieving process over the last five years. How it started with no tears, barely missing him at all. How it hid behind drunken nights out and awkward morning afters. How starting therapy last year made me see that I'd packed all the feelings away without looking, and that's a shit way to cope with anything. There's been a lot of crying since.

"This stuff's complicated," I say. "There's no right way to do it."

She lifts one eyebrow—doesn't have much patience for this kind of thinking, maybe—and takes another forkful.

"You and your dad, were you close, then?" she asks eventually.

I tilt my head, trying to catch her eye, but she's focused on her bowl. This is so weird. The world's strangest second date. The world's longest morning after. I know she wasn't interested in getting to know me yesterday, or this morning—she wanted fun, and then she wanted me gone. So now what?

"You don't have to tell me anything," she says, when I don't answer right away. "I was just making conversation."

"No, no," I say. "It's good, I want to talk. It's just a complicated question."

She shrugs, lifting her chin toward the open water. "We've got a bit of time."

I smile at that, but it makes me shiver, too.

"OK, well, Dad was . . . a character. That's what people used to always say about him. He was separated from my mum, so me and my brother and sister only visited him once a month. He had this big scruffy beard, believed in aliens. He was totally obsessed with puzzles, and he was always reciting lines from Bob Dylan songs, you know, like someone might wheel out a Bible quote for every situation?"

Lexi's lip twitches. "I think I might have quite liked him."

I'm glad she says that. People either got my dad or they didn't—I never met anyone who thought he was just *all right*. As kids, Jeremy and I were in the hero-worship camp—always willing to forgive his oddities while Lyra turned moody teenager and began to scorn them. But then Dad's weirdness started to seem less cool to me, too. I got a hint that he held things back, maybe. I realized he kept secrets, and I got to thinking about what those secrets might be.

When he died, I was seventeen, and we'd not spoken in three years. Our estrangement wasn't dramatic: just a slow, awkward drift. My therapist has suggested that it was more than simply a case of rejecting my dad before he could reject me—he thinks I distanced myself from Dad to ingratiate myself to my mum. As much as I hate the thought, I do kind of wonder. Mum's hard to win over. I've tried worse things to get her approval, or her disapproval, come to that—either would do.

Dad leaving me the houseboat felt like a message I completely failed to understand—typical of our relationship, really. I sold it as quickly as I could, just wanting it gone. Wanting him gone. And now here I am, spending most of the money my granddad left me to get the houseboat back.

"You said last night you weren't going to be in this part of the country for long. Is this where your family are from?" she asks.

"This?"

"Yes, this barren expanse of ocean—are your family not sea-dwelling mermaids?"

I laugh. Her lips press together for a second, as though she's irritated, but I reckon actually she's pleased. I'm starting to think that reading Lexi is kind of like reading something in code. All the gestures the rest of us use mean something different for her. So far, I've figured out that when she does lift the corners of her mouth, it's not a smile, it's more like an eyebrow-raise. When she frowns, she's not angry—she's thinking. And when she avoids my eyes, I reckon it's not because she doesn't want to look at me. It's because she doesn't want me to see what's in hers.

"I meant Northumberland."

"Yeah. My brother and sister—Jeremy and Lyra—and my mum, all my cousins and aunts and uncles . . . they stuck around the Alnwick area. They're all within half an hour of one another."

"And you're down in . . ."

"London," I say, just as she says the same word. "How did you guess?"

"You look like you're about two inches away from a man bun."

That makes me properly belly-laugh. I reach for my hair, tugging experimentally at the ends of my curls.

"Yeah, you're not wrong. And you? Did you grow up in Gilmouth?"

She nods, setting her bowl down under the deck chair and lying back. "How did you guess?" She gestures toward herself. "Small-town vibes?"

"No," I say, after a moment. "You just seemed at home. When we met."

She blinks quickly. I don't know what that means yet.

"Well, yeah. That pub where we met, it was mine, once."

"You owned the pub?"

"I inherited it from my mum. I got the pub, Penny got the houseboat."

"Wait, is Penny your sister?" I say, frowning. She said *friend* before.

"No," Lexi says, in a tone that makes me think she's had to answer that one a lot. "She lived behind the pub garden. But her homelife wasn't great. When I was . . . maybe seven, and she was about five, she started hanging out with us at the pub—she used to climb over the back fence. We were best friends. My mum raised her, really. When Mum died, Mae—Penny's daughter—hadn't even been born yet. The dad was a prick who didn't want anything to do with her, so . . ." She shrugs, moving to stand. "That's how I ended up owning the pub. Not what I'd planned, but with Penny and Mae to support . . . Anyway. It's complicated."

"You helped support your best friend and her kid? That's pretty huge."

Her face goes tight. She turns away from me. I get the sense I've touched on something important, something that'll help make sense of Lexi, but even before she speaks, I can tell she's going to shut me out again. It was like this last night: I'd catch little flashes of a Lexi she keeps hidden, then she'd go back under.

"I've not finished checking the boat over for any damage," she says. "Here. I'll wash up."

I feel her pause behind me as she opens the door.

"*Do* we wash up?" she asks.

"Hey?" I say, turning around.

"Well, if we're trying to save water . . ."

I swallow. For the first time all day, I've not been thinking about being lost at sea.

"I'll just leave it in the sink," she says. "Someone'll be along to rescue us in a minute anyway."

We've said that to each other a *lot* today. I reckon a solid fifty percent of conversations have been along the lines of, *Don't worry, we'll be rescued*. We've tossed it back and forth like a ball. Her turn, then mine.

She heads inside. I listen to the clatter in the kitchen and close my eyes. The one thing we've not said to each other is, *We might not be rescued at all*. But that sentence has been going round and round in my head since the moment I stepped out onto this deck this morning, and I'd be willing to bet Lexi's feeling exactly the same.

~~~~~~

The sunset's epic, a vivid satsuma-orange. There's just nothing in the way of it out here—it's all sky. The sea turns bright as the sun sinks, shining like it's candlelit.

Then . . . it gets dark.

"Well, it'll be easier to spot other boats," Lexi offers, pulling a hoody on and then tugging her leather jacket back over the top.

We're standing on the deck, looking out at where the sun went, as if maybe we can wish it back. The air smells cool and sharp. I shiver. It feels more like a wilderness out here when it's dark. Empty, but in a threatening way. Not in a nice, nothing-coming-to-get-you way.

"Though we don't have any lights, so it won't be so easy for them to spot *us*," Lexi continues. She says it briskly, as though she's just being practical, but I notice her shoulders drooping a bit. "We should do shifts. One of us keeps watch."

"Mm. That's a good idea. Do you want first or second shift?" I ask.

"You choose."

"I don't mind—you pick."

I hear her huff of frustration, and wince. It probably makes me seem young, being so indecisive. I'm just kind of used to someone else wanting to make decisions.

"Fine, I'll go to bed now, we can swap over at two," she says.

"Great."

She doesn't go. She turns her face up to the moon, breathing deeply.

"This is all so fucking mental," she says quietly. "And I know when you come in to get me there's going to be that moment you always get when you wake up somewhere new, you know? Where you haven't quite realized what's going on, where your brain and your body assume you're still where you'd usually be. And then there'll be the moment after that. When I remember."

"And you're scared of that?"

The low, wet *schlup* of the sea against the boat beneath us is so much louder now that it's dark.

"I'm not scared," she says.

I'm not sure whether to call bullshit on this. If she needs to tell me she's not scared, maybe I should let her.

"How about if I make it quick?" I ask eventually. "If I wake you up like, 'Good morning, it's two a.m. and you're stuck on a house-boat in the middle of the ocean with your one-night stand'? Just get it all out there?"

She snorts. "How kind."

"Or do you want that second where you forget about it all?"

She's quiet. "No," she says. "I'd always rather know the truth."

"Same."

"Then I'll bear that in mind when it's my turn to wake you." She shifts away from me, opening the door. "Good night, Zeke."

"Night."

Maybe I'm being ridiculous, but . . . I feel like I know the exact moment she falls asleep. It's just a different sort of quiet. The stars are properly out now, and they're crazy—they're not dotted around the blackness, they're covering every *centimeter* of sky. I convince myself I can see the Milky Way, but I've no idea whether I'm even looking the right way.

I have a bit of a cry around midnight. Thinking about my dad. Looking up at the sky and wondering if that's where he's gone, up into the universe, singing out Bob Dylan among the stars. I wonder if Jeremy's right—if all the answers I'm looking for are hidden on this houseboat somewhere. Up until now, I've been a bit too busy to go looking, but Lexi's right. We've got nothing but time.

DAY TWO

Lexi

"WAKE UP, YOU'RE trapped on a houseboat with an uncaffeinated, unshowered harpy."

Zeke opens his eyes slowly and looks right at me. He's on his back, his curls thrown outward onto the pillow like the lines from the sun in one of Mae's drawings. I expect to see the penny drop in his eyes, the way it did in mine when he woke me at two in the morning, but his gaze stays steady. Zeke seems permanently dreamy—maybe moving from asleep to awake isn't such a big deal for him, as if he exists in that space anyway.

"Hello," he says softly. "What's a harpy?"

I pause. After five hours alone on the deck, watching the dawn, my whole body is alight with panic. When I think of a survival scenario, I imagine it would be very physical—hiking across a barren rockscape, scaling a rainforest tree, sprinting away from a score of zombies. *This* survival scenario is the opposite. It's basically a long exercise in sitting still.

I am a pretty sedentary person, but I'm also someone who always has my phone out, or the telly on, or a four-year-old launching themselves at me from the other end of the sofa—I'm not somebody who should be left alone with their own thoughts. And whoever said that ocean sounds were restful had clearly never been lost at sea before, because that endless, repetitive noise in the cold darkness was a total mindfuck last night. I started hearing things *in* it—a rhythm playing out, *ta-ta-da,* and then a voice, on repeat, making a sound like a wolf: *a-whoo, a-whoo.* I'd huddled under two blankets and cried, grateful for the knowledge that Zeke was asleep and wouldn't ever know.

The result of all this is that I am pathetically grateful for human contact, even if the human is a twenty-three-year-old stranger who knows what I look like naked.

"A harpy is like a . . . wrinkly old woman? Maybe with wings? You know, I'm not actually sure. It's Greek or Roman or something."

"You're not wrinkly or old."

He's making no move to get up. I notice that he's slept without a top on—I can see the tan width of his shoulders. I stand, shuffling my way down the side of the bed toward the door, head bowed slightly to fit under the sloping sides of the ceiling.

"You think that now, but wait until we've been out here for a couple of days without my retinol cream."

"No wings, either," he says comfortably, sitting up in bed.

I turn in the doorway. "Are you not panicking? About all this?"

"Not right now. Right now I'm waking up."

I shake my head. I have this cruel impulse to scare him—to say, *We're screwed, don't you see? Not a single boat has passed us in more than twenty-four hours.* But another impulse swallows the words back. I don't want him to be afraid. Yesterday morning, it was him versus me, but something has shifted in the darkness, and now it's hard to say exactly how I see him. Still a stranger, definitely. But not an enemy.

"Come on," I say. "We need to eat something. And then we need to make a plan."

~~~~~

I gasp when I step out onto the deck, and the sound brings Zeke right up behind me in a few quick steps.

"Sorry," I breathe, feeling the heat of his body against my back as he moves past me into the sunshine. "Sorry, sorry, I've not seen a ship or anything, it's just . . ."

"I think it's injured."

Zeke is down on his knees already. Right in front of us, at twelve o'clock to the door, is a seagull. A little one, a baby, maybe. It's browner than I'd expect a seagull to be, as if it's not got its final feathers yet. It's floating on the back of something—a broken kayak, snapped clean, one yellow stripe still visible on its side despite the water's erosion. It was such a shock to step out here and find something other than blue water and blue sky.

"See how it can't stretch out its left wing?"

I lean on the railing, looking down at the bird. Does seeing a seagull mean we're close to land? Or is that just one of those myths, like my mum's absolute conviction that going out with wet hair would lead to me catching a deadly Dickensian-style cold?

The seagull lets out a small sound, half mew, half caw, and I'm shocked to feel my eyes fill with tears. There is a lot to cry about right now, and this seagull is extremely low down on the list, so I don't know what this is about. I blink them away before Zeke sees.

"We came out to make a plan," I remind him, waving a notebook in my hand. It's his—he dug it out of his bag yesterday for our inventory. I find the idea of him carrying a notebook around almost as strange as him carrying around a bunch of knives—I don't know any men who write things down by hand.

He doesn't look away from the seagull.

"Zeke? Hello?"

"Hi," he says, glancing over his shoulder, eyes narrowed against the sun. "You OK?"

"Yeah, I just . . ." I pause. "Are you thinking the kayak might be useful? Do you think we should try to get hold of it?"

He's slow to answer. I respect that about Zeke: he's not afraid of a bit of silence.

"No," he says finally. "I'm thinking, how do you save a seagull without Google?"

"You're not serious."

He frowns. "We don't have a lot to do, Lexi. I think we can spare half an hour to rescue a baby bird."

"How would we even do that? It's way out of reach."

He turns, sitting down, one forearm resting across his knees. "We came out here to make a plan, didn't we?" he says.

~~~~

Zeke is now down to a pair of boxers. They're bright red—I am unsurprised that Zeke does not have ordinary boxers—and they sit low on his hips. I look away, out to the water, where the seagull staggers a few steps forward across the broken kayak.

"I am wondering whether *get in the sea* is such a great plan after all," I say, eyeing the very amateur rope ladder we've just made so that he can climb back up again—or either of us can, if we ever fall in. "It's only a bird. Birds get injured and die all the time. We should be worrying about ourselves."

"I can do that, too. I can multitask," Zeke says.

"The bird will probably die anyway."

"OK." Zeke gives a one-shouldered shrug. "But we'll have tried."

Something shifts a little in my chest, like a block of ice breaking loose. Look at him, framed against the seascape with his abs and his chocolate-and-gold eyes, talking about saving an injured sea-gull. I may be a tough woman, but nobody is that tough.

"I won't do it," Zeke says, voice softening. "If you don't want me to."

I look at the bird. "Fuck," I say.

Zeke waits.

"You're just looking for something to save because we can't save ourselves," I tell him.

"Uh-huh," he says, not missing a beat. "Absolutely."

I blink. I don't know any men with enough self-insight to accept that without pause. The surprise throws me.

I look back at the bird. "Fuck," I say again.

"You swear a lot," Zeke says. And then, "Why do I like that so much?"

That makes my stomach flutter, a strange sensation after the heavy, sickening panic that's sat there for the last day and a half. I look at him sharply, but he's looking at the sea; I can't tell for sure if he's flirting.

"Fine. Let's do it," I say, turning my gaze away.

Zeke bends to grab the rope, the one we tied to itself—sometime yesterday he sorted that loop on the side of *The Merry Dormouse*, which I was grateful for, since every time I saw the rope snaking over the railing it made me want to scream at our own stupidity. Now that we've made a ladder from the only spare I could find on the boat, this is our one remaining rope. He ties it around his middle, shoots me a brief, almost exhilarated look, and then dive-bombs into the sea.

The moment he hits the water, he lets out a huge gasp, almost a scream. My whole body flinches at the sound.

"Zeke? Zeke?"

"I'm OK, I'm OK. It's just . . . cold."

I watch him smooth his sodden hair back, his legs kicking in the water as he adjusts to the temperature, still breathing hard. I am a lot more nervous about this than I'd realized. I know he's right there, only a meter or so below me, but now it's just me up here on this deck, alone, feet bare on its grainy surface, hands clinging to its flimsy railing. It's not a good feeling.

Still breathing hard against the cold, Zeke swims toward the broken kayak. The seagull squawks, flapping. Zeke tugs the kayak closer to the boat, until his back is against the houseboat's dark blue paintwork and the seagull is inches away from him, still clinging to its life raft.

"Lexi?" Zeke says, treading water. He has the kayak in one hand and the rope in the other. "What do we *do* with Eugene when we've got hold of him?"

"Eugene?"

He looks up at me, squinting against the sunlight. His breathing is steadier now.

"You don't like it? I think it suits him."

"We don't even know it's a boy seagull."

"You want me to check?"

"My plan this morning did not involve examining seagulls for penises. Can you remind me how we ended up here?"

"Uh, well, we basically tied the houseboat to itself instead of . . ."

"No, please, I didn't mean *that* part," I say, covering my eyes. "I do not want reminding of that. Eugene is fine. He can be a Eugene."

I find myself thinking of Penny, perhaps because she would have saved this seagull, and probably named it, too. She wouldn't have made a plan, though, or a ladder, or tied herself to the boat—she'd have thrown herself into the water without thinking, and I would have had to figure out how to get her back again. That's our dynamic: from the day we met, she became the cute baby sister I always wanted. Penny is all sunshine; she's spontaneous, perky, the human equivalent of a cup of coffee. *You need a hug, gorgeous,* she says to me sometimes, wrapping her arms around my middle, and then, *Succumb!* she'll command me, when I resist.

Thinking about Penny takes me to Mae, but that's too painful, too much, and my mind rears back from it like the thought has teeth.

I wonder if Penny's worrying about me. Whether they've sent out search parties yet. I hope she just thinks I'm not replying to her WhatsApps because she kicked me out; the thought of her being frightened makes my stomach bottom out. I know she'd keep it from Mae for as long as she could, but . . .

I shiver. How long does it usually take for people to report someone as missing? Surely the busybody neighbor at the marina would have sounded the alarm when she saw the houseboat gone in the morning. So why are we still here?

"I'm not sure . . . how much longer I should stay in the water," Zeke says, and I can hear his teeth chattering as he speaks.

"Sorry. Let me go find something to put him in."

I spin on my heel and step inside the boat, the little door swinging shut behind me. I head for the bedroom, which is a mess—in a space this small, it doesn't take much to make it look untidy—and I open the wardrobe. I've not hung up everything from my bag yet. Avoiding creases didn't seem a priority, and I'm reluctant to do anything that feels like moving in, which is obviously ridiculous, since moving *out* is currently impossible.

My first thought is my holdall, though a distant corner of my brain reminds me that it cost me fifty quid and will probably never be the same again if it's had a terrified seagull inside it. But while I'm emptying out the contents into the base of the wardrobe, I lose my footing and end up falling forward against the back wall, one hand slamming into the wood. And a panel comes loose.

I yelp, flinching back as it clatters to the base of the wardrobe. It's exposed a small, hidden cubbyhole, built into the wall of the boat, just wide enough to hold a cardboard shoebox on its side. The box looks old, its lid stained and warped; if it's Penny's, I don't recognize it.

I ease it out, wrinkling my nose at the fusty smell, and lift the lid. There are five, maybe six large notebooks inside, leather-bound and battered. *Ship's Log* is printed on the front of each one.

"Lexi?"

I stand up so fast I make myself dizzy. Zeke's bobbing around out there in the freezing cold sea while I'm getting all Nancy Drew in here. I tip the logbooks out on top of our bags and leave the bedroom, grabbing my towel from the bathroom as I go, then doubling back just as I reach the door to snatch the scissors out of the sink. Whatever the deal is with this shoebox, it'll make a better seagull holder than my bag, and that's all that matters right now.

"This is looking very *Blue Peter*," Zeke says, eyeing the objects I'm clutching. One of his arms is now wrapped around the back of the broken kayak. "Do you think Eugene is concussed? He's gone still."

I finish punching holes into the lid of the shoebox and lean over to examine the bird. It's sort of staring at nothing, but don't birds generally do that? What is a standard resting bird face?

"He's fine," I say firmly.

Zeke, on the other hand, looks worryingly cold. There's a faint tinge of blue to the edges of his lips now.

"Are *you* OK?" I ask.

"Just a bit cold, that's all."

I'm sweating through my long-sleeved tee—it was cool out here first thing, but now the sun is warming the deck, and the sea is turning a deeper, purer shade of blue. It looks like it *should* be warm, which I guess is probably what Zeke thought before he leaped in.

"Here," I say, "use this to hold him."

Zeke catches the towel above his head, then gently wraps it around Eugene, who flaps a little and lets out a single quiet *caw*, but nothing more. This feels like a bad sign. If I was a bird, and a giant human was trying to wrap me in a towel, I'd want to object a bit more than this.

"OK. Hmm. I didn't think about how few hands I'd have at this point, did you?" Zeke says, voice labored as he attempts to clamber onto the broken kayak, one knee up, like a spider trying to lever its way up out of a plughole.

This is all as per the plan we drew up in the notebook, complete with diagrams that I now realize gave us very little other than a sense of control over something, but at least I've found out I would be able to beat Zeke at Pictionary.

He keeps getting up onto the kayak, grabbing at the rail, then almost losing his hold on Eugene and splashing back again. It's like watching *Total Wipeout*. I can't quite believe he's doing this. The muscles in his shoulders and stomach are popping as he tries to balance—it's the strangest mix of sexy and daft, and despite myself, I'm smiling.

I lean over the side just as he manages to get into a standing position on the back of the kayak, surfer-style. He pretty much throws me the bird in its bundle of towel, and then he's twisting and losing his footing and splashing right into the water again, a proper belly flop. I'm laughing, the sea-splattered towel clutched close to my chest. The wind picks up the loose hairs at the nape of my neck and cools the spots of seawater on my bare feet. For a moment something seems to open up inside me, like a shell cracking, as though my slightly frantic giggling is setting something free.

I get Eugene into the shoebox as Zeke hauls himself up the rope ladder and then collapses on a deck chair, immediately drenching its blue-striped fabric. It's a while before I look around—I'm checking Eugene over, as though I think I'm some sort of seagull vet. Beak: present and correct. Wings: yes, two. Talons: unnervingly sharp.

The moment I turn and see Zeke's face, my stomach lurches.

"Are you all right?" I ask, alarmed.

"Fine," he says, but his chest is heaving and his face is drawn.

Reality seeps back in: here we are, stranded in this awful barren sea, and if the weather worsens before we're rescued, if it gets colder out here . . .

"Let's get you inside. You should change into something warm."

"Right," Zeke says, staggering slightly as he stands, despite the fact that the boat is barely doing more than a slow rolling dip on the water.

I carefully carry Eugene into the bedroom while Zeke heads to the bathroom. As I set the seagull down on the bedside table, I lift the lid and peek inside his box.

Eugene stares up at me, eyes ink black, soft feathers ruffled. He's so still. Maybe we should have left him out there—what if his mum was coming back for him? He doesn't look like a tiny baby, more like a teenager. Do mother seagulls still care about their babies when they're adolescents, or was his mother like Penny's mum, the sort who decides you're on your own once you're no longer cute enough to dress up like a doll?

I close the box and head to the wardrobe in search of something I can wear instead of this top, which is now sweaty, sea-splashed and smelling strongly of seagull. It's a mess in here, that weird loose panel leaning behind Zeke's duffel bag, dust everywhere, ship's logs upended across our bags. Those books are next on my list—they might say something useful. We could really do with useful right now. God knows the injured seagull doesn't qualify.

I strip down to my bra and trousers, ignoring my reflection in the narrow mirror inside the wardrobe door and choosing a blue shirt I bought years ago, now soft with overwear.

"Ah, sorry," says Zeke from behind me.

I spin around, clutching the shirt to my chest. He's only a couple of steps away from me—that's pretty much always true in this boat. He's wandered in wearing just jeans; one of his hands is still on his head, as though he's paused midway through rearranging his curls.

He can't see anything with the shirt where it is, but I'm aware of my bareness, the cool wood of the wardrobe pressing against the skin of my back as I step away from him. The boat sways beneath my feet, and the sight of him like this, wet and lean and gorgeous, makes my breath falter.

This is different from seeing him in his boxers on the deck. We're in the bedroom; I'm half-naked. Our night together flashes through me. Dizzy, slick desire. The way his dipped gaze met mine, slow and honey-sweet. How his breath caught when I touched him. I think of the Zeke I conjured up yesterday when I was afraid he might hurt me, and it seems so absurd now, after seeing him cradling a wounded seagull in his arms, after hearing him say, *You can have my knives.* There are so many versions of this man in my head.

Zeke turns away from me, dropping his gaze. "I'm really sorry. I went into the bathroom without . . ."

He gestures toward the wardrobe without lifting his eyes.

"Oh yeah, of course."

I step awkwardly to the side. He hesitates, finally glancing up again; I can't quite read his expression. He'll have to brush past me to get to the cupboard—there's not room for anything else. We say nothing, eyes locked, the hot, still air silent between us, and there's a weird sense of timelessness to it all, like we're caught somewhere between our night together and the reality of our lives as they are now.

"Listen, Lexi," Zeke says, looking down at the floor again. He clears his throat. "I just want to say—after yesterday—I—sorry, could you just pass me my T-shirt? I feel stupid saying this topless."

"Yes, yeah, of course," I say, spinning to grab his T-shirt and holding it out to him.

The moment has broken, but my heart is still beating too fast. I'm already braced to dislike whatever he's about to say—it has the tone of a rejection.

"I hope you feel safer with me now," he begins.

"I'm fine," I cut in. I still feel a bit embarrassed about yesterday, though I know if it was Penny saying that, I'd tell her she had every right to feel the way she did. "It's fine."

He frowns slightly, pulling on his T-shirt with one swift tug.

"But we're stuck here together. If you want to get away from me, you can't. I don't want you to feel uncomfortable." He takes a breath. "So I just want to say, just really clearly say, that I'm not expecting—I'm not going to hit on you or . . . I know things started that way between us, but it's different now. I think we should just . . . ban it."

My mouth is dry. "Ban it?"

"Yeah. No . . ."

For the briefest moment his gaze kisses the bare skin of my chest and shoulders, and the heat still pulsing under the surface flares up in me again.

"No sex," he says.

Well, that pulls me up short.

"Right," I say, trying to keep my face blank.

"No touching or kissing or anything sexual."

"Right. Great. Yeah."

"All sex acts strictly forbidden," he says, waving a hand in a *cut* motion.

"I've got it, Zeke," I say sharply.

Christ, sex acts? Where are we, the courtroom?

"Sorry. I was so crap for you yesterday. I want to be better today."

I melt slightly. He is being considerate, really. And he's absolutely right: the dynamic between us is complicated enough as it is. We *can't* sleep together again; that would be madness. I mean, there's no morning-after pill out here if the condom breaks, for starters. And the brutal reality is that in my experience, sleeping with a guy never ends with a positive relationship. I needed to hear him say all this.

But needing something and wanting something are different matters entirely, and even though it probably *does* have to be this way, I'm surprised to discover quite how much I wish it didn't.

"Right," I say briskly. "I'll just get dressed, then. Platonically. So . . ."

"Yeah, sorry," he says, spinning on his heel and heading out of the room. He pauses briefly in the doorway, glancing over his shoulder. "Thanks for having that conversation," he says quietly, and the hint of a smile tells me he's remembering me saying the same on the deck yesterday. "It helped."

Zeke

I'M HANGING OUT with a beautiful woman, and we're not going to have sex.

I don't really know how I feel about this.

I saw the way she was looking at me when I walked into the bedroom earlier, and my heart kind of sank, like, oh yeah, that's what she needs from me, isn't it? I should've guessed it would be. She made it clear that was all she wanted from the start.

But then I remembered what she said yesterday, about being a woman trapped somewhere with a man she hardly knows. I remembered the way she doubled over laughing this morning on the deck as I messed around trying to grab Eugene, and how good it felt to hear that sound, to know that it was me that brought it out of her. I remembered that I'm actually good for more than one thing, and that maybe that's *not* what she needs from me here, and maybe it can be me who sets that boundary this time.

And I'm kind of proud of myself.

For the last eight months, I've been working with a therapist. My flatmate, Brady, brought up the idea, and the suggestion was so out of character, I actually listened. *I just wonder if you're OK, mate,* he'd said, fidgeting next to me as we watched an old *How I Met Your Mother* rerun at nine a.m. He was just up, and I'd not slept, going from the restaurant to a nightclub, bringing another woman home to my bed, seeing her down to her Uber that morning the way I always do. *Like, it's cool to want a lot of sex and stay out all night with women if that's what you like, but . . . do you?* Brady asked. *Do you actually? Because you seem really fucking tired all the time, man. What's it all for?*

Turns out that was a very good question. The sex was a temporary fix, that's what therapy's taught me. It was a way to feel good about myself for a night without any of the risks associated with actually getting to know someone.

I don't know when it became a habit, but it did. Wanting to give people what they need from me so they'll like me better, and then wanting to leave when it's still my decision to go.

I've been making progress, though. I made a conscious choice to take a different path—fall in love, have a healthy, happy family, all that stuff. I'm worth more than just one night.

That's the mantra anyway.

I stand out on the deck, fingering the tarpaulin by the helm. I guess breaking my rules for Lexi meant I felt like I couldn't be totally myself with her. And now that I've set that boundary, now that I know we're not going to sleep together, I feel like a weight's lifted, even though—and this is so messed up—even though actually I'd *love* to sleep with Lexi again. I mean, she's so beautiful. And that night was . . .

"You're always standing there," she says, emerging suddenly through the door onto the deck.

She's in shorts and a T-shirt now, hair piled in its usual giant bun. Stripped back and gorgeous. I bet she has no idea how attractive this look is.

"Does it make you feel in control, or something?" she says. "Captain of your own ship?"

I realize I've got one hand on the completely useless helm.

"Oh," I say. "Umm."

"Co-captain," she corrects herself. "*Platonic* co-captain."

I wince slightly. "Did I go too hard on the platonic thing? Because . . ."

"What, you mean . . ."

She mimics the slashing gesture I made when I said, *All sex acts strictly forbidden.*

"I've not had a lot of practice at that conversation," I say, smoothing my curls down.

Lexi's mouth lifts in a quick smile. "You were very effective."

"But I came across like a bit of a dickhead," I finish for her.

She shrugs, moving past me to look out at the water. "We're all dickheads sometimes," she says, not unkindly.

I frown slightly. Her saying that, it snagged on something. Déjà vu again, maybe? Like I've heard someone use that line before.

"Seriously, though, I get it. Sorry if I was a bit prickly about it at first. Just, you know. A woman's got pride."

She's got her back to me, hands on the railing.

"But everything you said was right." She glances over her shoulder. "I think we're doing pretty well, you know. Not dead yet. Not killed each other yet." She looks at me in an evaluating sort of way, eyes narrowed a little. "You think you can survive out here for a while without me driving you nuts? If we have to?"

"Yeah," I say. "Yeah, totally."

I don't even have to think about it. I like being around Lexi. She's interesting, and she's smart, and even when I've pissed her off, she doesn't make me feel stupid.

"Same for you," she says.

I smile, leaning against the helm. I guess this is . . . friendship, then? Is that what it is? It feels more comfortable than anything we've had so far.

"So," she says briskly. I'm starting to get that Lexi isn't really the dwell-in-a-nice-moment type. "Any idea what the hell we do now?"

"I did have . . . I did think . . ." I bite my bottom lip. I don't know why I started either of those sentences. I was just thinking how nice it is that Lexi doesn't think I'm dumb, and now I'm about to suggest something she'll definitely think is stupid.

She turns, putting her back to the railing, arms folded across her T-shirt.

"Mm?" she prompts.

"This tarp," I say, tilting my head to the tarpaulin I was fiddling with when I first came out onto the deck. "I was just thinking, like . . . could we . . . make a sail? Or is that ridiculous? Because I have no idea how to . . ."

"Zeke," Lexi says, her eyes widening, "you're a fucking genius."

～～～～

All right. So Lexi *also* has no idea how to make a sail. This should make me feel worse, but it makes me feel quite a lot better, actually.

"I'm confident it should be triangular," she says, standing on the sofa.

She's trying to get a bird's-eye view of the tarpaulin we've just cut from the boat with my largest knife, which kind of made me want to cry, but: priorities. Still, it'll be totally blunt now. A blunt knife is a tragedy. A smaller tragedy than me dying at sea, but still shit.

"We can attach it to Dad's flagpole," I say, "but I feel like we need another pole . . . along the bottom, maybe?"

"Right," Lexi says, clicking her fingers and looking around her for an obliging pole. "Sorted," she says, pointing to the standard lamp.

I eye it. It's quite . . . small.

"Don't look at my pole like that," Lexi says, deadpan. "It's about what you do with it."

That makes me snort with laughter. I see the pleased glimmer in her eye before she turns her attention back to the tarpaulin.

"You know this isn't going to be any use right now, don't you, given there's zero breeze?" I say. I'm worried the idea's going to disappoint her.

She waves that off. "Yeah, but when there *is* a breeze, we'll be ready. Is there anything useful in the bedroom? The wardrobe hanging rail?"

"It's about thirty centimeters long," I point out, "but I'll check in case there's something we've missed."

She nods, not looking away from the tarpaulin. I head for the bedroom, glancing out of the kitchen window as I go. More sea, more sky, more nothing else.

I go to the wardrobe first, to take a look at the rail. But the first thing I spot when I open that door are the books.

The logbooks. *Dad's* logbooks.

They're scattered on the wardrobe floor, over my duffel bag and hers, as if Lexi just upended the box when she found them. And there's a secret compartment left open in the back of the wardrobe— a cubbyhole. One of my dad's classics. I recognize the mechanism.

My heart's hammering. Dad always loved his hidden compartments. When we were kids, he built us our own secret drawers inside our IKEA desks. Mine was filled with marbles, then scrawled song lyrics, then the little scraps of evidence that my father wasn't really my father.

"Zeke? You all right?" Lexi says from behind me. "Oh yeah, I totally forgot about those in all the Eugene excitement. I meant to read them as soon as we were done."

I whirl to look at her. "They're private, OK? You can't read them."

Her eyebrows shoot up. "They're yours?"

"No, they—they were my father's."

Dad filled those logbooks out religiously, the way he did most things. Meticulous and obsessive, that was my dad, and that's Jeremy and Lyra through and through as well, though it looks different on those two. For Jeremy, it's about getting everything just right: top marks in every exam, the perfect house, the perfect job. For Lyra, it's more like she's pissed off at the whole world for being so disorganized.

My dad's logbooks were private—he'd stop writing the minute one of us came in. I used to look at their thick leather covers and wonder whether those books would tell me what my dad actually thought—about me, but also about my mum, our family, why the whole thing got so broken. Dad was an enigma, with his quotes and his riddles and his secrets. As a kid, even before I got suspicious about him being my real dad, I thought he didn't really want me. He was always stilted around me, different from how he was with Lyra and Jeremy.

I bought this boat back to look for answers. But now that I'm staring at those old books, I feel like a child again, and the idea of finding out the real truth . . . it's terrifying. Better to wonder than to know you're not loved.

I slam the wardrobe door closed, leaving the logbooks scattered where they are.

"Just don't read them," I say, my back still to Lexi, my breath coming fast. "OK?"

"We've got to read them eventually, surely. What if they might tell us something useful?" Lexi says. "About the boat, I mean."

"They won't."

"Zeke, there are very few things on this boat. We need to make use of *everything* we have."

"Just leave it, Lexi."

"Can you tell me why?"

There's a gentleness to the way Lexi's pushing that reminds me of Brady. He's the one who suggested therapy, and who gave me the shove to apply to Davide's restaurant when I was just a grill chef at a fast-food chain. All of a sudden I miss him so much—I wish he were here to crack a dumb joke, chill me out, distract me.

I'm breathing hard. That childlike version of me is still here, scared and unloved. Everything's right on the surface and I can't shove it down, but there's nowhere to go, either, no way to walk away.

"I'm not going anywhere," Lexi says.

I realize I've been standing here saying nothing for ages. My skin starts to prickle. I hate it when I don't notice myself zoning out like this.

"As in," she clarifies, "when you want to talk about why those logbooks make you so uncomfortable, I'll be here." She stretches her hands out. "I *really* don't have anywhere else to be."

I swallow, keeping my face turned from hers. "Yeah, thanks."

"And I'm like a dog with a bone once I want an answer on something," she says, after a moment. "So sooner rather than later would save you some aggro."

Eugene makes a noise out on the deck, a kind of *haww–haaw–haaww*, and it's pretty earsplitting even from here in the bedroom. Both Lexi and I jump.

"Fuck me!" she yells, clutching her chest and glaring toward the door, but she's already moving to go check on him. "Saved by the seagull," she says over her shoulder at me as we cross the living area.

I breathe a little easier as the bedroom door closes, calming down now that the books are behind me. I knew rescuing that bird was a good idea.

We brought him out onto the deck to get some air while we were hacking away at the tarpaulin with my precious knife. I announced hours ago that he's already looking better, which he definitely is. Lexi said he's *looking the same, mainly because he's a bird and birds always look the same.*

"Zeke," Lexi says.

There's something about her tone. I don't know Lexi all that well, really, but I know exactly what it means when she says my name like that.

It means there's hope.

I climb up to the deck, and in two steps I'm beside her, over by the railing, waving my arms, jumping up and down as Lexi screams, "Hey! Hey!"

There's a ship.

When you've stared at the sea for hours on end wishing for something, actually seeing it there is totally surreal. The ship's massive, loaded with containers—from this distance it looks like a toy made of Lego blocks.

We're both jumping and screaming. Eugene's cawing by our feet. My throat already hurts, and Lexi whacks the side of my head as she sweeps her arms back and forth, and we just keep going and keep going, but so does the ship.

"It's not . . ." Lexi's breathless. She grips the rail, bending over for a moment, head down. "It's not coming this way. It's not changing direction. It's not seen us."

"Hey! Help! Help!" I scream, still jumping. I'm not giving up. This is it. This is our rescue. This is when we go home.

"Zeke, it's getting smaller."

"Help us! Help!"

My voice breaks. It hits me that from this distance they likely can't see us at all. Even if they can, even if we're a speck on their screens, we're not radioing them or sending up a flare—there's no reason for them to think we're in distress.

I've thought so much about what might happen to us out here, but it's not occurred to me once that a boat might come and we might *not* get rescued.

Lexi starts yelling and jumping again beside me. Eugene shifts from one foot to the other, stressed out. I scream until I'm hoarse and the cargo ship has silently vanished.

And then Lexi just goes wild.

"This cannot! Be! Happening!" she screams, kicking the folded deck chair and then doubling over.

I crouch down, pressing my hands to my cheeks. Beside us, Eugene keeps squawking, wings flapping.

"Hey," I say, as she sobs. "Lexi, it'll be OK. It'll be OK. Another ship will come."

"Shut up! You don't know! You don't know! It won't be OK, we're going to die out here and Mae will be traumatized and Penny will be alone . . . And there's so much . . . Fuck. I've not done anything! I've done nothing interesting in my whole entire life and now it's about to be over!"

Her face is blotchy and wet. I'd do anything to make her feel better.

"The ship just didn't spot us, but this is good, we saw a ship. That means there will be more ships, right? We've got tons of food and water. There's wood for the burner if it gets cold. The boat has held up until now. We'll be fine."

"You don't believe any of that," Lexi says into her hands. "One ship in two *days* and it didn't even come close to us. You know we're screwed."

I don't know what else to say. I'm all out. My heart's aching.

"Can I give you a hug?" I ask, still crouched opposite her with Eugene in his box between us.

"What? Yes, fucking hell, just because we've said no sex doesn't mean you can just squat over there while I'm having a breakdown," Lexi sobs, and to my surprise, that makes me laugh.

I stand as she unfolds herself and I pull her into my arms. She smells of that perfume I caught on the first night—kind of lemony—but she also smells of the houseboat, and of the sea.

"This is so bad," she says into my shoulder, her whole body shaking as she cries. "This is really, really, really . . ."

"I know," I say. I stare out at the water. It's so empty again, as if it's reset to screen saver. I'm angry. Furious. Shaking with it. That ship just *left*. That's not . . . It's not *fair*.

"I can't do this, Zeke."

"You can. You're doing it. You've been doing it for two days and two nights and we're still here."

She presses into me. I hold her tighter.

"I don't want to die," she says.

"Don't say that," I tell her, tipping my cheek to rest against the soft fuzz of her bun. "That's exactly what people say when they're about to die."

That makes her laugh. I smile. Not many people would have laughed at that, given the circumstances.

"Do you know what I really want to do right now?" she asks, voice still muffled in my T-shirt.

"What do you want to do?"

She pulls away from me with a sniff, wiping her face with her arm. "I want to get drunk," she says.

Lexi

WE'RE FLOATING IN the thick heat of the afternoon. There's a very particular kind of sunshine out here, whiter than the sunshine on land; it's mirrored back on itself in the water, and there's nothing to block its path, so it's just relentless.

I have a glass of red wine in my hand and I'm dancing barefoot on the roof, between the comedically shit sail we finished attaching to the flagpole with our second glass of wine, and the bicycle with its cute fake flowers woven around the handles. Zeke still has a little phone charge left—he's kept his on airplane mode ever since we realized we were lost out here—and we've decided to use it listening to one of his downloaded playlists on Spotify. I just wanted some noise, something that wasn't wind or lapping waves or a stressed-out seagull, something that wasn't my own thoughts.

Right now we're on "How Far I'll Go" from *Moana*—to my delight, one of Zeke's downloaded playlists is *Disney's Greatest Hits*, something I find completely incongruous with his cool-guy vibe. He just smiled when I asked him about it and said, *They're iconic. It's great songwriting. Don't shame me. Who doesn't want to be a Disney princess?*

It's hard to get to this spot, the flat roof on top of the bedroom, kitchen and living area, especially if you're short like me and can't hitch up from the deck. I have to inch my way around a narrow ledge on the side of the boat and hop up from there, but it suddenly, drunkenly struck me as strange that there's a part of this boat where I've not stepped foot, so I had to try.

The song switches to "We Know the Way." Down in the kitchen, Zeke sings along—he butchers the Samoan section, laughing at himself, but his voice is good. It's low and gritty, soulful. I spin to his song and lift my face to the open sky. It's the bottomless blue of true summertime.

Since that ship sailed off, I've been sliding deeper and deeper into apathy, and right now it feels great.

"Are you on the roof?" Zeke calls, throwing the kitchen window open.

It swings, smacking into the side of the houseboat.

"It kind of sounds like someone is tap-dancing up there."

"Yeah, that's me," I shout back, louder than I need to. There's nobody nearby to think about, no reason to quiet down. Why not shout?

"Can you dance?" Zeke asks after a moment, voice drifting up from the kitchen. "I feel like you can."

I twirl. "Oh yeah. I'm bloody brilliant. It's like *Strictly Come Dancing* up here," I say, attempting a few cha-cha steps. Penny and Mae love the show; I always watch it with one eye while scrolling through my phone. Mae likes to sit with her feet in Penny's lap and her head in mine. The thought of her little, precious, engrossed face makes the apathy a lot harder, so I try to focus on the movements of my feet and the blank heat of the sun.

"Are you actually? Can you teach me?"

"To dance?"

"Why not?"

"I mean, I haven't danced properly since I did classes when I was, like, thirteen. And that was a *long* time ago," I say, taking another slug of red wine.

"Did you love it?"

"Yeah," I say, then pause midstep, surprised at myself.

"Then I bet you remember how. Come on. Come down."

His voice still holds the throaty warmth of his singing. I feel weightless, just the right amount of drunk as I hop down and inch my way back along the edge of the boat. The ledge is a foot wide; there's a low railing along the flat roof that I can hold on to as I go, but the sea is one misstep away to my right.

I can swim, and the sea is perfectly still, so falling in would be fine. It might even be nice. It tugs at me, the temptation just to leap off into the water and swim, even though I know I wouldn't get anywhere. The sea is absolutely everything the boat isn't: it's enormous, edgeless, with nothing to duck under or bump your hip on.

And that ship just left.

I've never felt so trapped in all my life. The water pulls at me, glimmering, wide.

"Please don't jump?" Zeke says mildly from the deck, stretching out a hand to help me.

I snap out of it, looking away from the water. There's a gap between the railings and where the wheelhouse cover would come down if we hadn't sawed it off for our sail, and I slip through. My hand stays linked with Zeke's for just a touch longer than it should. I'm wine-giddy and sun-kissed and feeling desperate; right now I really do wish he'd not declared sex *forbidden*. It's one of those words that makes me contrary, especially when I'm tipsy.

Then "Let It Go" starts on the phone, and the moment I hear the opening notes, it's like Mae has stepped onto the deck. As the piano plays out across the water, I miss her so much it makes me breathless. The soft, trusting weight of her as I carry her, sleeping, from the car. The cadence of her brightest laugh, the one that tumbles out of her. The way she says my name—*Lexeeee*—when I'm telling her no more telly.

I gulp in a breath, eyes flicking to Zeke, who is watching me in that thoughtful way of his, as though he's trying to figure me out.

"I can just about slow dance," he says. "You want to show me how it's done?"

"I think you're really overestimating how much I can remember from dance classes that took place in an age when we were all wearing baggy jeans the first time around."

His lip quirks. "I think you're capable of pretty much anything."

He holds his hand out to me. I take it. He settles the other lightly on my waist, and we begin to dance, circling in the center of the little triangular deck as though we're on the dance floor at a wedding. At first it feels ridiculous, but by the time we hit the chorus, I'm resting my head against his shoulder, eyes pricking with tears, gripping his hand tightly. The floor moves beneath us, but I'm used to it now, that ebb and bob, the knowledge that the sea is always so, so close.

"Why did you stop dancing?" he asks quietly.

"God, I don't know, it was decades ago," I say, but the moment it comes out of my mouth, I *do* know. Dad was long gone. Money was tighter than ever. The pub was too quiet. Penny loved her football lessons, and I knew Mum paid for them, so something had to give.

As the last line of "Let It Go" plays out, I tilt my head to look up at him. His hazy maple-syrup eyes; the faint impression of dimples; the sensitive line of his lip, reddened by the wine. I know if I kissed him, I'd taste the merlot already on my tongue.

It takes me a moment to realize the song has shifted to "A Whole New World."

"I actually did learn a routine to this song," I say. "It was the first one we did at the class." I'd made Penny practice with me in the pub garden, cheered on by the summer tourists with their spritzers and sun hats.

Zeke smiles. "Yeah? Show me."

I snort. "It was very . . ."

I step back and fling my arms in the air, lifting my face dramatically to the sun.

Zeke copies me, ringlets flying, the tips of his fingers brushing my arm as he lifts his hands to the sky and bends his back. I press my lips together, and then, because I'm drunk, and because right now nothing seems to matter much, I start dancing.

The teacher called this *modern dance*, but I don't know if it quite fits in any category—it's just the sort of solo a child would perform in the living room. She pitched it perfectly, hence the fact that I seem to remember it two decades on. There's not a lot of footwork and there is a lot of arm sweeping. At one point I have to take three little steps backward, and go *thwack* into the steering wheel; Zeke reaches out to steady me, his eyes bright and laughing, and I don't even stop to wonder if he's laughing at me or with me.

I barely falter—it all just comes back to me, almost like it's skipped my brain altogether and the memory has stayed in my body. Just as I reach the finale, I remember how Penny and I adapted it that summer, making it a two-person performance.

"Catch me and lift me up!" I say, grabbing Zeke's shoulders and hopping.

He cottons on fast. He grips me around the waist and lifts me as I push off his shoulders. I am a lot bigger than I was when I last did this, and have considerably less core strength, but thankfully Zeke is a much better dance partner than eight-year-old Penny. He's holding me up as I tentatively stretch my arms out to either side, one of my feet popped in full Mia–in–*Princess Diaries* style, and we're wobbling, teetering here on the deck, already starting to laugh. The sun is in my face and my heart is pounding—this is the first time I've raised my heart rate with something other than terror since we left dry land.

I look down at his face, tilted up to mine. He's smiling, those crossed teeth showing, his eyes narrowed against the sun's glare; he looks gorgeous. As he lowers me to the deck, I feel every inch of our bodies touching. His eyes grow warmer, smile subsiding to the crooked one that draws a dimple in his left cheek. His chest is rising and falling, his curls mussed.

Then he drops his grip on my waist, reaching for the phone on the shelf above the steering wheel and hitting replay on "A Whole New World."

"OK," he says, "so step one is . . ."

He starts dancing.

I'm still out of breath, and he catches me completely by surprise. I laugh as he tries to mimic my performance, complete with pointed toes, expressive hair flicks and a move that takes him dangerously close to hurling himself into the sea.

"Careful!"

He grips the railing, bent over, laughing.

"What's next?" he asks. "How am I doing?"

"You're a natural. It's the shimmy," I tell him, demonstrating, and then wincing slightly—this move is a bit different now that I'm a fully grown woman.

I think I catch a flicker of heat in his eyes as he watches me dance, but he smiles it away and starts shimmying right back at me.

"No, oh my God, what are your hips doing?" I ask.

"I don't know, what are my hips doing?"

"They're meant to just . . . They don't really get involved," I say.

Zeke's whole body wiggles side to side, as if he's an overexcited puppy wagging its tail. I am not sure how, but even his knees are shimmying. I laugh so much I snort, which makes him laugh more, which makes his dancing even more shambolic.

"Just stop waggling so much!" I say, wiping tears from my cheeks. "You're—oh my God, no, why is your bum so . . ." I copy him, sticking my bum out behind me.

"My bum is just where it wants to be, thank you," he says, though he does try to pull it in a bit.

When I first saw this man lounging in his armchair in The Anchor, I never, ever imagined he would dance like this.

"There you go, you look less like you're pretending to be a chicken now, this is good!" I say, reaching for his hips. "Now just . . . stop. With these. The hips need to be used sparingly. Like . . ." I try to think of an analogy that'll work for Zeke. "Like salt."

"I'm lost," Zeke says. "Are you saying I dance like oversalted chicken?"

I tighten my grip on his hips, the black leather of his belt digging into my palms. He stills for a moment, holding on to the railing on either side, looking me in the eyes. He's bright-faced and breathless and we're barely a foot apart. All of a sudden, I want to kiss him—not one of those fierce, heat-seeking kisses from that night in Gilmouth, but a kiss with eyes open, where you're still half laughing, where you don't want to stop looking at each other for even a moment.

He lets out an unsteady breath, and then holds out a hand for me. I assume we're going to dance again—the music is sliding from "A Whole New World" to "Go the Distance"—but instead, he tugs me inside the boat. It's cooler in here, and a little stuffy. I can smell washing-up liquid from Zeke cleaning the barbecue and plates with a bucket of seawater, and there's dampness in the air. Probably just the sea leaching in from somewhere, no big deal.

The door slams behind us.

"Where are we going?"

"Cocktails. My hips are a lot better after a negroni," Zeke says, with a tiny smile, heading for the kitchen.

He fiddles with one of his newly storm-proofed cupboards. Earlier today, he fixed them all closed by looping a string around each handle—*storm prep*, he said, which made my stomach turn over. But now he's tipsy and it's taking him forever to undo them.

"Fuck's sake," he says, but he's still half dancing to the Disney song playing from the phone out on the deck, swaying his head back and forth, foot tapping. "That's your influence, you know. The swearing," he says over his shoulder.

"Yes, I'm sure you were all 'dangs' and 'dashes' before you met me," I say dryly, but I'm remembering what he said when we were rescuing Eugene: *You swear a lot. Why do I like that so much?*

The string comes loose. I watch as Zeke pulls out all the drinks I picked up in Tesco, and feel a sobering twinge of nerves as I headcount the bottles: half a liter of rum, half a liter of gin, one liter of soda water, two liters of tonic . . .

"We shouldn't be wasting all this stuff," I say.

"What, the gin?" Zeke says, voice warm. "Here, look, this is going off anyway," he says, handing me a packet of cut mint from the fridge.

I bought this to make myself mojitos. It was juvenile, really: mojitos are Penny's favorite, and she's always begging me to make them for her—apparently mine are better than hers. I'm not sure when I imagined I would make myself a solo mojito. Maybe by the time I went to Tesco I already knew that after a day or two alone on the houseboat I would come to my senses and message Penny. I'm sorry I walked out like that. You didn't really want to kick me out, right? I would have said. You've got to give Penny an opening to apologize—she gets herself stuck in corners otherwise, digging her heels in because she's too ashamed to admit she made a mistake.

The mint leaves are turning dark and limp against the plastic. I guess there's no harm in using these, and it's not like rum is a particular staple of survival. I grab a knife from the drawer and break open the packet. Standing here in the kitchen with Disney tunes playing and the crisp, artificial feel of supermarket packaging in my hands, I can almost pretend I'm in the real world. I'm still warm from the dancing; I feel better than I have in days. Maybe longer.

"Hey, is that how you chop?" Zeke says after a while, nudging me.

"No, I'm just pretending for the live studio audience."

I catch his smile in my peripheral vision, my gaze fixed on the mint leaves spread out on the counter.

"You know . . . if you keep your finger across the back of the knife like that it'll make your hand cramp up faster. If you just . . ."

It happens so fast, so easily. The houseboat is barely moving, but still, the floor *is* always shifting underneath us, enough to throw you a touch off balance if you're not ready for it. We're drunk. And the knife is one of Zeke's chef's ones—it's sharp.

I turn toward him to tell him off for mansplaining just as he moves toward me to guide my hand on the knife. Its tip slices clean through his T-shirt. I feel it cut the skin underneath as easily as if it were moving through warm butter.

For a moment we freeze, both silent, as the wound begins to lazily drool blood from the gaping slit in Zeke's green T-shirt.

"No," I say, more disbelief than denial. "I . . ."

Zeke claps a hand to the wound and then lets out a raw *ah* of pain. The blood seeps between his fingers, a vibrant, childish red. His T-shirt is already darkened and wet. I look up and meet his frightened eyes.

"We need to . . ." I don't know what to say. What we need to do is ring 999. I've just sliced his midriff open. But there's no 999, no phone at all. There's just me and Zeke. "Stop the bleeding," I manage. "Can you—can you walk? Bathroom?"

I slide the door open—it jars and catches, and I swear under my breath as I shove it back. Zeke steps through behind me, bent over himself, as though he has a stitch. I scrabble for the first aid kit and unzip it after three tries, my careful inventory forgotten—I haven't a clue what we've got in here, or even what I'm looking for. As I dither over plasters and little tubes of cream, fear singing through me, Zeke grabs his towel from the rail and presses it against his stomach, then lowers himself to sit on the lid of the toilet.

"Yes," I say, meeting his eyes fleetingly in the mirror above the sink, and then looking away. "You should . . . Yeah. Sit down."

"I'm OK, Lexi," Zeke says, voice labored.

I look down at my shaking hands and realize I've not put the knife down yet. I drop it in horror, and it clatters into the sink, leaving a thin streak of Zeke's blood against the bowl.

"Honestly, I'm OK."

"I'm so sorry," I breathe, bracing myself against the sink. "What the fuck were we doing, drinking all that alcohol?"

I'm still drunk; my thoughts won't seem to come into line. What do we do? What do we do?

"I'm sure it's not as bad as it looks. It doesn't even really hurt," Zeke says, moving his legs gingerly. His foot brushes mine. "Should we wash it? Maybe with seawater—would that stop it getting infected? Or is that stupid?"

The word *infected* passes through me like it's made of steel. You need antibiotics if a cut gets infected. We've only got a tiny first aid kit, plasters, one out-of-date tube of antiseptic cream.

"I don't know," I say, scrubbing at my face to try to sober myself up. I stare at my reflection in the mirror—I look awful. Pale and red-eyed, my hair desperately in need of a wash. "Seawater has salt in it, which is good for infection, but it's also got bacteria in it, too, right?"

I look down at the miniature first aid kit in the sink and pull out a tube of Savlon. Its use-by date says it expired in 2020. I chew the inside of my cheek, trying to work out the relative risks. How bad can antiseptic cream go? Will it just be less effective, or does it go nasty?

"The alcohol," Zeke says suddenly. "The gin, and the rum. Alcohol sterilizes stuff, right?"

"Yes!" I'm already heading for the cupboard, abandoning the Savlon in the sink.

The door to the drinks cupboard is still hanging open. I present the two bottles to Zeke, who stares at them, blank-faced with shock.

"The rum?" I say, when he says nothing. "I'm not sure you want a load of fragrant botanicals in there."

He takes the rum, breaking the seal with a grimace.

"Do I just . . . chuck it on?" he says, lifting up the towel slightly, averting his own gaze from his stomach.

"Yeah, I think so?"

It occurs to me that it might hurt, but before I can warn him, he's done it, and he *screams* between his teeth, hunching over himself. His pain is so audible I can almost feel it.

"Oh my God," I say, pressing my hands to my face.

"It's OK, it's OK." His breathing is labored. "The burn's easing off already."

I turn back to the sink. I can hardly bear to look at him. I did this. Me, waving a razor-sharp knife around when I've been drinking red wine since lunch. It's so irresponsible it takes my breath away.

"Lexi, will you just stop for a second?"

I'm fumbling around with the Savlon again, trying to open the jammed, dried-up tube. The lid comes off and flies out of my hands, skittering off toward the base of the toilet.

"It's OK. The alcohol just hurt, that's all. It's not so bad now. It's only a cut. Look."

"I don't want to," I say, but my eyes are drawn to him in the mirror as he lifts the towel away from his stomach.

I turn. His T-shirt is bloodstained from the ribs down, a solid, unpleasant shade of brown. He lifts the fabric to reveal the skin beneath, shifting his weight with a wince, and the blood runs fresh as he moves, another quick, slick gulp of dark red. The wound is stretched wide, grotesque and meaty, as broad as a smiling mouth.

"Hmm. When I imagined doing this," Zeke says, "I sort of thought you'd be able to see less of my insides."

I can hear the effort it's taking him to keep his voice light.

"Oh, God," I say, turning my face away. "That's not just a cut. Put the towel back on, Zeke, you need to apply pressure."

He does as he's told and stays quiet, slumped there, head bowed as he looks down at the darkening towel. How much blood can he lose? How much has he already lost?

"Please don't feel bad, Lexi. None of this is your fault, OK? I said we should make cocktails even though we were drunk and . . . you know . . . on a boat. Lexi—are you OK?"

"Stop being so understanding." I close my eyes and take a deep breath. I can smell blood, tinny and frightening. "I'm fine. I just feel . . ." *Awful, awful, awful.*

"You aren't responsible for this. For me. Lexi, look at me."

I meet his gaze. He's steadier now, not so afraid, not so young-looking, but I can see the pain there. As the adrenaline eases, it'll start to get worse.

"Painkillers," I say, swiveling back to the first aid kit. "We've got ibuprofen, paracetamol. You should have both. But maybe not at the same time, we should space it out . . ."

"I'll just have some paracetamol," he says. "We shouldn't . . . We don't want to get through the medicine too fast."

He's right. These small calculations are so difficult when we have no idea how long we'll be out here—how much do we eat, drink, use, save up?

I fetch him a glass of water to take the tablets. He knocks them back with a wince, and I wince, too.

"How long should it take for the bleeding to stop?" he asks. His voice is level. The tone of a man telling himself to remain calm.

"I have no idea. I don't know about any of this stuff, Zeke. I did a basic first aid course about ten years ago."

"I've done some as part of a kitchen safety course," Zeke says. "But a lot of that was about how to prevent this stuff. Like, don't cut on an unstable surface. Such as a boat, I guess."

I turn to face him, leaning back against the sink. It's so cramped in here that his feet are framing mine, his knees spread so I can stand between them. The shower curtain tickles my elbow. My heart is still racing.

"I do remember learning what it'll look like if it gets infected, though," he says, swallowing with difficulty. "It'll get red and raised, with little lines running off it, maybe."

"OK. OK. So we know what to look for."

"And then what?" Zeke says, glancing aside.

"Should we . . ." I point to the Savlon, abandoned next to our toothbrushes on the edge of the sink. It seems a bit ridiculous in the face of his wound, like considering applying Polyfilla to a hole made by a wrecking ball.

"I don't really want to move the towel again," Zeke says, almost apologetically.

"No. Yeah. OK."

So we stay where we are. Zeke keeps pressure on the wound. I stand with him, my thoughts wine-fogged and slow with panic. Minutes pass. The towel turns darker. It's been perhaps twenty,

twenty-five minutes since I casually sliced his midriff open with a kitchen knife, and the world feels like a completely different place.

After a while, Zeke eases his hand from the towel and shakes it out at the wrist, breathing heavily through his nose. We wait. I stare at the bloodstained fabric.

"I feel like we need a game plan that isn't just me sitting on this toilet," Zeke says, moving to stand.

I open my mouth, but to my surprise, he's not waiting for me to come up with something.

"If you put that green blanket over the bed, I can prop myself there," he says. "Less strain if my feet are up, and we can wash the blanket more easily than the sheets if I, like . . . bleed everywhere."

"Right! Yes. Good idea."

I hover for a moment, wondering if he needs my help to walk, but he grips the doorframe and then takes a few unsteady, short steps to get himself to the kitchen counter. I move past him into the bedroom, grabbing the green blanket from the end of the bed.

We get him settled back on the pillows. I end up lying beside him, hands on my belly, staring up at the wood-paneled ceiling. When I close my eyes, the skylight leaves its rectangle there, glowing black. We've never been in this bed together before—we've always taken it in turns. Well, except for the first night.

"It's wide," Zeke says, his voice strained. I glance over, then down to the towel. He's feeling around underneath it; his fingers come back shining with new blood. "It's sort of stretched open? I don't know if . . . I feel like a cut like this, at home, it would need stitches."

At home, we would be in A&E right now. He'd probably be bandaged up already, just waiting for a doctor to be free to suture him. We wouldn't think twice about the painkillers he'd pop on the drive to the hospital.

"Do we have a needle and thread?" Zeke asks.

"Oh my God," I say, lifting a hand to my face.

"It's OK. I'm sure I can do it myself," he says, raising his head to look down at himself. "Do we have anything like that? A needle?"

"There's actually a mini sewing kit in my bag," I say. "One of those hotel ones." From a stay in the New Forest for a friend's wedding.

"OK. Well . . . We'll wait awhile. Maybe it will look better in a bit," Zeke says.

His voice sounds strained, and I look at him closely, tracing his profile on the pillow. He's sweating and drawn. Maybe that's the infection setting in, the bacteria already zipping through his bloodstream.

It is totally possible that Zeke will die. Blood loss, infection—without modern medicine, those things kill you.

I have been so afraid out here on this houseboat, but I don't think—until now—I have truly understood the danger we're in. It's not just the sea, the possibility of running out of food . . . it's everything. Anything. The tiny dangers we encounter every day aren't tiny here. Splinters, snagged nails, a bout of food poisoning: any one of those could feasibly kill us.

I watch as Zeke swallows, and I am hit with a sudden, searing pang of emotion. It's not love, obviously—I barely know the man. Of course it isn't love. But it's akin to it: fiery, low, sweet. Somewhere between desire and grief, as bitter and strong as the way I feel for Mae.

"You'll be OK," I say, and I reach across to grab his hand. "I'll wait with you."

Zeke

IT HURTS. A lot. I'm still just on paracetamol—every time the pain gets bad enough that I consider asking Lexi to fetch me some ibuprofen, I imagine her having a fall or something, and needing it, and I bite the question back.

The bleeding does stop, but whenever I move around it starts again. I know what I need to do. I just . . . don't know if I have the balls to do it.

Neither of us is drunk now. It's late—Disney killed my phone, so we've only got the corgi clock in the kitchen to tell us the time, but I reckon it's after ten. The stars are out, running edge to edge of the skylight. I can't sleep. I wonder about reading the ship's logs, like I'm looking for something that'll hurt worse than this, but I know I'm not going to do it. I shift a bit and can't help moaning at the pain.

"Zeke," Lexi says. "Take some fucking ibuprofen."

"No."

"Please."

"No. I'm fine."

"You're not fine. Please." Her voice rises. She turns her head to look at me and her expression makes me cold. "I can't bear this. It needs stitches. It shouldn't still be bleeding like this."

"I know."

I've known it for ages, really, but I'm so fucking scared of what happens next.

"I'll do it," she says, but her bottom lip is shaking slightly. "You shouldn't have to do it yourself."

I shake my head. That lip quiver. Lexi's always hemming herself in, putting other people first. I don't want to be yet another person she has to look after.

"I'm not squeamish, it doesn't bother me," I lie. "I'll just do it myself."

I take the ibuprofen and wait forty-five minutes. The cut still hurts, but it's slightly duller, kind of like an aching tooth. Lexi boils the two thinnest needles in a pan on the gas hob, and she pours the boiling water on the thread, too, in case that helps. We chose dark purple thread. Lexi vetoes red—*It's very hard to look good in red*, she says. She keeps trying to make me smile, and I do appreciate it, but fuck. It's hard to keep smiling.

I tell her to go out on the deck so she can't hear me. *God*, she says, eyes pained. *If you scream, I don't think I'll be able to bear it*. And I can see she means it—she has real empathy. I feel lucky that of all the strangers I've gone to bed with, Lexi's the one who ended up here.

I manage to slosh more rum on the cut, though even that's excruciating, but I only get one stitch down before I think I'm going to throw up or pass out. I must make some sort of noise, because the moment the needle's through my skin, Lexi comes shooting through the door.

"You're not doing this on your own," she says, voice shaking. "Lie back down. I'll go wash my hands."

DAY THREE

Zeke

THE NEXT MORNING, I doze in and out of sleep, only waking properly when I find Lexi perched beside me, on the edge of the bed. Her wide eyes are fixed on my midriff.

"Good morning," I say, smiling, even though my stomach hurts like hell.

"Have you looked at it?" she says.

When she sewed me up last night, she'd breathed as if she was feeling each pinch of the needle herself. But she didn't hesitate once. She was incredible.

"Not yet," I say, shifting up the pillow a little with a wince.

"How does it feel?"

It burns. I'm due more painkillers, but I'm trying to stretch myself. Use fewer. Get by. The wound is so hot I keep wanting to check the temperature of it with my hand, but I know I should touch it as little as possible.

"Bit sore," I say. "I'm not feeling sick or anything, which is good."

She hands me a chocolate digestive. "Breakfast."

"I can't tell you how glad I am that these were on your shopping list," I say.

I take it from her carefully. Got to look after every crumb of these biscuits. We opened the packet yesterday, after the shock of the knife. There are these and some of those dry amaretti biscuits that're never as nice as you hope they'll be. That's it for sweet foods.

"Shall I look at it? So you don't have to?" Lexi says as I nibble at the edges of my biscuit.

I consider this. "You'd have to do a really good facial expression. If you look freaked out, I'll freak out."

"Christ, right, so how do you want me to look?"

"Pleased?" I say, after a moment's thought.

She unfastens the belt we used to hold the towel in place, and a tiny, testosterone-fueled corner of my mind manages to think dirty thoughts for just a second as her fingers move across the buckle.

"Well?" I prompt, trying to read her.

"This is my pleased face," she says, still examining me.

"You're frowning quite a lot."

"I'm thirty-one, Zeke," she says. "A frown is just drawn on my face in perma-marker now."

"You know thirty-one is really young, right? You act like it's eighty."

"I have almost a whole decade on you."

"Eight years."

"Right. That's basically half your life."

"Which half? The first one flew by."

That makes her eyes smile.

"And it's actually a third of my life, thank you," I say. I try to sit up and her hand claps down on my shoulder, holding me in place.

"You need to eat more than a biscuit. Keep your strength up. Could you manage some cereal? Cornflakes are pretty good dry.

Don't pull a face, you food snob, we're surviving at sea, you're not getting eggs Benedict."

This is all said at speed. I smile up at her, and I watch her face soften as she looks at me, the way the skin around her eyes crinkles.

Last night changed something between us. I think maybe . . . we're a team now.

Lexi

HE'LL SAY HE'S not, but he's weak from the blood loss, and the pain of his wound is drawn all over his face. Earlier, when he got up to pee, he almost collapsed and ended up hunched over the kitchen counter for a full five minutes before he could stand properly again.

He's good at pretending. But he's not OK.

"You're hovering," he says mildly, as I adjust the cushion behind him.

"I'm helping," I say. "You're welcome."

"You're hovering," he repeats, a little more firmly this time. "And I can tell every time you look at me, you're wondering if I'm going to die in a minute."

"And you're telling me that's *not* relaxing?"

I get a faint, tired smile for that. His eyes have turned kind of hollow; there's a grayish semicircle beneath each one, a thumb-swipe in charcoal.

"Honestly, I'm fine as long as I stay lying down," he says. "I just need rest."

I am *craving* Google. The thing I want to find out most of all is when I can stop worrying. I want to know when the danger will have passed—the moment a doctor or a nurse would say, *He's made it through the first however-many hours, so the worst is over now.*

"This place needs a tidy," I say, turning my attention to the bloodstained towel still sitting in a heap in one corner, and the wardrobe door hanging open to reveal the mess inside. "I'll just get it sorted around you and you'll hardly notice I'm here. I'll be popping out to check for boats all the time anyway."

He says nothing, but when I glance over my shoulder at his face I notice his expression—I think he's just clocked I don't want to be alone. I flush, grabbing the dirty towel and taking it out onto the deck to wash with seawater when I next haul up a bucket.

When I return to the bedroom, Zeke has his eyes closed. He opens them when I arrive, but it looks like an effort, like he's lifting something heavy.

"Big ship out there, right? Waiting to rescue us?" he says.

"I told them now's not a great time, can they come back later," I say, though I don't enjoy the joke. The very thought of rescue makes my whole being ache for it. We are both working so hard to stay strong for each other today—the strain is like a constant white noise in the air between us.

I examine the mess in the wardrobe. Both Zeke and I have half unpacked, but left various things in our luggage, too—a halfway house between settling in and being impractical. Those ship's logs I found when we rescued Eugene are still sitting lopsidedly on top of our bags; one has slid down the back, another almost ending up in the inside pocket of my open holdall.

"You know," I say, "you've got some reading material, if you feel up to it today."

He doesn't answer. I figure I've pissed him off—he's been very clear about not wanting to discuss the logbooks, after all—but when I turn, I realize he's unconscious.

"Zeke! Zeke!"

I'm at his side immediately, my hand gripping the bare skin of his upper arm. There is an awful, time-stopping moment when he just lies there, sallow-faced and still, and then his eyes flutter open.

"You OK?" he says, his voice sticky. "Did I drift off? Sorry."

"God, no, sorry," I say, staggering back and leaning into the cupboard next to the wardrobe. "I shouldn't have woken you. You rest. You . . . I'll just . . ."

"I thought you wanted to tidy," he says, frowning slightly. "Are you all right?"

"Yes," I say, crouching down and reaching blindly for my holdall. "I'll just take this out onto the deck and sort through it properly, check there's nothing I missed in the pockets, OK? Go back to sleep."

By the time I reach the deck chair in the thick, midday sunlight, my heart is still thundering like rain on a tin roof. Eugene is out here, sunning himself in his box, unfazed by our ongoing state of disaster. The door slams shut behind me and I jump, even though that sound is now as familiar to me as the *click* of Mae easing my bedroom door open when she can't get to sleep.

Zeke looked dead. He looked dead, and for a moment, I thought he'd left me.

The idea of being alone here, of Zeke being *gone*, and just a— just a *body* . . .

I sit, dropping the bag to the deck between my feet. I'm trembling all over. I need to calm down. He's not dead, we're still afloat, and all is about as well as it can be, given the circumstances. Panic is useless. I loathe being useless. But *fuck*. His face, all smoothed out and still against the pillow . . .

I stare down at the holdall. My makeup bag is in there—I've ignored it up until now, but maybe there's something useful inside it that I've not considered. I unzip it, rifling through the concealer, foundation, blusher, brushes, mascara. Unless this tube of lipstick is one of those cool James Bond gadgets that turns into a helicopter or something, this is all totally redundant. I briefly despise myself for being a woman who packs three shades of foundation instead of useful things like tissues, or snacks, or a small inflatable dinghy.

I can't bear this. I know Zeke needs rest, and I should really be out here watching for boats, but I don't want to leave him alone. I don't want to *be* alone. I want to get off this boat, off off off off *off* it, and as I press my hands hard against my face, I think to myself, *Would I survive if Zeke was gone?*

Yes. I ball my hands into fists. I would survive. I *would*. I'm strong. I'm still here. I would do what I had to do, just like I did when I stitched Zeke's skin up.

I reach into the holdall again and find the hard edge of one of the logbooks. It must have slid fully into that inside pocket as I dragged the bag from the wardrobe. I pull it out and let it lie on my knees, smoothing the surface of the leather cover.

Just don't read them, OK? he said. But why? This is a ship's log—won't it contain information about the houseboat? It might tell us the exact capacity of the water tank, something we're always trying to guess at; it might say there's a phone hidden in some other secret compartment Zeke's dad created way back when. It's *something*, and we have so little out here.

I'll just look. I'll flick open the first page. It would be crazy not to. I've got to be sensible—I can't be sentimental. Zeke is injured. There is no room for emotional decision-making right now.

I open the book.

It's obvious within just a few pages that this isn't really a logbook—it's a diary. I scan pages of cramped, tiny writing: *The rain is endless today, and the sound on the tarp reminds me of camping in the garden with the boys, Lyra refusing, of course, sitting indoors watching Charmed . . . I ate well tonight, a stew. The children would*

have hated it no doubt, too many vegetables ... If I had known sooner,
would it be different, could it be different, I wonder?

I should stop reading. There is no detail about the boat here. But
I keep turning the pages, telling myself I'm just scanning for information, not really reading, not really taking in anything personal.

There is such a freedom to this life. No tethers. Only me, the
water and my puzzles. I am doing just fine today. Even the
problem with the sump for the shower hasn't got me down—
the valve needs replacing, but I keep forgetting because
the children have been here. I know I'm getting it wrong
with the three of them, I can feel I am, with Zeke especially,
but of course, he's different ...

I blow a loose strand of hair out of my face. My heart thumps as
I scan on.

Paige thinks I should tell him the truth ... I sometimes long
to, but I know when he finds out, he'll never come back to
this boat, and ...

"Fuck," I whisper, slamming the book closed.

Why have I done this? I hate secrets. Knowing things I shouldn't
stresses me out, and there's plenty of stressors in my life right now—
I do not need an extra one.

Eugene suddenly lets out an outraged squawk. I startle, then
turn to glare at him.

"What?" I say.

He stares back at me with his judgmental little bird eyes.

"You know what?" I say to him. "You should just go. We should
just chuck you back into the bloody ocean. We can't afford to keep
giving you stale bread. We need the stale bread, OK?"

He remains infuriatingly unblinking.

"This isn't some CBBC show," I tell him, my voice rising. "You're not our cute animal sidekick. Scram. Scram!"

I've started to cry.

"I know you can hop around," I yell at him. "I've seen you do it so you can shit on our sofa cushions. Get out of the box. Go. Just go."

"We gave him food, so he'll probably stick around as long as possible now," comes Zeke's mild voice from inside the boat.

I spin around, wiping my face, shoving the logbook back into my bag.

"What are you doing up?" I say with horror, standing and yanking the door open to find him leaning against the kitchen counter again, head bowed, a fresh towel bunched up beneath his T-shirt.

"I needed the bathroom," he says.

His voice sounds too light and breathy. He turns his head to look at me, still bent over, forearms resting on the counter's edge. "We need Eugene. He's good for morale. He's our therapy animal."

I want to say, *Lie down. Please. Rest. I am so, so afraid you'll die.* But instead I say, "Bloody hell, could you be any more Gen Z?"

He chuckles slightly, then winces. I think he's swaying more than he should be, even taking into account the movement of the boat.

"He'll be well enough to hunt fish for himself soon—look, he's on the move," he says, nodding behind me.

I turn. Eugene is right by my feet, taking uneven steps and letting out a faint, chatty *bok bok* sound, like a chicken.

"Oh, so now you get out of the box, you little shit," I say through my tears, and when I turn back, Zeke's smiling at me.

"Please lie down," I say. "I am not a woman who says 'please' very often. But—*please.*"

He sobers, eyes steady on my face. "I'm OK, Lexi."

"You think you're OK. But you look terrible. I *need* you to rest."

He straightens up slowly, taking a step toward the bedroom and gripping the doorframe with both hands.

"When I'm better," he says, voice almost too quiet to hear with his back to me, "I'm going to make you a proper breakfast."

"Zeke, we're . . ."

"Lost at sea, rationing food, I know. Let me have this, OK?"

I stay silent. I'm not really one for fantasies and daydreams. I don't want him to make plans—it feels like tempting fate.

"We don't have a lot of brunch ingredients," I say eventually.

"I like a challenge." He leans forward to crawl onto the bed. "And all's not lost yet. We still have a cafetière."

DAY FOUR

Lexi

IT'S EARLY EVENING, the low light before sundown. We're out on the deck, watching for boats, but really just watching the water. You can lose hours to the sea. It shimmers and fractures—I can't find names for all its shades of blue. Sometimes it seems closer to purple, or gold, or green, and sometimes I can imagine it's the skin of a living beast, breathing underneath us, muscles sliding beneath the surface as it braces to pounce.

Right now it's so serene out there, and I don't know how to feel about it. That still water is keeping us trapped in this particular patch of nowhere, coordinates unknown. But it's also keeping us steady. Still water means we're still alive.

I can't quite believe that another whole day has slid away out here. Zeke is resting on a deck chair beside me, but I do feel encouraged by the progress he's made today: he's now able to move around without feeling like he'll faint, and that aura of sickness that clung to him, the sallowness, it seems to have eased in a way I can't quite define. He just looks more himself again.

"Want to play a game?" he says, eyes still closed.

Our makeshift bandage—a strip cut out of one of the T-shirts in my luggage—forms a discreet lump beneath his top; I keep glancing at it.

"We've already ascertained I'm crap at charades," I say. Though actually I blame Zeke for being unable to guess that I was *clearly* taming a horse, not having a seizure, which would have been a very insensitive choice of charade.

"Not charades. Would you rather," he says.

I raise my eyebrows. I've only ever played this as a drinking game, and we're not really in a position to be wasting fluids. I think about the wine we cracked open two days ago and wince.

"Would you rather be lost at sea on a houseboat with your one-night stand *or* . . ."

I snort.

"Or," Zeke continues, "go back to secondary school?"

"Ooh," I say, turning to face him and leaning on the railing. "Interesting."

Secondary school would have been awful if it hadn't been for Penny. She was my lifeline: she was prettier than me, skinnier than me, and boys liked her, which meant she had power. The one time the boys in my year tried to nick my lunch box—*Hey, pub girl, what have you got in there, pork rinds? Salted peanuts?*—she told them if they didn't back off then she'd tell everyone how small *their* peanuts were, and the whole school had talked about the showdown for weeks. A Year 7 with a pink unicorn rucksack scaring off four Year 9s—that was my Penny.

"Secondary school," I say. "Worse outfits but less likely to die. You?"

Zeke smiles slightly, eyes still closed. His curls are frizzing and greasy at the roots; the unkempt hair sweetens him a bit. He looks very young, lying there on the deck chair, and I feel a twist of discomfort at that, though it shouldn't matter now. All sex acts have been strictly forbidden, after all.

"I'd rather be here than there," he says.

"Seriously?"

"If you're the stupid kid, school isn't fun."

I frown. "There's no way you were a 'stupid kid.'"

He smiles, but it doesn't touch his dimples.

"Trust me. There're two things I'm good at in life, and you don't get graded on either of them at school."

"Cooking," I guess, because I know that's one thing he's confident about—since he's not strong enough to stand and cook himself yet, he's been directing me from the sofa, but between us we have managed to make some genuinely delicious meals out of my random, overemotional Tesco shop.

"Yep."

"And . . ."

He cracks one eye open and looks at me.

"What?" I say.

"Huh," he says, sitting up slightly to give me a wry look. "I kind of hoped you'd remember."

"Oh. Oh." I swallow. "Well, yes, you were very good at that. But come on, what are you, a Stepford wife? You can do more than cook and have sex."

His face goes blank. I pull back slightly, surprised at the suddenness of his reaction—I'd been joking, obviously, but it's clear from his face that I've hurt him.

"Sorry, I just meant—you really talk yourself down," I say.

I hadn't registered it until now, actually. He's the sort of good-looking that tends to come hand in hand with self-assurance, and he'd been so confident getting me to bed. I just hadn't imagined he could have low self-esteem.

"Would you rather be a mermaid or a centaur?" he asks. A firm change of subject.

"Are you seriously asking me that? What good is a hoof right now? I'd be *thrilled* with a fish tail." I've never liked my legs anyway.

"Right," he says, a smile forming as his shoulders relax slightly. "You go, then."

I mull it over. I've felt myself slowing down a bit in the last day or so—when you're forced into inaction, you have to lean in eventually or you'll go mad. Or maybe it's Zeke, his steadiness, his thoughtfulness. He never rushes—it might be rubbing off on me.

"Would you rather eat a rat or eat a donkey?"

"Rat," he says, without hesitation. "Donkeys look so sad all the time. I don't want to give them something else to worry about."

"Mae loves donkeys, so it's rat for me, too," I say, glancing over my shoulder at the horizon. It's become a habit to check the full 360 degrees, even when there's two of us.

"Mae's your friend's child? The one you help look after?"

I nod, already wishing I hadn't said her name out loud. I miss her so much I could break with it. Her absence is raw and gaping, a hole in the very core of me, and the only way to cope is to force my mind away from her however I can.

"Tell me about her," Zeke says softly.

I look back at him, heart hitching in my chest.

"No," I say, swallowing. "No, I don't want to talk about her."

His eyebrows rise a fraction, but there's nothing judgmental in his face.

"I hear you, I just . . . We have nothing but time, and I get the impression you're missing her a lot? I think . . . it might help you to tell me about her."

I look back out at the water. Zeke has no idea what Mae is to me. Telling him means showing him one of the deepest, most significant parts of myself. For a moment I resolve not to do it, but then I glance at him, and he's so familiar to me now—soft eyes, the ghost of a dimple—that it feels a little strange he doesn't already know. He's seen me sobbing and drunk and covered in his blood. What's the use in hiding myself from him now?

"I'd be missing her even if I weren't here," I say. "I don't live with her anymore."

"But you did?"

"For her whole life. Until this week."

He stands carefully and joins me, leaning on the railing. I'm not sure how much of this is for companionship and how much of it is because he needs something to take his weight.

"She's four," I say. "Loves books, elves and gymnastics." I grit my teeth tightly against the wave of pain that comes with the image of her in her leotard and shorts, hair plaited close to her scalp by Penny, who's always been better at hairstyling than I am.

"She's not just your friend's kid, is she?" Zeke says softly. "She's yours, too. You've raised her."

All of a sudden, that sets me off. I don't have time to hold back the tears—they're already running down my cheeks, so I just let myself cry.

"Yeah," I say through the tears. "I *have* raised her. I'm just a family friend, really. That's all I'll be now. But I *was* more than that. I gave her half her bottles at night, and I changed a thousand nappies, and she's—she is mine, in a way, even though I know she's Penny's."

"You said the other day her dad's a bit of a . . ."

I sniff, jaw tightening. "Scumbag? Yeah. The sort of man who knocks a woman up and then wants nothing to do with the baby."

"I'm sorry. That's . . . Every kid deserves better than that."

I glance at him. I know his relationship with his own father is complicated. I wonder about asking, and then I remember the diaries. This isn't a conversation I should be starting unless I'm willing to confess that I know more than I should.

"So what happened?" Zeke asks. "Why did you leave?"

I swallow. I don't want to talk about this, either, but Zeke's right: I think about it all the time, and without the option of messaging Penny to make up again, I've got nothing to do but stew over it. It might feel good to talk it out.

"Penny's got this boyfriend. He's fine. Ryan. Whatever. They're getting serious, and Mae does like Ryan, and I'm sure he's . . . fine . . ."

I wipe my cheeks. Ryan probably *is* fine. But Penny has had so many bad experiences, and every time she dates an arsehole it has an impact on Mae. And Ryan will never be me. He doesn't know the Cheerios song I sing for her every morning. He doesn't know instinctively when Penny needs a break; he doesn't know how stressed she gets when there's too much on her plate.

"They wanted you to move out?" Zeke guesses. "So he can move in?"

I nod. "Penny did this whole thing about how it was for me. How I basically gave up half my twenties to look after her and Mae, and she wants me to get a life of my own. But really she just wants the place to herself with Ryan. She wants me gone."

"Really?" Zeke says after a moment. "Are you sure?"

I step aside, moving away from him, suddenly irritated. "You wouldn't get it."

"OK," he says, voice gentle. "I guess I just think if I was Penny, I'd feel a lot of guilt about how much you'd given up for me. Maybe she's trying to give you something back."

"By kicking me out?"

"By offering to take some of that . . ." He searches for the word. "Some of that responsibility away. Maybe she doesn't know you want to stay."

I stare at him. "Are you serious?"

"Well, have you ever told her?"

I widen my eyes. "She knows," I say, though a current of fear has just passed through me at the question.

I'm not totally sure when I last told Penny how much it means to me to be such a big part of Mae's life. And sometimes I do wish that I could have something that's mine—a job I like, a boyfriend, time off that actually feels like a holiday. But I only have those thoughts very quietly, usually when I'm worn out or tired, and I feel guilty for them every time.

Because I'm so grateful for Mae. I would give up a million things for her. If Zeke said, *Would you rather stay single forever and be part of Mae's life, or have your own place and a boyfriend and lose her*, I wouldn't hesitate: I'd choose Mae. She's brought so much to my life. She *is* my life, really, or she used to be.

"She'll be so glad to see you when we get home," Zeke says softly.

I drop my head, tears returning. "Oh, God," I say.

He touches my back, just lightly, like he's testing whether I want to move away again. I stay put, and he presses tighter, as if he's holding me steady. He's right: it was a huge relief to speak about her out loud. She's burned in my chest like a secret every minute out here, and in some small way, sharing that with Zeke has changed the way it feels to miss her.

"I'm so glad I know now," he says. "And I can't imagine how much harder this must be when you know you have your little girl waiting for you."

"Please," I say on a sob. "I can't bear to think about it like that."

His hand grips the fabric of my T-shirt for a moment, then loosens, as though he's remembering himself.

"We will get you home to her." His voice is as soft as ever, but there's steel in it, too. "OK? We will get you home."

"You can't say that," I choke out.

"OK," he says, after a moment. "Then I'll say . . . there's nothing I won't do to get you back to Mae."

The sunshine weighs hot on my shoulders. I press my forehead against my hands and close my eyes. It's hard to feel lucky out here, but hearing Zeke say that—for a moment, he makes it easy.

DAY SIX

Lexi

A DAY PASSES, and then another. It genuinely astonishes me every morning to wake up and find that we are still floating here. Sometimes it seems *so* bleak—and sometimes it almost seems funny, like we're the punch line of a very long joke.

We're rationing the food more now, being extra careful with water. We've finally figured out the water tank systems monitor, a small screen set into the wall behind the steering wheel. You're meant to input the tank's capacity when you install it, but whoever fitted it didn't bother, so it doesn't tell us how many liters we have left. It just has four lights for the freshwater tank, four lights for the wastewater one. Full, three-quarters, half, a quarter. And empty. Late yesterday, the light for the freshwater tank flicked from a half to a quarter, and Zeke and I finally opened the bottles of tonic and soda water we had been saving up until now. It hadn't felt good.

I've got into a daily routine of sorts, and I always spend at least an hour checking the houseboat meticulously for damage, looking for ways to make her safer. You'd think we would spend our whole time considering our imminent demise, but days are long, and there's only so much panicking you can do before you get sick of yourself. So in reality, I spend a lot of my time thinking about other things: whether Eugene has feelings; what I might order if I had fifty pounds to spend in Papa John's; and Zeke. Naked.

That's a bad one, obviously. I don't let myself do it much. Hardly ever. And definitely not when he's there, because he's starting to get to know me really well, and I worry he can tell what I'm thinking.

By day six, I've stopped waking up and going through the horror of remembering where we are. Instead, I wake up and think: *I have to wash my hair.* The shower doesn't work, obviously—no power— and though I wash myself every day with hand soap and a bucket of seawater, I've not figured out how to do my hair. It's almost sticky with grease now, and it makes me feel disgusting.

I declare this to Zeke as I march out into the living area. It's late, nearly midday according to the corgi clock—I was on first watch last night. Zeke prefers to sit indoors in the heat of the day, because although it's nauseatingly stuffy inside, it's a little cooler.

I can't believe the weather we're having. It feels like we're in the Mediterranean, not the North Sea. Both Zeke and I have caught the sun in the last six days, and we are turning browner now; when I look at myself in the wardrobe mirror, I'm already so different. My tanned skin makes my blue eyes pop like someone's edited them on the computer, and the grease almost turns my bleached hair back to its original mousey brown. I've lost weight—my chin doesn't slope into my neck, it juts sharply, and my upper arms aren't so wobbly. It's interesting how little I care: back home, I'd have been delighted, but now the exact proportions of my body feel completely irrelevant as long as it's still in one piece.

Zeke's different, too. He's not lost weight the way I have, but his hair is slicked back now, and he's growing a beard. I like it, though I've not said so—it would feel kind of inappropriate. Since our con- versation forbidding anything happening between us, he's been fastidious in friend-zoning me. I find it a constant source of irritation. The more he politely keeps a distance from me, the more I want to press close and make him change his mind.

Which is terrible. He's being a nice man. I *agreed* that we should keep things platonic.

But still, I'd love him to just sit up on that sofa, snag his T-shirt over his head, pull me in with one hand on the back of my neck the way he did in bed on that first night and—

"I'd say you could go for a swim with a bottle of shampoo," he says, "but I don't think it's worth the risk."

I sigh, settling down on the opposite end of the sofa from him. Neither of us has been near the water since the accident with the knife—it's changed our whole perspective. We've discussed the possible dangers in the sea: sharks, jellyfish, the sheer coldness of the water. And we've both seen movement out there, though neither of us can be sure that it isn't just a trick of the light on the surface. But it looks so *inviting* right now. Glittering, azure, cool, fresh . . .

"Could you throw a bucket of seawater over my head?" I suggest.

"Weren't you the one telling me to stop lifting things?"

I pull a face. He's healing well—there's no sign of infection yet, and my anxiety is slowly easing by the day. But the wound still restricts his movement, and I *do* fuss about him doing too much. He's a very pliant patient, really—he doesn't get annoyed when I tell him to sit still. But he does always end up standing again two minutes later.

"Right, yes. Sorry."

I watch him sip his drink. We're both thirsty all the time. The pot of Vaseline in my makeup bag has been an unexpected godsend—you feel so much thirstier with dry, chapped lips. We give ourselves four small glasses of water per day now, and we use the seawater bucket for everything we can.

"I could maybe wash your hair for you if you leaned over the bucket," Zeke says thoughtfully. "Shall we try? It's not going to make it any dirtier."

"Oi," I say, shoving his shin with my foot.

He doesn't wince, and I relish that small sign that he's not hurting so badly anymore.

"You're not looking much better," I tell him, "and you got to swim in the ocean with Eugene on day two."

"We can do me after," he says, unoffended. "No shortage of shampoo—or seawater."

This is true: we have plenty of seawater available. A lot more than we'd like.

~~~~~

"Your spa is prepared, madam," says Zeke, once I thump a full bucket of seawater down on the deck and begin untying the rope from its handle.

I glance up to see him topless in his now-battered velvet trousers, with a new clean strip of one of my T-shirts tied around his midriff. He's got a washing-up sponge in one hand and his bottle of shampoo in the other. It's a manly black-packaged one, called *Recharge* or *Ravage* or something equally masculine, like the mere fact of washing is inexcusably feminine and must be counteracted by all means possible. It's not really Zeke's style, and the way he's examining the label makes me think it wasn't his.

"Nicked it from Brady, my flatmate," he says, seeing my expression. "I'm a terrible packer. Hate it. I leave it to the last minute because I know I'll forget ten things anyway."

He's mentioned his friend Brady before—the name always conjures up a loping, teenage roommate, thoughtless and yawning. I find these peeks into Zeke's real life both fascinating and unsettling; it's almost impossible to imagine. I wonder if he's different back home. I wonder if I am.

"How are we doing this, then?" I ask, diverting my attention to the sloshing bucket on the deck. "I kneel like I'm about to be beheaded?"

That makes Zeke laugh. He crouches down beside me as I throw my hair forward over the bucket and lower my head in as best I can. The water is much colder than I expected, but I'm sweating with the exertion of pulling up the rope, and the sun is so hot I don't mind the shock of it.

"Hold still," Zeke says, dunking the sponge in the bucket and then squeezing it over my head.

I shriek as a rivulet comes jetting down my neck, soaking the top of my T-shirt.

"Sorry," Zeke says, but I shake my head.

"No, this is great."

Zeke starts to rub the shampoo through my hair, and I let out a moan. It just feels so good—the clean, cologne-ish scent of the shampoo, the feeling of the water on the skin of my scalp, his fingers massaging me.

Zeke stills for a moment, shifting slightly, then resumes. I close my eyes, forget all about the fact that I'm bent over a bucket of seawater, and just think about his thumbs rubbing over the muscles at the base of my skull.

He clears his throat. "You need to . . . OK. Hmm. You need to not make those sounds?"

My eyes fly open. "Oh. Umm."

"Sorry. It's just . . . quite . . . distracting."

I can't decide whether to laugh or blush. "Got you," I say, pressing my lips together.

I shouldn't be gratified, but I am. Sometimes, when I look at Zeke, it strikes me as totally impossible that he slept with me. He's so gorgeous, so young, so . . . I don't know, the word that comes to mind is *special*. I bite down on a smile. It's nice to know that I'm a distraction, even if I am essentially the only woman on the planet right now.

He rinses my hair out carefully, cupping his hand at the back of my neck to stop the water drenching me too badly.

"Lexi! I'm not even rubbing you."

I start laughing. I hadn't noticed myself making a sound.

"Sorry. It just feels really good. Shutting up now."

Zeke's bare forearms move on the edge of my vision, muscles bunching, water droplets shining on his tanned skin.

"You want me to wring it out?" he says eventually. "Untangle it?"

My hair is long—it reaches down to my waist. It's very impractical hair, and a total vanity thing, as Penny always likes to point out to me. *You kick around all day in stained trackies but you groom that hair like it's your pet*, she told me last week, when she caught me running oil through the ends after my shower. So many elements of this memory feel alien to me now: Penny, showers, the luxurious smell of hair oil.

I should say no—I can wring out my hair myself.

"Would you?" I find myself saying instead. I like being like this, with his hands in my hair, and knowing he likes it more than he should.

He hesitates for just a moment, then shifts the bucket aside.

"Sit back," he says, fingers combing against my scalp.

I do as I'm told. He comes to sit behind me and twists my hair in his fist, squeezing gently to wring out the droplets. I close my eyes, heat lancing through me as he begins to comb out the tangles with his fingers.

"When was the last time you did this?" he asks.

His voice makes me shiver.

"Washed my hair?"

"No. Let someone do something for you."

"Oh." I blink. "I mean . . . Well . . ."

Answering this question is harder than it should be.

"Penny makes dinner sometimes?"

"Don't you guys live together? I feel like that's just . . . normal."

"Oh, maybe . . ."

His fingers are firm and gentle.

"I mean, when was the last time you let someone treasure you? Look after you?"

"I wasn't really raised that way," I say. "My mum was not big on spoiling us."

"Well, OK, you're thirty-one now, not five."

"Are you saying it's too late for me?"

"Yes, Lexi, for once I am saying it's too late for you," he says, laughter in his voice. "You're unspoilable. I don't think there's any danger in letting someone . . ." His fingers slip through my hair as he thinks. "I don't know, letting someone give you the night off from looking after Mae just because. Or letting someone . . . give you a massage. Make you your favorite food for dinner. Cherish you."

I swallow. The idea is so alien to me. It feels totally decadent, almost shamefully so. I associate doing things for yourself with the way my father behaved, I suppose—when we talked about him, he was always the selfish one who abandoned his responsibilities. My mum was the woman who stayed; she fought to keep the pub afloat, and she fought for me, and she took Penny in because she saw a little girl who needed help. She was my hero, and I never once saw her treat herself—always other people.

But the feel of Zeke's fingers in my hair is so delicious, and the idea of someone wanting to do this for me—to make me feel good just for my own sake . . . it's almost impossibly tempting.

"It sounds too good to be true," I whisper.

"That," Zeke says gently, "is just about the saddest thing I've ever heard."

Zeke

SHE PLAITS HER hair herself. I watch her fingers, still sitting behind her, still thinking about all the ways I want to make Lexi feel cherished. Some PG, some . . . less so. It's getting hard, being together twenty-four/seven. The injury slowed me down some, and obviously I stand by the decision to keep things platonic, but I'm still me. My sex drive's an issue, and Lexi is . . . she's . . . Hmm. Even more gorgeous and fascinating every day I get to know her.

"Your turn? Shall I get a fresh bucket of water?" she says, turning to look at me over one shoulder.

"It's fine. I'll use this."

I clear my throat, wincing slightly as I straighten my legs in front of me. Sitting at an angle like this, my feet stick out under the railings.

"Do you want me to go so you can strip off?"

No, I think. *No, I want you to be the one to strip me down.*

"Yes," I say. Trying to sound convincing. "Yes, that would be . . ."

I trail off. I just checked under my bandage.

"Zeke?"

I can hear in Lexi's voice that I'm not doing a very good job of looking unfreaked.

"It's fine," I say, repositioning the fabric so she can't see.

"Zeke, you have to show me."

It's the stitch where Lexi started. It's swollen and red, with a lump about the size of a garden pea. Maybe a petit pois. Important distinction, but either way too big, and it didn't look like that a few hours ago.

"It's OK," Lexi says after a moment. "It'll be OK. It's not that bad."

"No," I say. "It'll be fine."

Eugene flaps his wings. I think he's got a bullshit sensor—he always pipes up when we're pretending things are all right. He's still in his box, but he hops out a lot now. Checking for crumbs from lunch, that sort of thing. He even made it up onto the railing yesterday evening. We thought he might leave us, but he didn't; he just stretched his wings out and lifted his beak. Very Kate Winslet.

"Do you think we should take out that stitch?" Lexi asks.

I thought she'd sew up the wound the way you'd stitch a torn piece of clothing or something, you know, in a zigzag, but she did each stitch individually. She's smart like that. If she'd just knotted the thread once, we'd only have the choice to take out all the stitches or leave them.

"I guess they'll need to come out sometime."

"I think it'll be a lot nicer than it was having them put in," she says. "Can I?"

I nod. She runs a finger lightly over the wound. I breathe in sharply between my teeth.

"I'll sterilize the scissors," she says, swallowing.

"We should use a knife," I say. "It's sharp, and it's got a fine point."

I'm better at speaking up with Lexi when I have an idea now. I don't know what it is—maybe just because there's only two of us, maybe because of the way she listens when I talk, maybe because she never rushes me.

"You want me to come at your stomach with that knife again?" she says.

"You've not been drinking this time, have you?"

"I wish. I'd kill for a vodka lemonade with ice."

"Whisky and Coke, a pint." Just saying it makes my mouth ache—it wants to water but I've not got it in me.

"Just a pint of Coke, to be honest. A pint of anything."

We've started having these conversations—foods we miss, things we're craving. At the beginning you think it'll keep you sane, but it's like . . . scratching a mosquito bite. Amazing for a second, way worse one minute later.

"Do you feel different?" Lexi asks worriedly. "Hot? Cold? Dizzy?"

I immediately feel all these things at once.

"I feel fine," I say.

She doesn't look convinced, but stands and heads inside to get the knife. I breathe out slowly, taking the time to clear my head. This is probably going to hurt.

I remember the bucket of water and slip out of my jeans, grateful that Lexi's inside—this isn't a sexy move to do sitting down, especially with the injury. My hand hovers over my boxers, but I leave them on. I don't back myself to get dried and dressed quickly enough before she comes out again.

The water feels amazing—so cold it makes me hiss. It calms me down a bit. I turn as the door opens behind me.

Lexi looks different with her hair plaited. She almost always wears it scraped up in this big tight knot on the top of her head, and the low plait makes her look more relaxed. More at home. I like it. But then, I like the high bun, too. I like it all, way more than I should.

She takes me in: I'm stripped down to my boxers, wet, leaning back on one hand, the other holding the sponge. Her T-shirt is falling off her shoulder, and I know she's not bothered with a bra today, and it's driving me crazy—she's driving me crazy. I absolutely will not touch Lexi again, I've made that promise, but she's always so close, and it would only ever take one step to get there.

I reckon she knows what I'm thinking. Her eyes are hot and watchful. She does this: looking at me like she wants me even though we've agreed we're not going there. It's a headfuck, but I don't really mind. I'd rather have those looks than not.

In a moment of weakness I let my gaze slip down to her shoulder, bared by that oversized T-shirt. And then my eyes catch on the knife.

"Ready when you are," I say, looking away.

Lexi

LIFE IS FULL of extremes right now. Either I'm doing absolutely fuck-all for hours on end, or I'm dashing around panicking. Either I'm lazily daydreaming about Zeke, or I'm thinking he might be about to die. As I sit down next to him and place a hand on his bare chest, I take a moment to appreciate the human brain and its capacity to cope with absolutely mad shit, and then I get on with the task at hand.

Slicing through the thread is difficult—the area is so swollen that the stitch is deep in the flesh, and I can see it hurts Zeke when I finally manage to slide the knife under the thread. Fresh blood blossoms the moment it's done. I reach blindly for the flannel I brought out and press it down, imagining all the other stitches popping, the wound gaping open like it did at the start.

Zeke lays his hand over mine. "Thank you," he says, breathing hard.

The contact is unusual; I feel it more than I should, as if he's stroked me or pressed his lips there. I love it when he touches me— a swift hand on my waist as he moves past, a thumb to my cheek as he wipes something away. Sometimes I long to lean into him, cat-like. He keeps his hand where it is, and I hold still, hoping he can't tell how it's making my body heat.

"Here," I say, handing him a mug with the other hand. "I used the boiling water to make us little hot coffees as a post-surgery treat."

"Am I drinking espresso with a hint of sterilization?"

"You are. Bet you'd pay three pounds sixty for that in some wanky London coffee shop," I say, and he nearly spits out his mouthful.

I'm funnier with Zeke. He laughs so readily it makes me braver about saying the little things that pop into my head.

"That is so delicious," he says, closing his eyes as he swallows.

I do the same. It really is phenomenal. I think of all the times I knocked back a coffee on my way out of the door, or left an inch of it cold in the bottom of my mug, and it makes me truly furious with myself.

It's strange, the things that get to me. I am so pissed off that I didn't pack a better spare bra, for instance. The two I've got are both underwired—I can't be doing with that nonsense right now. And I wish I had more than two tampons rattling around in the inside pocket of my bag. I'm not due on for another two weeks, so it's not my period I'm worrying about, it's just that tampons absorb liquid, and I've already decided that they might stop a small hole for a while if there's a leak.

I keep my hand under Zeke's, pressing down on his wound. I have no idea how long you're supposed to do this for, and already the temptation to check if it's stopped bleeding has set in, like the urge to cough when you've got a tickle in your throat. The warmth of his hand is a soft, quiet reminder of how close we are, how bare he is.

"Well," Zeke says, closing his eyes, "if I'm going to die, at least the weather's nice."

"Shut up," I say sharply. "You're not going to die. Don't joke about that."

He cracks an eye open, watching me. "It's a coping mechanism," he says after a moment.

"Well, pick another one. Do denial, that one is my favorite."

"No thanks," he says, closing his eyes again. "I don't like lying."

My stomach tightens as I think of the words I saw in his father's logbook.

Paige thinks I should tell him the truth . . . I sometimes long to, but I know when he finds out, he'll never come back to this boat.

I've never been one for making a distinction between lies and withholding the truth: the fact is, *I'm* lying to Zeke. But what do I say? *I suspect that there is a big dark secret about you in your father's logbooks?* The man does not need that right now. And surely he'll read them eventually. It's crazy to me that he's not cracked and binged them all—I know I would have.

"Tell me about your family," I say suddenly.

If he's surprised, he doesn't show it. "We're like most families," he says. "Bit complicated."

"You have two siblings?"

"Yeah," he says, eyes still shut. He's lying back now, head resting in the crook of his arm, knees pulled up in an upside-down V so he can fit on the deck. "We're quite different. Jeremy and Lyra are super smart, for starters. They both went to uni, whereas I got shitty exam results. Their careers are, like . . . things they built for themselves. Jeremy's in insurance, and Lyra's a lawyer. Me, I hung around doing pond-life jobs in kitchens until my friend Brady gave me a kick up the arse to apply for a junior chef job at Davide's, which is a proper fancy restaurant in Putney. Jeremy and Lyra were a team, two peas in a pod, and then there was me. The youngest, tagging along. I was always the odd one out."

Of course, he's different, the logbook had said. I swallow. I can so see Zeke as the people-pleasing youngest sibling, jogging to keep up with the others; it makes me a little sad.

"What about your mum? What's she like?"

"She's . . . she's great. She's good. She wants the best for me."

He's uncomfortable—with the question, not his wound, I think. I wait.

"We clashed quite a lot," he says eventually.

He begins absently stroking my hand beneath his as he talks; I'm not even sure he knows he's doing it. I'm slightly ashamed to note that I feel each movement of his fingers low in my belly.

"I was one of those teenagers. A difficult one. She's quite . . . I don't know. Helicopter parent. Always hovering, always pushing me. She was an academic before she retired—she studied plant cells, it was all super technical. That's how she sees the world as well, in black and white, and I'm kind of . . . gray, aren't I?"

I tilt my head. I know what he means, actually. I remember how hard I found it to define Zeke when I first saw him at the pub, with his old-soul eyes and his cool necklaces and his self-help book.

"I was pretty disappointing for her, I think," he continues. "But she was as patient as she could manage to be with me. She was a good mum, basically."

"Was?"

Zeke opens his eyes, looking disturbed. His hand stills on mine.

"Is," he says. "No, is, sorry. I don't know why I said that."

I get it: people have started to feel past tense to me, too. It's hard to imagine a world outside of the confines of this boat.

"I was only four when they split up, so I don't really remember Dad at home—he's always been on this houseboat," Zeke says.

I wonder what that must feel like—not just the strangeness of being on this houseboat again, but the feeling of only really having known your parents apart. My dad walked out on us when I was seven years old. I visited him and his new girlfriend a few times before everyone decided it was better for those visits to stop. I watched him go from the father who lived with me to the person who sent me presents in the post, and then cards, and then nothing at all. It's not hard to trace the impact he's left on my life, and every guy who has walked out on me or Penny since has only made me more convinced that you can never count on a man to stick around when things get hard.

"I still haven't got a clue why he left the houseboat to me instead of Jeremy," Zeke says. "But the minute all the probate stuff was sorted and I'd turned eighteen, I came up to Gilmouth, sold the boat, drank too much, and left the next morning without looking back."

A thought occurs. "You must've met my mum," I say, shifting my wet hair to the other shoulder. It's dripped down me, and the fabric of the T-shirt sticks to my skin, cool in the day's heat. "If you sold her the houseboat?"

He turns his head to look at me. His gold-brown eyes are almost orange in the sun, fire-colored.

"Yeah," he says. "Yeah, I must have, briefly. We met in the marina. I can't remember the woman's name, but she was maybe . . . fifties? She had a cool hat on, a pink beret."

I tear up, then blink, shocked to find the emotion so close to the surface. Mum's been gone for more than four years now, and it's rare I cry about her death. For a good six months, I couldn't seem to cry about it at all. I pull my hand out from under Zeke's and rub my eyes.

"She thought this boat was so cute," I say, then clear my throat as my voice comes out strangled. "She thought everyone in the world would want to stay on it—when she first listed it to rent, she tried charging a fortune." I laugh wetly. "We make a bit of money on it each month, but I don't know if we've ever earned back what she paid you for it."

Zeke's hand flickers on the flannel, as if he wants to reach for me but holds himself back.

"Anyway. So weird you met her. I kind of like that she knew you, in a way," I say, then I frown, surprised at myself. "What was it that made you want to buy the houseboat back now? Why not sooner?"

He gazes out to sea, thinking. "Last month, me and Jeremy went for a pint together for the first time in . . . I don't know, years, probably. We do talk, we're part of each other's lives, but it's complicated. We hardly ever manage to catch up properly without arguing about something. And we *never* talk about Dad. But this night in the pub, I don't know what it was—Jeremy seemed more open than usual. We ended up getting a bit drunk together and telling each other all the secrets we'd found out as kids. I told him Dad smoked sometimes, out on the deck, when he thought I wasn't watching. He told me Dad believed the moon landing wasn't real. I told him Dad put in a fake insurance claim on his van. He told me he knew I always thought Dad wasn't my dad, and he thought I was right."

My mouth falls open.

"You always thought your father wasn't really your father?"

My mind has gone straight to that logbook. *When he finds out, he'll never come back to this boat.*

Zeke nods. "As a kid, I was sure of it. Dad said something once when he came to pick us up—*I won't tell him, all right? I promised you that.* After that, I looked for evidence of it everywhere—proof my mum cheated, anything that might tell me who my real dad is . . ."

He smiles slightly.

"I just never belonged, and it turns out I wasn't the only one who knew it. Jeremy suspected the same. He was an expert at figuring out Dad's hiding places. When we went for that pint, he told me he always knew Dad hid stuff on the boat, and if I really wanted answers, I should've looked there. So I googled it. Your mum and Penny didn't change the name of the boat—it was easy to find. And it looked just the same. Knowing Dad, he would've hidden the truth somewhere only he could find it. I thought, odds are, whatever it is might still be on there, if the current owners didn't do more than add a bit of paint and some new cushions."

"How could you afford it?" I ask. "A houseboat, cash?"

"My granddad left us each some money when he died. I've been sitting on mine. Waiting for something." He shrugs. "Something that felt important enough, I guess. Something I cared about."

"I sometimes wish my mum had sold up and left me the money rather than leaving me the pub," I say, then I bite my lip.

I don't think I've ever said that out loud before. When Mum's cancer was finally picked up by the doctors, it was so late, and things happened quickly—we only had two weeks to say good-bye. It was unspeakably awful, the worst time in my life; I can still hardly bear to think of those final days. The idea of selling The Anchor was the last thing on our minds.

"Obviously the pub was her dream, and I wanted to carry that on for her," I add quickly.

Zeke looks at me, thoughtful. "It's not what you chose, though," he says.

"I chose them. Mum, Penny, Mae." I shrug. "They're my family. And my mum was amazing. Even though she was run off her feet *all* the time, even though she had a pub to look after, somehow she always made me feel like she had time for me if I needed her."

It used to be so hard to talk about my mother, and it still makes me ache with missing her, but it feels good, too. I don't ever want to forget a fraction of her: I want to remember the daft songs we'd make up in the car, and the exact smell of her hair after she'd washed it, and the way she'd chuck my chin if I was scared and say, *Hey, I've got you, OK?*

"She sounds amazing," Zeke says softly. "And she looked after Penny, too?"

"Like she was her own. Penny stayed over most weekends from the age of about . . . six, maybe? Her mum was a singer, when she was clean enough to work, so she was often out late or disappearing off to some other town for a gig. Eventually, when Penny was ten and pretty much living at ours, Mum just turned our spare room above The Anchor into her bedroom. For most of her teens, Penny never went to her mother's—she called the pub home."

I remember the first time she did it, and what a thrill I felt—like we'd finally managed to steal Penny away for ourselves. I loved the nights when Penny slept over. We'd watch cartoons together on the living room rug in our pajamas; we'd make friendship bracelets and all sorts of wild promises about being together forever. Then we'd wake up in the morning and tumble down the stairs to eat our cereal at the bar while Mum got the pub ready, and I'd feel like all my favorite things were in one place.

"Did it ever bother you that your mum left the houseboat to Penny? Even though she wasn't her kid?" he asks.

"Mae's not my kid, but I'd leave everything I had to her."

Zeke's eyes widen slightly. I might have sounded a bit snappy there.

"Sorry," he says.

"No, it's OK, I just . . . There's more to family than blood. In my opinion," I say, tipping back my coffee mug and catching one last drop from the bottom, letting it moisten my dry mouth.

"Definitely. Sorry." He pauses, thinking. "You guys grew up together at the pub, then? What was that like?"

It was loud and warm and chaotic. It was toddling between bar stools and petting dogs by the fire and watching Mum pulling pints, hair falling back as she laughed her big, rough, dirty laugh. It was cold leftover burgers for dinner and homework at the always-empty table by the toilets, then it was shifts that bled one day into the next, with only a short trip upstairs to sleep in between.

"It's a way of life all of its own," I settle for. "Pub life."

"Did you drink a lot?"

I shake my head. "Not me. Penny did, for a while. She leaned into the whole sexy-young-barmaid thing, always doing shots with cute tourists. She only really snapped out of it when she got pregnant. Before that, she was all about the late nights and one-night stands."

"Late nights," Zeke says, pressing his lips together to hold back a smile. "*Wild.*"

"You know what I mean."

"Let me guess." He cracks an eye open. "The sensible one?"

"Guilty as charged."

"I bet you could be wild," Zeke says, opening his other eye, lifting his forearm to shade the sun so he can look at me properly. "I feel like it's in there. Just kind of . . . trapped."

"Oh yes, I am Eugene in his cardboard box," I deadpan, but I like that he's said it. I like that he sees me that way. "Shall we?" I ask, tilting my head toward his midriff. We're sitting with our thighs almost touching now, facing each other, flank to flank on the deck. The sun is getting fierce: I lift a hand to my wet hair and find that it's almost dry at the back already.

Zeke moves the flannel. The wound is red, and there's pus leaking from the end where the stitch had been infected.

"It's OK," I say quickly, because his face has fallen. "It's good that it's coming out."

"Yeah," Zeke says. "Yeah. Maybe I should let it breathe?"

I really have no idea. We're so completely clueless. I hate these moments—I can kid myself that we're coping fine out here when we're sipping espressos and talking in the sunshine, but when I'm staring at the vicious red line of Zeke's wound, I feel like a child. Sometimes I fantasize about waking up from this to a soft bed and a person in a white coat saying, *It's going to be all right, Lexi—it was all a bad dream.* I rub my eyes with my thumb and forefinger; my head is feeling a little fuzzy in the heat.

"You need a water," Zeke says, looking at me closely, sitting up on his elbows.

"I'm fine." I drop my hand.

"When did you last have one?"

Eight o'clock this morning. I try to take less than my four cups per day—I'm conscious that Zeke is healing and must need it more than me.

"A bit ago," I say vaguely.

"You look pale. Lexi . . ." Zeke sits up, bringing a hand to my cheek, looking right into my eyes.

I breathe in. The sensation of his thumb smoothing over my cheekbone as he examines my face only makes the light-headedness worse.

"Let's get out of the sun. We shouldn't be sitting out here."

He levers himself up, his body brushing mine, and something flutters in my throat at the contact. I'm a bit dizzy when I stand; I try not to let Zeke see me stumble, and as I do so, I notice him doing exactly the same—catching himself on the doorframe, glancing quickly at me to check if I saw.

"I'm fine," he says, at my expression. "You don't need to look after me, Lexi."

I frown. "Of course I do."

"I can cope."

The door swings shut behind me. It's fusty in here—it smells of sleep and the warm, rotten fridge. I wrinkle up my nose. It is literally impossible to get that fridge clean, for reasons I cannot understand.

"I know you can cope. That's not what it's about. I'm looking out for you because you're my person."

He goes still.

"As in," I say, heart beginning to thud, "you're the only person I have. You're my one person on this boat with me. That's all I meant."

He looks at me over his shoulder for a long while. I hover on the bottom step, adjusting my hair, feeling my gaze slide away from him to the windows. Things must have got really uncomfortable if I'd rather look at the empty ocean than Zeke's face.

"You're my person, too," he says eventually, and the corner of his mouth rises in a crooked, closed-mouthed smile.

DAY SEVEN

Zeke

I'M WATCHING THE darkness out here on the deck, and I've got this weird ominous feeling. Like something bad's coming, maybe because actually today *hasn't* been bad, except for that swollen stitch, and at times I've felt genuinely happy. Chatting to Lexi on the deck with a coffee felt kind of perfect. And out here, perfect can never last.

I pull my blanket closer around my shoulders, my eyes gritty with tiredness. It's so cold at night—I'm wearing all three of the pairs of socks I packed, and a jumper of Lexi's under mine. It smells of her, lemony and sharp. I wonder if I could capture that in a lemon tart, a meringue pie, even a zingy, fresh dressing for a rocket salad.

I've enjoyed cooking here. Davide's kitchen has a great atmosphere, and I'm so lucky to have got that job, but somewhere over the past year I've lost the excitement I get from conjuring up something beautiful with whatever I find in the fridge. Most nights I just eat at the restaurant, or get takeaway from whatever kebab shop's still open. I've not cooked my own way for too long, and it's been nice reconnecting with the part of me that just loves to play around with food. I'm getting to know Lexi's palate a little, and I like that, too. Cooking with her in mind, seeing her love the food I've made her.

I take a clear, cold breath of night air. I need the toilet, and to check the corgi clock. Not having a clue of the time is so annoying, though otherwise I've got pretty used to not having my phone. I don't like to look at it much anyway, back home. A couple of days ago, if she saw me sitting and zoning out the way I do, Lexi would say, *You bored? Want to read the logbooks?* And I'd smile about it, laugh it off, but it made me feel like a coward, because no amount of boredom would be enough to make me take that leap. She's stopped asking now, so I guess she's figured that out.

The miniature torch from the first aid kit in the bathroom is beside me. I grab it and head inside to the bathroom, though I hardly need the light now. I reckon I could find almost anything on this boat blindfolded.

It's not until after I've used the manual pump to flush the toilet that I realize my left sock's wet.

Really wet.

The floor's covered in water.

"Shit! Shit, shit, shit!"

I kneel. My knees are instantly cold. It's wet all over the floor by the shower, and my torch beam catches the way it's darkened the bottom of the shower curtain, too, how it's filling the base of the shower enough to overflow. I dip a finger into the cold water and press it to my tongue. Salt.

Seawater.

Lexi bursts into the bathroom, slamming the concertina door into the frame.

"What? What's shit? Are you OK?"

She's breathing hard, and her bun has slid all the way to bob down by her left ear. And . . . she's . . . uh.

She's wearing nothing but a pair of black knickers.

"Oh, fuck," she says, eyes rounder than ever. She clutches her hands to her breasts and spins around.

"You sleep . . . like that?" I say.

My voice is suddenly very high-pitched. Like thirteen-year-old Zeke. I should be thinking about the water, but for a second, right now, I'm really, really not.

"It was hot in the bedroom. I was going to put a T-shirt on when I heard you coming in. You always get yourself a glass of water first, so there's usually time, but . . ."

She reaches to grab her towel and wraps it around herself.

I've seen Lexi naked before. I've touched her almost everywhere. But I didn't know her then like I do now. And somehow it makes her nakedness . . . different. She's *so* gorgeous, every bare curve, and it's *Lexi*, not just a beautiful woman, but the one who made us sterilization espressos and who feeds Eugene on the sly. I've never looked at a woman naked and known that she cares about an injured seagull even though she pretends she doesn't, and turns out it makes a hell of a lot of difference.

"Why did you shout?" she asks.

I avert my gaze—maybe a second later than I should have—and keep the torch shone down at the water on the shower tray. Before I can explain, Lexi's clocked it, and she's swearing, too.

She steps into the wet shower, patting down the walls, looking for a leak. I'm crouched here on the floor—there's not much room, and there's a lot of towel in my face. She's very close, and it's really not been long since I saw her topless, so this is . . . distracting.

"I was wondering if maybe the showerhead's leaked," I begin, straightening up just as she turns. "But . . ."

Her towel slips. She grabs for it as I stand, her elbow flying up—and she knocks the shower handle.

Whoosh. Just like that, the shower's on.

It's only a few seconds' worth of water—I guess whatever's trapped in the line, since the shower's not actually working. But the water's freezing, and the blast of cold makes us both cry out.

I step backward out of the shower, get tangled in the curtain, almost trip. It wrenches my cut, and the sensation's like someone taking a hot poker to my skin. I breathe in sharply between my teeth. Lexi's hand is on my back in less than a second.

"You OK?"

"Fine. We need to find the leak," I manage, leaning back against the wall, breathing hard. My trousers are sticking to my thighs and my hair's dripping down my neck. My wound throbs with my heartbeat. "What I was going to say is, it's not from the shower-head, because it's salty. It's seawater, not fresh water."

She assesses me for a moment, scanning me over. I can see her deciding that the bigger threat right now is the water, and it freaks me out that she even hesitated to check on me. We can't afford to think that way out here.

That said, I know if she was hurting, I'd be exactly the same.

"Now everything is all wet, we'll never be able to tell where the water is coming from," she says, her voice shaking. "Why isn't the shower draining?"

She's right—the water's still just sloshing in the base of the shower. I remember from staying here as a kid that there's an automatic pump that drains the water out, but it won't work without power.

"What if—could that be how the water's getting in? Up the drain?"

My heart beats faster. I've no idea how the drain works, but eventually that water must end up out in the sea. There's a freshwater tank under the bed, and the toilet waste collector's built in under there, too, but there's no tank for used shower and sink water that I've seen, so it must be getting pumped out. What if that system's gone wrong? What if—what if it's letting water in?

"We should bail it out," I say, my mouth dry. "All this water. Dry it as best we can and then see . . . if it comes back."

"Good idea." Lexi breathes out shakily. "OK. OK. Well, if it was *really* bad leak, surely we'd have doubled the amount of water or something by now, and even with the shower coming on, I don't think there's much more."

She turns, and my torch catches her straight on. Hair damp, bare shoulders dewy with droplets. We pause for a second like this, her eyes wide with fear, her skin glowing, her face so beautifully familiar to me now. I want to fix this for her. I want her to be safe.

Lexi bites her lip and turns her face away from the glare of my torch.

"I'll get dressed," she says, "and then let's start bailing."

It takes us a while—the last dregs of water are trickiest to get rid of, but when we've finally dried the shower base, it's obvious we're right about the issue. The boat dips slightly and as it tips back, a little slosh of seawater comes over the edge of the drain.

Lexi lunges for the water with the corner of a towel, as if she's swatting an insect, then she hesitates, leaving the towel there.

"Can we block it?" she asks.

"Cut-up fabric, maybe," I say, already moving away to head for the bedroom.

"Tarp on top," she calls after me. "It won't soak through that so easily."

In the end, stuffing the hole is the easy part—the hard part's fixing the tarp in place. We end up using clothing tape—tit tape, Lexi calls it—from her makeup bag.

"I *knew* something in here would come in handy," she says

triumphantly, smoothing the last piece down. "This won't hold for long, but . . ."

I don't say anything. I don't have to. Lexi saw that light blinking on the tank system monitor yesterday—she knows we've already used three-quarters of the fresh water we have on this houseboat. She knows *we* won't hold for long, either.

DAY EIGHT

Lexi

ZEKE'S HAIR IS officially long enough for a topknot—well, a half one. He was complaining about missing the band he usually wears to keep his hair back from his forehead when he's working, so I used a black scrunchie from my makeup bag to create him a little half bun on the top of his head. Instead of looking comically cute, as I'd hoped, he actually just looks like he's starting a trend. Put anything near that face and somehow it turns out stylish.

"Like the new look, do you?" he says, smiling crookedly at me from the kitchen.

He's making something undoubtedly delicious from our remaining raw peppers and the pasta we boiled in seawater yesterday. I try to focus on the thought of the food, not how desperately I want a drink. It is taking at least fifty percent of my energy not to notice how thirsty I am right now.

"I actually do," I say. "You look . . ."

He looks relaxed. Sun-kissed and sexy and tousled. And always, always, like he's just slid out of bed.

"You look good," I settle for. "It works with your style."

He smiles slightly. "And what's my style?"

"Oh, I don't know, world-weary pop-star chic?"

He laughs, and I bite down on my smile.

"Not what you're going for?"

He shrugs. "I just like playing around with clothes. Wearing what *I* want to wear."

"Have you always been that way?"

I pull my bare feet closer and run a finger over the chipped polish on my toenails, trying not to think about the sunny Saturday afternoon I spent doing "nail art" with Mae the week before we got lost out here. She wanted hers polka-dotted—I messed them up, and Penny turned them into little flowers, and Mae had been so delighted. I close my eyes. I would *kill* to see her smile right now.

"Nah. I started doing a lot of things differently about six, maybe seven months ago," Zeke says. "I guess that was when I changed my look a bit."

He's stopped talking, but I've got a lot better at telling when Zeke's done talking and when he's not. It is always worth letting him think for a moment, because whatever he says next is invariably extra interesting.

"It was when I started seeing a therapist about my sex life," he says.

I knew it. *Extra* interesting. I look up at him, open-mouthed. He laughs at me over his shoulder. I rearrange my expression, trying to look less gobsmacked.

"I'm not some kind of sexual deviant. Just . . . was having a lot of sex for a lot of unhealthy reasons."

I am still staring. I've never known a man who goes to therapy, let alone one who goes to talk about his *sex* life. He chops the peppers so fast his hands are a blur, and I am too distracted by this conversation even to worry about the proximity of the knife to his stomach. What is acceptable to ask him, here, without just being incredibly nosy?

"So the night we met," I say eventually. "That was a regular day for you, then? A one-night stand with a woman you just met in a pub?"

"Not for a while. I have rules now. I never have sex on a first date. Never sleep with someone if I don't think we'll speak the next day. And I never sneak out the next morning after spending the night." He ticks them off on his hand as he goes. "No judgment on anyone who finds that stuff makes them happy, but it was making me really sad, so . . . yeah."

"Oh. But you broke your rules? With me?"

"For you. Yeah."

I pull my knees in against my chest as he seasons the peppers and tosses the veg over the pasta.

"There was me joking about you leading me astray," I say, a little weakly. "And . . ."

He laughs. "It was worth it."

This has thrown me. I did assume Zeke was pretty well-accustomed to a one-night stand—it was obvious in everything from his confident approach at the bar to the way he kissed me. But . . . I can't quite fathom the idea that he didn't want to do that anymore, and chose to break his rules for *me*.

"I can see you doing a lot of thinking over there," he says. "Looks tiring. Pasta?"

"Umm, yeah," I say, standing to reach for the bowl. "Thanks."

He meets my eyes as he hands it to me, the corner of his mouth lifting slightly. His beard is getting thicker; it makes him look tousled and rugged, as though he's spent a few months backpacking somewhere hot.

"I don't regret it for a second," he says quietly. "Not even now, with everything that's happened since."

"That's mad," I say, before I can stop myself, and his smile widens.

"Maybe," he says. "But I can't help hating the thought of never having met you."

He moves past me with his bowl of pasta, heading out onto the deck. I stand for a moment by the sofa. I hate compliments. They make me want to squirm away or redirect the person's attention; right now I have the weirdest compulsion to point at the window and go, *Hey, look, a whale!* But as I move to follow Zeke, I realize that since we woke up at sea, I've not felt the unworthiness that dogs me on land. I've not felt like I'm less.

Maybe it's the lack of context. Nobody on Instagram to compare myself to; nobody to ignore me and talk to Penny instead. Just Zeke, who says things like *I can't help hating the thought of never having met you* like it's no big deal to tell me that I matter in my own right.

So instead of shrugging off the compliment, I let myself absorb it. He's glad he met me. That's lovely. I'm so glad I met him, too.

I pull one of the extra blankets out from under the deck chair as I sit down beside him with my bowl, settling into our usual companionable silence. It's a bit cooler today, and the sky is dotted with fluffy clouds, the kind Mae would draw with her crayons.

This, I suppose, is the first clue things are about to change.

~~~~~~

I take a nap in the bedroom after the pasta—it's the natural order of things—and wake to find myself about five inches from slamming into the floor.

My hands fly out just in time to catch me as I land. I just . . . rolled out of bed. I can't make any sense of this, but as I lie here face down with my forehead pressed to my arm, I realize I'm not feeling good at *all*.

I just about make it to the toilet before vomiting. On the way there I whack myself into the door, then the sink; I stub my toe on the toilet. It's not dizziness, though at first it feels like it. It's the boat.

It's moving.

"Zeke!" I shout, flushing the toilet.

"You're up," he says, appearing suddenly in the doorway with bright eyes and messy curls. "Can you believe we're moving? Oh, hey, are you OK?"

He steps into the bathroom, eyes widening.

"Shit—is it food poisoning? Or seasickness, because of the waves?"

I long for a glass of water to wash my mouth out. The thirst is becoming harder to bear—my body is *craving* water now, and it's even worse after being sick. For a wild second I think about just flipping on the bathroom tap and lapping from it like a water fountain, and the fantasy makes me close my eyes and groan.

"I don't know if I get seasick. I've never been at sea before," I say. "Except on a ferry. And that was not like this. There was more ice cream and fish and chips, for starters."

The joke's weak; it's the best I can do. I pull myself up and sit down on the toilet seat, leaning forward on my knees, trying to take deep breaths. Throwing up has helped with the nausea—it's less intense now. I remember last night—the shower—and turn my head to look at the drain.

"Don't worry, I already checked it this morning," Zeke says, stepping past me to reach my toothbrush and toothpaste, which have rolled into the sink. "You weren't sick when we first got swept out, and we're eating a lot of old food that should probably have been in a fridge . . ."

I take the toothbrush from him gratefully. The timing seems a bit coincidental if this is food poisoning, and I'm not sure that option is all that much better than seasickness. The danger either way is all the fluid I could lose. I stand unsteadily and peer through the kitchen window.

"How big are the waves? Are we properly going somewhere?"

I look back at Zeke. He nods, dimples showing.

"Wherever we were stuck before, it obviously wasn't on any sort of shipping route—only that one ship ever came by. But now . . ."

He's breathing faster—excited, I think. Zeke is so understated it's hard to tell. I attempt a smile back at him, trying to ignore the way my head is pounding from dehydration. I want to be positive, but I'm thinking about this boat and what it was designed to do— float down canals, sit in the marina, bob around with the ducks . . .

"She made it through that first night," Zeke says.

I don't have to tell him: he knows what I'm thinking.

"She can do this, Lexi," he says.

I don't know when we started calling *The Merry Dormouse* "she." I've always found referring to boats as women a bit pretentious, but I get it now. This houseboat is a living, breathing thing, the third person trying to survive out here. Or the fourth, if you count Eugene, who was hopping around the deck this morning while Zeke watched for boats, like some kind of rangy stray dog who doesn't want to join in but doesn't want to be left out, either.

"Yeah," I say, as we move unsteadily through to the living area. "She can do this. Absolutely."

I glance at the kitchen, where the horizon line moves in and out of view in the window. Zeke's storm-proofing is already being put to the test. There's a cupboard door partly open, one of our precious tins of baked beans pressed to the gap but held in place by that small loop of string. I feel a fierce wave of appreciation for Zeke and his brain, the way he thinks of things that would never cross my mind: the sail he dreamed up from the tarpaulin; his securing doors with string; rescuing a useless seagull who's made me smile more times than I'll admit.

We head out onto the deck and the wind touches my face. I grip the frame around the wheelhouse. The sea has completely changed, no longer glassy and shimmering. Now it's ruffled and thick, like icing piped on a cake.

"God, that breeze feels nice."

I stumble slightly and Zeke puts his hand on my waist to steady me. Even with the nausea still clinging to me and the deck rising and falling beneath us, his touch zings through me. If the boat can make it through another day, I know I'll think about his hand on me as I sit and keep watch for ships in the dark. For now, though, I pack the feeling away, like I always do.

"The sail," I say suddenly, turning to look at the pole with its fabric wrapped tightly around it, waiting for this moment.

"I know," Zeke says, already moving to lever himself up onto the roof. "I was waiting for you to get up before I . . ."

Just as I say a reprimanding, "Zeke!" he winces and drops back to the deck, a hand on his stomach.

"Sorry," he says ruefully. "Forgot."

"I'll do it."

I go around the edge, the way I did when I drunk-danced up there. As I climb up onto the roof, I flash back to the moment I hitched myself up here with a glass of wine, and I'm almost stunned by the carelessness with which I did it. So much has changed since then.

I open the sail out. It catches and gets buffeted by the breeze; I think I even feel the houseboat shift underneath me. I swear under my breath, trying to angle it in a way that feels helpful—a way that will propel us forward, not slow us down.

"I feel like we need some ropes," I say after a few ineffectual moments. "Doesn't this normally involve ropes? We just need to be able to move the . . ."

"Boom," Zeke supplies. "I think that's the horizontal one."

"Right, OK, the boom—we need to be able to shift it side to side from the deck and then fix it in place."

It takes us almost three hours, in the end. We start by deconstructing our ladder to get the rope we need. Neither of us is particularly handy, and it turns out there's a reason why sailors are so famous for tying knots. It's *really* hard to fix everything where it needs to go, and the more we get into this, the more obvious it is that we're essentially trying to learn how to sail from first principles, which is patently ridiculous.

Eventually we end up with something that means there's tension in the sail and we can manipulate which direction it faces, but I'm starting to wonder if we've created a monster here.

"I think we might be going around in circles," Zeke says bleakly, looking over the side. His voice is sticky and dry with thirst, just like mine. "Maybe we can use the helm now? Steer . . . into the wind? Not into the wind? I don't even know. We just want to go *somewhere*, don't we?"

"Maybe we put the sail down for now. Just have it for if we need to navigate around something."

"*Around* something?" Zeke says, eyes widening. "Why have I not worried about that yet?"

I hate scaring him, but the shower drain leak has made me so much more nervous about the boat's integrity, and with these waves, there are a whole host of new things to be terrified about. Still, I liked using the word *navigate*. It was pleasingly nautical, and gave me a fleeting and very misplaced feeling that I might know what I'm doing.

"Let me make us some food," Zeke says, opening the door.

His classic coping mechanism. As he heads inside, I stare out at the water, this new sea, as unfamiliar to me as a new town. The sun is low in the sky, only a few minutes from setting, and it's right in front of me here on the back deck, which presumably means we're heading east.

I close my eyes and imagine a map of the UK. We were in the northeast of England when we were first carried out to sea, so if we wanted to go home, we'd need to head west. Right now we're presumably being carried toward Denmark or Norway, depending on how far we've traveled north or south while we've been drifting.

Surely we'll cross paths with some ships now that we're on the move. *Surely*. We just have to—we can't keep going like this.

Once I've put the sail down, I notice how much safer the deck feels than the roof of the boat—ridiculous, really, when there's nothing remotely safe about any of this. I put away the deck chair we pulled out for Zeke to rest on, and brush a droplet absently from the back of my neck. The waves are leaving a steady spray on my shins, so I assume it's seawater until the second drop lands on my shoulder, and then a third and fourth and fifth hit my arms.

"Zeke!" I scream, stumbling to the door.

He comes, wide-eyed, hopeful. "What? What?"

"Zeke," I say, gripping the doorframe. I beam down at him where he stands below deck. "It's *raining*."

~~~~~

We collect the water in everything we can think of—even Zeke's stolen trilby.

The issue is securing things with the boat moving. We lose one cereal bowl over the side, and I almost cry as I watch it bob away behind us, spilling its two precious inches of rainwater into the sea. We have to wedge everything in or tie it down. My brain goes *Leaks, leaks, what if there are leaks in our hull, what if the water is coming back up the drain*, but I'm too busy to look—it'll have to wait. If we start sinking, I guess that will be my answer.

Zeke sets up an amazing system with the leftover tarpaulin and a makeshift funnel he creates from cardboard toilet-roll tubes. It gets soggy pretty quickly, but it fills the bucket within a few hours; I carry it to the kitchen sink the way I'd carry Mae to her Moses basket when she was tiny, taking every step with the utmost care.

"To your left," I say, spotting a bowl that's beginning to overflow.

We're out on the deck, and darkness is drawing in now; it's becoming difficult to see what we're doing. The rain patters sloppily on the deck and beads on the railings, shining in the moonlight. I'm less queasy out here, but I've vomited overboard twice since we messed around with the sail, and every time it scares me. I'm losing calories and nutrients, and I really don't have a lot of those to spare.

"On it," Zeke says, bending down to lift it to his lips.

At first, we were careful not to gorge ourselves on our new water—we don't know how long this will last. But since we've got the sink as full as it can be without overflowing when the boat moves, we've allowed ourselves a whole pint each, sipping slowly and licking our lips, a trick that we've learned makes it easier to take the water steadily.

I stumble into the steering wheel as I try to move between water bowls in the darkness. *The Merry Dormouse* seems to be doing us proud—she's bobbing along, taking each wave in her stride—but all the same, whenever a larger wash of spray reaches up to the railings, my stomach lurches and my faith wobbles.

We make it inside and collapse on the sofa in the darkness. Zeke's arm brushes mine and I wince—we're both soaking wet, but I don't have the energy to get up again and change clothes.

"We're doing really well, you know," Zeke says, pushing his wet curls back from his face. "It's been over a week. We're still here."

"Lost at sea for *eight days*," I say, with genuine wonderment.

"And barely a scratch to show for it," Zeke says.

I glance at his stomach. I hope he's not put it under too much strain with all this activity. His lip quirks; he knows I'm fretting about him. He nudges my shoulder, like, *Stop it*, and I cut him a sidelong look in the darkness, like, *You really think I'm ever going to quit worrying about you?* His shoulder stays resting against mine for a few moments, his eyes liquid in the darkness, and then—as always—he shifts away.

"I'll get dry towels," I say, pushing myself up to stand, trying not to feel disappointed.

I'm tired. My fingers are still too numb from the cold. I'm distracted and emotional and sick to my stomach, so I do something stupid, the way you do when you're so drained you can hardly function, like when Mae was three weeks old and I poured milk over Penny's toast instead of over my cereal. My mind is kidding itself that it's working, but really, it's barely got anything to give.

As the boat bobs beneath me, I reach to steady myself on the bathroom door. The concertina folds back on itself, the way it always does—I *know* it does that, and I should know it isn't a steady handhold.

I lose my grip.

It's not a straightforward fall. First, I whack my shoulder against the wall, then the boat rocks me the other way and I go tumbling backward toward the kitchen counter. I think my head hits the fridge door before it hits the floor, but it's hard to tell for sure, because everything goes blurry—and then it goes black.

DAY NINE

Zeke

TWO IN THE morning. She's curled on her side on the bathroom floor. She keeps saying, *I'm fine. It's just the seasickness.* But she hit her head so hard. I'm sure she wasn't vomiting this much before the fall. I wish I knew how to tell if she's concussed or bleeding in her brain or . . . or . . . any of the thousands of bad things streaking through my mind right now.

I play the fall over and over. I was too slow. So stupid. I didn't get to her side in time. By the time I was there, she was unconscious. It was just a few seconds, but she was definitely out. I shook her shoulder, and she didn't respond, and I thought, *You can't die, I'm not sure I can live if you die.* I look down at her now—eyes closed, cheek lying on the tiles—and this great balloon of emotion expands inside me. So big it hardly fits in my chest.

I don't know if I've ever cared about another human being the way I care for Lexi. I tip my head back against the wall. I'd throw myself overboard if it would help her right now. I'd give her every scrap of food left, the clothes off my back, just *anything*. I guess this is what all those self-help books were on about. Here's my "authentic connection," right here on this bathroom floor.

No wonder people say that love is torture.

~~~~~~

I should probably be out on the deck keeping watch, but for now I'll have to settle for checking through the windows as dawn creeps over us. I can't bear to leave Lexi on her own like this.

The rain's thrumming on the roof of the boat. Our tarp and cloth covering for the shower drain gave in about an hour ago under the new challenge of the rocking waves. I've stuffed it with fresh fabric, but it's already soaked, and I know I'm going to have to start using the towels, maybe even bailing. There are three leaks in the ceiling now, too: one in the bedroom, right over the bedside table, and two in the living area. But they're small, and I've plugged them as best I can. We're still afloat. We're still OK.

As long as Lexi's not dying.

"Hey." She sits up carefully on the bathroom floor, reaching for the thermos of water tucked between my back and the wall. "I feel a bit better for that sleep."

"Good." I try to remember what I've seen about head injuries in films. "How many fingers am I holding up?" I ask.

She's not focusing on my hand at all. Her eyes skitter to the side over and over, like she's watching fast traffic from a car window.

"Somewhere between two and four? Three? Three point five?" she says.

Hmm. Not good.

"Just . . . lie back. Rest. And get better. Please."

I wonder if I should be keeping her awake, but I'm sure I read somewhere that it's a myth that it helps, and she looks so tired.

"If I tell you something now, when I am probably dying from a bleed on the brain, will you promise not to be angry with me?" Lexi says, laying herself slowly down on the tiles again.

She pulls her knees up, her socked feet pressed to the side of my boots. I eye the darkening fabric stuffed into the shower drain.

"That's a fairly manipulative bargain you're trying to strike, there."

"I know. I'm an arsehole. This is not news," she says, closing her eyes. "But you've got to admit, I'm in a position of strength here on the bathroom floor, and I'd be a fool not to use it."

"You're not an arsehole, Lexi. You're lovely."

She rolls her head to the side, pressing the center of her forehead into the tiles. She's still in those damp, rainy clothes—I've laid a blanket over her, but she's shivering.

"Let me get you a jumper," I say, moving to stand.

Her hand flies out to grab my leg.

"I looked in one of the logbooks," she says.

I slowly lower myself back to sit on the bathroom floor again.

"I'm so sorry. I was scared. I wanted information. I saw it was basically your dad's diary, and I did it anyway. I told you I'm an arsehole."

"Lexi . . ."

I rub my forehead. My heart's pounding. I don't know what I'm feeling, but it's not pretty.

"I had no right," she says, eyes opening and finding mine. "I'm sorry. I can't even explain why I did it."

I breathe out slowly. I'm not surprised she doesn't know why she did it. Lexi has so many walls up, it's like entering a maze, and I don't think she knows her way around herself, either. It makes it hard to be angry with her, but . . . I am, I think. And sad. And scared. And . . .

"I didn't see anything explicit, just something about your dad not telling you something, but I do think it might be in there," she whispers. "The answer you wanted." She rolls slightly so she can get a proper look at my face, then bats the shower curtain as it catches in her bun. "But honestly, I can't believe you've not read them yet. That level of self-control blows my mind."

I shake my head. "It's not self-control. It's . . . cowardice."

Her eyes are soft. "You're scared to find out for sure? That your dad isn't your dad?"

"I guess," I say, but I don't think that's all of it. Opening those books means actually *listening* to my father, a man I've chosen to shut out for most of my life, and I don't know what he'll say, but I'm pretty sure it'll hurt me. I know he never cared for me the way he cared for Lyra and Jeremy. Turns out I'm just not ready to see that written in black and white.

"I mean, does it matter if your birth father was someone else?" Lexi says. "Because your *dad* is your dad, right? I don't think the scumbag who knocked up Penny has any right to be part of Mae's life, personally, and on the same basis . . ."

"I think, if my relationship with my father had been better . . ." I clear my throat. "Yeah, maybe I'd feel that way. But I feel like there's something missing. I've always felt like that. That I don't belong. And maybe finding my real dad . . ."

Lexi closes her eyes again. "I worry about that all the time, you know," she says. "With Mae. That she feels that absence."

I want to tell Lexi that I'm sure she's enough for Mae, that her little girl's not missing anything, but I *had* a dad and I still wanted another one, so . . . I'm not really one to talk.

"I don't think everyone feels the way I do," I say eventually. "Lyra calls me *perpetually lost*." Lyra likes using words like *perpetually*, words I'd never be able to spell. "Always grass-is-greener. Maybe this is just that."

Lexi moves suddenly, pulling herself up and retching into the toilet. Her shoulders slump in exhaustion.

I reach over and smooth her hair back, then pause, hand hovering. But she leans back into my palm like a cat wanting to be stroked, so I do it again, careful to avoid the lump on the back of her head.

"God," she says, as she reaches for the pump handle to flush the toilet. "I would never, ever let a man see me like this usually, you know."

"Not even your boyfriend?"

She raises her eyebrows, taking a sip from her thermos. The houseboat lurches beneath us—a bigger wave, I guess—and Lexi and I lock eyes. We hold our breath for a second. This has happened a few times now. We're getting into the new rhythm. Got to roll with the punches out here or you'd spend your whole time screaming your head off, basically.

"I don't date men nice enough to hold my hair back when I'm throwing up," she says, setting down the thermos and pulling her blanket closer.

I've wondered about Lexi's dating life. She's thirty-one—she's had eight years of dating on me. She must've had men lining up to take her out. So why's she single? Who was stupid enough to let her go?

"What kind of men *do* you date?" I ask.

I take a sip from my own thermos. Water is seriously underrated. I guess when I get home I'll gulp it down without thinking again, but right now I can't imagine seeing a glass of water as anything other than a miracle.

"You want the short history of my dating life?"

"Or the long one." I want it all, really—everything about her.

"Well, there was Johnny, in Year Eleven. He was the one everybody wanted, so I hung on to him at all costs, and the cost was fairly substantial," she says, shifting into a more comfortable position. "Then there was Lee. He was very nice until he wasn't. He taught me why 'crazy' is a bad word even if they're laughing when they say it. Then there was a string of casual ones, all as bad as one another, and then Theo, who left me after I took on supporting Penny and Mae, and then I just gave up, really."

I stare at her in horror. She snorts.

"Believe me," she says, "this is not an unusual story, tragic as it is. Every thirty-something single woman has at least a few nasty ones in her history, even if she doesn't recognize it. Good men are hard to find."

"How old did you say Mae is?"

"Four. Four and two months, to be precise, which she always prefers you to be."

"And Theo left you before she was born?"

"Yup."

"And you've not dated since? Not . . . at *all*?"

She snorts at my expression.

"Sorry," I say, blinking fast. "I just thought . . . that's a really long time to go without . . ."

She shrugs. "I had the odd encounter at The Anchor that ended up in bed. Two or three times, maybe. But yeah. Didn't you clock that I was a little rusty?"

I think about that night. Kissing the skin of her stomach, feeling her nails scrape my shoulders. Burying myself inside her and just *losing* it as the world seemed to fall away around us.

I clear my throat. "No," I say firmly. "You did not seem . . . rusty."

I catch the ghost of a smile before she swipes it away.

"Do you mind if I lie down again?" she asks, her voice a little weak.

"Course not," I say, moving as close to the door as I can to give her some space.

I feel embarrassed now. Only two or three one-night stands for almost five years? It'd been four months since I'd last had sex when I took Lexi back to this boat, and I felt like a monk.

"Penny's dating life was enough to put me off every time I considered dipping my toe in again. She's only ever had a string of terrible men who left her the second things got serious." She sniffs. "You know, this one guy walked out because she asked him to pick her up a Mooncup from Boots?"

I laugh.

"He just said, *Look, love, no offense, but this isn't really my scene.* I know I shouldn't generalize, but it just seems to me like men can't handle the nitty-gritty. Real-life stuff, shit happening, the grind. Over and over, that's what I've seen. I think if any of the other men I've encountered in my life had been on this houseboat with me, they'd have . . ." She pauses—nausea getting worse for a moment, maybe. "They'd have taken charge to begin with," she continues. "Then they'd have got angry because they were scared. Then they'd have given up and sulked and gone to pieces. But you've not done any of that. I don't think you would have left me out here even if you could have."

"Of course not," I say, shocked that she'd even think it.

She lies down with her head in my lap, which surprises me, but no complaints here. I stretch my legs out as best I can in the tiny space as she wriggles her hairband free and then massages her scalp. Her eyelids dipping in pleasure. I swallow. She looks so gorgeous, even after vomiting all night. I want to say, *I would never, ever leave you*, but I can't, because that's not what this is.

"What about you? Come on," she says, snuggling in, knees curled up to her chest. "Entertain me with tales of your exes. I know you've slept around a bit, but what's your dating history?"

I stay quiet, chewing my cheek. She cracks an eye open, turning her head to look up at me.

"Come on. First serious girlfriend? There must have been *one*."

I don't often think about Nicky. She's come up in therapy a bit—how could she not, really—but these days, it doesn't hurt to remember her. Just makes me kind of curious. Who would I have been, if I'd never met her?

"Oh, there *was* one," Lexi says with satisfaction.

"Just one, yeah."

"Broke your heart?"

"I mean . . ."

I guess she did, really. Or changed it. I was just a kid, looking for someone to make me feel at home, and for a while, I was hers—installed in her flat, hardly ever out of her bed, as obsessed with her as she seemed to be with me. But it barely lasted two months. *I've taught you everything I know, cuteness,* she'd said. *You knew this wasn't going to last. You're* very *pretty, but we were never going to be anything serious, were we?*

"How old were you?" Lexi asks.

"I was sixteen."

"And she was . . ."

Lexi's so good at reading me now.

"Twenty-eight," I say reluctantly.

Her eyes snap wide open. "*Twelve* years older than you?"

"Mm."

"How did *that* happen?"

"We met when I was waiting tables at a golf club one summer."

She'd caught my eye with a glass of wine dangling between finger and thumb, at lunch with her father and his new wife. Draped in her chair, languid, beautiful. I'd seen her straighten at the sight of me. When I'd reached the table to take their order, she'd said, *I don't suppose you could show me to the bathroom?* By the time we'd reached the corridor outside the restaurant doors, her body was already brushing close to mine. *I'm Nicky,* she'd said. *I'm here all summer and I'm* ever *so bored.*

"You totally have a thing for older women."

I frown and shake my head. "I don't *have a thing*, I just . . ." But I trail off, because I kind of do, really. "I just always feel more connected to women who are a bit older than me. They know what they want, they're . . . They just seem more interesting."

"If by interesting you mean damaged and jaded, yes."

"That's definitely not what I mean. That's so . . . that's so far from how I see you."

She says nothing for a while. "I don't know whether it's better or worse that you've been with older women before."

I smile slightly. "Why does it bother you so much? The fact that there's an age gap between us?"

"It doesn't."

I wait.

"All right, it does a bit. A woman over thirty with no home of her own, who goes back with a twenty-three-year-old she meets in the pub . . . she sounds a bit of a mess."

"Not to me," I say, running my hand up and down her arm. I remember doing this in bed, how soft her skin had felt. It's difficult to match the woman in my lap with the woman I took home on that first night. She'd been a stranger then, and this is my Lexi, my only person in the world. "She sounds like someone who didn't really get her twenties. It makes sense she'd want a person who's at a similar stage."

Her eyes fly open again. Wide-wide.

"You're not at a similar stage to me," she says, staring at the bathroom wall instead of up at me.

"No?"

"Zeke, I'm a thirty-one-year-old woman. I want kids of my own. I should be with someone sensible to father my children, not a beautiful twenty-something who makes me feel alive for a night, or whatever."

"What, I'm not sensible? And how do you know I don't want to have kids soon?" I say, my hand stilling on her arm.

At last, she looks at me. She doesn't say anything, and her eyes are still dizzy-looking, but they're sharp, too. Missing nothing.

"There's more to a person than their age," I say quietly. "You can't just decide who I am because I'm twenty-three. I wouldn't say every thirty-one-year-old woman wants, like . . ." I reach around for a handy cliché. "To get married, or to have a baby, or to get Botox, or something."

"No," she says after a moment, with slight amusement. "I wouldn't advise saying any of those things."

I give her a small, tight smile. She frowns.

"That's fair. I'm sorry," she says.

I watch her swallow. I can see it hurts her, and I wish I could smooth that away.

"*Do* you want kids?" she asks.

Her wide eyes are vulnerable. Maybe defiant. It's hard to tell the difference with Lexi.

"I can't wait to be a dad," I say. "I think about it all the time."

She breathes in, a sort of two-part hiccup. The way she might inhale if I'd just got down on one knee.

"It's part of what made me go to therapy. I didn't think I could handle a relationship, but knew I wanted kids, a family, and . . . it didn't add up." This is harder to talk about than I thought it would be. "I think Nicky—the woman I really fell for when I was sixteen— I think she just confirmed for me that I wasn't worthy of real love. But she did make me feel like I was good at sex. So . . . I did a lot of that." I shrug. "I wasn't being honest with myself about what I wanted. Or I was too scared to go out and get it. Sex, that's easy," I say.

I feel her tense slightly and I wince.

"I mean, like . . . I know I can . . ."

"It's OK," she says. "I get it. You were saying: sex is easy . . ."

I take a deep breath. "Trying to fall in love? Find that one person, raise a family with them, trust them to love you forever? That scares me. That's hard."

She nods.

"But yeah, I want kids. I can say that now. I want to be a dad who does everything. Middle-of-the-night get-ups and school drop-offs and all the heart-to-hearts. I want my kids to know I'm always there for them."

Her eyes are fixed on my face.

"But . . ."

"But?" she says, her voice barely a whisper.

"One of the things I worry about is that I'll . . . mess them up. I tend to mess stuff up."

Lexi frowns, lifting her head from my lap and straightening to sit against the sink.

"What does that even mean?" she asks.

"Like . . . I'm kind of stupid." I cringe, closing my eyes, tipping my head back to the wall again. "I never live up to people's expectations. It's OK, I'm used to it. But I wouldn't want my kids to be disappointed in me."

Lexi doesn't speak for so long that I open my eyes to check she's not fallen unconscious or something.

"Did you mean all that?" she says, disbelieving.

I stare at her. "That's what . . . yeah. Yeah, I mean it. I'm not looking for you to make me feel better about it or anything, I just . . ."

"Zeke. You are not stupid. Oh my *God*. Did you see the contraption you built to collect us water? You thought of that in half a second. You've been so brilliant and inventive surviving out here with me—you're the ideas person. You're the one who figures everything out."

I close my eyes again. It feels so, so good to hear her say that. Just like when she called me clever at The Anchor. And I want to believe it so badly. But I'm not the ideas person. As a kid, I was the tagalong, doing whatever Jeremy and Lyra told me to—whatever it would take to fit in. Until it became clear that I never would, and then I just tried not to mind.

"I'm really not, but it's cool. I've made peace with who I am," I say. "Velvet trousers, remember? I don't mind being a bit different."

I can feel the embarrassed thumping of my heart in the flesh of my wound.

"We don't need to talk about all this," I say, forcing myself to open my eyes and look at her.

She's bracing herself against a wave of nausea that I can almost see moving through her. She shakes her head, frustrated, taking another moment to collect herself.

"Everything you've told me about your life," she says, "it doesn't sound like you let people down. It sounds like you've not found people who make you feel like you're enough."

"Nah, I . . ." I trail off.

Because she's named it exactly. That quiet sadness in the back of my mind. The certainty that there's no way to make myself into the right shape to fit in. I don't remember ever feeling any other way—except lately. With Lexi. As terrifying as life is out here, I'm not straining to live up to something or acting out before I have the chance to disappoint. I don't get that nagging sense that I'm just not quite *right*.

She makes me feel at ease.

"That was . . . deep," I say, tipping her a look. Trying not to let her see how much she's shaken me.

"I know," she says, raising her hands to run her fingers through her hair, beginning to work on some of the tangles. "It's the wisdom of age."

"Lexi . . ."

"Mm?"

"You're not that old."

"I feel ancient," she says, dragging the word out. "Especially right now. I feel like they took eighteen-year-old me and put her through one of those old-fashioned coffee-grinder things."

"What was eighteen-year-old you like?"

"Sharp. No bullshit. A woman who got things done."

"Sounds like thirty-one-year-old Lexi."

"No, no. Thirty-one-year-old Lexi is jaded and insecure and tired." Her eyelids are drooping.

"Right now thirty-one-year-old Lexi is really dehydrated, which probably isn't helping," I say, holding out her thermos. "Drink. And rest."

"Will you . . ."

I nod. I know what she's going to ask. She's sent me out to check for leaks every couple of hours or so. I haven't told her about the holes I just stuffed with cotton wool in the ceiling.

"Zeke?" Lexi whispers.

"Mm?"

"You've surpassed all my expectations," she says, her voice fainter now, as if she's about to fall asleep. "Every single one."

Lexi

IT'S A ROUGH night.

I crawl to the bedroom sometime around midmorning. There's an endless, dull throbbing in the back of my head, a low bass note that won't let up. The sound of the waves is even louder in the bedroom—it's as if we're in an echo chamber down here, and it seeps into my dreams, turning into womb sounds, the rhythmic ache of a heartbeat.

At some point I stumble to the toilet, catching a gray-white sky through the windows as the walls and cabinets slide in my vision. The houseboat isn't cute now, with all its slightly-too-small chairs and drawers and cupboards. It's hellish, like a dollhouse in a horror film. I fall on my way back into the bedroom and Zeke is there, catching me, though I'm not one hundred percent sure I'm awake, because that seems like the sort of thing I'd dream up.

I wake in the afternoon with a horrible taste in my mouth and a sheen of sweat all over me—by the time I eventually stripped out of my damp clothes, I was ice-cold, and Zeke layered me in blankets. I think of him calling himself stupid, and it makes me not just sad but *angry*. Who fucking dared make him feel that way?

"Hey, you're up," he says softly, pushing the door open. "How's your head feeling? And your stomach? Could you eat something?"

"I knew you'd say that," I say, lifting my head and shoulders to look at him. "Are you like this when you're *not* rationing every last grain of rice?"

"What, always planning the next meal? Yup. You should see my recipe notebooks from when I first started at Davide's."

His hair has dried—it's softer and fluffier than usual. He's wearing his battered, stained velvet trousers, and a pin-striped shirt of mine, which he has French-tucked into his waistband to disguise the poor fit. I find this nod to fashion completely adorable.

"I hope I will see them, one day."

I look up at the skylight as he tidies around me. The rain has subsided to a light, airy drizzle, like the fine spray that creeps past the shower curtain. God, what I'd give for a shower.

"Isn't it funny that you and your dad both wrote down your thoughts? You with your recipe notebooks, him with his logbooks?"

He keeps his face averted. "Guess so. I'd never thought about it like that."

I watch him as he shuffles around the bed, head ducked. It says so much about his relationship with his father that he still hasn't dared to open one of those logbooks. My heart aches for him. I think he's more afraid to confirm what his dad thought of him than he is to know the truth about his parentage. I almost want to say, *It's not so bad, you know, watching your father turn away from you*, but I'd be lying. Dad leaving us the way he did, it made me who I am, and not in a good way.

"So. What could you manage to eat?" Zeke asks, chucking the blankets into the corner.

I am immediately itching to fold those.

"Digestive?" I say. "How many are left?"

"Plenty," he says, and I know he'd give them all to me, and it makes me want to weep, that kindness, all his kindness.

I should get up and fetch some food myself, my brain says, but I'm too tired for that old crap, and right now it's easier than usual to say, *Actually, why not just let someone else do the work for a minute?*

Zeke heads into the kitchen to bring me a digestive, then reaches for the moldy bread that he keeps in a plastic Tesco bag in the back of the left-hand cupboard. "I'll just go see if Eugene is about. Bucket by the bed in case the biscuit turns out to be a bad plan."

"We should not be giving that bread to the bird," I say half-heartedly, resting the digestive flat on my palm, just contemplating it. The idea of eating moldy bread makes me want to vomit again, but before the rain came, I really felt the perilousness of our limited supplies. "There's no way to get more food, Zeke."

"I'm working on making a fishing pole," he says, but he looks torn. "All right. No bread for Eugene."

He puts back the plastic bag and starts checking the storm-proofing on the cupboards. The nausea rolls in the base of my empty stomach like something we've left loose on the deck.

"He can catch himself fish to eat now," I say. "He's up and about again."

"Right, yeah, exactly," Zeke says, not looking at me.

"And we might actually starve, you know. This is serious."

"Of course."

The same voice that told me to rest says, *You love that bird.*

"Just don't give him loads, OK?" I say. "Hold some back."

The smile Zeke shoots me could melt chocolate. "Yeah," he says, reaching for the bag again. "I'll be sensible."

I settle back into the pillows with an exhale as I hear him step out onto the deck, the door swinging shut behind him. The rainwater I've been drinking all night seems to have worked a small miracle on my body—I can almost feel myself plumping up, as though my blood is flowing faster. I nibble at the edge of my precious digestive and my mouth even manages to generate a small flood of saliva.

"Lexi!" Zeke roars.

My nausea evaporates for a moment, replaced by something sharper: panic.

"What? Zeke?"

"Can you come out onto the deck?" He's already back in the bedroom doorway, hair wild, eyes wilder.

"I think so?" I say, swiveling my legs out of the bed and standing gingerly, reaching for the arm he offers me.

Everything wobbles around the edges when I stand, as if I've just twisted a camera lens and lost focus. We move through the living area so slowly, and I keep saying to Zeke, "*Tell me, tell me,*" but he just says, "*Come on, you have to see.*" The deck is slippery; I have to step over our various rainwater-collection bowls, registering the volume in each one even as I follow the path of Zeke's finger.

"*Look,*" Zeke says, pointing to the horizon above the body of the boat.

It's . . . a building. That's what it looks like. A strange gray building on thick stilts in the water, distant, but directly ahead of us, at twelve o'clock to *The Merry Dormouse*'s nose. It looks monstrous, like something out of a *Transformer* film, and as I stare at it, I begin to see that it's a platform with metal structures on its top. The legs are reddish; there's some kind of crane on there, tilted at an awkward angle, like a bird's neck looking down into the water below.

"An oil rig," Zeke says. His voice is thick with excitement and his hands are gripping the rail. "It'll be full of workers, Lexi. *People.* We're safe. We're saved."

I double over—knocked by the boat, and by the shock of it.

I fall to my knees. We're safe. The cold seawater soaks into my socks and the deck scrapes my bare skin.

"Oh my God, oh my God," I chant, pressing my forehead against my arm. There is nothing like this—nothing like the rising, growing, exploding euphoria of believing things will actually be OK. A bowl of rainwater tips against my thigh, dousing me, and I hardly feel the cold, like it's happening to somebody else.

Zeke's laughing. "We did it. We did it. We didn't die!"

The realist in me sits up at this. "We still need to get there," I say, resting back on my heels and reaching one hand out to hold myself steady.

Zeke peers over the side of the boat. I hate it when he does that. He always leans so far, like a little boy who can't resist going right to the edge.

"Honestly, it looks like the current is taking us roughly the right way," he says. "Can we use the sail and the helm? They'll send someone out when we get close enough anyway."

I get to my feet and stare out at the water, the oil rig, the water, the oil rig. I can't believe it's real. For a second, I think to myself, *What if we've gone mad and it's a mirage?* before realizing that I have no idea what an oil rig looks like, so this would have been some seriously inventive imagining on my part.

Zeke and I busy ourselves unfastening the sail. I pull my hair up into a tangled bun with the band around my wrist, wincing as I tug at the tender skin of my head injury. I imagine the people on that oil rig, what they'll think, how they'll greet us. How they'll look at the bump on my head and the cut across Zeke's stomach with first aid kits to hand, how they'll sterilize them, give us bottled water . . .

Zeke's talking, not really saying much in particular—"*Oh my God, I knew we'd do it, I knew we'd be all right*"—but I feel as though I'm floating, only half here. I'm going to see Mae again. I'm going to get home. I cling to the flagpole as *The Merry Dormouse* lurches her way onward and I feel a pang of genuine love for her. What a boat. She's been a hero, and her job is almost done. Thank God— I'm not sure how many more ways we can plug up that shower drain, and though Zeke's not talked to me about it, I know he's been fixing up holes in the ceiling ever since the rain started.

The next hour is another crash course in sailing, if you can even call it that. There are a terrifying few minutes in which we steer ourselves the wrong way in the wind, and every so often *The Merry Dormouse* seems to rear forward when the sail fills with air, and my stomach drops, because I'm sure we've gone too hard and she'll dip her nose into the sea and upend us. I'm dogged with a total conviction that something will go wrong any second: we'll hit something, or capsize, and the people on the rig won't get to us in time to save us.

Eugene squawks anxiously as Zeke and I alternate between grappling with the billowing sail and turning the wheel; both of us hit ourselves with the boom hard enough to bruise our already-battered bodies, and we're slow, breathless, weak. But we're heading the right way. We're heading toward safety. For the first time in so long, we're not just floating helplessly—we're doing something to save ourselves.

The closer we get to the rig, the more detail we can see: the gaps between the metal structures, showing tiny fragments of sky; the worn-down stripes on the great concrete legs, battered by the sea. At some point Zeke hands me a slice of sweating cheese on a stale cracker and I eat it without thinking, hardly noticing the taste until it makes me nauseous again and I gag over the side of the boat.

As the rig looms larger, we each snatch a moment to go inside and pack up our belongings. It's bizarre. I stand in the bedroom, and for a moment I am genuinely unable to fathom the idea of leaving this tiny space.

I meticulously repack my bag with everything I hung up in the wardrobe. I find my purse at the back of the bedside drawer and unzip it, looking at my driving license, my credit card, all these little plastic symbols of a life that feels completely alien now. I imagine paying contactless for something and it makes me want to laugh.

Zeke's bag is by the bed, packed exactly how I'd expect Zeke to pack—haphazardly. The end result is a duffel bag so full he's only been able to half close the zip, and as I carry it out onto the deck with mine, I see what's sitting in the top.

The logbooks. They're all in there.

I look at him standing beside the sail, up on the roof, wind in his curls.

"Did you . . . ?" I begin.

He clocks what I've seen.

"No." He gives me a lopsided, closed-mouthed smile. "I tried opening one of them and slammed it shut again. I dunno. There's a lot going on right now."

I tilt my head as I look up at him from the deck, like, *All right, I'll give you that.* We've barely stopped for the last two hours, and this small pocket of stillness in the frenzy of the day feels almost nostalgic now, as if we're going back to the time when we were frozen and floating with nowhere to go. All of a sudden I feel dizzyingly emotional.

"I'm glad it was you," he says, so softly I almost don't hear him over the wind. "On this adventure with me."

"Is that what we're calling it now?"

"Uh-huh. Adventure. Quest. Mission."

"Not two clueless arseholes drifting around?"

"Definitely not," he says. "Have you seen yourself right now?"

My hand is on the wheel, my feet planted on the deck, my hair whipping in the wind. I can't bear how he's looking at me—there's something sweet and tender about it, and this is starting to feel like a good-bye.

"You look amazing," he says.

For a moment, up there on the roof of the houseboat, his eyes are just like they were on that first night: hot, intense, fixed on mine like they don't want to let me go. I've seen glimmers of that desire on his face in the last week, but he shuts it down so effectively I sometimes think I imagine them.

He shifts to the edge in a crouch, sliding so his feet hang over the door, and reaches a hand out for mine. I think he's asking me to help him down, but once he grips me, he just stays there, holding my hand. The sensation of his skin against mine starts at my palm, but it spreads in warm sparks, up my arm, through my chest, right to the core of me. He slides his thumb slowly across mine, as if he's tracing the shape of me to memorize it.

Then he drops my hand. "Sorry," he says, eyes widening. "I'm sorry. I shouldn't have done that."

"It's OK," I say, but he's already getting back up on his feet, dodging the swinging sail.

"No, it's not," he says, and I can't see him now behind the tarp. "I made a promise about what would happen on this boat, and it wasn't that."

I look at the approaching rig. I don't argue the point with him. Not because I give a damn about that rule we made anymore, but because in a matter of minutes, *everything* will be different.

We won't be on this boat, for starters.

~~~~~

The nerves set in the closer we get to the rig. I expected to see some-one up there by now—we're near enough that we'd be able to see figures, and I imagined they'd be waving to us, maybe even sending out a life raft. But the rig is silent and still.

We're so close now that I can see the rust and peeling paint. It's cooler here in the rig's monstrous shadow, and the quietness is eerie. I'm beginning to feel afraid.

"Lexi?" Zeke says.

"It's fine, it'll be fine," I say, and then: "We need to get closer, and they're not . . . sending anyone out, or anything . . ."

I frown. We're drifting onward, but the rig isn't quite where I expected it to be in my line of vision. I *thought* we were heading straight for it, but . . .

"Are we . . ."

"Yeah," Zeke says grimly.

He's already turning the wheel, but the breeze is slower here; it doesn't seem to move us at all. We're now about twenty feet from the rig's structure: I can see a ladder, tantalizingly close, and a gathering of crustaceans just above where the water touches one of the pillars rising out of the sea. A seagull caws, and Eugene stirs in his box, seeming tamer than ever compared to the birds looping above us.

I swear, looking up at the slackness of the sail, then back to Zeke, who is twisting the wheel, sinews standing out on his forearms. Could we make a paddle big enough to help us steer this houseboat? Suddenly the boat that has seemed so small for the last week seems absolutely enormous. I clutch at my chest, clutch at the railings, because we're drifting on by, and there's the ladder, there, there, sliding away from us in horrible slow motion.

"We're going to miss it," Zeke says. "We're going to—"

"Help!" I yell, tilting my head up. My voice is so small compared to the awful grandeur of this place. It echoes, but the sound is lost under the *slap* and *whoosh* of the waves. "Help us! Help!"

Nobody comes. The boat drifts on. This is the slowest, most torturous way to lose all hope.

I clench my jaw and bend to unfasten my boots. "I'm going to do something."

I pull my shirt off over my head, then grab the rope curled on the deck, the one we use to lower our bucket in and out of the sea, the one that started this mess in the first place. I begin to tie it around my waist.

"Lexi?"

"I'll swim across."

My hands are shaking so much it's hard to secure a knot; the rope is too tight, cutting into the bare skin of my midriff, but I'm already readying myself to dive into the water. The breeze sends my skin goose-pimpling, and a wave touches my bare feet, startlingly cold.

"That's—Lexi, no—you'll get hurt!"

"What the fuck else are we going to do!" I yell, hating the way my voice is shaking, hating how hard it is to force myself through the gap in the railings onto that ledge at the edge of the boat, the one I walked along, drunk, wondering what it would feel like to let myself fall.

I'm only a few meters away from something to hold on to. It's not like I'm diving into the open ocean, the way Zeke did to save Eugene. But all the same, I'm so scared I can't form a cohesive thought, like all the parts of it are scattering in the wind.

I dive. The cold grips me a second after I hit the water, like the pain did yesterday when I hit my head—it strikes with the same hammer blow, and I gasp, mouth burning as I swallow seawater. I'm afraid I'll be too cold to swim, but my limbs move, sluggish but insistent. One stroke, another. My muscles begin to burn. The rope is slack, and it tangles around my left leg—for a moment I panic, but I manage to kick it free and forge on, letting it float behind me.

Zeke is shouting something I can't catch. This is the hardest thing my body has done in a very long time. I'm so broken from the last twenty-four hours—I'm astonished I have any strength in me. I let out a roar as I get close, a hand's width from the ladder, my nose and mouth full of seawater. When my knuckles strike metal, I almost go under with the relief of it. I hold myself there with both arms wrapped around the bar, wet rust painting my arms, flaky and blood-red. Zeke whoops across the water. I have just enough breath to manage a laugh.

"Lexi Taylor!" he yells. "You just did that! You really just did that!"

I look back. It is so strange seeing *The Merry Dormouse* from the outside after all this time—it looks rougher than when I saw it last, its paint dulled and worn, that wonky, wild sail sticking out of its roof like a flag on a kid's sandcastle.

And it's still moving. If this rope around my middle strains taut, then I'm about to be pulled into the tide with the weight of a whole houseboat.

I swear, scrabbling for a foothold on the ladder. Now that the adrenaline of the swim is easing off, I'm so cold and my muscles are so strained that even moving my own weight through the water is an effort.

"You can do this," Zeke calls, and it shouldn't help—what a ridiculously banal thing for him to say in the circumstances—but it does.

I'm up now, on shaking legs, knees knocking against the metal, my numb hands already fumbling to undo the rope around my middle.

I don't know how to tie a rope properly. That much has been made fairly obvious. I don't even know what I do, looping bits around other bits and through metal bars, all the while trembling all over, standing there on a ladder in the North Sea in my M&S bra and some knickers that almost but don't quite match.

The rope groans, and the boat begins to turn as it pulls taut. I can't watch; instead, I rest my head against the ladder, close my eyes and start to cry.

Zeke

SHE RESTS FOR maybe two minutes before she begins trying to pull the boat in.

"Lexi," I call across the distance between us. "You can't do that. It's just—it's not going to be possible."

My voice echoes under the rig. She's wrenching on the rope one-handed because she needs to hold the ladder, arm muscles popping, an agonized grimace on her face.

"Lexi, stop!"

"How the hell else am I getting you here?" It's half sentence, half sob.

"I can just swim over. We can leave the boat to . . ."

"Crash into one of those pillars and go under? No. No. She's coming here and we're going to get her secure."

Lexi looks like a superhero right now, braced there on the ladder, drenched and bare, the rope in her hands.

"Just stop a second," I say, gripping *The Merry Dormouse*'s railing. "What if you use your body weight on it? One arm around the ladder, stand on the rung where you've tied it . . . and then do a sort of one-legged squat? Push down on the rope with your other leg? It should create some slack, and then you could tie it up again . . ."

It takes her a few more tries after the first one, but it *works*. The houseboat is about a foot or so closer to the ladder now, definitely.

"You," she says, her voice hoarse. She says nothing else, but there's a lot in that word, and all of it makes me glow.

The untying and retying is such hard work, I can see her legs shaking from here. I keep saying, "*Let me swim over and do it,*" but she shakes her head, teeth gritted, and I don't want to say to her that she can't do it herself, because look. She's amazing. She can.

"Don't you dare jump in and swim the last bit," she says, when I'm just a couple of meters from her. "We did not come this far just to open up your wound again and get a load of seawater in it."

The exhaustion's rolling off her. She's shaking so much, red-faced and sweaty and sea-soaked. I want to hold her so badly, want to wrap myself around her. I'm useless over here. I shove Lexi's abandoned boots into her holdall, sling both our bags over my shoulders, and glance at Eugene in his box. We'll have to come back for him. It's stupid how much the thought of leaving him hurts.

When I finally leap across to the ladder, pain sears through my stitches so sharply that I can't avoid crying out.

"Zeke!" Lexi shouts down. She's climbed up to give me space to get on, but I can hear she's paused on the ladder.

"I'm OK," I call back, forehead to a rung, pain still lancing through me. "Keep going up. I'm OK."

Every step to the first deck of the rig hurts. When I finally get there, we don't say anything; she just turns in to me as I drop the bags at my feet. She presses her face to my chest. I hold her bare, trembling body. One minute, three minutes, five. We stay like this in the wind and the quietness, and I try not to notice how empty the rig feels around us.

Lexi steps away eventually, reaching for her bag and pulling out some dry clothes, along with her boots. I glance around as she yanks the jumper over her head. Everything looks so massive after the boat. I feel miniature, like an ant. And the bleakness, the echoing caws of seabirds . . . it's freaky.

It looks a hell of a lot like this rig's deserted.

Once she's dressed, Lexi takes my arm, and we pick our way across the mussel shells covering the rusty grating beneath us. The shells pop and crack under our feet. Lexi's shaking all over. I need to get her somewhere warm and dry. We head up a set of steps and reach a concrete level—firmer ground.

"You're OK," I tell her.

"Right. So are you," she says, but her eyes keep flicking to my T-shirt, and I know she's looking for blood. I'd like to do the same, but I don't want to freak her out.

"There," she says. "Try that door."

It's an emergency fire door. I try the handle—it's unlocked, and there's a gloomy corridor on the other side. Lexi's hand tightens on my arm. It sends a warm feeling through me—even though she's holding on to me for comfort, it's working the other way around.

The corridor has that cheap, temporary vibe you get in institutional places. It's all made with pale cream panels, and there are signs everywhere. EYEWASH, it says on the wall, above some kind of contraption a bit like a handwash dispenser. EMERGENCY EXIT, says a big green sign, pointing back the way we came.

"Are you scared?" Lexi asks quietly.

"Nah. Not me."

"Not even a little bit?"

"I'm mostly cold," I say. *And worried about you.*

"*Bah!*" she says in my ear, and I jump about half a meter.

"Lexi! Jesus."

She's laughing. A thin, wobbly laugh, but a real one.

"I knew you were scared."

"Fine, yes, this dark, derelict oil rig has given me the creeps a tiny bit, OK?" I say, pulling her closer to me with her arm on mine as we take in blank walls and dirty floors.

"Your toxic masculinity is showing," she says, with a smirk in her voice.

I laugh, then my laugh trails off as a great creak rumbles through the structure around us.

"Umm," Lexi says. "Did that sound . . ."

"Ominous?"

"Structural?"

I pull a face. It didn't sound *great*.

"We're going to be fine," Lexi says, swallowing. "There'll be a phone. A radio. Something. Then we'll be home in no time."

She tries a few handles and finds locked doors. We turn a corner, catching more laminated signs and wall panels in the dim light—and another door. This one opens.

"Oh, shitting hell."

Lexi gets a look inside before me. I peek over her shoulder and pull right back out again. It's some sort of sick bay—empty beds with lights over them, a bit like desk lamps but fixed to the ceiling.

"Are we in a disaster movie? Can you just tell me this is real, please? I feel like I'm in a bad dream."

"It's real. Sorry." I swallow, forcing myself to take in the dark room again.

There'll probably be useful supplies in here—bandages, creams. But it looks so creepy. I wrap an arm around Lexi's shoulder, desperate to stop her shaking.

"Maybe another room will be better," I say, steering her away. "Maybe there's one filled with all our friends and family waiting to surprise us."

"Don't say that. Don't joke about that."

I wince. "Sorry. Stupid."

I know she misses Mae in a way I can't comprehend. I want to see my mum, Brady, even Jeremy and Lyra, but Lexi's like a woman with a hole in her heart right now, and I just stuck a finger in it.

"Not stupid," she says, glancing up at my face. "It's hard to say exactly the right thing to someone who's shit-scared and doesn't even know what they want to hear. It's not stupid to sometimes hit on the wrong thing, Zeke. We all do it."

She remembers that conversation in the bathroom, then. I'd hoped she might not—mild concussion, or something. I look away, embarrassed. Not because of what she said, but because of how good it makes me feel to hear it.

The next door leads to a staircase with the same clinical feel as the corridor we just left behind. As we make our way up the steps, with Lexi leaning on my arm, I figure out why I feel so weird. I'm unsteady on my feet, like the steps are moving underneath me. No wonder Lexi's dizziness has got worse—we're both having to manage our sea legs.

Plus I'm still a bit light-headed from the blood loss, and my wound's hurting like hell right now. Not that I'm going to mention that.

As we round a bend, it gets lighter. There are windows, showing cranes and sky. I never thought I'd be so relieved to see the sea again.

"Do you need to rest?" I say, glancing at Lexi.

She shakes her head. "I want to keep going."

"I could keep exploring, while you . . ."

Her grip on my arm gets twice as tight.

"We stay together. Please. Don't leave me."

I give her hand a quick squeeze.

"Never."

We check every door. We find bare bedrooms, mostly, like dorm rooms in a school. There's even a games space with a snooker table and some of those chairs that you find in waiting rooms, the uncomfortable ones with curved wooden arms. Deeper down the maze of corridors is an inventory room filled with tall metal shelves, carrying endless boxes of screws and pipes and bits of metal.

"A treasure trove," Lexi whispers, running her hand across a dusty shelf. "Or maybe . . . absolutely useless."

I know what she means. If we were in a survival film, then all these pieces of equipment would probably be a lifeline. We'd cobble them together to start up our engine or something. But it turns out being lost out here hasn't made me any less *me*. I'm still a man who has no clue what to do with any of this stuff.

The last—very last—room we find is our real treasure trove. A radio room.

Lexi lets out a sobbing gasp when she sees the sign on the solid metal door, and then she tries the handle. It's locked.

She falls forward into the door, half collapsing. As if this barrier has sucked all the energy out of her at last.

"We can break in," I say, reaching for her arm, trying the handle like she did, just in case. "We're so close. We can just . . . Surely we can . . ."

We yank at the handle. Hammer at the door. Go back to the tall shelves and look for something—anything—that might help us. We bruise our hands and toes. And the door just . . . stays locked. A big, thick, gray metal obstacle between us and the rest of the world.

Lexi sways on her feet. I move to catch her.

"You need rest," I say.

I wince. As I steady her, it tugs on my stitches, and the pain is fierce.

"You have to lie down," I manage.

"Not on those beds," she says, shuddering. "I want . . ."

She stares at the door, tears in her eyes. I gather her into my arms, and she melts against me, damp and sea-smelling, the most precious person. My mind's going full tilt, trying to think of a place I can take her that won't feel so much like somewhere that might feature in a first-person shooter game. It's all so *bleak* here. I have this weird out-of-body moment and imagine a world where I could take Lexi to a café, or a shop, or my flat, and it's almost painful.

"Did you see that helicopter pad through the window in the office?" I say. "That's where our rescuers will be dropping in. We can write a message on it. *Help us, we had a one-night stand on a houseboat and ended up here!*"

I get a laugh for that, and honestly, it's better than a bath would be right now. Better than a hot piece of toast. Better than a pint of Coke.

"Or something shorter," she says into my chest. "And less like a BuzzFeed article."

"Right, yeah, we can edit it down, sure."

She loops her arms around my waist, pressing in. Letting me take the weight of her body. I back up until I'm against one of the cream-paneled walls and we can both just lean there, her head on my chest.

"Do you think we could take a break from trying to cope with all this?" she says.

"You want to freak out for a while?"

"Yeah. This is just all completely fucking *awful*."

I stay quiet. I totally get that she needs to say that out loud right now, but I really don't, and I trust she knows that, too. The wind whistles through the gaps in the edge of the windows, and I wonder if there's anyone else I would prefer to have with me in this nightmare than the woman with the gorgeous eyes who said *I'm not but thanks* when I told her she was beautiful. It doesn't even take a second to realize that no, there isn't. Not Brady, not my brother, not Bear Grylls. I just want her.

"Do you think chocolate goes off?" she says eventually.

"Hmm?"

She pulls back to meet my gaze.

"Chocolate. Do you think it actually goes off? Or do they just put sell-by dates on chocolate bars for insurance reasons or something, and actually you can eat it forever?"

"Like cheese?"

She does one of those hemmed-in smiles. The kind she wears when she's trying to act like she doesn't want to laugh.

"Since you're the person in charge of all our meals, I sincerely hope you're joking right now."

I smile. "Is there a reason you're asking about sell-by dates?"

"I saw chocolate bars in an open bedroom drawer. Snickers and TimeOuts. They were obviously someone's secret stash."

"TimeOuts," I say, salivating.

"Aren't you too young to—"

"Lexi." I'm laughing.

"Sorry, sorry. I think eating them would probably be bad, though."

"Bad, like, morally?" I ask, looking down at her.

"Bad, like, intestinally."

She gives me a tiny smile when I laugh.

"We're going to be OK," she says.

"Absolutely," I say. "We're going to be fine."

And right now, with my arms around Lexi, it doesn't even feel like I'm pretending to mean it.

Lexi

"YOU DON'T HAVE to call me a culinary genius," Zeke says from behind me, "but I have just conjured up an absolutely banging dinner from fossilized tins."

I am standing in a pool of seawater and cracked old mussel shells, staring out at the waves between the metalwork on this side of the rig as he picks his way across to me. Seabirds swoop and caw above him—it's clear they've colonized this place, and they're not sure about the visitors. Zeke's holding two plates on one arm, like a waiter, and two glass bottles of Coke between the fingers of the other hand. The steam rising from the food swirls away on the wind. He's wearing someone else's faded jeans with a leather belt; he's shorn the jeans to finish just above his boots and found a moss-green knitted jumper that makes him look like he might distill whisky in the Scottish highlands. Only Zeke could try out oil-rig chic and make it happen.

He's moving more gingerly—he thinks I've not noticed, but I know his wound is hurting. I try not to let the worry show on my face.

"You got the hob working?"

"Yep—whichever generator powers the kitchen seems to still have some juice. Not sure how long we'll have it, but . . . let's make the most."

When he's close enough, I peer at the contents of the plates, stomach tightening with hunger. It's some sort of stew—it smells strongly of Bisto gravy, which makes me nostalgic for home, and it has those little round boiled potatoes in that my grandma used to eat for her dinner.

"This looks . . ."

"It tastes better than it looks, I promise you."

"I was going to say it looks fantastic."

Zeke smiles, already tucking in, Coke bottle now balanced on a giant concrete bollard to his left. There are so many giant things around here. After the smallness of the boat, this rig feels oversized and garish, with yellow and red lines painted on the concrete and blaring instructions laminated on walls. The machinery all around us is caked in sea salt, rust and bird poo; it's like standing in a metalwork graveyard.

I look back out at the water, trying a forkful of the stew. It's delicious—hot, laced with salt, and just the right sort of wholesome.

"So. What now?" Zeke asks.

"Now . . ."

I stir through my plate, noticing chopped green beans, wondering if they really can survive this long, even tinned. We can't figure out when this place was abandoned, but it feels like a time warp. Even the fonts on the signs look dated, and the curtains in the bedrooms are all a shade of nineties mauve.

"Do we hit the radio room door again? Try to knock it down?" I suggest.

"It's solid metal, Lexi," Zeke says, his voice gentle. "I don't know what more we can do."

I clench my jaw. "Then we look for clues as to where we are. There might be a map somewhere with coordinates."

Zeke looks pensive, still chewing. "Do you know what to do with coordinates?"

"No," I admit, looking back out to the water. It's so different from all the way up here on the rig platform—I'm used to the horizon sitting close to us, a warm blue line across the windows of the houseboat, but suddenly we can see so much more water. The sky blends into the sea in the distance, as if someone smoothed a thumb along it.

I glance up at the machinery that reaches into the sky. The rig has several cranes, painted a battered red and white. There's a tower, too, a sort of crisscross metalwork structure to the right of us. Inside it there are thick, rusty cables leading down toward the water below. I squint, lifting a hand to block the glare of the low sun. It's hard to see what's at the top of the tower, but I think there's a ladder running up its side.

"If we got higher . . ." I take a shaky breath. "If we got higher, we could see more."

Zeke nods. "Maybe see boats, or even land . . ."

I keep my gaze fixed to that tower, stark and steely against the sky. When I close my eyes for a moment, I can still see its shape, inverted, white against darkness.

I hate heights. As a kid, I wouldn't even go up on the monkey bars; if a building has more than three stories, I avoid the view from the windows.

"Only one of us should go," I say. "It'll be dangerous. I'll . . ." The sentence sticks to my tongue.

I want to say I'll go. I'm a woman who steps up when things are hard or a decision needs to be made—that's who I *want* to be. And Zeke's injury has clearly worsened since we got here. The last thing he needs is to climb a gigantic ladder. But I am starting to sweat at the very thought of going up that tower.

"It has to be me that goes," he says. "Your body's been through so much today. No way am I letting you do that."

I drag my gaze away from the ladder and watch Zeke knock back his Coke, throat working, eyes closed against the bright sky.

He's a beautiful man. Thoughtful and kind, with just a dash of darkness to him. When I'm with him, I feel different: like I'm worth what I used to think I was worth. Like I'm *someone*. That's the gift he's given me out here, and despite every horror we've been through, I feel genuinely lucky to have had this time with him. That's how special he is.

I don't want Zeke going up that tower. Getting onto the rig was hard enough for him. I know his wound is hurting, and I live in constant terror of it opening up again, or worse, getting infected.

"I'll go," I manage.

"Lexi, that's crazy, you can't—"

And then I say the one thing that I know will make him back off.

"Don't tell me I can't. I *want* to do it."

~~~~~~

To begin with, the ladder is nice and sturdy, with wide rungs covered in chipped yellow paint. It's not too badly rusted—I feel safe. In a deeply unsafe sort of way, of course.

I'm out of breath by the time I reach the platform that leads to the next ladder. It's broad, with thick metal railings. *This is OK*, I think, gripping the rail tightly as I pick my way across to the body of the tower, the birds cawing their protest around me. *I'm doing OK.*

"All right, Lexi?"

Zeke's voice is distant now. I glance downward, then let out a quiet, terrified *oh* as I realize how high above the main platform I am already. Zeke looks minuscule down there, his upturned face no bigger than a thumbnail.

"Oh, God," I say, gripping the railing with both hands as my vision starts to swim and the ground morphs below me.

This next ladder is not as sturdy. It's thinner, with a sparing curved framework around it, a pretty cursory nod to safety. I wonder if the people who'd normally climb this tower would be in harnesses, secured with ropes. I've got nothing, just my bare palms on the metal, my black boots on the rungs.

"You OK?" Zeke calls.

I almost wish he knew how afraid I am of heights. I wish I weren't doing this. For a traitorous second, I decide I don't care about Zeke at all, and I'd rather he were going up this ladder than me.

"I'm OK," I shout down. "I can do this."

I keep saying it as I get set on the first rung. It feels so flimsy, and the wind can reach every part of me as I climb now, with only the caging around the ladder and the sparse structure of the tower to shelter me. It tugs at my clothes, making my jumper buffet my body.

"I can do this," I say.

Up another few rungs, and another. The sea unfurls beneath me; I can hear it, but all I can see is metal and sky. My thigh muscles are beginning to burn, my palms getting sore.

"Five more," I say to myself. "You can do five more rungs, can't you?"

My foot slips. It's the tiniest movement, a miscalculation by no more than a centimeter, and I find my footing within seconds, but my stomach clenches and my heart hammers and suddenly I am too aware of it all: the open sky at my back, the smallness of Zeke's voice, the gap between living and dying.

I lean my forehead on the ladder. It burns cold against my skin, an icy brand running from my eyebrow to my cheekbone. As my heart rate slowly steadies, I tilt my head so I can glance out at the horizon. I am *so* high. Then I look up at the triangle of the tower above me, and it's clear there's still so, so much further to go.

I don't know whether I can see Zeke—I'm too afraid to look down. There is a constant butterfly-lightness in my stomach, and my breath doesn't seem to make it to my lungs. It just flutters in and out of my mouth.

I go higher. Higher. For a while I sing to myself to pass the time, "How Far I'll Go" from *Moana*, and I think about dancing drunk on the deck with Zeke. We knew we were in danger then, but it was different—with hindsight, it was a less pressing sort of danger. We might die, but not *imminently*. Whereas right now . . .

It gets windier the higher I go, the breeze buffeting my ears with the sound you hear if you crack a window in the car on the motorway. I look up: I don't think I'm even close to halfway.

My foot slips again. Properly this time, the result of tired legs and endless repetitive motion. I jolt forward and whack my nose on a rung of the ladder. Pain blooms. I cry out, clinging on, and suddenly my breath isn't just fluttering in my mouth, it's catching helplessly on the wind, too fast, out of control. *I'm going to die*, I think, and the moment I've let the thought in, it floods through me. *I'm going to die. I'm going to die. I'm going to die.*

The pain in my nose has made my eyes water, and the tears on my cheeks seem to set something off—I'm crying in earnest now.

"Oh my God. I'm going to die." I say it out loud and it gets truer, and I'm staring down now; I couldn't resist, because the fear said, *Go on, just check, just once.*

The rig platform looks like a child's toy down below me. I can't see Zeke, just a lacework of machinery and swathes of color below it: rusty red, gray concrete, the speckling blackness of all those mussel shells. Bird poo forms vivid green tie-dyed patches on the rig floor, spread and reshaped by the glinting puddles.

It swims, shifts, like a reflection in water. I can see the edges of the rig—that's how high I am. The full width of it lies below me, and then sea. Vomit rises in my throat. I tilt my chin up and force myself to look at the top of the tower, its apex black against the sky.

I can't go up any more. I just can't. I shift one trembling foot, planning to climb down, but I don't know that motion; I don't know the distance to the rung below—I only know up, up, up.

I can't go down. I can't go up. I'm stuck here. The panic is all-engulfing; it takes me under. I cling and I sob, useless, in an absolute frenzy of terror. Sweat runs down my back and tears drip from my chin, spiraling downward into the tiny bird's-eye landscape below me.

"Lexi, you're OK."

I inhale sharply at the sound of Zeke's voice.

"Lexi? Listen to me. I'm right below you. OK?"

"*Why?*" I choke out. I'm angry, because why have I done all this if he was just going to come up anyway and risk himself? But I'm relieved, too, because thank God, thank God, I'm not alone.

"You telling me you'd let me enjoy the view up here all on my own, if the roles were reversed?"

"Zeke," I say, shoulders shaking as I sob, "I can't do this."

"Course you can." He sounds so calm. "You're the person who threw herself into the ocean half-concussed to get us here. The person who carried an injured seagull in a shoebox from the boat to the rig because you didn't want him to get lonely."

"*You* didn't want him to get lonely," I manage, my words catching on a sob halfway. "I said leave him in the fucking boat."

"You said that, but then there he was in the mess room when I came back out with dinner," Zeke says, with a smile in his voice.

"I was just keeping busy while you cooked," I say, voice thick.

"Uh-huh. Of course."

He sounds as though he's just below me, but I can't possibly look down—my gaze is fixed on a patch of white sky. While I'm looking into nothing, then I can almost imagine I'm not here.

"Zeke . . ."

"Lexi."

"I can't."

"Of course you can."

"I can't."

"Take a breath. You've done amazingly. We're almost at the top."

"You shouldn't be here," I sob. "It's all for nothing if you rip open your stitches or fall off and die, you selfless moron."

"Can you look at me?"

"You want me to look down?"

"Only at me. Not all the way down. I'm right below you. Look, here, I'm going to touch your leg."

"Oh my God, don't."

He already has, just a gentle, firm hand on the back of my left calf, where my boot meets my jeans. I shudder with sobs, but that hand, it helps.

"You should . . . You need to put both your hands on the ladder!"

"Apparently not, actually," Zeke says, as he rubs soft, reassuring circles on my calf with his thumb.

I focus on the place where our skin touches. My sobs are ebbing a little. Maybe I'm just running out of tears.

"What can I do?" he says.

"Just stay," I whisper. "For a moment. Just don't . . . don't leave."

He keeps touching me. He stays. I'm calming slightly with each assured swipe of his thumb.

"We can head down now," Zeke says after a while, as my breath slowly steadies. "There's a pretty sensational view from where we are, and I don't know about you, but I'm just seeing a lot of sea."

With a deep breath, I move my gaze away from that patch of sky. My eyes are aching, dry from the wind and sore from the tears, and it takes a second to focus on the horizon. My view is bisected by a cable, thick as a tree branch and edged with the silver of the ladder. Zeke's right. It's just endless, breathtaking ocean.

Zeke's thumb is still resting on the skin of my calf, beneath my jeans. I feel an acute, almost painful desire to be held, and I make a vow that if I get off this tower alive, I am going to kiss the man who climbed up here to tell me I'm amazing, rules be damned.

"Lexi?" he says. "What do you want to do?"

I grip the ladder tightly. Zeke's right: I have done *so much* today, and all things that I never thought were possible for someone like me. I'm a tiny speck in a giant ocean right now, but I don't feel small.

"Let's keep going," I find myself saying. "We'll see more from the top."

Zeke

I CAN'T BELIEVE she convinced me she wanted to do this. I can't believe I *let* her. But by the time I figured out she was scared of heights, she was already on the second ladder.

It was torture watching her climb from the platform. It's better now that I'm here, too, close enough to reach up and touch her. Whenever she pauses, or when I hear her breath start to speed up, I talk.

"Ask me a question," I say, when I run out of things to ramble on about. "Any question."

Lexi hesitates slightly, then keeps climbing. One steady step after another. My wound throbs nonstop, and my head feels tight, but I bet she's suffering worse.

"How many women have you slept with?"

. . . Oh, God. Not that question.

"Hello? Zeke?"

I'm going to have to give her a ballpark. I start doing some rough math, gripping another rung, taking another step, trying to figure out how badly this'll change her mind about me.

"Hang on. You don't *know* the answer, do you?" Her disbelief cuts through the fear that's laced her voice since she left the platform.

"Just give me a second," I say. Wondering where the line is between rounding down and lying.

"You're twenty-three. How much sex can you have fitted in?" she asks, breathing hard as she climbs.

"Quite . . . a lot?" I say, biting my lip.

She glances at me. It's the first time she's looked down.

"I'm not going to judge you, Zeke."

Maybe she sees my doubt.

"Seriously," she says, "I know you. Maybe if we'd just met and you told me you've slept with thirty women . . ."

I bite my lip harder.

". . . I'd be a bit eye-roll about it and make some assumptions about the kind of guy you are, but . . ."

She pauses, and I watch her hands tighten on the ladder. She takes a shuddering breath. I'm about to say, *Let's just go down*, when she takes another determined step up the ladder.

"But I know you're respectful, and kind, and that you've taken a look at what that sex was about for you, and I know you'll have made sure the women you slept with were on the same page as you. So, no. Not judging."

I swallow. I don't think I realized how much I needed to hear her say this.

"Was I close with thirty?"

"Mm," I say.

I reach for the next rung, arm muscles starting to shake.

"Higher?"

"Bit."

"OK, fifty? Higher or lower?"

She's out of breath from the climb, but her voice is starting to sound stronger. I guess I should be pleased that my body count is distracting her, but it's making me hot with embarrassment. I wish I were one of those people who could say, *I don't regret those nights,* but I do. I know I slept with those women for all the wrong reasons.

"Higher."

"Wow, right, a hundred?"

"Lower," I say, with relief.

It's almost easier to talk like this—not looking right at her, and moments away from probably dying. Really helps you open up.

"Seventy?"

"You're close," I say, and then I gasp.

She's reached the top. Suddenly she's falling forward onto her hands and knees, disappearing from my view as a bunch of outraged birds swoop away from the summit.

"OK?" I call, grabbing at the last few rungs.

The platform at the summit is really a walkway around a central pulley that drops down the middle of the tower, all rusted and rank with bird poo. Behind the machinery, there's the most insane view. It's like being on a plane. The horizon's fuzzy, like the edge of a torn sheet of paper, and the sea's so vast I can't get my head around it.

"Behind you," Lexi says, still down on all fours.

Her voice is different: hoarse and choked up. But I can hear how relieved she is—the relief you feel when you thought you were going to die and haven't yet. I've got really familiar with that feeling lately.

I turn to see what she means, gripping the pulley at the center of the platform to keep myself steady. There's just more sea, more sky.

No. Something else: another rig.

"That one might not be abandoned," Lexi says, voice hushed.

She's still kneeling, as if she can't quite bear to stand up. Today's been so hard on her body—she needs rest. I hope she can make it down that ladder again, a thought I'm careful to keep off my face as I look over my shoulder at her.

"It feels like we're so close to life," I say, letting go of the machinery and moving gingerly toward the railing. "Being here, seeing this . . ."

I stare and stare at the rig. Imagining the people who might be there.

"Please step away from the edge," Lexi says, voice choked.

I don't want to say it, but there's not really anywhere to be except the edge—the platform is maybe three-by-three meters, but the mechanism takes up most of the space. I grip the freezing railing, my hair whirling in the wind.

"Maybe they'll check on this rig," I say. "The people in that one."

"This place doesn't feel very checked-on to me," Lexi says, wiping her face with one hand.

"Here," I say, moving to help her up.

"No!" She flinches away from me, crouching lower. "No. I'm good down at floor level, thanks."

She shuffles in a fraction before realizing that only brings her nearer the hole in the center, where the cables plummet to the sea below. She lets out a whimper and crouches even lower, her cheek to the grating. Her face is tear-streaked and pale. I sit down slowly beside her. I'm not scared of heights, but I'm still moving slowly—there's a bad vibe up here, a sense that the teetering platform might tumble sideways if we don't step carefully enough. It doesn't help that the grating is gappy and you can see through it to the structure beneath us.

"Just think of the deck of the houseboat," I say softly. "There's more space here than there."

"The deck wasn't a million miles up in the *air*, though," she says.

"Yeah, but you didn't fall over the edge and into the sea for over a week, so why would you do that here?"

"That is helpful, but also really annoying," she says.

I smile. "Reckon you could at least sit up?" I ask. "Like this?"

I nod down at myself—I'm sitting with my knees up, back to the railing, facing the rusty orange pulley. It blocks out a fair bit of the view, which I think might help Lexi right now.

She sniffs and pushes up slowly on her arms, then clenches her eyes shut when she glances over the edge.

"Ugh," she says.

"Just look at me," I say, pushing my hair back from my forehead. "Hi."

She opens her eyes and meets mine. I can see her temptation to shift her gaze to the skyline, but I keep our eyes locked, and slowly, slowly, I watch how she softens. Her shoulders drop ever so slightly. Without breaking eye contact, she reaches to grip the railing and rises to sit cross-legged.

We stay like this for so long I lose track of time, just looking at each other, the bare sky whistling around us. After those days cramped in a tiny wooden box with her, all this space makes me feel light-headed. But whatever else changes, Lexi's still Lexi: brave, frightened, strong, soft, warm, cold. I've never met a woman who's so many things at once. And I want her, even here, after this mad, wild day. I want her like I've never not wanted her, like every other time I've wanted a woman, I've been looking for Lexi.

"Sixty," she says faintly.

"Pardon?"

"Women. Sixty women?"

"Oh my God," I say, breathing out a laugh.

"What, you thought I'd drop the topic without getting an answer out of you?"

"Well, no, I mean, I do know you. But . . ." I swallow, finally breaking eye contact to stare down at the grating beneath us. "Sixty-five. There you go. And I'm not even sure it's right. It's a guess. That's how . . . That's how messy it all got. There're women I don't even remember."

She sobers, looking at me with those wide, icy-blue eyes.

"I'm sorry," I whisper.

"Don't say sorry," she says. "Not to me. I was just thinking how easily I could have been one of those women you don't remember."

I shake my head. "You wouldn't've been."

Her eyebrows rise slightly.

"No, seriously. It wasn't like that. If this . . ." I nod at the sea, then wish I hadn't—it makes her glance through the railings and blanch. "If this hadn't happened, yeah, maybe we would have just gone our separate ways and never seen each other again, because that's what you wanted. But I wouldn't have forgotten you."

"No?"

"No. And I never wanted you to leave that morning, you know."

"I seem to remember you thought I was trying to steal your houseboat."

I smile. "Well, yeah. But even so. I knew there was something about you even then." I look down, the sea tugging at the edges of my vision. "Maybe I've had sixty-five one-night stands, but I've never once had this."

"What, you've never once ended up lost at sea with a woman you slept with? Does it even count as sleeping around if you don't tick that one off?"

I cut her a look. "I've never had *this*." My voice shakes slightly as I say, "I've never felt like this about a person before."

She inhales, as though I've shocked her. My heart pounds. I love her. It's obvious to me. Not like some blindsiding bolt from the sky—I just know it in my gut, in the way I know it's right to be kind. It's an instinct.

"Zeke," she whispers. "Don't. You can't mean that."

"Why not?"

"I just . . . I don't . . . you . . ." She's shaking.

"Can I touch you right now? Can I hold your hand?" I whisper back.

She stretches out the hand that isn't gripping the railing, and I twine my fingers through hers.

"Does this change the rules?" she says quietly. "Between us, does this . . ."

"I don't know. Does it?"

"I don't . . . I don't really know *what* I want to say right now, and my brain feels like mush, but . . ." She takes a deep, unsteady breath, watching my thumb smooth over hers. "I think we might die on our way back down this tower, and if we do, I'm pretty sure I'll be out there in the afterlife thinking, *Why the fuck didn't you kiss Zeke Ravenhill when you had the chance?*"

I smile slowly, something warm spilling through me. Her eyes slide back to meet mine. I don't give her another moment to second-guess herself, to remember the sheer drop and the terror and everything that'll pull her away from me. I just lean forward and kiss Lexi Taylor on the top of the world.

It starts tender and slow. Then her tongue touches mine, and my body is so full of pent-up adrenaline and desire that the sensation just floors me, and now it's passionate and fierce, every bit the kiss that might be our last. The wind wraps around our shoulders and the sky falls away beneath us. The world stretches out and out and out. And still none of it's big enough for the way I'm feeling. Lexi makes another sound in her throat, and I close my eyes, forgetting the empty skyline. Knowing that no matter where we were right now, it would feel like nobody else mattered.

Lexi

THAT KISS.

It turns me inside out. I am condensed down to the purest essence of myself today; that's what it feels like, and that kiss is the same: concentrated joy, desire, sweetness and a dash of vertigo, all in one moment.

As we pull apart and I rest my forehead against his shoulder, I think of what I've done today, from waking up with a head injury to throwing myself into the sea to scaling the tallest tower. And all those things that seemed impossible back home, suddenly they seem tiny. Do I want to stop working in my mum's old pub? Do I want to set up a café, the little place serving shit-hot coffee that I'd dreamed of creating before my mum died? Do I want to do my own thing, start my own life?

Yes.

So go the fuck on, then, I think. *Do it.*

Because right now I feel like I could do absolutely anything.

~~~~~~

Climbing down from the tower puts this new epiphany to the test. It's *awful*. Not as bad as the climb up, but physically harder, and I'm so tired that I'm terrified I'll slip. At least every rung makes falling a little less dangerous. That's what I tell myself.

"You get a biscuit when you get to the bottom," Zeke calls down to me at one point when I stop for a break, clinging to the ladder.

"What am I, a golden retriever?"

"I would *not* give those biscuits to a dog," Zeke says.

"Please. You'd sneak one out for Eugene in a heartbeat."

"You calling me soft?" he says.

I'm getting good at knowing when Zeke is joking about something that matters. He does it all the time, like how he throws around the word *stupid* when he's talking about himself.

"You know," I say, moving again, "I didn't know soft men existed. Not really. Not until you. The world is full of hard edges—we don't need any more of that. So yeah. Maybe I'm calling you soft."

He doesn't say anything to that, but I know he's smiling.

In the end, I do fall. The last couple of rungs seem so impossible I just tumble down the ladder into a heap and lie on the concrete, bruised, my muscles trembling, my shoulders shaking with either sobs or laughter—I couldn't say which. Zeke stands over me, a hand outstretched. When I don't have the strength to reach up to him, he bends down and takes me in his arms. I immediately wriggle, trying to get loose.

"Zeke! Your wound! I'll be too heavy!"

He rolls his eyes and says nothing, just carrying me with steady steps toward the emergency exit.

"I am taking you to bed," he says, and the words send a shiver of heat running through me. He pauses midstep. "For rest. Not sex. In case that needs saying after that kiss."

Could I . . . ? Maybe I could . . . ?

"No," Zeke says, laughing at my expression as he shoves the door open with his shoulder. "Your body has been through way too much today. You need rest."

There is *so* much we need to talk about, and there's no way I should be having sex with Zeke—it's no more sensible an idea than it was a week ago. But . . . God, that kiss. That *kiss*.

Zeke smiles just enough to show his crossed front teeth. "I'm lying you down in the first bed I see, and I bet you are going to fall straight to sleep. OK, no, not one of those beds," he says, jerking a head toward the infirmary door. "Too horror movie. And not that bed," he says, when we reach the first bedroom. This one looks eerily lived-in—the duvet is thrown back as though its occupant just stepped out to use the bathroom. "Same problem. Just hold tight."

"You should *really* put me down," I say weakly.

"You weigh next to nothing," he says. "And I am extremely strong."

"I don't weigh next to nothing," I tell him, and saying it makes me realize that I haven't thought about my body this way for days. Perhaps it's the lack of a full-length mirror, or perhaps it's the fact that there have been significantly more important things to worry about. "You've lost blood, you're exhausted, you've not eaten, I *know* your wound's hurting . . . You're not exactly at full strength, Zeke."

"And I wasn't actually particularly strong to begin with," Zeke says, laughing at himself. I know so few men who do that—it's one of the ways he seems much older than he really is. "I'm not going to lie, my legs are wrecked after going up and down that ladder."

"Put me down," I say, kicking my feet as we approach the stairs.

"Can't," Zeke says, voice strained and thick with laughter. "Got a point to prove."

"What point?" I say, still kicking. "Whatever it is, I'm pretty sure it's problematic."

"Really?" Zeke says. "Thank God for that." He sets me down on my feet and leans against the wall. Then he pulls me toward him. "To be clear, I think your body's perfect," he says. "It was the day I met you, and it is right now."

"It's changed a fair bit in that time," I say dryly, leaning into him, bringing my hand to my hip to show him what I mean. "The lost-at-sea crash diet."

"It's still yours," Zeke says. "So: perfect."

I close my eyes and press my face into his chest as he gets his breath back. His heartbeat slows against my cheek.

"Have you fallen asleep?" he asks after a while.

I make a sound that is intended to be a no, but isn't particularly convincing.

"Come on," Zeke says. He presses a single, open-mouthed kiss to my shoulder, bared beneath the loose neck of my jumper, and it makes the hairs rise on my arms. "Let's just get you to bed."

We finally settle on a room that is only "medium creepy," according to Zeke. As I climb into one of the bunk beds, Zeke moves to leave, but I grab his arm. He looks down at me, his face shadowy in the low evening light.

"Stay," I whisper.

"Yeah?"

"Stay."

He climbs in with me, tucking his body behind mine. I hold his hand to my chest and close my eyes. I'm scared and tired and broken, just physically *wrecked*, but it doesn't matter, not right now. Right now I feel safe.

DAY TEN

Lexi

WHEN I WAKE the next morning, the sunlight is blindingly bright against the cream-paneled walls of the dorm room. Zeke is sitting by the boxy window, his hair disordered, one of his knees drawn up in front of him on the chair. He looks gorgeous, and a little wild, a new rough-edged version of the well-groomed man I met at The Anchor.

And he's reading.

He's reading one of the *logbooks*.

"Oh my God," I say, sitting up too fast and wincing as the movement makes my head thump.

Zeke looks up at me, and I feel as if I'm looking through his eyes to the little boy who came to that houseboat hoping to find a father who'd make him feel loved.

He clears his throat. "Hey. Morning."

"You're doing it," I whisper, my gaze dropping to the book.

"I've read four so far," he says, nodding to the pile on the chest of drawers beside him. "And went down to check on *The Merry Dormouse* as well. I freshened up the drain blocker and bailed the water out a bit . . ."

I blanch. "Bailed? How bad are we talking?"

"She'll be fine. I think we just need to go down every . . . eight hours or so."

I breathe out. "OK. That doesn't sound too bad." I redirect my gaze pointedly to the book in his lap. "And . . . have you got . . ." I am about to say *an answer*, but instead I say, "what you wanted?"

He smooths the page, eyes downturned. "Some cryptic stuff that looks pretty obvious to me, but he's never actually *said* he's not my father. And he's not said who my dad really is."

"I'm sorry."

I wait, give him time.

"It's so weird, to be honest. Reading it. It makes me remember . . . all the other sides of Dad, the ones I've forgotten about. I focus so much on the times he excluded me or favored Lyra and Jeremy. But I'm actually mentioned in here a lot." He looks up with a half-hearted smile. "Mostly stuff about him not understanding me, but still."

"Not understanding someone and not loving them are not the same thing."

He swallows. "Maybe. Anyway, I've started reading them. That's something. I was sick of being too scared to open the books, and after yesterday . . ." His smile turns genuine as he looks at me. "I felt kind of inspired to be brave."

I look down at the duvet cover, half-pleased, half-embarrassed. I *was* brave yesterday. I can hardly believe what I did. I hope one day I can tell Mae all about it, and that she'll be proud of her auntie Lexi. I'm pretty proud of me.

"But I'm glad you're up," Zeke says, snapping the book closed. "No more logbook angst. We've got big plans."

"Have we?"

"Oh yeah. Full agenda. Because today we're on holiday."

"I beg your pardon?"

"Holiday," Zeke confirms, with a definitive nod. "In an exclusive resort."

I prop myself up on my elbows, looking at him. His eyes turn warm.

"I want to make today . . . good. I want us to have a good day, like the day we might have after a kiss like that if we *weren't* stranded in dystopia. So. Stay there. Relax. Enjoy the fact that you can't drown right now. I'll be back in a minute with your flat white."

He heads out of the door as I say, "What do you mean you'll be back in a minute with my . . ."

He's gone.

I lie back against the pillow and pull the duvet up to my face to hide my smile.

~~~~~

He makes us coffee with a tin of condensed milk that should have been used by 2020. My attitude to best-before dates has really flexed since this trip started. I drink mine with my legs in his lap in our bunk bed, and we catalog which of our muscles are currently hurting.

"What's this one called?" he says, wincing as he pokes his upper thigh.

"Oh yeah, I've got that one," I say, massaging mine. "And my calves. They're *dead*. And, weirdly . . . my toes?"

He cocks his head, directing his attention to my bare feet. "Your toes?"

"Don't touch them!" I yelp, withdrawing my legs so fast I almost spill my precious, delicious coffee. I put it down. "Oh my God, Zeke, I've not had a proper wash since Thursday, you *cannot* touch my feet."

He looks amused. "I don't care about that."

"*I* do."

He reaches for one of my ankles. I flail, scrabbling back against the pillow, but he lunges for the other so fast he almost catches it.

"Zeke! You do not want to touch my feet!"

"Do too. And I'm quicker than you."

"No, you're not. You're recovering from an injury," I say sternly, as he flashes me a cheeky grin and grabs for me again. "And I'm more motivated!" I shriek, sticking my feet up in the air.

Zeke sits back on his knees at the end of the bed and tilts his head the other way, eyebrows raised. I realize I am now lying back on the pillow with my legs up in the air, wearing nothing but knickers and a giant plaid shirt I found in the bedroom cupboard. I make a sound a bit like *arp* and wrench up the duvet to stick my legs underneath it instead. My heart is galloping, but Zeke doesn't come closer; he sits back on his heels, and his expression reminds me of the little, wicked smile he wore when he chatted me up at The Anchor.

Then he pulls a piece of paper out of his pocket with a small flourish. I lean forward to peer at it, but he tweaks it so I can't see what he's written.

"First holiday activity," he says. "We're going for a seaside stroll."

⁓⁓⁓

"This is incredibly weird. You know that, right?"

Zeke adjusts his ridiculous hat, and then mine.

"I'm shooting for 'quirky.'"

"It's giving 'I lost my mind at sea.'" I pause. "Did I use 'it's giving' right?"

He grins, and a pulse of joy goes through me at having made him smile. We're close, a little closer than we'd usually stand, even on the houseboat—and now we have what feels like all the space in the world, out here at the edge of the rig with the wind around us. But I just want to *touch* him. Even if he has made me wear a "seaside strolling hat," otherwise known as one of the half-squashed straw hats he found in someone's dorm room.

We're in that delicious sliver of time in which nobody yet feels the need to clarify anything—to ask what we are to each other, what we're doing. There's a small, awful part of me that's already saying, *Come on, Lexi, he's only looking at you that way because there are no other women on earth at the moment,* but I'm giddy enough to ignore it. Right now this is just lovely, and after everything that happened yesterday, staying in the *right now* feels like the only reasonable thing to do. There might not be a *later* anyway.

"Just look at that," he says, spinning on the heels of his boots. They're considerably more battered than they were when we first met, marred with lines of white salt left when the water dries, scuffed from endlessly stubbing his toes on the houseboat.

"Look at what, exactly?" I say, inspecting the moldering mechanics, the endless blank sea, that god-awful tower. Behind it, a solitary cloud rests against a sky the color of washed-out denim.

"That view. Lexi, look. A three-hundred-and-sixty-degree sea view. We've stopped seeing it, but it's still there, and when I came back up here from the houseboat this morning I just . . ." He trails off, the way he often does. "This morning I felt lucky. When we were on the boat, I kind of forgot we're lucky. I kept thinking how *un*lucky we are, the stupid series of mistakes that got us stranded . . . But now that we're here, it feels genuinely possible to live in the moment. I thought, people pay so much for that feeling. Yoga retreats, gap years, meditation apps . . ."

I want to stand on tiptoe and kiss the triangle of his chin, so I do, and he smiles, reaching for my waist.

"What was that for?" he asks.

"Just for your brain," I tell him. "And for keeping me positive."

He kisses me—the first time he's kissed me properly since the moment on the tower. My stomach swoops, my tired, broken body suddenly alight with energy, and he chuckles against my mouth.

This time I'm the one to pull back. I want him—I want us to go to bed together, any of these hundred beds, and I want to spend all day with him there, reminding myself of the details of his body, the ones I've tried to recall in minute detail more times than I can count. But I want to savor today, too. I want the silliness of Zeke's "holiday," more stolen hats, more kissing. I want to feel lucky.

"You reckon that one's him?" Zeke asks, pointing at an entirely random seagull.

Eugene left his box sometime yesterday afternoon—Zeke is convinced he tried to fly up and help us climb the tower, which is an adorably ridiculous idea, but I have to admit, I kind of like the thought that Eugene might have been one of the birds I heard on my way up the ladder. That healed-up seagull is so much more than just a bird—he's proof that sometimes daft humanity can win out after all. I miss him already.

"My expertise stretches just about far enough for me to say, that is *probably* a seagull," I say, and Zeke laughs.

"It's him," he says. "I know it."

We start walking again. Or strolling, as Zeke is insisting it shall be known.

"You're right, you know. There *is* a kind of mindfulness to this. The near-death experience: your pathway to Zen," I say.

Zeke laughs. His hair gets buffeted beneath his straw hat, catching against his beard; there's a smear of dirt along his neck like a shadow.

"Shall we sell it?" I suggest. "A week absolutely shitting yourself in a decrepit houseboat? A weekend trying not to die on a rusty oil rig?"

His smile turns serious. I watch the little muscle beneath his ear that tenses and flickers when he's hunting for what he wants to say. There is something about this man, his warmth, his depth. He is unlike anyone I've ever known.

"That's not what you'd need to sell," he says eventually, looking down at me. "That's not why I feel lucky."

I look away from him, but he turns my face back to his gently, with one finger on my jaw. We've come to a stop on a rusted walkway on the far side of the rig, the sea stretching out before us.

"It's you," he says, "by the way. It's less cute if I spell it out, but I feel like if I don't, you'll tell yourself I'm talking about something else."

He's right: I'd tell myself, *He doesn't mean me.* Nobody ever does. Except . . . maybe Zeke. Maybe this beautiful, gentle, extraordinary man really does look at me and feel lucky. The thought is so tempting I can hardly bear it.

"Come on," I say, taking his hand. "Aren't we meant to be strolling?"

Zeke

WHILE LEXI PLAYS tinned-food roulette to decide the ingredients for our holiday lunch, I head back to the houseboat to check on the shower drain and fetch the spatula. In all the weird stuff left on this rig, there's not a single spatula, and I just can't cook without one. It's like trying to cook left-handed. You can take my clothes and my good-for-curls conditioner, but I can't survive without a spatula.

The water's different here underneath the rig. Quieter, darker. And the houseboat's so *small*. The little bench-sofa, the narrow kitchen cabinets, the ceiling barely an inch above my head. As I check my new makeshift drain plug—I found masking tape in the storeroom of the rig, which has been a game changer—I find myself thinking about showering in here as a kid, elbows tucked in, head ducked to fit under the spray.

Being alone changes how I see this place. Heading back out into the living space, I don't look at that sofa and think of Lexi trying to get comfortable as she waits for dinner; I think of sitting there myself, age ten, knees drawn up to make room for Jeremy, watching

Dad burning fish fingers on the hob. Penny's not even changed the kitchen handles that Dad whittled and painted himself—small Rubik's cubes in brown and white.

Without Lexi here, it really does feel like Dad's houseboat, and he's in my head, after reading those logbooks. He seemed different on the page—softer, almost, than I remember him. I think of Dad as so frustratingly hard to get through to, and I guess I felt he wasn't *trying* to connect with me, but the man in those logbooks was muddled and wistful, a bit lost. Never sure of anything but his puzzles. I wonder what would have happened if I'd opened up to him, just once, instead of pulling away. He wrote that I was a mystery he wanted to solve, and it was so weird to read that, because that's exactly how I see him.

Lexi's right: he was my dad. One way or another. And he died. And yeah, maybe there's some biological dad out there who could fill that hole for me, but even if there is, who's to say he's going to be the father ten-year-old Zeke had wanted? I'd probably be better off if I could just say, *I had a dad. He wasn't perfect, but he was mine. Then he died, and just like that, I lost the chance to know him.*

I blink away tears and look down at the floor, registering what I've failed to see as I've been standing here feeling sorry for myself.

The planks of the kitchen floor are shiny.

Shinier than they should be.

Wet.

~~~~~

I don't tell Lexi.

It's not that I want to deceive her—I *really* want to tell her, because to be honest, I'm scared. If there's water coming in from somewhere other than the shower drain, then there's a real chance *The Merry Dormouse* will go down before the day's out. I couldn't find the leak, but the water didn't come back when I wiped it away, so I'm hoping it was some rogue rainwater that snuck in through a ceiling hole I missed.

The reality is, that houseboat's our only escape route from here if a ship or helicopter doesn't turn up. We found spaces around the rig where we're sure there were lifeboats once, and there're signs everywhere pointing to them, but no actual boats. Kind of terrifying to know that when they left this rig, they left it in a hurry, but we've always felt all right about it because if worst comes to worst, we've got *The Merry Dormouse*.

I'll just keep checking on her. I'll keep drying her out, then drying out the towels, then drying her out again. It takes a lot of water to sink a boat, right?

"What is it?" Lexi says, looking at me over her lunch—broad bean stew, not my best dish.

We're sitting out on pillows on the concrete, facing each other, her back to the door we first entered through when we came to the rig. She's looking better. Less . . . gaunt. Every time she clears another plate or drinks another glass of water, I relax a bit more. The weather's pretty mild today, but we're both in jumpers—it's windier up here on the rig than it was down on the boat. Lexi's jumper swamps her, its sleeves covering right up to the first knuckle on both hands. I like this look on her. It makes me want to spend lazy Sundays in bed together; it's that kind of vibe.

"Nothing. It's fine. I was just thinking how whenever I'm on holiday, I always do the big-picture thinking. What do I want from my life? All that stuff."

She smiles slightly. "Oh yeah? And? What *do* you want from your life?"

I think about my last holiday: four days in Barcelona with Brady, Will and Emiliano. The big-picture stuff that holiday had been about relationships. Women. I'd brought up that I was looking for something serious, trying to work out how to find the one, and Emiliano had laughed at me. *Who'd have you now?* he'd said, slapping me on the arm. *You hoping a good woman will make an honest man of you?*

It had annoyed me. I've never been anything other than honest.

"I want to open my own restaurant," I find myself saying. "Fresh food, different menu every day. I know it's stupid, but the way we've been cooking out here, making do with whatever we've got, that's my favorite way to work. I love the challenge, the way it takes the pressure off because you can only do what you can do . . ."

"Can I just ban the word *stupid* once and for all?"

I blink at Lexi as she settles back against the heap of pillows. "Hey?"

"You said, *I know it's stupid*. It's not stupid. You're a chef. What's stupid about wanting to open your own restaurant one day? That's a really reasonable ambition, Zeke."

"Junior chef," I say automatically. "But . . . yeah, I . . ."

I didn't actually notice I'd used the word *stupid* at all. I swallow back an instinctive apology and reach for her hand. I want to touch her all the time, but especially when she does this—when she looks at me in a way that makes me see myself differently.

"Thank you," I say.

"Why do you think it feels stupid to you?"

"I guess I just feel like it's unrealistic for someone like me."

"Someone young, talented and driven . . . ?"

I pull a quick face, dropping her hand. Nobody has ever called me *driven*. Talented in the kitchen, maybe. Talented in bed. But running a business like a restaurant . . .

"I've not got that sort of brain," I say. "Like, I'm always . . ."

"What are you doing with your hands right now?"

"Showing you what my brain looks like," I say, as I wave my arms around between us in a sort of whirly cloud of chaos.

Lexi tilts her head to the side. "This is your brain?"

"Imagine smoke from a fire, only it's windy and it goes everywhere."

"Sounds beautiful," she says, holding my gaze.

"It's messy. I wouldn't be any good at running something. I can follow orders, but that's about it."

"I wish you'd see the Zeke I see," she says, pulling her pillow closer, so our legs are touching. "I wish you'd see the person who's keeping me alive."

I think of that wet floor in the houseboat and try not to let the wince of fear show on my face.

"It's weird," she says, shifting to lean back on her hands, legs still touching mine. "Our lives are so different in so many ways, but . . ."

I like this *but*.

"But?"

"But I've always wanted to run a café."

"No way," I say, sitting up straighter. "Seriously?"

I suddenly feel horrified.

"Have I been—have you wanted to cook this whole time, are you also really into cooking, and . . ."

She laughs, knocking her knee against mine. "No! I love you cooking for me. It's not really about the food. It's about the people. Growing up in the pub, I got to see what a place can do for bringing people together, and the weird connections that get made when you all overlap somewhere—people who'd never usually chat, all in one room. But I also saw the bad stuff. The drunks. The fights. What alcohol does."

Her eyes flick to my stomach, and I know she's thinking about what alcohol did to us.

"So I want to have that, but with coffee instead of booze." She does one of her frowns that's actually a smile. Lexi language for *This is big for me and I feel kind of embarrassed and excited at the same time.*

"I love that." *And I love you,* I think. *I love you, I love you, I love you.*

But I bite it back. Too soon. Too . . . much. She'll write it off as something I'm just feeling because I'm stuck with her. I know Lexi, and I know she'll be waiting for me to leave her the minute we hit dry land. So *that's* when I'm going to tell her. Once we're home, and she sees I'm not going anywhere.

"When we get back, I'll open my cute café in Gilmouth and you'll open your swanky restaurant in . . . London? I guess?" she says.

I smile, watching her look away from me. I love that we were clearly thinking about the same problem at the same time.

"The whole we-live-in-different-places thing seems kind of . . ." I am about to say *stupid.* "Kind of unimportant given what we've already survived, no?"

She shrugs one shoulder, the breeze catching a loose hair on her cheek. "Not really. Your life, your job, it's all in London, and mine is where Mae is."

"Lexi."

"Yeah?"

"I want to be where you are. I can get work in Newcastle—I've got a good CV."

When Lexi smiles, she looks as if she's trying not to—like the smile's growing despite her best efforts to hold it in. But right now she's smiling as if she doesn't see a single reason to stop, and that makes me feel amazing.

"Come on," I say. "We've got an afternoon of art therapy ahead of us."

Her eyebrows shoot up. "*Art* therapy?"

"Mm-hmm."

"I thought this was a holiday. Are we actually just in a really elaborate kind of rehab?" she says, looking around, as if she's checking for doctors.

I laugh, pulling her up by both hands. She stumbles into me slightly, and I relish the feeling. I love the way we're taking things slowly—this is new for me. We're not rushing to bed, but we both know today's really the two of us meandering there. Every time she touches me it's like low-key foreplay, even if she's just tucking one of my curls behind my ear.

"We're on a retreat," I tell her. "It's going to chill us out. Relax us."

I let myself kiss her, then get drawn in a bit more than planned. We break apart slightly breathless, and I rest my forehead against hers.

"I'm a very relaxed person already," Lexi says, deadpan. "I'm so laid back, Zeke. I'm extremely chill."

"When I first saw you, you had your arms folded *and* your legs, like, double folded," I say, shifting back to demonstrate the bind she'd twisted her legs into at The Anchor. "I've never met someone so tense."

"In fairness, you're not seeing me at my best." She waves a hand to capture the whole near-deathness of everything.

"God save me when I do," I say, pulling her in the direction of the storeroom. There's paint in there—just dried-up scraps in the bottom of a tub, but enough to mess around with. I like the idea of seeing Lexi loosen up.

"If you're going to ask God to save you at some point," Lexi says dryly, "could you maybe ask Him now?"

Lexi

I PAINT SOMETIMES with Mae, but this is different. Zeke lives up to his whole "I'm creative" image by becoming immediately absorbed in a sophisticated seascape, but that's fine; a man who wears velvet trousers can't very well *not* be artistic. I faff about painting a house, like I am five, and then start again on something new, a bunch of blobs and lines. It takes me a minute to realize that I'm trying to do what Zeke did when he waved his arms around to show me his brain. This is *my* brain. Lots of straight lines and corners. Lots of worst-case scenarios. And, in the end, when you look at it all crowded in on the page like this: no less chaotic than Zeke's charming smoke in the wind.

We take a brief step back into real life after this, because we discover an unopened tin of paint in the store cupboard. Zeke points out we could put this to better use, so we spend the rest of the afternoon writing SOS across the helipad and the main deck of the rig. It's kind of sobering at first, but after a while we forget what we're actually writing and just chat as we slop down the paint. Zeke tells me more about his family; I even talk a little about my dad, what I remember of him from my childhood, the spitting argument we had at Mum's funeral when I cut him out of my life for good.

It's amazing, to be honest. It's the sort of heady, gorgeous day that you get when you let yourself believe that a wonderful man might actually want you. I haven't stopped feeling scared or sad, but I've started feeling a lot of other things, too, and some of those things are louder. Joy. Hopefulness. Love, maybe, if I were the sort of person who could let myself call it that so soon.

Zeke's organizing us a "date" for tonight. I head back to the room to get ready, digging my makeup bag out of my holdall. Putting on makeup with butterflies in my stomach makes me feel like I've thrown a line back in time to the Lexi who lives on land, and the moment of connection makes it so obvious how different I am now. That Lexi moved through life without looking. Now I'm scared and desperate and drained, but I'm also living so hard it's like I'm doing it in Technicolor. If I survive this, I'll look back on these days as the making of me, I know I will.

The outfit isn't as special as I'd like, but at least it's not something I've worn before. Zeke has seen every item of clothing I have, and worn a fair few of them himself, too. I'm going for an oversized, bright blue T-shirt that I found in the rig laundry room; I cut the sleeves and neckline, so it plunges in a raw-edged V, as low as it can go without showing the bow on the front of my bra. I wear it with my leather jacket and black boots, and use a thin, age-darkened rope as a belt.

As I fuss with my rope belt, I'm struck by the ridiculousness of this, how hard I'm trying for a man who's seen me in sea-drenched, unwashed underwear, but caring about mascara instead of provisions feels *so* nice. I'm going to let myself have tonight.

Zeke doesn't say anything as I step out into the corridor; he just breathes out slowly, taking me in for so long I start to twist inward, folding my arms.

"Don't," he says, reaching for me. "You are so beautiful."

I shrug him off. "You with all the chat-up lines . . ."

He frowns, reaching for me again; this time I let him take my hands.

"I wish you'd listen when I say things like that. I wish you'd hear it."

Actually, I do feel kind of beautiful today, with nobody to compare myself to except another version of myself, and Zeke's warm eyes on me, and the knowledge of all that my body has done for me in the last week.

"What's it about? Why can't you take a compliment?" he asks softly.

I shrug, avoiding his eyes. "It just feels kind of wrong. Like it shouldn't be about me."

"What shouldn't?"

"I don't know. Anything?"

He's quiet for too long. I risk a glance at his face. He looks very sad all of a sudden, and just as I'm starting to feel embarrassed, he says, "I think it's amazing how you're always there for other people—me, Penny, Mae. But being there for other people doesn't have to mean . . . erasing yourself."

"Is that what you think I do? What I've done?" I ask. I can't decide whether that's pissed me off.

"I think you deserve to be cherished," he says, stretching out his hand to me. "And I can't wait to show you what that looks like."

My frown smooths away—it's impossible to scowl at him when he says things like that.

"Come on," he says, smiling. "Let me start by feeding you."

I take his hand and follow him through the network of corridors, out into the duskiness before sunset. The breeze picks up my hair and shakes it loose; I'm glad of my leather jacket. The butterflies are still fluttering high in my stomach as we climb the steps to the helipad. We skirt this afternoon's painting—circling the word SOS scrawled in red paint should be a buzzkill, but it isn't, it really isn't. This is my life right now. My eyes are fixed instead on the nest of duvets and blankets set up in the very middle of the helicopter pad, on the central bar of that H.

Zeke has made us a picnic. I can see at least six bowls of different dishes, and even two wineglasses that I suspect have come up from the houseboat.

My eyes prick. This is so lovely. He didn't have to do this. But he did, for me.

"OK?" he says, looking at me a little nervously.

"Perfect," I manage, settling in on one side of the picnic.

He smiles, passing me a plate. I'm not entirely sure what any of this is, but I see macaroni, and thick dark sauce, and something flecked with bright green peas and the muted orange of tinned carrots. All of it looks incredible.

"Oh my *God*," I say through my first mouthful, and I watch his face brighten.

"You like that one? I used the last of the Worcester sauce, that's where it gets the depth from, and . . ." He trails off, embarrassed. "Anyway."

"Don't stop," I say, nudging his knee with mine. "I love it when you talk food. You get all . . ." I wave my fork at him. "Glowy."

"Glowy?" he says, with a dubious eyebrow-raise, but one of his dimples is showing as he fights a smile.

"It's very sexy," I inform him, taking another forkful and letting out a moan as the flavor hits my tongue. It's a zingy, peppery pasta dish, and I have no idea how it tastes this delicious. "How good is the food you make when you're *not* working with expired tins only?"

"I actually think expired tins might be my thing. Second dates, though . . . less so," he says, voice as light as always, but he's not looking at me as he reaches for another bowl. "How am I doing with the picnic? Is that appropriate?"

"It's good, actually," I say. "Low pressure, not too showy . . ."

"Right, well, I did think about taking you to the Ritz, but . . ."

I snort and he gives me a lip-quirk smile that makes my stomach tighten. As we eat, his eyes keep holding mine; he shifts nearer, then I do the same, and even though the food is incredible, I almost wish it away.

He clears the picnic up once we're done, and then settles back beside me, pulling two of the duvets over our bare shins as the sun begins to sink toward the sea. I feel like every minute of today has been leading us gently here, and the anticipation has built to this slow, delicious feeling that the moment he kisses me, I'll be lost. The hairs on my arms rise as he reaches across me to tuck the duvets a little higher up my legs.

When the sunset comes, it's one of the best we've seen. It's luscious and red-gold, as though the sun is dripping hot into the water. There's a faint fog to the west, fading one edge of the sky into haziness.

"Do you ever think about our one-night stand?" I ask, looking out at the water.

Zeke turns his gaze from the skyline to look at me. "Do I ever think about having sex with you?" he asks, incredulous.

I start to laugh. He snakes a hand out and places it on the back of my neck, but he doesn't move; he just looks right in my eyes as the laughter fades on my lips. It reminds me of that first night, in the pub, when I'd almost dared him to kiss me and he'd held back, watching me instead.

"Yes, Lexi, I do."

My stomach turns over. I shift into him, bringing our faces close as the sun dips. I don't want to rush this, not after the delicate slow build of the day that brought us here. The one thing we have right now is time.

With two duvets layered on top of us and three underneath us, everything feels soft and languid. The fierce desire I felt for him on that first night hasn't changed, but it's spread and deepened, like the rich orange sunset stretching across the sky. Zeke's thumb sweeps the back of my neck, and I shiver.

"It was incredible, that night. But I wish . . ."

"That is a very unfair point to trail off," I say, as he dips his head, presses a kiss to my neck. My body sparks up as soon as his lips touch my skin, as if he's found a button set in the curve of my neck, the exact spot to bring me to life.

"Sorry. It's hard to find words for it," he says. "I just feel like I didn't know at the time how important that was. Our night together. It was amazing, but I wish I could go back and tell myself . . . this woman, she'll be your everything. Then sometimes I wonder if I sort of did know. The moment I keep playing over and over is when I . . . Can I say this?" Zeke's voice is husky now.

I tilt my chin back, letting him press a kiss to the base of my jaw, the patch of soft skin beneath my ear. I can feel every place where he's kissed me—they're bright spots of icy coolness as the wind sweeps over us.

"Please," I say, swallowing.

"I unfastened your bra, and you held it there with your hands across your chest," he says, his lips so close to my skin that his words vibrate there, caught between us. "You were sitting at the end of the bed, and I was kneeling, and I saw just an inch . . ." He presses his thumb to the top of my breast, showing me, and I arch despite myself, wanting more. "And you said, *I like how your eyes go.*"

He presses a slow kiss to the place where his thumb was. It goes cold the instant he lifts his mouth, and the sensation makes me quiver.

"I said, *Go what?* And you said, *Don't mine? When I look at you?*"

I remember it. How his eyes seemed to turn to hot sugar, to caramel. How they made me melt.

"And I looked you right in the eye, kneeling there in front of you, and I got exactly what you meant. Your eyes had turned so soft. The way you looked at me. It made me feel like I was all there was."

His voice catches a little; he presses another kiss to my neck, and I turn into him, sliding myself closer. I lift a hand to his jaw, tracing it through his beard, pulling back so that I can kiss him lightly on the lips. Even that—just the faintest featheriest kiss—makes my heart quicken.

"You know," I say, "I don't remember when I let go of my bra."

He hums against my throat, tracing a slow, hot path. I reach for his belt and rest my fingers there, feeling the warmth of his toned stomach above it.

"You're right, I was holding on to it." My voice is breathy and unfamiliar as my hand shifts over the buckle, sliding the belt free. "I generally prefer to keep as many clothes on as possible. But I don't even remember dropping it. Like it wasn't even a thing."

"It was a thing," Zeke says. "*I* remember it."

He shifts away to pull his T-shirt over his head. The heat of his skin as he comes back to me is an exquisite shock, and I shrug out of my jacket, fumbling with my rope belt, wanting it all gone.

"I'm just saying that . . . I felt comfortable." I whisper the last words as I raise my arms and let him pull my T-shirt dress slowly up, up. "I let you see me, even then."

I feel a hot flush move up my body at the confession, as though somehow that's the most revealing thing, even as he takes me in, every curve. His smile is slow and whisky smooth. It makes my lips move, too, like he's tugging the joy out of me with that slight lift of the corner of his mouth.

"That's all I want," he whispers. "You. All of you."

We kiss again, a drugged, consuming kiss, and that's it: the sun is down, the horizon line melting into pure heat and darkness. I throw my head back, lost already, and it's like that first night, but it's different, too. I'm different. When I meet his gaze, rocking, gasping, I feel all the depth of what we've been through between us. It makes every moment fiercer and brighter. By the time he moves inside me, I'm the same as everything else out here: a little wild.

DAY ELEVEN

Zeke

WE SLEEP IN the bed that's become ours now, her head on my chest, her leg over mine. I'm happy. Happier than should be possible when you're in this much danger.

I never realized sex could feel the way it felt last night. It was as if I could finally express that huge emotion in my chest, the expansive one I don't have words for. I've always felt a connection through sex, but I've never felt closeness like that, never felt like I was . . . making love, I guess. The first time was hot and fast, forehead to forehead, so intense I thought I might cry, and the best part was that it wouldn't have mattered even if I had—Lexi knows me so well, I didn't have to hold a single part of myself back.

I slip out first thing to go and check on the boat while she gets some more sleep. It's raining today, and it's breezier, too. I bite my lip the minute I open the door from the houseboat's deck. That water patch on the kitchen floor is back, about the same size as when I last looked, maybe bigger. And when I check the bathroom, the shower drain cover's floated off, too—the sea must've got rougher last night. I fix it all back, cold dread in my stomach as I wipe up the water in the kitchen and check again and again for where it could be coming from. There's just . . . nowhere. Maybe the hole's so small I can't see it?

When I get back to the dorm room, Lexi's sitting up in bed, round-eyed, duvet drawn close to her chest. I sit down beside her.

"You OK?" I say, frowning.

She leans into me, closing her eyes.

"I woke up and you were gone," she says.

"Shit, sorry—I should've left a note. I just went to check on the boat, I didn't want to wake you." I reach for her hand.

"It's fine, I just . . . need you, I think," she whispers. "Probably more than I should."

I kiss the top of her head. "I need you, too, you know." My voice is husky. "And I'm not going anywhere."

A loud *bang* cuts across the end of my sentence. Lexi freezes. Her hands gripping my jumper. A *bang*. Another *bang*. Both of us turn to the window.

"What do you . . ."

"Come on." She's already flying out of the door, grabbing her leather jacket as she runs into the corridor.

There've been a hell of a lot of surreal moments in the last ten days. The word's almost lost meaning. But I don't know what else to call it as I step out and see a walkway crumpling into the sea as if it's a model built of paper.

The sound's so enormous it makes me think of a dinosaur's roar. Metal buckles as though it's melting, and Lexi swears, grabbing for me, stumbling back toward the shelter of the emergency exit door. The noise is deafening. A bone-shaking crack, the scream of steel on steel. Chunks of metal slide and topple, then the bulk of the tumbling walkway must hit the sea, because there's a deep crash, and then, a few seconds later, a slow-motion wall of water reaching up into the sky.

It's white-gray and deadly. Lexi and I realize the danger at the same moment, fumbling at the door handle, throwing ourselves inside and slamming the door behind us as the wave comes looming across the concrete, slapping down so hard it shakes the windows in their frames. Lexi is saying something, clinging to me, and it takes me too long to process it, so she says it again, louder, eyes even wider.

"Zeke. Zeke. We *have* to get off this rig."

~~~~~

The last few bits and pieces tumble—broken pipes, chunks of grating, a cord of cable spiraling down into the water. We watch it all through the window by the door, holding each other tightly. Lexi's shaking in my arms.

"It's settling. It was just that one part of the rig," I say.

"Look at the damage it's done to the platforms below. Who knows what it'll have done to the rest of the rig. And the *houseboat*. Oh my God. Zeke . . . What if the houseboat is damaged?"

I close my eyes, but the rig seems to lurch beneath me, so I open them again, grabbing at the windowsill. Lexi looks at me weirdly—maybe that lurch never happened. I'm shaking, too, I think. Am I? I'm so used to this kind of fear that I guess I've switched into survival mode again without noticing.

"I didn't tell you because I didn't think you needed to know," I begin, and Lexi is already saying, "What? Zeke, what?"

"There's a leak on the boat."

"No, no, no," she says, burying her face in my chest.

"And it's getting harder to block the drain. The rougher the sea is, the more seems to come up."

Lexi makes a moaning sound in the back of her throat. Outside, the seagulls have come to inspect the broken corner of the rig, hopping casually between severed pillars. It's the platform we crossed to go from one ladder to the next when we were climbing the tower.

Lexi stood on that platform two days ago. The thought makes me want to throw up.

"If the boat's not safe, we can stay here," I say. "Someone will come."

"Nobody ever comes!" Lexi shouts, balling her fists as she draws back to stare out of the window again. "We can't stay here. It's too risky."

She bites her lip and reaches up to re-do her bun. She ties it tightly, the way she does when she wants to feel in control. Her fingers are still trembling.

"You know what we have to do," she says.

I close my eyes for a moment. If that houseboat's damaged, if it's gone under . . . I pull Lexi close again.

"You have to be OK," I say roughly.

"Zeke . . ."

"No, I mean it. You *have* to be OK. OK?"

She presses her head to my chest. "I'll try," she whispers. "I don't know that either of us can promise more than that."

〜〜〜〜

I've never felt so glad to see *The Merry Dormouse*.

She's still there under the rig, bobbing on the spot, looking so— I don't know. Harmless. Helpful. Ready to rescue us, like she didn't cause this whole nightmare in the first place.

It's dim inside the boat. Above us, the rig lets out a jarring creak, and I shiver.

"This is it?" Lexi says, pointing to the small pool of water on the kitchen floor.

"I just can't figure out where it's coming from."

Lexi frowns, checking the ceiling, the walls.

"Me neither." She sighs, rubbing her forehead. "What do we do? Stay or go?"

I know what I'd always pick back home. I know what she'd choose, too. Lexi's the person who stays, the one you want in your corner, and I'm the drifter.

But no part of me wants to sail away right now.

"The rig's so big. Even if bits of it keep falling off, surely it's safer than this?" I say, moving through to the bathroom. "I mean, Lexi, look."

She swears under her breath. The drain cover has floated off again, and there's at least two inches of seawater in the base of the shower.

"We watched a platform we've walked on falling into the sea," Lexi says from behind me, reaching for the little cup and bucket I've been using to bail out the shower water. "We've done days at sea with this drain leaking. And the other leak is small—if we find it, we can plug it."

I close my eyes and lean a hand against the bathroom wall for a moment.

"Zeke?"

"It's just weird being back here again."

"I know. I really thought we would never get back on this bloody boat. But . . ."

She comes over, nudging under my arm and wrapping herself around me. I let the warm fluff of her giant blond bun bat against my cheek, the way it always does when she holds me like this. The smell of the houseboat is making me feel a million things. They're not good things. I breathe in Lexi instead.

"We'd have to leave Eugene behind," I whisper. "He's up there with all the other seagulls now and I don't even know which one's him."

"Oh my God, Zeke . . ."

"I know. I know. I'm an idiot."

She grips me tighter, that bucket still in her hand, pressed to my back. "Shut up, you're not, you're just . . . You get attached. Eugene lived with us here, and you ended up loving him even though he's a selfish little shit who ate loads of our bread. There's probably a name for it. It's probably a syndrome, falling in love with someone just because you're stuck with them."

I wonder if we're really talking about Eugene here.

"This isn't even a choice, Zeke. Staying feels like the safe option, but it isn't, not anymore. The boat got us this far," Lexi whispers into my T-shirt.

"Let's just dry out the shower and see if we can plug the leak," I say. "Then we can take it from there."

Once we've resecured the drain cover as best we can, we get down on hands and knees in the kitchen and check every inch of the place. It's so hard because *everything* is damp—it doesn't help that it's raining today. Houseboats are always a bit wet; that's what Dad used to tell us when Lyra complained about her clothes smelling of damp.

"Here, this plank looks like it's been fixed before," Lexi says, voice strained as she leans into one of the lower kitchen cupboards. "And it's definitely wet."

There's a small *clunk*.

"Zeke," Lexi says.

I stiffen. "What?"

"There's something . . . else. In here."

I sit down next to her, shuffling so I've got my back to the fridge and my feet wedged against the wall by the bathroom door. She turns, still crouched, an A5 plastic wallet in her hands.

It's filled with papers. They look like printouts from an old computer—there's something about the font and the spacing that'd make it obvious even if the paper wasn't all worn and yellow.

"Oh," I say, staring down at the wallet.

"Secrets?" Lexi guesses.

"Very Dad," I say. "So . . . yeah. I guess so."

"It could be about anything," Lexi says. "These could just be tax returns."

"I'm not sure my dad paid all that much tax," I say dryly.

"Insurance forms. Some random stuff that he didn't mean to hit print on. Spare paper, basically."

I say nothing. I'm certain the plastic wallet in Lexi's hands holds the answer to the question I've been asking my whole life, and I don't have a clue what to do about it.

"On the plus side," Lexi says, "I've found the leak. It's a pipe. I can tighten the join—I'll go get some tools from the rig. I'll . . ."

She stands, but I reach up and grab her hand.

"Do I read it?" I ask.

I look. The top piece of paper seems to be an email. I try not to read it, but I see my dad's email address, and one I don't recognize, and a few words, two of which are *Paige Lowe*. As in, busybody neighbor Paige. What the hell's she got to do with anything?

"You know what?" Lexi says, sitting down again, keeping hold of my hand. "I think there is absolutely no right answer to that question."

"I feel like if I don't read it now, I'll spend another week ignoring it, like I did with the logbooks. And I don't want to do that."

She smiles slightly. Her eyes are as icy blue as always, but they're at their absolute warmest.

"I think you bought this houseboat because you had a whole bunch of questions, and that wallet looks to me like a whole bunch of answers," she says.

Now that I'm holding the wallet, I'm not sure I really did buy this houseboat because I had a whole bunch of questions. I think maybe I bought it because I miss my dad.

My finger slides to the snap holding the flap of the wallet closed. I hover there, a shot of fear hitting my stomach. Sometimes the big moments in your life are disguised as nothings. The cold, drunk minutes I spent with Paige and Lexi on Gilmouth marina. The sight of Jeremy's name popping up on my phone five and a half years ago, the call that told me my father had had a heart attack.

But right now I know I'm sitting inside a moment that'll change my life. It's eerie, like standing between two mirrors, or looking down from the top of the rig tower. Like facing something vast.

I click open the snap.

Lexi

I WANT TO tell him that whatever he sees in that wallet, it won't change anything. That he may not have noticed it, but he's a whole person of his own, more than the sum of the people who made him. I know he fears he'll find out that his father wasn't truly his father, and perhaps it's because of my relationship with Mae, but I want to tell him it doesn't matter.

Zeke is Zeke, wherever he came from. And he's perfect just as he is.

He reads in silence, dropping each paper on his lap as he finishes scanning it. "Paige," he says eventually, without lifting his head.

"Paige?" I stare at him. "Paige as in . . . Paige off of our rope fiasco?"

"She found out," Zeke says, unfolding the last sheet of paper with steady hands. "And told my dad, and that's what ended my parents' marriage."

"Told your dad . . ."

"About Jeremy."

I blink. "Your brother?"

"About my mum and Paige's brother."

"Wait, sorry, you've . . ."

I'm lost, and Zeke looks so broken by this, I'm desperate to understand. I crouch in front of him, resting my hand on his.

"Zeke, what does it say? What did Paige tell your dad?"

"Jeremy's not my brother. He's—he's my half brother. Jeremy wasn't my dad's son."

"Jeremy?"

He breathes out slowly, and then lets the papers go, spewing them out across the wet floor, dropping his head into his hands and starting to cry.

"It was never me. It was Jeremy. I wasn't . . . It was . . ."

I've heard envy in Zeke's voice every time he talks about his brother. Jeremy, who understood his father's interests, who was meticulous and fastidious and the perfect son.

And all along, it was Jeremy who was the secret.

Zeke breathes in, tipping his head back against the grubby fridge door.

"I am such an idiot."

"What? No, you're—"

"Moping around half my life over some secret that wasn't even about me?" He presses his hands to his face. "What does it say about me and Jeremy that he never once felt out of place, and I've been looking for an excuse for why I don't belong my whole life?"

I ache for him, pulling him into me.

"And my dad . . . I never thought he was . . ."

He sobs against me, his whole body shaking. I grip him tightly, and then even tighter as something hits the roof above us with a quick hard *crash*.

We both swear and break apart, ducking, as if whatever is coming at us might be inside the houseboat rather than out. I scrabble to my feet first, then Zeke follows me onto the deck.

Most of our time on the water was spent out here; under the looming weight of the rig, I feel like I'm in a dark version of a scene I've lived before. There's the sea, there's the rickety railings, but the sky is overcast by this great, cabled ceiling above us. I can smell metal and rust and rot. I draw the sides of my leather jacket close around me, folding my arms.

"Whatever it was that fell, it's cracked the roof," I say, my voice shaking. "Look, there, by the bike wheel."

"We shouldn't be out here," Zeke says as he glances up again. "We could get hit."

He tugs me back to the door, but I resist, looking back to the knot of rope at the far end of the deck.

"We have to go, Zeke. It's not safe."

He shakes his head, but he's no longer pulling me toward the inside of the boat. He's staring at that knot, too, and following the track of the rope across to the steel bar we chose as one of our mooring points, reachable from the ladder where I first clung after we got to the rig. When we were still hopeful. Before all of the wild, extraordinary things that have happened between us here: the kiss on the tower, the condensed-milk coffee, the incredible sunset-drenched night on the helipad.

This place has been spooky and hellish and awful. But it's also been so very beautiful. And for all its horrors, it is the place where I fell in love.

"Once we're untied . . ." Zeke trails off.

"I know. There's no unmaking that decision."

"No."

"And then we're just . . . back into the unknown."

He shakes his head. "There must be a way to improve our odds. Something we can do here to . . ."

I watch him. He's thinking. I like watching Zeke think. I could do it all day. He gets this adorable indent between his eyebrows, not quite a frown, kind of like a question.

"I've thought of something that is probably very stupid," he begins, and I cut him off.

"I bet it's genius," I tell him, holding his gaze. "Whatever it is, I trust you. Let's do it."

Zeke

IT TAKES US about an hour to get set up. With the rig groaning around us and the seagulls circling above, we take our bags and as much water and food onto the boat as we can without risking weighing *The Merry Dormouse* down. Then we get every sheet off every bed in the whole rig and tie them together.

"I feel like I'm at a hen party," Lexi says. "Here, pass the rum, would you?"

I hand it over. She sprinkles the sheet in alcohol before reaching for the next one.

"There's always some kind of bizarre booze-fueled crafting activity involved in a hen do."

"This bizarre?"

"Maybe not *this* bizarre. Though this is a lot more useful to me than a flower crown."

The rig creaks again. Both of us glance at the heap of untied sheets, then at each other.

"Do we call it?" she says.

I'm hating every second of being here. I don't know if the rig always made these sounds and I just got used to it, or whether it's got a lot noisier, but I can't help feeling like any second now we're going to be crushed under a falling crane. So yeah, I want to leave. But I also know this is a real shot at getting rescued, and I don't want to miss it because we lost our nerve too soon.

"One more," I say, grabbing for another bottle of alcohol.

Our hands touch—she reached for that one, too. I look up at her and she smiles briefly. She's wild-haired, sweat glistening across her nose and forehead, and I can feel her terror, but Lexi has this fierce energy to her in a crisis, too. She's just . . . amazing.

"You ever made a Molotov cocktail, Zeke?" she says.

"No." I look back at the bottle of rum. "But I have played a lot of video games featuring them?"

"That'll do," she says, her eyes widening slightly as the rig lets out another roaring groan beneath us. "Now. Where are the matches?"

~~~~~~

This is the wildest, craziest thing I've ever done.

"Well done!" Lexi says, her cheek twitching slightly. "No, really, it's great."

"Why's it not . . . bigger?"

"It's the perfect size!"

I cut her a look. She blinks back, her cheeks still giving away the smile she's trying to hide.

"Will you stop taking the piss?"

She flashes me a quick-fire grin.

"Taking the piss? Whatever do you mean? I'm here to make you look fanciable, aren't I? And to fluff your ego? This is an action film, right?"

I grab for her, and she dances away, then sobers as a distant rumble sounds somewhere deep in the rig below us.

"I'm pretty sure we broke a lot of laws for this," I say, eyeing the gently smoking building in the center of the rig.

We're standing by the ladder down to the houseboat, watching our handiwork in action. The action's just a bit . . . low-key. When I threw the flaming rum bottle into the alcohol-soaked building, with its trail of sheets running toward the basement, I fled to the ladder hand in hand with Lexi, heart in throat, blood pounding. But . . . nothing really happened. So now we're hovering at the ladder, wondering if we need to try again.

I figured a burning oil rig was a sign nobody could miss. Nothing says *We were here* like arson. But this little trail of smoke's just getting snatched by the wind.

"I wanted more drama," I say, squinting against the bright white-gray sky.

"Oh well. If I've learned anything these last two weeks," Lexi says, patting my arm, "it's that drama is overrated."

Boom.

Flame, brightness, sparks, something flying through the air—something metal, maybe, rearing toward us, screeching as it hits the grating—and a flurry of seagulls screaming, rising up through a thick cloud of smoke billowing dark against the sky.

"Oh, fuck," Lexi says, scrabbling backward, hand flying to grab my jumper. "Go, go, go!"

We almost throw ourselves down the ladder as that chunk of metal goes tumbling over the side a meter or so to our left. I can smell fire and the bitter sharpness of alcohol, and something flat and nasty that smells a lot like gas.

"Get on!" I shout down at Lexi, already fumbling with the ropes.

I don't have time to think about how this'll work. I just untie the second rope and then leap before the houseboat can swing away from me, landing on the deck with a knee-jarring thump, stumbling into Lexi and pushing us both into the helm with the impact. My wound wrenches and I gasp.

"We need to move, we need to *move*! Why isn't she going faster?" Lexi says, then she ducks and screams as something drops into the sea beside us with a hiss of sparks meeting seawater.

It's dark above us and flickering with firelight. I can hear the fire's sinister low crackle through the sound of the waves and the scream of the rig as it burns. The seagulls are already gone, black Vs in a distant patch of sky. I spare a fleeting thought for Eugene, heart hurting. I hope he's gone with them, away from the smoke and the ash, off to the open ocean.

"We're getting somewhere," I say, voice raised. I lean over the side to look at the waves, as if I can will the current to carry us faster. "We're moving, Lexi, we are. Here, get inside."

"Is that even safer?" she says, voice thick with panic.

We both duck again as another sizzling chunk of steel goes plunging into the sea.

"Inside," Lexi says, already wrenching the door open. "Got it."

<center>~~~~~</center>

So here we are. Back on the fucking houseboat.

I stare at the rig, now a distant, burning pillar on the horizon. We definitely made an impact. Smoke stains the sky, and I can still see the orange-red-yellow of flames licking at the tower we once climbed, can still hear the occasional roar and rumble as something collapses. It's midafternoon—three or four, I'd guess—and there's a tie-dye effect to the horizon, white to blue behind the blazing rig. The sea's smoother than it was when we arrived, rockier than it was when we first woke up after our one-night stand. I'd call it a solid three out of ten, zero being dead-lake mode, ten being we-are-dead.

"Are you OK?" Lexi asks, coming up behind me on the deck. "Or as OK as a person can be when . . ."

"I'm fine."

I don't know what else to say. I feel like this is all happening to someone else. We're both a bit high on the adrenaline, maybe. And I know I'm shell-shocked from finding out about Jeremy. I feel almost nothing at all when I approach the thought, just a kind of . . . blankness, like the whole area's numb.

"Fine," Lexi repeats, sounding unconvinced.

"I'm . . . compartmentalizing." I gesture in one direction. "Over here, we have the fact that I spent my whole life believing my father wasn't my father. Over here"—I gesture in the direction of the sun—"we have the fact that said father is dead, so I can't tell him I'm sorry. And over here, straight ahead, we have the likelihood of dying at sea."

"Is there a nice compartment? For puppies and rainbows?" Lexi points to a random bit of sky. "Maybe over here?"

I point to her. "The nice compartment," I say, before pulling her into my arms.

"Oh yeah, I am so puppies and rainbows. Really, though, you're processing something huge, and you're having to do it in very . . ."

"Damp conditions?"

"I was going to say stressful conditions. You *did* just flee from a burning oil rig."

"Excuse me. I just *set fire* to an oil rig."

"Well, yeah, that, too. But now you're back on a smelly, leaky houseboat with a big crack in the roof, so I get it if you don't feel like you're coping right now, given everything. I mean, I'm not sure I'm coping, and I didn't just find out something massive about my family. I'm purely dealing with the fact that I hate this bloody boat, and that's hard enough."

I kiss the top of her head, bun-dodging. "You don't mean that. You called this boat a hero two days ago."

"OK," she says reluctantly. "I don't hate her. But . . ."

"Go on?"

"No. It's embarrassing."

"Is it as embarrassing as tying a houseboat to itself?"

"Is anything that embarrassing?"

"Well, then."

She sniffs. "I just miss Eugene a bit," she says, lifting her chin. "That's all. It's not the same on here without him." She whacks my arm. "Don't do that face."

"What face?"

"The 'I knew you had a heart of gold all along' face."

"This is my 'I set fire to oil rigs' face, thank you very much."

"No, your 'I set fire to oil rigs' face is much more regal." She adopts a serious expression to demonstrate. "See? It's akin to but subtly different from your 'this houseboat fridge still smells' face."

I love you, I almost say. *I love you even though I have only known you for eleven days, and I know that's mad and I don't even care.*

"I miss Eugene, too," I settle for, as the oil rig shrinks away.

~~~~~

Three hours later and the wind's picked up. *The Merry Dormouse* is rising and falling now—I have to grip the railing. The rig isn't even a gray smear on the horizon behind us. It's gone.

Lexi and I stand on the deck, quiet and tense. There's so much more noise when the wind is blowing. Tarpaulin rattling, sail slapping against its ties, contents of the kitchen cupboards clashing like cymbals. I've had to borrow a couple of Lexi's hair clips to hold my hair back from my face. The sea's sparkling and creased like crumpled tinfoil. If you stare at each wave at a time, they don't look like much at all, but the boat's already creaking and shaking, and we've had to bail out the shower twice.

"We should have stayed on the rig," Lexi says, voice small.

"This weather isn't bad. If we weren't so used to being on the water when it's really still, we wouldn't even notice it," I say.

"You mean, if we weren't in a rickety, leaking houseboat, then we wouldn't even notice it," she says dryly.

I hug her close. I feel like if I keep hold of Lexi, I can keep steady.

"We should get inside," she says. "We need to do as much storm-proofing as we can before it gets dark."

"Don't say the S word." I kiss the top of her head. "It's just a bit windy, that's all."

"Do you think we might get rescued this time?" she asks after a moment, looking out at the water. The sun's just dipped into the sea. The world's turning grayish, still tinged with the sunset's red. I don't want darkness to fall.

"Sure," I say. "Why not?"

That makes her laugh. "Because we haven't been rescued before, in all those days on the water? Because we're a tiny, rubbish boat on a very big sea? Because shit happens?"

Beneath the laughter, beneath the swearing, I think Lexi's serious. There haven't been many moments in the last eleven days when she's genuinely lost hope. She's a fighter, and she's always looking ahead. It's kept me going—she's kept me going.

"Think of Mae," I say quietly.

"I'm never not."

Her tone is sharp, and I squeeze her tightly, trying to take the sting out of what I've said.

"We don't give up. Because of Mae."

"I know. I know." She lets out a long, growling sigh. "I was so angry with Penny when I pitched up at this houseboat. But our argument seems *so* meaningless now. I know when people come back from extreme situations or nearly die from pneumonia or whatever, they say, hold the people you love closer, life is too short, all of that. But you can't feel it until you've lived it, can you? You can't feel how small those things are until you've stood here in something so fucking bad you can't even comprehend it."

She grips the railing as *The Merry Dormouse* collides clumsily with another wave, dousing our already-soaked feet on the deck.

"The truth is, I want to move out, sometimes. Not all the time, but sometimes. I love living with Mae, but I would also love my own life. I've been a bit part in Penny's for five years now, and it's been great, I wouldn't change it. But I got kind of lost along the way. If you're the sidekick for long enough, you forget how to lead your own life."

"Look at yourself, Lexi."

She's magnificent. Dirt- and oil-stained, with filthy hands and her hair flying in the wind. Black boots, leather jacket, icy shark-blue eyes.

"If this is an action movie," I tell her, "*you* are definitely not the sidekick."

Lexi

IT'S WINDIER. WAVIER. Worse. With every hour that passes, my adrenaline ratchets up, and so does the weather. It's raining now, thick, hard, ceaseless rain that eats its way into the houseboat, sliding through that crack. It's almost dark, but I can still see that there's white on the water, a fine spray like spittle from an angry mouth.

Things are bad.

"Lexi," Zeke says after a while, as I shrug on a jumper, the chill from outside creeping into my bones. "You need to eat something."

I want to brush him off—there's no *time*, I have to secure the bathroom cabinet, I have to bail out the shower base again—but then I look at him, and I realize he's scared.

"Of course," I say, sagging back, steadying myself against the wood burner. My nausea is manageable at the moment, as I've taken some out-of-date seasickness tablets from the rig, but I have not missed the feeling of the world lurching beneath me.

"Here." He hands me something on a plate.

I look up at him. "No. *No.*"

"I think the time's come," he says.

"The last digestive? The *last digestive*?" My voice rises. "You're giving me the last digestive right now? Is this supposed to make me feel better?"

His eyes widen slightly as I slam the plate back down on the countertop. It immediately slides off and I have to catch it again.

"No!" I snap. "We do not eat the last digestive! There is *always the last digestive*. Do you understand?"

An object shifts inside our kitchen cupboards and we both instinctively duck.

"I . . . sort of understand?" Zeke says, reaching for my hip. "But I think maybe . . . we need sugar . . . and there's a biscuit going spare . . . so . . ."

I bat him off.

"If you eat this biscuit," I say grimly, "I will kill you myself. Now get back to staying alive."

~~~~~

"Can I tell you something?" Zeke says, his voice a little hoarse.

He's taking a breather, standing against the kitchen counter, one foot braced on the floor, the other against the door of the fridge. The boat rocks beneath us and moisture gathers on the ceiling in slow, sinister drips. It's more than just the crack now—the rain is getting through in so many places I've lost count.

"Yep," I say, running a cloth down the side of the leakiest window, braced on the sofa cushions. Things have become increasingly frantic—Zeke and I are mostly communicating in bursts.

"Go," I prompt him, glancing up. "Now's good."

"I love you," he says. "Sorry. I had hoped to do a big buildup and everything, you know, wait for the perfect moment. I was going to tell you once we'd got you home to Mae, but . . . now I'm wondering if we might be short on time, so I figured, I'd better just let you know."

I am crouched on the tatty sofa, my greasy hair scraped up into a bun, wearing a striped jumper ransacked from the rig—it sags from my collarbones, stretched by open-sea winds and overwear. I am afraid, and tired; I am simply living, doing, being. Right now I'd say I'm my rawest, truest self.

I look at Zeke. His hair is thickened by salt and dirt, his beard framing his jaw, his eyes a soft, hopeful shade of amber. The waves are reaching hungrily to our windows, but for a moment, I don't even care.

"I love you so fucking much," I tell him, my voice catching.

The boat rocks violently, and I have to grab for the back of the sofa to keep from falling. For a fleeting moment, I think of the romance I wanted when I was a little girl with a pillowcase on her head like a veil, dreaming of her wedding day—the fairy-tale ending. And I think of the romance I've had: dirty, gritty, bare, laced through with danger and wildness. If we're going to die on this houseboat, I'll die knowing I lived a love story far better than any I could have dreamed up.

"Come here," Zeke says, so softly I almost miss the words over the rain and the rattling cupboards.

I climb down unsteadily from the sofa. He takes two steps to meet me halfway, and he gathers me up and kisses me, as hungry and desperate as the wind beating against our windows. The boat tilts backward and we lose balance, stumbling, but when my back hits the wall we just keep kissing, his arms braced around me.

We strip down fast, our hands frantic. I'm shaking with panic and desire. There is a lastness to this, a sense of ending. Everything is heightened. This need I have for him has a new depth to it, and if I had to name it, I'd call it *grief*.

"I'm so sorry," I choke out. "I'm so sorry if we die because I thought it was brave to get back on this boat instead of staying on the rig."

He pulls me down to the floor. "I love you," he says again, as we tug off our trousers, cold hands finding warm skin. His voice is hoarse and dry. "Don't you dare even think about dying."

We don't wait. I'm slick and shaking with want even as the fear courses through me. I feel sure that if anything will kill me right now, it's not having Zeke.

As he reaches a hand between us, the boat tips so far that I think we're gone. We're rammed against the bathroom wall, every inch of us touching, and in that endless second where the boat waits to plunge into the sea or to right itself, Zeke presses into me, his eyes full of fierceness, as if he's denying it all, as if he's saying, *There's just us, nothing else.*

I cling to him. I'm feeling everything: his hard body, the terror of balancing on the precipice, the sharp thud of my heart against his chest. I don't know how long the moment is—two seconds, ten—but I have never felt this alive before. It's as if I've woken up and found my whole life was a lazy dream, and in reality, *this* is living, this quick flame-bright thing.

When the boat tips back, it carries us with it. We slam into the kitchen cabinets, my elbow cracking on the edge of a cupboard door even though I can feel Zeke turning into the impact to try to soften it for me. We don't part, not even for an instant. I'm crying, crying out. Behind us I hear something break, perhaps the glass of a window. I don't care. I have him, his body enveloping mine, mine enveloping his. We're part of the boat now, our bare skin pressed to her straining, creaking boards.

"Hold on for me," Zeke breathes roughly into my ear. He's still moving, still sending that heat coursing through me as the waves beat hard at our sides. "Just keep holding on, Lexi. Keep holding on."

Zeke

WE STAY THERE, naked, together. The boat rolls us like we're coins in a jar. Lexi's body starts to chill against mine. At some point in the darkness, our flagpole snaps, and the noise of the sail going flying is terrifying enough to get us up off the floor. What we see brings a sound from Lexi I've not heard before and never want to hear again.

There's no way we'll make it through the night. Dim moonlight leaks through the broken windows and lights long pools of water across the floor, staining the sofa cushions in streaks, and the bathroom floor's slick with water coming up the shower drain. The crack in the roof's running like a tap. You can smell the sea everywhere—it's on us now.

"We're lower," Lexi says, voice raised over the rain and the wind. "We're lower and rocking . . . we're going to sink."

I can't even reassure her. Usually, we take it in turns to freak out, but there's nothing else to be done in the face of the facts.

"Get a bowl," Lexi calls, already scrabbling for her clothes in the darkness. "And start bailing."

I pull a muscle in my shoulder and break a nail, which sounds like nothing, but is actually bloody and excruciating. Lexi's sick. Eventually, I am, too. Every so often in the madness and darkness we find each other and press our shaking bodies together, her chin tucked to my chest, her bun bouncing against my jaw, and then we break apart again to try to stay alive.

Then the boat starts to list, nose rising, bedroom dragging backward into the deep. I grab for Lexi in the darkness, my feet slipping on the drenched planks.

"I love you," I shout, holding her as tightly as I can.

"I love you," she says. "I love you, Zeke."

Only this time she doesn't spin away to keep bailing and scrambling and fixing what's broken. She sags into me. As if she's the thing that's breaking.

"Don't give up," I say, but my voice is so hoarse I don't know if she can catch it.

"I can't keep going," she sobs. "I'm just—I'm out. I can't keep going."

"You can. You *can*."

"What's the point? We're sinking, we're . . ."

I grip her arms. "What's the point? Are you serious right now?" My fingers tighten. "Are you telling me you don't think we're worth fighting for?"

Her head drops, her shoulders shaking. We stumble together, hit a wall, right ourselves. Something smashes somewhere. I am so profoundly scared I can't believe I'm still able to function.

"This, us . . ." I begin, but she's shaking her head.

"This is how it has to end, maybe," she says, still sobbing. "Me and you. It's been so beautiful. I've loved you so much. But I don't want to go down apart, fighting the sea like we've got a fucking chance of winning, when we could be holding each other." She looks up at me, her eyes desperate, and lays both her palms on my cheeks. "I think this is it, Zeke. This is it."

"No," I say, voice ragged, but I'm sagging, too. If Lexi's out of hope, I don't stand a chance.

I start to cry. She kisses me, desperate, tear-drenched. I know she's right. I can feel it, smell it, hear it in the roar of the waves. We've lost. What we're fighting, it's just too big. And all of a sudden I get what Lexi means when she says, *This is how it has to end*, because what we've gone through's been so wild, and this is how wild things go. Brutal and sudden. Swept under by something too strong to fight off.

So I just hold her. Feel every ounce of the love I have for her. Let myself sink in it, and the pain of knowing it's over, and the abject searing torture of knowing that if I go, it means she's going, too, and *all* I want is for Lexi to live the happiest, safest, fullest life.

But this is it. This is it for us.

The end.

And then.

Voices.

Voices.

A great bulk blocking the moonlight for a pitch-black instant, then—

The glare of searchlights blazing through our shattered windows.

The soaring sensation of hope surging back.

～～～

"Is anyone alive in there?"

A male voice. Loud and clear above the waves and the wind. I've not heard a single voice but Lexi's for almost twelve days. A face appears in the window for a split second as the lifeboat manages to get alongside us, and the sea sends us tipping. It's a man, but it might as well be an alien. I cannot comprehend it. Everything's disjointed, snapshots caught in the lifeboat's beams.

"Help!" Lexi screams, pulling away from my arms and scrabbling to the window.

The lights flood through our broken boat. Shards of glass, pools of water, our abandoned bailing bowls sliding toward the bedroom.

"Can you reach the aft deck?" the man shouts over the wind.

"Yes! Yes!"

Lexi whirls around to grab me and we scramble our way there, stumbling against the strange tilt of the boards beneath us, yanking at the makeshift barriers we fixed in front of the door to keep out the storm.

Outside, silver shows on the waves like the whites of an animal's eyes in the dark. The lifeboat seems huge, blocking out half the sky. I think I'm dreaming, a drowning man's dream, maybe, but then I see the figures on the lifeboat deck and they look so *real*.

We cling to the railing, wind snatching at our clothes. I hear Lexi let out a wild, high-pitched laugh as the lifeboat swings in beside us like the storm's nothing at all. And then arms are reaching across the broken railings and pulling us—"*Lexi first,*" I scream, "*Lexi first*"—and suddenly the ground is so steady beneath us I think for a second we must've been pulled to land.

"You're safe now," someone says, their voice close and warm.

But I don't feel it, not until I turn and feel Lexi collide with me. Sobbing, grasping, soaked. She smells of salt and sweat, and of *Lexi*, my person, not torn from my arms and swept to sea, but *here*.

I grip her shoulders, check her over, kiss her tear-soaked face and taste sea salt. For a moment, after all that terror, after being so sure it was over . . . I feel completely awed. We *survived*. I can't believe it.

"Look," she whispers, eyes on the sea behind me.

I turn. *The Merry Dormouse* is sinking. As we watch, a wave sweeps over the deck, where the railing hangs half off, jagged and wrong-looking, like a broken bone. Our bedroom's already under the water. As I watch, something goes tumbling past one of the shattered windows, and it feels completely surreal to be standing out here, looking in. It would've been us tumbling backward into the depths in there.

She fights—she rears against the force pulling her down, but there's no saving her now. For a few short breaths, she disappears, reappears, disappears, her nose breaking through the waves. Then she's gone.

My eyes sting. I turn back to Lexi and press my forehead hard to hers.

"She was amazing," Lexi says, choked through her tears. "That boat. She was our lifeline."

"I know. I know."

"She saved us."

"*We* saved us," I correct her, but I'm crying for the houseboat, crying to see her gone. "We did this. OK? All right, Lexi? It doesn't end for us." My voice is so hoarse I don't know if she can hear me, so I say it again, my skin clammy and cold against hers. "It doesn't end for us. Not like this, not ever. Do you understand me?"

She nods, forehead still pressed to mine. She gets it. We faced the storm and we've survived it. I know she understands. Because if we've got through this . . . what the hell could ever tear us apart?

DAY TWELVE

Zeke

THEY INTRODUCE THEMSELVES. Kiki, Steve, Gareth, Paddy, Ash, Madur, smiling as they pull life jackets over our shoulders and pass us bottles of water, asking questions about injuries, asking us what we need.

There's only one thing Lexi needs, though.

"A phone," she says, gripping Kiki's arm. "Please."

The woman pauses, ducking down—she's almost six foot, and Lexi seems smaller than ever with her shoulders hunched against the cold wind.

"Lexi needs to warm up," I say, looking around me.

Everyone's moving so . . . comfortably. Like there's no rush now. Steve's speaking into a radio, Madur's gently trying to usher Lexi inside the boat, but the urgency we had in the houseboat's gone, and with it, the edge seems to have eased away from the storm. The waves are choppy, but standing here on the lifeboat deck in the steady rain, it doesn't even look like a storm. I bet this wouldn't make the news—probably doesn't cut it for a storm name. Not even an article about blown-over dustbins.

"Here," says Steve, wrapping a foil blanket around my shoulders.

I shake my head, impatient, trying to pull it off so I can give it to Lexi, and he smiles.

"Gareth's got one for her," he says quietly. "We'll get her inside in the dry, all right? And have Madur check her out. Then you."

I nod, making eye contact for a moment. He gets it. I fought so hard for Lexi for all this time, and I'm not done yet.

Steve's got one of those mild, open faces, the kind I associate with vicars and middle-aged dads. He's wearing a camera on his forehead, and I find myself staring into its blinking red light instead of at his eyes. I glance away, toward Lexi, pale in the lights of the boat. She's now bundled under at least two foil blankets and is talking fast to Kiki, who's pulling out a weird-looking phone, more walkie-talkie than mobile. Looking at Lexi makes me feel less crazy. Her hair's completely soaked, lying in stripes on her bare neck. I need to touch her, hold her, check she's really there.

"You remember the number?" Kiki says to her. "Let's get inside—Lexi, right?"

Lexi snatches the phone like a starved person grabbing at scraps. Kiki looks startled, glancing over at Madur, who already has an arm hovering around Lexi, trying to direct her down the steps into the area labeled *Survivor Space*.

"Lex, come on," I say, grabbing her hand and pulling. "We need to get off the deck."

She looks up at me. Her eyes are wild. "I don't know if I remember Penny's number," she whispers. "I taught it to Mae, but I can't . . . is it oh seven *six* four nine, or . . ."

"Lexi, I need to sit down," I say.

Her eyes sharpen. She glances around, as though coming to.

"In there," she says to me, pointing to the survivor space. "Now."

"What a good idea," says Madur.

I lead us down the narrow flight of steps into the body of the lifeboat. It's glaring down here, lit by overbright strip lighting. There're seats lining each side, with padded straps and grips dangling from the ceiling to keep yourself braced. I sit, and Lexi stumbles into the seat opposite me, eyes down on the phone. The boat's engine is deafeningly loud down here—the sound's so comforting after the chaotic roar of the wind.

"I can't remember," Lexi says tearfully. "I can't remember if it's . . . oh seven, oh seven six . . ."

Madur glances at me, eyebrows slightly raised. "Can you help her? I really need to examine you both. That's our number one priority right now."

He reaches for her wrist and pauses, head cocked, listening to her pulse. On the floor beside him he's laid out a series of cards in bright colors: I catch the words *casualty* and *lifesaving interventions*.

"Lexi, I need you to take a breath. Just in for four, out for eight. Can you try it with me?"

She shakes him off, eyes glued to Kiki's phone.

"Oh seven . . . Oh seven seven? Oh seven six?"

"Lexi."

She looks up. I feel a little dash of pride at being able to cut through to her.

"You're going to see Mae so soon," I say softly. "It doesn't matter if you can't call home yet. Because you're *going home* now."

Her eyes instantly fill with tears. "Oh, God, don't say it," she says. "What if it isn't true? What if we . . ."

"Lexi," Madur says, crouching down in front of her and steadying himself with a hand on the floor. "Looking at what-ifs will have really helped you survive on that houseboat. But you're safe now. The most important thing to do is to let me look after you, so that when you get home to your little girl . . ."

His eyes fly to me, checking he's got it right. I nod.

"You can be the best you can be for her. OK?"

Lexi lets out a shaky breath. "What is it?" she says, in the tone that means, *Fine, I'm listening.* "In for four, out for what?"

Madur smiles. "In for four, out for eight."

I lean back into the seat and watch her try it. The phone's trembling in her lap—her hands are shaking. I look down. Mine are, too. I'm feeling kind of . . . weird. Disconnected. It's like I won't let myself believe it, whatever I say to Lexi about how we're going home. I guess there've just been times before when I thought we were rescued—that ship we saw, the rig—so I've got used to never trusting what looks like a miracle.

But there's Madur, a proper qualified person wearing plastic gloves and checking over Lexi's injuries. If that doesn't count as a real miracle, I don't know what the hell does.

"Is this meant to be doing something?" Lexi says, cracking open one eye. "This breathing thing?"

For the first time in a while, I laugh. My voice sounds creaky, as if I've kind of forgotten how to do it.

"I think it's meant to calm you down," I say. "Right, Madur?"

"That's about it, yeah."

Lexi scowls. "What would I want to calm down for?" she says. "Are we not being rescued? Is this not rescue?"

"Yeah, it is," Madur says. "That's exactly what—"

"Calm is for a crisis," Lexi says, leaning forward in her seat. "Calm is for when we're trying to work out how the hell not to die. I'm *alive* now. You're telling me I'm safe. I don't want to be *anything* but buzzing."

"Right," Madur says after a moment, breathing out a laugh. "OK, well, as you were, then."

Lexi meets my eyes, and for the first time since the storm started, her fierce intensity breaks, and she smiles.

"Tell me again," she says.

"We're going home."

"Again."

"We're going home."

"Again."

"Home," I say. "Home, home, home, home, home."

She leans back and closes her eyes, still smiling. "I have imagined this moment so many times," she says. "And this is it." Her eyes open again and meet mine. "Right? This is really it?"

"Right," I say, and seeing her believe it makes *me* believe it, and just like that I'm crying again.

"I'm sorry to ruin this moment," Madur says, "but I really would feel a lot better if I could take a closer look at some of your injuries. That, for instance," he says, pointing at my bloodstained finger, the one where I lost a nail.

"Oh my God," Lexi says, eyes widening as she seems to come around again. "Check his wound. His stomach. *Now*—please—I sewed it up myself, and . . ."

"May I?" Madur asks me.

I nod. To his credit, he hardly reacts to the sight of the clumsily stitched wound across my stomach.

"You did a fabulous job there, Lexi. Let's clean that up a tad, eh?" he says calmly, already reaching for a bottle in his kit. "This might sting a bit, but looking at what you two have been through, I can't imagine you're scared of a little pain."

"Right," I say, and then I laugh again, remembering Lexi on the rig, saying, *Your toxic masculinity is showing.* "Actually," I say, "I'd love a paracetamol right now."

Everything hurts, now I think about it. The finger's the worst, but there's also my wound—a dull, persistent throb—and the muscles of my legs and arms, and the back of my throat, and . . .

"Sure!" Madur says, already rummaging.

"Wow," Lexi says, watching him produce a packet of paracetamol. "Wow."

It suddenly seems to hit her. She reaches forward, grabbing Madur's shoulder.

"What food have you got?" she says, her voice a little hoarse. "Have you got—have you got chocolate?"

"Thought you'd never ask," comes a voice from the steps, and Kiki ducks in, already holding two bars of Galaxy.

"This is heaven," Lexi says to me, wide-eyed as she grabs the outstretched chocolate. "It's heaven, isn't it?"

Kiki chuckles, passing me my Galaxy. "You really have been to hell and back, haven't you? It's not even the caramel one."

~~~~~

Dawn properly breaks today. It just smashes against the sky. Orange, pink, blue.

We watch it come up from the lifeboat deck. They wanted us to stay in the survivor space, but I couldn't stand how trapped I felt down there. I needed to see it—I needed to know we were moving. We stand hand in hand as the lifeboat forges on, cutting through the waves, taking us home.

I look at Lexi and feel a bottomless sensation that *relief* doesn't cover. More like . . . ecstasy. For the first time in two weeks, I can stop worrying about something happening to her, and the pressure lifting makes me feel like I've just surfaced after twelve days holding my breath. Everything else—the nightmare being over, knowing I'll see my family again . . . it's all small compared to really believing Lexi will be OK.

"Here, I can't offer you tea, which I bet is just what you fancy right now," Gareth says cheerfully, handing us each our third protein bar of the night, "but I can give you pretty much an endless supply of these. You must be famished. What've you been living off in there?"

"We ate pretty well, actually. You'd be surprised what Zeke can do with out-of-date cheese," Lexi says, with a small smile. "Thanks for this."

She's still wearing two blankets like a cloak on top of her life jacket, the top one crinkly with silver foil. Her hair is drying now the rain's stopped, and she's moving better, as if she's got energy back in her limbs.

"The world's a bit obsessed with you two," Gareth says, coming to stand beside us and adjusting his hood against the wind.

I have this weird compulsion to touch him. I can't actually believe he's here—all solid, bearded six foot of him.

"What do you mean?" I ask.

"You've captured the nation. The houseboaters lost at sea. Once your neighbor raised the alarm, everyone fell in love with the story, I think—the one-night stand, all that."

He looks briefly panicked, like he might have overstepped in mentioning that, even though absolutely nothing this man says could annoy me right now.

"Anyway," he goes on, with a slightly anxious side-eye at me, "when a military plane reported a burning oil rig yesterday, with SOS painted on its helipad, everyone went wild, especially when the plane had to turn back because of the weather. Then there was all the suspense with us lot setting out to the marker they'd sent us . . . Not that we had much hope, I must say. We'd written you off. Sorry," Gareth adds, patting me on the arm.

"Please never, ever say sorry to us," Lexi says, her mouth full of protein bar. "You saved our lives. We will love you forever. *Forever.*"

Gareth smiles. He's in his fifties, maybe, the sort of average-looking guy you'd overlook on a bus.

"Just what we do," he says, glancing back toward the cockpit, where his fellow volunteers stand.

Gareth, Kiki, Madur, Steve, Paddy, Ash—they don't know me and Lexi. They had no reason to save us. They volunteer to do this job because they want to help people. I don't know if there's anything bigger or braver than that. I keep saying, "*Thank you, thank you*," but it seems to embarrass them, so I'm trying to rein it in.

"Oh my God," Lexi says, suddenly clinging to my arm. "Oh my God, Zeke, look!"

At first it looks like a shadow on the horizon, a thickening cloud. Then it grows and lengthens and darkens.

"It's land," Lexi says. "That's land!"

Gareth smiles beside her. "Not just any old land. Gilmouth harbor."

I'm crying again. The world's waiting for us. I can hardly believe it still exists.

"Whatever happens when we get back," Lexi says suddenly, her grip tightening on my arm, "I don't want us to lose this."

"I'll give you a minute," Gareth says, slipping off and leaving us alone on the deck.

"I love you," I whisper, laying my hand over Lexi's on my arm. "I meant what I said when we got off the houseboat. There's literally nothing that could happen on dry land that would change how I feel about you."

She swallows, eyes brimming. "Same. And me neither."

I kiss her gently on the forehead, breathing in the smell of salt and sea and Lexi.

"Oh my God," she says, pulling back a little and shaking her head. "You're going to meet Penny and Mae. You're going to come around to our flat. Which isn't really my flat anymore. I need a flat. Shit, I need a flat."

I laugh, pulling her snug against me with one arm. "We can go shopping for food. I'm going to make you black truffle pasta sauce. I'm going to make you *dessert*. Oh my God, I'm going to get a McDonald's."

"We can watch TV. What do you even watch on TV? Do you

watch TV?" She looks up at me, briefly terrified. "You're not one of those men who spends all day watching sport, are you?"

"You two holding up OK?" Steve calls out to us from the helm. "There's a bit of a crowd on the dock, apparently, but the coastguard has made sure that your family are there to greet you, and the rest of the rabble are behind the barriers, all right?"

Your family. It surges through me. Mum. Jeremy. Lyra. My *family*, real and alive and *there*.

Lexi's doubled over, crying into her hands, her half-eaten protein bar dropping to the deck between her feet. "Oh my God," she says. "Mae. I get to hold Mae."

Lexi

IT'S LIKE AN out-of-body experience, perhaps because I have one single focus as we step off this lifeboat. Everything else is dreamy and strange, too bright and loud. There is only Mae.

Her face as she sees me across the pontoon.

Her pigtails bouncing as she starts to run.

Her perfect little arms as they are thrown around my neck, and the smell of her, that indefinable essence of Maeness.

I sob into her shoulder, breathing her in, feeling every single gram of gratitude that a body can hold.

"Auntie Lexi! Auntie Lexi!" Mae says, hugging me tighter than she's ever hugged me before, sinking into the firm padding of my life jacket.

I will never, ever, ever take it for granted that I get to be loved by this precious little girl. I pull back to look her over: the quizzical pale brown eyebrows, the freckles on her left cheek, her hair trying to weasel out of its long curly bunches. I'm dimly aware of Zeke behind me, of the people rushing to hug him, of the real world at the edges of my vision, but I don't have space in my brain for all that. Not yet. Just Mae.

"Look," she says, bouncing excitedly, radiating joy. "Look what I made!"

She's drawn me a sign: *Welcome Home Lexi, I Love You*, it says, and I cannot think of a single more beautiful thing.

It takes at least three minutes for the world around Mae to come into focus. Penny, who pulls me in tightly and tells me she loves me. Marissa, her tears clouding her glasses as she swoops down on me for a hug. Ryan, Penny's boyfriend, who to my surprise is crying, too. And Alyssa from the flat next door, a person I genuinely haven't thought of once in the last two weeks, but am delighted to see, because she is so normal and so real.

Then the rest of reality starts to seep in slowly as I grip Mae's hand. The press with their flashing cameras, and the crowds behind the makeshift railings constructed by the lovely people of Gilmouth marina, many of whom have come to hug me, too—I get the sense that they feel our houseboat's adventure was theirs.

I take a deep breath. The air tastes so different. I can still feel the sea on my tongue, but there's the flat taste of car fumes, too, and the dull warmth of a crowded place. The world is vivid and noisy: everyone is in color, their sunglasses and their phone screens shining in the morning sunlight.

"I can't imagine what you've been through," Penny says, still crying, pulling away from what must be our tenth hug of the last two minutes. "My beautiful, wonderful Lexi. I can't believe you . . ."

I draw back to look at her. Her face has gone pale.

I'm still so poised for disaster that I feel my whole body stiffen in readiness for whatever it is she's seen over my shoulder.

I spin. It's Zeke, emerging smiling and ringleted from the crowd of his family. Rocking his life jacket, of course—he could've stepped off a fashion week runway. He catches my eye, and I can't believe I ever worried about a single thing changing. The moment we're looking at each other, it's back to the two of us again, and right now

I cannot *wait* to feel him slink an arm around my waist as we step into real life together.

"*That's* Ezekiel?" Penny says in a whisper.

I look back at her. My eyes widen.

"Penny? Are you OK?"

She's reaching for Mae.

"What's going on?" asks Marissa.

"Penny," I begin, but she's pulling me back, away from the water, away from Zeke. "Penny, what are you *doing*?"

"Lexi, just *move*," she snarls, then she grabs at someone in a high-vis jacket. "We need to get through," she says. "Lexi needs to get to the ambulance."

"What? I'm fine," I say, looking back over my shoulder. "I don't want to get in the ambulance."

I catch sight of Zeke once more before he's whirled away in another hug, and then Penny is shoving me through an opening in the crowd, and someone is yelling at me, *Did he kidnap you? Were you kidnapped? Smile, Lexi! Over here!* And we're running along the pavement to the pub, Penny scooping a confused Mae up into her arms.

She doesn't stop until the door of The Anchor swings shut behind us.

"Mae," she says, putting her down. "Marissa is going to take you upstairs so you can watch all the police cars out of the big window!"

Marissa kicks into gear, slightly breathless from the run here. "Come on, sweetheart," she says, a hand on Mae's shoulder. "I've still got your elves and dragons coloring book up there, too."

"I want to stay with Lexi," Mae begins, but Penny shakes her head.

"We just need five minutes, sweetie," she says. "Then Lexi's all yours again!"

Penny strides to the bar as Marissa pulls a reluctant Mae to the flat upstairs. The Anchor is always strange when it's like this, silent and still. It's not a place built for solitude, and the quietness makes it shabbier: you see all the chips on the wooden tables, the old beer stains on the carpet. It is unspeakably odd to be here. The ground feels like it's slipping underneath my feet.

"What the fuck?" I ask, with force.

Penny pours herself a large tumbler of whisky, even though it's barely eight in the morning. Her hands are shaking. She looks way too thin, and my stomach lurches as I realize that the lankness of her blond-streaked hair and the new hollows beneath her cheekbones are probably from worrying about me. She's wearing a gray tracksuit that I'm pretty sure is mine, though living together for so long has meant that my and Penny's wardrobes have mostly merged into one collection of similar sweatshirts.

I have a horrible, twisting sensation in my stomach. For a second, I contemplate just walking out and leaving Penny there with her whisky, secrets unspoken, but I know I won't. I always want the truth.

"What's going on, Penny?"

"*That's* Ezekiel?" she says, voice trembling. "That man on the dock, that is the man you've been at sea with? That's the man you met here?"

"Yeah. That's Zeke, yeah. Why?"

She takes a shaky breath and knocks back the rest of the tumbler, reaching for the bottle again.

"Whoa, easy, Pen."

She hardly drinks these days. After going cold turkey during pregnancy, she decided never to go back to the heavy drinking—*No more bad decisions*, she'd said, then she'd put her hand on her belly and said, *Not that I could ever regret this.*

"His family only released one photo of him, and they didn't call him Zeke, they called him Ezekiel, and . . . His hair was short in the photo, he didn't have a beard . . . He didn't look like that. He wasn't on social media or anything, and . . . He didn't look . . . I didn't realize it was him."

"You didn't realize he was *who*, Penny?"

I'm gripping the back of the nearest chair. I can sense that whatever's coming, I'll need something to keep me steady.

"That man. Lexi . . ." Her voice drops to a hushed, awful whisper. "He's Mae's father."

AFTERWARD

Zeke

I LIFT MY face to the sky. I can't believe this is the same sun that beat down on us on the water. This one's so much . . . gentler. The tame sunshine of pub gardens, SPF 50, ice creams.

Everything here is so ordinary it's crazy. I don't know how else to describe it. I'm just blown away by all the normal stuff that's been going on without us. Mobile phones, cars, the hum of a plane overhead . . . It's so neat and controlled, as if I'm standing on a toy marina and invisible hands are arranging all the pieces.

Lexi's off with her family, and mine are here, around me, hugging me, talking fast, all smiling wide. I realize that I love them, obviously I do, even if that's hard, and I hold them tightly and force myself to tell them, because you don't know when you'll get to do that, you don't know that you'll get another chance.

"Love you all," I say, choked. "I love you all."

I look at my mum as I say it. When I last saw her, I didn't know that she'd betrayed my father, torn our family apart, kept that secret from us all. I suspected it, but I didn't *know*. It feels different to look her in the eye when I have the whole story.

She's got smudges on her glasses and tear tracks down her

cheeks. Her trademark neat bob is a fuzzy gray mess. She's staring at me as though I've come back from the dead, and she looks so exhausted, so *human*.

A long time ago, my mum messed up. Something we have in common at last—I've done that plenty. As I pull her in for another hug, I feel her frail, shaking shoulders and think, *I'm not letting resentment lose me another parent.*

"Love you, Mum," I whisper.

She doesn't say it back—we're not that kind of family, never have been—but she squeezes me even tighter.

"I am so glad," she manages. "Just so glad."

"You gave us quite the scare, little brother," Lyra says. She's got her arms around me, too, from behind. I can't remember the last time my sister hugged me.

"Welcome back, Ezekiel," says Jeremy. "Welcome home."

Welcome home. I'm so relieved I might collapse under it. *We did it*, I think, as my mother checks me over with her hands on my upper arms, demanding answers about injuries, lifting her head to summon over a paramedic. *We got home. We got Lexi home to Mae.*

～～～～～

I'm sitting in the backseat of Jeremy's latest fancy car, with Mum beside me, a bottle of lemonade in my hand, and Joy Williams singing out from the radio. Every part of this is wild to me. The song, the lemonade, my mother. I feel that this *can't* be real. Not in an I-can't-believe-it sort of way; more that it's all too good to be true.

"Oh, Ezekiel," Lyra says from the front passenger seat, breathing out slowly. "You always did love the drama, eh?"

I swallow, that vast grateful feeling in my chest shrinking slightly. How long has it taken for my sister to recast my traumatic experience as me making drama? I check the clock. An hour. Nice. All those huge emotions I felt on the pontoon have ebbed a bit. The idea of telling my family I love them already seems kind of strange again, the way it would have before I went to sea.

Jeremy's taking me to the hospital—Mum's insistence, even though the paramedic said there was no sign of infection in the wound on my stomach. I wish I was still with Lexi, but I think she went off somewhere for some quiet time with Mae, and I'm not surprised she's forgotten about me for the moment. I want her to enjoy every single second of being home with Mae, and if that means the two of us have to be apart for a little while, I'm cool with that. Still, it felt wrong leaving the harbor without her, like leaving a bit of myself behind, and now that I'm here with Mum, Lyra and Jeremy, I'm feeling weirdly like . . . I've gone back in time or something. I don't know. I just feel odd.

"We are so happy to have you back," my mum says. "Aren't we, Lyra?"

"Yeah," Lyra says, checking her blunt fringe and then snapping the visor back flush to the car roof again.

At twenty-nine, she's exactly who she was at ten: hard-edged, hard-nosed, always the first person to speak up or step forward. She would've done well on the water. Better than I did.

"It is great to have you back," Jeremy says, as though he's welcoming me home from a trip to Florida. My high-handed big brother, always in formal mode.

I'm happy. I think I'm happy. I must be happy, mustn't I? I'm *back*. I just wish I'd seen Lexi again before leaving.

"You'd better take the B roads to the A1, Jeremy," my mum says. "There was a crash near Warkworth last time I looked."

I stare at the back of Jeremy's head, trying to figure out what the hell's going on in my brain. I'm feeling . . . scattered. Everything's too much, even though I'm just sitting here, doing nothing.

I press my hand to the wound on my stomach, my broken nail throbbing. Somewhere back there at the marina, with Mum bossing

around the paramedics and Lyra disposing of hovering news report-
ers as though she'd been getting rid of journalists her whole life, I
started to feel the way I used to feel. Fidgety, uncomfortable, sad.
Like I'm always in the wrong place.

I sag back in my seat, turning my gaze to the world outside. Sitting here among them all, the reality's still that I don't fit in. I guess
that whole childhood fantasy about having another father was
wishful thinking. An explanation for why I don't belong. Embarrassing, really. Especially as it turns out there's no excuse for me
being the way I am—there's nobody else to blame.

"What did you miss the most, Ezekiel?" my mum asks, with
forced cheer.

I wince. She's trying to make conversation. She did this all the
time when I was a kid, because I was so quiet—she was always trying to get me to speak up when all I wanted to do was listen.

"I dunno," I say, trying to turn my thoughts that way.

I see the slight tilt of Lyra's chin and I know she's rolling her
eyes. She's never had any patience for my slowness.

"You, probably," I tell my mum after a moment.

It's true, but the part I don't say is, there wasn't all that much
else I missed. I had so much on that boat, and now that I'm back,
seeing the huge ripple effect we left behind us . . . I feel kind of
guilty for not thinking more about home. For me, out there, it was
all about getting Lexi back to Mae. That was my focus.

My mum starts to cry.

"Oh my God," Lyra says, without turning around. "*Don't*, Mum."

Mum never cries. She just doesn't hold with that sort of thing.
Straight-backed, sharp-eyed, she's a push-on kind of person. But
here she is, weeping, and reaching to clutch my hand. I see it again,
just a flash of it: she's not the disapproving figure I built up in my
head as a child. My mother's a full person, as messy as I am, as

messy as the version of my dad that I found in those logbooks. I grip her hand tightly in mine.

"Pull it together, Mum, he's back now," Lyra says, glancing over her shoulder. "Look, he's right there, see?"

"Let her cry, Lyra," I say sharply. "Not everyone copes the same way you do."

The car goes very quiet. I can feel the collective shock. This is not a thing I would usually say. In fact, I'm not sure I've ever snapped back at Lyra like that before.

"All right," Lyra says after a moment, and though I can't see her face, I can imagine her expression: eyebrows raised, slight amusement on her lips. "I was just trying to save you the sight of what a wreck you made your family, actually, but sure, I'll zip it."

"You don't have to save me from anything," I say, turning to look out of the window again. "I can save myself these days."

"Noted," Lyra says.

This time, when she looks over her shoulder at me, her expression is almost . . . I don't know, interested. She's never looked at me like I'm interesting before. Maybe if I'd had the balls to stand up to Lyra before, instead of following her and Jeremy around like a lost puppy, my childhood would've been a bit different.

Mum sniffs, looking straight ahead, wiping her cheek with her spare hand. "I do apologize," she says. She squeezes my hand again. "It's just been a little bit of a stressful time."

"Don't be sorry," I say, my voice rough. "*I'm* sorry. You must have been so scared while I was gone."

I hate the hurt I've caused her. Not just the last two weeks—she's dealt with a whole lifetime of crap from me. I fought her whenever I could, broke the rules, disappointed her so many times she must've wanted to give up. Thing is, I always thought she was lying to us—and I guess I was right. She *did* have an affair, and she never told us that Jeremy had a different biological father from me and Lyra.

But now that I know the truth for sure, I wonder if it was really the lie that bothered me, as a kid. I remember once I told my therapist that my mum probably regretted me—the kid she shouldn't have had, the proof she cheated. It was an offhand remark at the time, but seeing how much my mum is feeling right now, seeing the pain she's been through since I've been gone . . . in an awful, twisted kind of way, it feels good. I can see how much she cares. And that feels new.

"We were rather worried, yes," she says, her voice still wobbling slightly. "Was it dreadful? Was it just—was it torture? I understand if you don't want to talk about it. But I have to ask. I've imagined every kind of horror you can think of."

This time my answer comes instantly. "No," I say. "No, it was amazing."

The car goes silent again as Jeremy pulls onto the motorway, joining the stream of traffic. The wind thunders against the windows. I flinch. I wonder if it'll ever stop feeling make-or-break when the breeze picks up.

"I mean," I say, skin prickling, too aware that they're all waiting for me to speak. "I mean, it was awful. But I fell in love. So . . . that bit was amazing."

"You fell in *love*?" Lyra says, incredulous, turning her whole body to look at me over the back of her seat.

The flow of traffic on both sides is starting to make me feel a bit dizzy. I see a sign for the hospital, and suddenly I can't wait to get there.

"Of course you did," Mum says. "What an experience to share with someone. It's only natural that the two of you would bond."

"It wasn't just that," I say, looking down.

The network of knobbly veins on the back of Mum's hand is the color of seawater at dawn. The traffic's the wind, not letting up. My

body's completely tense, every muscle bunched up, as if I've been elec-
trocuted. I've got that disconnected feeling again, the one that took
hold of me on the lifeboat for a while. As though I can't believe the
bad thing has really ended, or I'm just waiting for the next one to start.

"Let yourself settle back in before you think too hard about any
of it," Mum says. "A checkup from a proper doctor, a few days at
home, and you'll be back to your old self again."

I stare down at my mother's hand against the filthy, cracked
velvet of my trouser leg. I'm not sure going back to my old self is
something I want at all.

~~~~~

It's not until I'm back from the hospital, bandaged, pinpricked and
in possession of some strong antibiotics, that I realize I don't have
Lexi's number.

I'm standing in my childhood bedroom in Alnwick, looking out
at the street. Normally when you want to talk to someone it's kind
of an impulse to reach for your phone, but I don't have that with her.
We've never messaged. It feels more like I should turn over my
shoulder and say, *Hey*, but all I see back there is the solid white bedroom wall. This house feels so massive after the houseboat, and so
boxy. Why do we all choose to live in these big squarish things?
Why is there so much floor space in this bedroom? What's it all for?

I rub my chest. Lexi and I didn't swap numbers—our phones
will be at the bottom of the sea now anyway. I have no way of getting hold of her at all. The realization washes over me like ice-cold
water.

"Mum," I call down the stairs, as though it's 2010 and I'm a kid
again, wondering where Lyra and Jeremy are, whether they've gone
out without me. I feel like all the different versions of me are clashing right now. "How can I get hold of Lexi?"

"Sorry, darling?" she calls. Mum never hears you the first time.

"Lexi."

"The houseboat woman?" Her voice is a bit too high. "I don't know, Ezekiel, are you sure that's a good idea?"

"It's not," Jeremy says, coming up the stairs with a cup of coffee.

He hands it to me as he walks past, into my bedroom. He sits down on the edge of the bed and watches me critically, forearms resting on his knees.

"You need a bit of space, Ezekiel. This has been a traumatic experience."

I stare back at him. "Are you actually telling me what I've just been through?"

"Of course, I can't imagine it," he says, raising his hands.

"No." I put the coffee down on the desk. "You can't."

He sighs, rubbing his eyes behind his glasses. "I should have known when you said you wanted to buy that houseboat back that it would all end in tears."

End in tears? I nearly died about ten times. It's not like I got lost on my way back from school or something.

"It was your idea for me to buy the houseboat back," I choke out. "You said Dad always stashed his secrets, and that boat was his bolt-hole, and it was bound to have the answers."

Jeremy frowns. "I know. I stand by that. I wanted to help. You do understand that, don't you?"

Jeremy always wants to help. He just wades in there, helping left, right and center, and if you happen to be in his path when he's helping, you'd better be ready to dive out of the way. I remember the truth—which of us has a dead biological father we never met—and simmer down a bit.

"Well, whatever." I fidget with the new bandage on my finger, hating the whine in my voice. It's this bedroom: I'm regressing to fifteen-year-old me with every minute I spend here. "I just want to see Lexi."

"I've got a number for her boss, Marissa," Jeremy says reluctantly, leaning back on the bed to pull his phone out and find the contact.

I glance out of the bedroom window at the street while I wait. There're a few more vans out there than there were before. And men with cameras. I stare. I'm feeling less weird than I did in the car, but the world's still so strange. People everywhere. Noise all the time. I can hear the motorway's *whoosh* even with the window closed—I don't know if I've ever noticed that here before. And everything smells. Not bad, just . . . distinct. This whole house has a scent to it that I'm not sure I ever knew was there.

One of the people below clocks me and lifts the camera to their face. It makes me think of a sniper in a film, that's how quick it is. I yank the curtain across.

When I eventually get through to Marissa on Jeremy's phone, I remember her voice. It's the woman from the pub, the one who slipped out from behind the bar when she noticed me looking over. She kind of set me and Lexi up, I guess.

"Hi," she says. There's a guardedness to the *hi* that I don't like.

"Hey. Can I speak to Lexi?"

The silence is too long. And just like that, I know the bad thing's not over at all.

"I'm sorry," Marissa says. "She doesn't want to speak to you."

My heart starts to hammer. I lower myself down in the desk chair, the seat where I tortured myself over GCSE textbooks that never made sense.

"What do you mean, she doesn't want to speak to me?"

"I mean, she's told us all to tell you that, if you get in touch."

"She said that? She said she doesn't want to . . ."

I trail off in the face of Marissa's silence. No. No. I press my fingertips to my forehead. I saw Lexi a few hours ago. We held hands, gripped each other so tightly. *I love you*, she'd whispered, before she'd stepped off the lifeboat.

I should never have let her go. All the time out there on the water, we never split up, we never parted. I feel like I'm back on the boat, only this time, the wind's managed to tear her from my arms.

"Did she say anything else? Is she OK? Am I allowed to know why?"

My voice is bitter and sharp. I'm so tired. I'm so—lost.

"No," Marissa says after a moment. And then: "I'm sorry."

"Are you kidding me?" My voice rises. "No, I'm not allowed to know, or no, she's not OK?"

She sighs. "Look, you seem like a reasonably nice kid. So I'll just say, think about one thing you might have done that a woman like Lexi could never forgive, and then, yeah, it'll be about that. And she's not OK about it. *Capeesh?*"

I stare at the wall. What have I done? What could it be? There's . . . nothing, I don't think. She knows me better than anyone ever has.

"I don't know what you mean."

I can hear the hopelessness in my voice, and maybe she can, too, because she says, "Get some sleep. You've been through something unspeakable. Rest. We're looking after her."

She hangs up. I lie on top of the duvet and stare at the familiar landscape of my old bedroom ceiling. I feel completely . . . I don't know. I don't know. I'm wiped out, blank.

Lexi doesn't walk away from someone she cares about, not ever. So, what, she doesn't care, then? I can't believe that, either. I *know* her, I've held her in my arms and I've seen her so close to the brink and I . . .

I press my hands to my face. All at once it comes rushing in: the grief, fear, sadness, the loss. I'm worn out—I've got nothing left. It just crashes over me. I can't survive without Lexi.

So many times on that houseboat I felt like I was living inside a nightmare. But I'd take a night in the storm over this.

Lexi

"HE'S AT THE bar," Marissa whispers into the phone.

I close my eyes, snuggling deeper into the sofa. *No, no, no.* The image of Zeke standing at the bar of The Anchor, like that first day we met . . . it makes me want to cry, and I just don't have the energy for more tears. I'm sapped.

In my head he's still in those velvet trousers—I can't quite see him in anything else. It's a nice metaphor for the fact that I have only ever known one very specific version of this man: the version who didn't confess to knocking up a young bartender and then telling her he wanted nothing to do with her baby.

"Don't ring me and tell me these things, Marissa," I groan into the phone.

Mae's in bed, so life is happening at low volume—not quite a whisper, because Penny and I always vowed we wouldn't live our lives like that, but we turn the telly down and wince if anyone drops something. She's been a light sleeper since the day she was born; waking Mae is a crime punishable by serious chores.

It's amazing, really, how I've slipped back into this life. Mae's made it easier, I think: there's something so grounding about a child. Their needs are so immediate, and they're so physical—scuffed knees, sticky fingers, tangled hair. It's easier to be present in the here and now when there's someone beside you who knows no other way to be.

"What's Marissa saying?" Penny asks, poking her head out from the kitchen, where she's preparing her classic Saturday-evening treat for me and Ryan—a KitKat broken up over a bowl of vanilla ice cream. I fantasized many times about this KitKat ice cream on *The Merry Dormouse*.

I wave a hand at her, like, *Not important*, and she narrows her eyes, but steps back into the kitchen again. We've not talked about Zeke since she told me he was Mae's father three days ago. We've also not talked about the fact that I have moved back into my old bedroom, or the fact that in my absence Ryan clearly moved into our flat, or the fact that I wake every night sweaty and terrified, convinced I'm going to die. We've talked a lot about what we're going to order for dinner every evening, though, and she's fully caught me up on *Married at First Sight*, so it's not like we're in complete denial or anything.

"What's he wearing?" I whisper into the phone.

"Oh my God, I am not playing go-between for your late-night sexting with this man," Marissa says. "I'm just telling you that he's here, desperate to see you, and if you want to talk to him . . ."

"I can't. How can you even suggest that? Whose side are you on?" I hiss, glancing at Mae on the baby monitor.

She's too old for it now, really—if there's anything wrong, she marches out of bed to come and get one of us to sort it. But Penny and I like to see her sleeping. There's something so comforting about the sight of her curled up with her plait squiggling across the pillow and her bare feet poking out from under the duvet.

"I am on the side of everyone getting all the information," Marissa says. "I'm the BBC, all right? Just . . . remember that people change."

"It doesn't matter," I say, voice hollow. "It doesn't matter if he's changed since he made that choice, because he didn't *tell* me."

"Weren't you guys a bit busy?" Marissa says.

"There was time."

"He was a kid when he got Penny pregnant. Eighteen. Do you remember what you were like at eighteen?"

I think back. I was different, sure—feistier, more idealistic, more hopeful for the future. But I would never, ever have abandoned my child.

"He was so full of admiration for how I supported Penny," I say bitterly, glancing back toward the kitchen door to check she's not in earshot. "That just seems so ridiculous now that I know he abandoned her. Had he *forgotten*?"

"I think that's unlikely," Marissa says.

I hear the familiar clink of glasses behind her and feel a pang of nostalgia for the pub. It's a comfort-place for me, much like this sofa, and I resent the fact that I can no longer go there because it's the one place Zeke would know to find me.

"I would say 'You've got me pregnant' isn't the sort of conversation you forget, even if you're a thoughtless eighteen-year-old manwhore."

"Don't call him that," I say, pulling a cushion up to my chest.

"Whose side are *you* on?" Marissa asks. "I think the most likely option is that he just hasn't made the connection between you and Penny. Or hasn't realized the Penny he, you know . . ."

"Impregnated?"

". . . is your Penny."

"How many Pennys has he had?" I say, and then instantly regret it. "Please don't try to answer that."

"*I* don't know, do I? But you know who does, and is currently looking very mournful at my bar? Zeke."

I imagine his face, one curl falling into his eyes, eyebrows drawn together in a worried frown. It makes me want to run down the street to the pub, pull him into my arms and tell him I love him.

But then I glance across at the baby monitor and see Mae, and my heart hardens again. That girl deserves everything. She deserves a father who had the decency to at least *try* to be there for her, whatever that looked like. If Zeke's hurting, fine. He'll move on. He would never have stayed with me anyway. He's clearly got no loyalty.

"I'll talk to him when I'm ready," I say, swallowing. Right now if I look at him, I'll crumble. "You can tell him that."

"Tell him yourself."

"I *can't*, Marissa."

I hate the way my voice breaks. I glance toward the kitchen again. I don't want Penny to see how crushed I am by this. We've spent nearly five years merrily cursing this man—he's been the butt of every joke, the archetype of a cruel, useless man, and the idea that I *slept* with him, fell in *love* with him . . . I feel as though I've betrayed her in the worst possible way.

Marissa gives a frustrated growl. "I've got customers. But please get off that sofa and come and see me tomorrow."

"How do you know I'm on the sofa?"

"You've got sofa voice."

"What's— Never mind. I'll be there. Message me the best time."

"Gotcha. Try to get some sleep tonight, all right? See you, Lex."

I hang up. I haven't left this apartment since getting back from sea. All day, I've played with Mae, savoring every second of her, letting her put all her butterfly clips in my hair and watching *Frozen* with her in my lap. But whenever she and Penny go out, I stay behind. I can see Penny thinks it's because I'm having trouble adjusting to the big wide world again—I know she's been reading about how people recover from surviving extreme experiences because I saw the open tabs on her laptop. But it's not that. It's not even the journalists and photographers hanging around the place. It's that every time I envisaged coming back to reality again, I imagined Zeke doing it with me, and now I'm doing it without him.

Ryan comes down the corridor from the bathroom, and I wince—Penny's boyfriend is so loud. He's just a big man: gigantic arms, broad shoulders, blockish head. I can't exactly object to him on these grounds, but he does take up so much *space*.

Still. I suppose he probably thinks the same about me, the childhood friend of Penny's currently installed in the flat he shares with his girlfriend.

"You all right?" Ryan says, taking the armchair and reaching for the remote.

"Not really, Ryan, no," I say.

He pauses and looks at me. I look back at him. The silence stretches.

"I was really worried, you know," he says. "When you went missing."

"Really?" I say, interested.

I have reflected very little on how my disappearance affected Ryan, mainly because in my brain Ryan features only in the role of General Inconvenience. I am aware that this is potentially unfair, but experience has taught me it's best not to get attached.

"You know, you've actually never asked me a single question about myself," Ryan says, carefully placing the remote control back on the arm of the chair. "And that's meant I sort of think you're a bit of a prick, really. You've never once given me the idea that I'm welcome here."

I am too drained to feel much at all, but I do feel a wave of guilt at this. It's true. I've been waiting for Ryan to leave since the moment he arrived.

"But I know you've seen all the blokes before me who haven't stuck around, and I know that's why you keep me at arm's length. I know you're looking after Penny and Mae. I respect that."

"Thanks," I say, looking pointedly at the remote. Where's Penny? How long does it take to get the ice cream out of the tub?

"And just so you know, I never wanted Penny to suggest you move out."

My gaze flies to his face. I *had* always assumed he had a part to play in that whole drama. He looks back at me steadily. There's something very simple about Ryan—not to say that he's not smart, more that he's straightforward. I don't know if I've ever consciously registered that about him before, but now I think of it, I realize he's never tried to bullshit me. He doesn't suck up or try to make me like him. He's just stolidly tolerated me.

"As far as I'm concerned, the more parents Mae has, the better," he says. "You'll always be welcome in my life as long as she'll have me in hers."

I open and close my mouth. That hit me somewhere in my chest.

"I'm not trying to replace you, that's what I'm saying. I never have been. And Penny asking you to move out, that really was— well, she can tell you."

I follow his gaze to the kitchen doorway, where Penny stands with two ice cream bowls in her hands. Her eyes are wide and pained. She doesn't want to have this conversation. I suspect she's been dodging it for days. I know she hates that she hurt me; I know she feels guilty; I know she wishes she could take it back, as she so often does when she's lashed out or said something she doesn't mean. I also know that she hates to say *sorry*—not because she isn't sorry, but because she can't stand to feel shame. She'd rather live with a mistake than confess to making one.

"It's all right," I say, before she can speak. "I know you were try-ing to—"

"I was trying to set you *free*, Lexi," she says, and a tear spills over her lash line. She hurries forward with the bowls, putting them down on the coffee table and heading back into the kitchen for the third one.

"I'll do that," Ryan says, getting up and putting a hand on her arm. "You talk to Lexi."

Penny turns slowly to face me. I pull my knees up, making room for her on our beloved turquoise sofa that sags in all the right places. Wordlessly, I flick my gaze to the empty space. She drags herself there and sits down.

"I'm awful," she whispers. "I'm an awful friend. It's my fault you got lost at sea. It's my fault all this happened."

"What?" I sit up, chucking the self-pity cushion off my chest. "What are you on about?"

"If I hadn't told you to move out . . . Or if I'd confessed to selling the houseboat, so you'd have known you couldn't go there to crash that night . . ."

"Penny. I chose to go to the houseboat without asking you. That's on me. And I'm the one that bloody *tied it to itself.*"

She looks at me, eyes still forlorn and wide.

"Did you actually?" she says. "But Lex, that's so fucking stupid?"

I burst out laughing. It's the first time I've laughed in four days. If you'd told me two weeks ago that I'd *stop* laughing when I got off the houseboat, I would never, ever have believed you.

"I know," I say, reaching to stretch my blanket out so it covers both our legs. "Why *did* you sell it? *The Merry Dormouse?*"

She chews her cheek. "This guy popped up online asking to buy it—Ezekiel," she says, flushing slightly. "Obviously I had no idea who he was, and I guess he didn't know who I was, either, but any-way, he offered loads more than it was worth. And it was such a ball-ache, that boat—the maintenance agency was *always* sending bills for stuff that needed doing to it, varnishing, fixing leaks, another trip to the shipyard . . ."

"For that," I say with fervor, "I thank them."

"But I just thought . . . oh, go on, then. I didn't tell you because we talked about Mae inheriting the boat one day, and I felt like I was being super selfish, but you know I've wanted to knock through and redo the kitchen for ages . . ." Her eyes fill with tears again. "See? Awful friend."

"Don't be daft. But you should've told me. I wouldn't have cared, Pen! It's your boat."

"But it was your mum's," she says quietly, fiddling with the sofa cushion.

"And she gave it to you."

"Do you ever kind of hate me for taking so much of your mum? Now she's gone?" Penny says, in a very small voice.

I stare at her. "What? No!"

"You didn't resent me?"

"*Resent* you?"

She shrugs helplessly. "She treated me like her daughter, kind of. But I'm not. I wasn't. And I feel like you were used to expecting so little from people by then, what with your dad and all, so you took it in your stride, but . . . Your mum was amazing, but she was always so busy, and the last thing you two needed was someone else to look after."

"You treated me like a sister," I say, reaching to grab her hand. "I didn't lose something, I gained a sibling. And Mum just had a lot of love to give, I think. I never felt like I went without."

"She was like you," Penny says, with a small smile. "A natural nurturer."

I laugh. "Oh yeah, that's me. Mother Teresa. Where the fuck is Ryan with those spoons?"

"Just lurking in the kitchen, really," Ryan says, loping out again with the third bowl and three spoons.

"That argument, the night I asked you to move out," Penny says, with a big, shaky breath. "I want to explain. I'd been thinking for ages about how you should get a place of your own, not because I want you to go, but I just . . . I feel so *bad*, Lex. I should never have moved in with you all those years ago. I should never have let you do so much. But I was scared and on my own and it was so easy to take the help you offered."

"I'm glad you did."

"Yeah, but . . . It was selfish, wasn't it? To ask so much from you. And lately I've had these fantasies, sort of imagining the life I want for you, where you're happy and doing your own thing, running your café, meeting a gorgeous guy, having a kid of your own . . ."

I swallow. I'd imagined that future for myself, too, a few days ago. Now it feels farcical.

"I want that for you so badly. And that day . . . you took Mae out to the park, and I stayed home and pissed around watching a guy on YouTube talking about skincare and I just thought, what the hell am I doing? I felt so guilty."

"I don't care what you did while I was taking Mae to the park," I say, staring at her. Where's all this coming from? "Penny, I was giving you a bit of time to yourself. You get to choose how to spend it."

"Yes, but that's all you do, isn't it? Give me time. Give me things. And I don't give you anything back."

"Of course you do!"

"I don't," she insists, gripping her spoon with both hands. She hasn't looked at me in far too long; I nudge her with a foot, trying to catch her eye, but she keeps her gaze downturned. "I take advantage of you. And all of a sudden, I felt so bad, and I just—I wanted you to *go*. Take the leap, pull off the plaster. And I knew if I didn't say something then, I'd get comfortable again and let you stay forever. So I said you should move out now that Ryan wants to move in."

"Oh," says Ryan, through a mouthful of ice cream. "I didn't know that bit."

"I know." Penny's crying properly now. "I shouldn't have used Ryan as an excuse."

"I get it," I say. I've thought about this so much over the last two weeks. "It kind of *is* about Ryan."

"It's not," Ryan and Penny say in unison.

"No, it is." I'm talking slowly, picking my way, and this makes me think of Zeke, which makes my heart throb with pain. "Because Ryan is the first guy who's come along who wants to be a family with you. He doesn't see Mae as baggage. She's part of you, so he loves her."

Ryan nods at this. Just a little *Yeah, that's it* nod.

"And that means you don't need me as much."

"Lexi, I—"

"It's OK. It's good. It's good that you don't *need* me. I'd like you to still *want* me around, though. I'd like to still be Mae's auntie." My voice is getting thick. This is hard to talk about.

"Always," Penny says, finally looking at me. "Always, always, always. Do you know how heartbroken that little girl would be if you weren't part of her life? I never *ever* wanted that. I should have made that clear. I screwed up the whole thing. It was just so hard for me to let you go, I . . . I was trying to be selfless and I'm not . . . a natural at that, so I . . . ballsed it up, really."

I smile. I don't feel any of the anger and heartache I felt when I first walked out of this flat. It got lost somewhere out there on the water. I know where she was coming from—I think even back then I knew it, really.

"Just to be clear," I say, "you and Mae, you give me *so much*.

Helping to raise her has been the greatest joy and privilege, and seeing you become the amazing mum you are now . . . I'd die for you both, Penny. And I say that as a person who has recently done a lot of nearly dying."

She throws herself at me, sobbing.

"I'm an awful person," she says, as I let out an *oof.*

"You are not an awful person."

"I am. Lexi, you don't even know. I'm selfish and weak and cowardly and—"

"Penny! This is crazy! Will you stop?" I smooth her hair back and shoot Ryan a look, like, *A little help, here?*

"Come on," he says, easing her out of my lap and into his arms. "You're all right, love." He looks at me. "It's been a hard few weeks for her," he says quietly.

"I know," I say, with a twist of guilt. "I know it has."

"Viktor in Flat 6 is moving, you know," Ryan says after a moment. "If you wanted your own place, but without going far."

The kindness of this almost brings me to tears. I smile at him. Maybe Ryan really *is* fine. More than fine. Maybe Ryan is one of the good ones.

"Mummy?" Mae says from the doorway.

"Hey!" Penny says, whirling out of Ryan's arms, wiping the tears from her face. "Hey, Mae-Mae, did we wake you?"

"Why are you crying?" Mae asks, pulling Harvey the bunny a little closer to her chest. "We got Auntie Lexi back."

I bite down hard on my bottom lip. There are so many things that have been terrible in the last fortnight, but I think the very worst thing is knowing how frightened Mae was when I was at sea. The thought of it makes me want to crumble.

"We absolutely have," Penny says, smiling at me, eyes still wet. "And we are so lucky to have her."

"So why are you crying?"

Penny thinks for a moment. "Because I did something I shouldn't have done," she says. "I said something I shouldn't have said. And I've been trying to be brave enough to say so."

"Oh," Mae says, looking relieved. "That's easy. You just have to think about what Lexi would do. Lexi's always brave."

"Come here," I say, as my heart breaks. "Come give me a cuddle and I'll take you back to bed."

As we walk hand in hand to her bedroom, I have to grip the banister to keep myself together. There is no greater gift than this little hand in mine. It was simply too much for me to hope for more, that's all. The universe couldn't give me Mae *and* Zeke—it's more than I could possibly deserve.

Zeke

"YOU'RE DIFFERENT," BRADY tells me, cocking his head back to drink his beer from the bottle.

"Probably," I say, staring at the living area of our Putney flat, with its secondhand leather sofas and the rug we got from the Aldi middle aisle.

It's smaller than I remember. And darker. And . . . moldier. It's actually kind of making *The Merry Dormouse* look good. Did we usually leave the place this dirty?

"You've always had that slightly, you know, wounded vibe," Brady goes on, sliding a beer my way along the kitchen countertop. "But now you've gone proper dark."

I catch the beer with one quick hand, like a cowboy in a bar. I think about how Lexi would tease me for that, what she'd say about me drinking lager when we all know I'm a gin and tonic guy. I mean, who am I trying to impress? Brady? I slide the beer back down the counter to him, ending up whacking it into an unwashed bowl. Brady has to scramble to save it from falling over the edge.

"I nearly died," I say, going to the fridge for tonic water. There isn't any. "That changes you."

"All right, Jason Statham," Brady says, watching me over his beer. "You sure it's not just that you didn't get the girl for the first time in your life, and it's made you pouty?"

I stare at him. He smiles, head tilted, face warmer than his words make him sound. I know what he's doing: trying to snap me out of this, the way he does when I'm mopey or overthinking.

But this . . . is a little more than that.

"She just won't even speak to me," I say.

My voice rasps. I've been drinking too much, staying up too late. Everything feels so irrelevant. I've not gone back to work yet—journalists keep camping out at the restaurant, and Davide thinks it won't be good for me to be back in the kitchen environment yet. What he means is, the restaurant will be full of gawkers, and that'll be crap for everyone.

We're all just waiting for the world to lose interest in me. It won't be long, especially with Lexi staying completely off the radar, too. There are only so many "Are the lost houseboaters in love?" articles that can run when the two of us won't give them any new photos.

"What did you do? That's the question," Brady asks, leaning against the countertop. "Or, because it's you, let me rephrase. Who did you sleep with that you shouldn't have?"

"Piss off, Brady," I say. Suddenly I can't bear to be around him. I know he's trying to help, but it's like he's got the wrong script, like he's shooting lines meant for someone else.

"All right, Zeke, whatever you need," Brady says softly, and I close my eyes for a moment, then reach for the beer I chucked his way.

"Sorry," I say.

"That's all right. You're probably a bit, you know, PTSD and shit."

I don't say anything. I am—I'm constantly on edge, as if at any moment someone's going to jump out at me with a knife, which is weird, because I don't remember feeling that way on the houseboat. But that's not why I snapped at Brady.

"Is this what real life is?" I say suddenly. "Sitting around and drinking beer, talking shit?"

"Yeah, pretty much," Brady says. "Why?"

"I don't know," I say. "I don't know. I think I just . . . remembered it being better."

~~~~~

Mum couldn't believe I went back to London. She only let me go when I said I'd be back in two days, and I felt a bit bad, because I'm not back up north for my family.

"You again," is how Marissa greets me when I enter The Anchor on Friday night.

It's quiet. The journalists and trauma-tourists have all left now, probably chasing some other poor person living their personal nightmare.

Marissa pours me a gin and tonic without asking and sets it down in front of me as I settle in at my favorite bar stool.

"Just so you know," she says, "you've become an old regular. That is *very* sad at your near-prepubescent age."

"How is she?" I ask, sipping my drink. I'm still hungover from drinking beers with the boys yesterday, pretending to enjoy myself.

"Healing," Marissa says after a moment.

I nod. That's good. I want that for her.

"Zeke?" says a man beside me.

I feel Marissa stiffen, and I flick my gaze her way before I look at the man who's pulling up a bar stool next to me. He's got sensible glasses and short hair, kind of city smart, but there're holes in his ears where piercings used to be, so I'm guessing he had a different vibe once.

"Nicholas," he says, holding out his hand for me to shake.

"Journalist?" I ask, not shaking it.

"Sort of. Researcher." At my raised eyebrows, he adds, "I work for *Morning Cuppa.*"

Morning Cuppa is probably watched by millions of people a day. I look to Marissa.

"This one's been hanging about like a bad smell," she says. "I've seen him here most nights since you got back."

Interesting. He's waited until now to come over and talk to me.

"Your story, what you've been through—honestly, Zeke, it's incredible."

Nicholas has a real candor to him. A kind of intense earnestness. I imagine he's very good at his job.

"Our viewers would love to hear from you and Lexi. When you're ready to talk."

"Not interested," I say. "But thanks."

"That's such a shame," he says. "Especially when I've got Lexi on board."

My gaze flies up to Marissa again. She blinks. She didn't know, either.

"Lexi said yes? To going on TV?" I ask, finally giving Nicholas my full attention.

He nods. "Absolutely. The money was too good to pass up, I think. Obviously you know she's looking for her own place, and she's got her niece to look after . . ."

"Not her niece," Marissa says abruptly.

"Oh, no?" Nicholas says.

"Not her niece," Marissa repeats. She rubs emphatically at the glass she's drying with a cloth. "Lexi wouldn't say yes."

"Call her," Nicholas says. "She'll tell you."

Marissa narrows her eyes and pulls out her phone. Lexi's number is in that phone. Marissa's messaging her right now, just throwing a few words out there like it's nothing at all, when every moment of the day I'd kill for the chance to talk to her.

While we wait for Lexi's reply, I inspect Nicholas. He looks very relaxed. He smiles at me.

"Honestly, I have so many questions," he says. "But I don't want to put that on you right now. Not until you're ready."

I say nothing. In the last week I've encountered a full range of people who want things from me. It's incredibly weird. Most people like the story of us, I've realized—they aren't really interested in talking to me, they're just interested in telling other people they have. So when it comes to the actual conversation, they don't really say much.

Journalists are different. They want sound bites. They want to walk you into a little trap that gets them the exact arrangement of words they need, so they ask questions like, *And do you feel like loving Lexi made the journey harder, or did it keep you going?*

Basically, they don't want to know about the oil rig or the storm, they just want to know if Lexi and I were having sex.

"She's doing it," Marissa says in surprise. "She says . . . yeah. The money. It would mean she could move out and buy her own place, and there's somewhere for sale in the same building as Mae and Penny, so she wants the cash fast."

I cling to all the details this gives me. Lexi's stuck to her decision to move out and find her own place: good. She's rebuilt things with Penny and is prioritizing what matters to her most, time with Mae—also good. She's ready to talk about what happened on the boat to the entire nation, but won't talk to me: less good.

"You want me and Lexi on at the same time?" I say, turning to Nicholas. "Together?"

"Absolutely," he says.

I study him for a moment. Wondering how much he knows.

How much he's figured out. He's seen that it was Marissa, not me, who messaged Lexi—that probably tells him plenty.

"I'll do it," I say. "Just tell me when."

~~~~~~

"You look miserable," Jeremy says, as we walk through the grounds of Alnwick Castle three days later, looking for the perfect picnic spot.

Lyra has very strict criteria. No direct sunlight—she burns easily. No bugs. Nothing prickly. Basically, Lyra prefers not to go outdoors unless it's absolutely unavoidable, so she likes her picnic spot to be as indoorsy as possible.

"Is this why I'm here? Sibling intervention?" I say.

"Bonding time," Lyra says. "Mother's insistence."

"Ah." I should've guessed.

I catch Jeremy shooting Lyra a look, like, *Play nice, would you?*

The day after I got back, Lyra announced she was sick of walking on eggshells around me and I'd just have to tell her if she said something "triggering" (her quote marks) because she was no good at this weird fake thing everyone was doing. I've never felt more grateful for Lyra's bluntness. The weird fake thing's horrible. People fix on a smile when I turn up, and then they exclaim everything. *Zeke! How are you! Wow! So good to see you safe and well!*

"We would also like to spend time with you," Lyra adds, widening her eyes as though this should have been obvious. "Here, this'll do," she says.

Jeremy spreads out the blanket on the grass in a spot shaded by the castle wall.

"Would you like to . . . talk about it?" Jeremy asks eventually.

You can hear the effort it takes him. The strain in his voice. We're all a bit tense, especially Lyra, who has already announced she's on her sixth coffee of the day.

"The boat, you mean?"

I think of the ship's logs. The secrets once tucked into the houseboat's walls, now deep in the ocean. Everything Jeremy doesn't know, and whether it's my responsibility to tell him. My therapist's response to this question was an annoying *Only you can know, Zeke.* I keep turning up at his office and waiting for him to make me feel better, and he keeps saying, *You know therapy is a slow process,* and I want to scream at him that there's not time for slow. I can't go on like this, without her.

"What else would we mean?" Lyra says.

"I dunno," I say, but I think, *Lexi.* Everyone assumes it's the trauma of getting stranded at sea that's got me so lost and depressed, but I know it isn't that.

"You bought the boat looking for answers," Jeremy says after a moment. He glances sideways at me. "Did you find them?"

"Yeah, your whole Dad's-not-your-dad thing," Lyra says, turning her body toward me, the way she does when she's really listening. "How did that play out?"

My eyes flick to Jeremy. I didn't know he'd told Lyra about this. He looks back, unapologetic. Of course—the two of them share pretty much everything.

"It's all under the sea now, I guess," I say, looking down at the bag of food between us.

I start unpacking. I'm surprised to find my eyes pricking at the thought of Dad's logbooks being gone for good—I didn't realize that was bothering me. But it'd been like meeting him again, reading those passages, and I wish I'd had him for longer.

"I always thought it was a bit of a mad theory," Lyra says, reaching for a Scotch egg. "Jeremy's thing about Dad hiding stuff in the boat. The idea that something would still be there."

"They were still there," I say, noncommittal. "Some of Dad's logbooks, and some papers."

"Oh! So?" Lyra pushes. "What did you find out?"

"Lyra," I say.

"Yeah?"

"I don't think we should talk about it now."

"You say that about literally everything at the minute."

"Yeah, well, I'm not feeling chatty."

"How unusual!"

"Can you not?" I snap. "I've had a difficult fortnight, in case you didn't know."

She rolls her eyes. "I liked you better when you'd just got off the boat."

"Excuse me?"

"This," she says, waving her hand at me. "Sad victim Ezekiel. Lonely you-don't-get-me Ezekiel. He's come back over the last week. But when you got off that boat you had some grit to you for the first time in your life."

"Lyra." It's Jeremy this time. He sits forward, taking a can of lemonade. "Back off."

"No, you've always gone too easy on him, Jer." She rounds on me. "You have so much potential. You could be someone. And you just waste it dossing around and whining. This whole experience could be the making of you."

The making of you. Like I'm currently unmade, a messy bed.

"I know you're different from me and Jeremy. I know you don't have the focused gene—I know you missed out on the Ravenhill IQ, but— What?"

I think I sort of snorted.

"Nothing."

"No, what? That wasn't nothing."

"It doesn't matter. Go on. I'm useless, you and Jeremy got all the good genes . . ."

"That's not what I said at all."

"She's just trying to say she gets that you're not quite like us, Ezekiel," Jeremy says. "It's not your fault. It's just the way you were made."

His tone is so patronizing, and suddenly it just doesn't seem to matter, holding this back. I don't *want* to. I'm miserable, and for a nasty split second I don't see why I should have to be miserable and everyone else gets to live in blissful sunny ignorance.

"Actually, I wasn't made different. *You* were."

Jeremy frowns behind his square glasses. He used to wear dorky round ones, but his wife, Veronica, chose him these. She's been slowly improving him, polishing him up to shine like the successful man he is.

"What?"

"You weren't Dad's kid."

As soon as I've said it, I regret it. This is all wrong. Jeremy's everything I'm not, but he's still my brother—I still love him. And I don't want to hurt him.

"Jer, I'm sorry," I say, rubbing my forehead. "I shouldn't have told you like this."

He lowers his drink. Behind him, a group of children run by, yelling something about invaders coming to the castle. One straggles behind, using his sword as a walking stick to help him scale the slope.

"You're serious?" Jeremy says. "Dad? He . . ."

"I'm sorry. It was all . . . He had this folder of documents hidden on the boat. Paige knew, you know, his neighbor?"

"The weird one?" Jeremy says. He sounds slightly strangled.

"Yeah. It was her brother. He was your biological dad." My heart pounds. "Mum had an affair with him in the nineties."

"*Mum* did?" Lyra says. "I mean, obviously Mum did. I just can't . . ." She trails off, staring blankly at me. "I cannot imagine that. Are you *sure*?"

"I'm sure."

I guess this part'll be harder for them than it was for me. I always thought my mum had cheated on Dad. I always thought she was a liar. It was never particularly hard to believe, either: my mum's good at secrets, one of those stiff-upper-lip people who'll never show you even a hint of their trauma. Her emotions are so packed away I'm not sure she'd know how to start talking about them. The idea of her making a bad decision is pretty mind-blowing, but the idea of her hiding it from us? Not so much.

"But . . . Paige's brother died," Jeremy says. His forehead's wrinkled.

"Yes," I say quietly. "He did."

I'm pretty sure he died before I was born. I don't know if it's better or worse to know that the man was gone by the time he wrecked my parents' marriage, but it hurts to think that he never had the chance to know Jeremy.

"Oh," Lyra says.

She reaches for Jeremy's hand. I look away. Lyra's never once held my hand. I don't know how it happened—how the two of them became a two. But I'm so sick of desperately wanting to worm my way into the space between them when they've never left me room.

"So my dad wasn't my dad," Jeremy says slowly. "He was your dad."

"Yes."

"And Lyra's dad."

"Yes."

"And my dad . . . He's dead."

"I'm sorry."

"Right," Jeremy says, blinking rapidly. "Well. I suppose I've still got a dead dad, so it's not all that different, really."

I stare at him. Lyra's nodding.

"Right, totally," she says, patting his hand. "That's such a good way to look at it."

They're like . . . they're a different species to me. The thought that my father wasn't really my father ate away at me for years—it changed me. But Jeremy's taken it on board as though I've just re-scheduled his Waitrose delivery.

"Thank you for telling me," Jeremy says. He clears his throat. "I'll go for a walk, I think."

"I'll come," Lyra says, already standing, but he waves her off.

We watch him walk away for a while, and then, on impulse, I stand and chase him.

He looks around in surprise. He'd expected Lyra, I guess. He should've known better. I've always been the one chasing be-hind him.

"I really am sorry, Jeremy," I say. "I know this is a lot."

He nods. "I suppose it is," he says. He looks toward the castle, squinting in the sunlight. "Right now it just seems a bit odd."

I feel a moment of kinship with my brother. Things've been feel-ing a bit odd for me lately, too.

"It'll need to sink in."

"I'm sorry as well," he says, glancing at me as we walk. "I *did* always think it was . . . you. That you were the odd one out."

"I am," I say. "I'm kind of realizing now that this really doesn't change that. It was an excuse, I guess. I wanted something to ex-plain it. Other than me being, you know, basically just shitter than you two."

Jeremy frowns. "Ezekiel. You're not 'shitter' than me and Lyra. You're different. You're the creative one. Your brain works in ways the two of us don't understand. That's not worse, or better, it's just not the same."

He's never put it like that before. To be honest, we've never really had a conversation like this before. The closest we've ever come was that pint we had together, the night when we discussed buying back the houseboat.

"Look. Things have—Veronica and I have been going through a bit of a tough patch over the last few months," Jeremy says, without looking at me. "And she's asked me to do some work on . . . feelings, and expressing them, and . . . She's asked me to step up, actually." He shoots me a quick glance. "It's made me look at myself rather differently."

"God, I'm really sorry to hear that," I say, a little shaken. Veronica and Jeremy have been together since I was a kid. I don't know Veronica well, but the two of them have always seemed unshakable— the young suburban power couple.

"We're working through it. But I'm learning some rather uncomfortable things about myself in the process," Jeremy says, pressing his lips together. "It's occurred to me lately that as children . . . Lyra and I weren't always as kind to you as we should have been. I'm sorry for that."

I swallow down on the sudden tightness in my throat and resist the temptation to brush that off.

"Thank you," I say instead. "Thanks. That's . . . yeah."

"This Lexi," Jeremy says. He's still not looking at me, just walking, eyes downcast against the sun. "She's what's getting you down?"

"I know you think we just had some kind of weird . . . trauma romance . . ."

I see him wince at that and it almost makes me laugh.

"But I fell in love with her. I love her."

He nods. He's trying.

"And she's gone completely silent?"

"She won't speak to me."

"Perhaps she can't bear to, after what happened to you both. It *was* a trauma, Ezekiel."

"I know," I say.

I'm actually kind of grateful to hear him say that—Lyra's been acting like I went on a sailing trip and keep complaining about it, and she's right, it's bringing out the victim in me. I don't know what I want people to say, really. What I need seems to change all the time.

"But I don't think it's because of the trauma. When we got back, Lexi was with all her family, and then suddenly, she just . . ." I flatten down my curls, trying to think. "Someone pulled her away really fast. At the time, I thought she was just going for some quiet time with Mae—that's Lexi's best friend's kid. Lexi helped raise her, she's almost a mother to her, really. But the more I think back on the whole thing, how quickly they pulled Lexi away . . . I don't know. I wonder if something *happened*. Brady said this stupid thing about how I must've done something wrong, and now I can't stop thinking about it."

"Done something wrong?" Jeremy asks.

"Actually, he said I probably slept with someone I shouldn't have," I say, with a laugh I don't mean.

Jeremy says nothing for a while, just walking along, hands linked behind his back.

"Lexi helped to raise her friend's child?"

"Yeah. I told you, she's amazing."

Jeremy adjusts his glasses, pausing to look out at the view over the green fields surrounding the castle. The sunlight's lower now, giving each tiny blade of grass a shadow.

"Where's the dad? Is he not in the picture?" he asks.

I shake my head. "A one-night stand who didn't want anything to do with the baby, apparently."

Jeremy *hmm*s again.

"When you came up to sell Dad's boat," he says, "did you stay in Gilmouth for long?"

He's using that measured voice he slips into when he's solving a puzzle.

"Just one night," I say, watching a family clearing up their picnic below us. The castle looms behind, and for a strange second its bulk reminds me of the shadow of the oil rig.

"Alone?"

"Pardon?" I turn to stare at Jeremy.

"Did you sleep with someone that night? If I remember correctly, during that year after Dad's death, you were out every night with a different woman."

There's only a *hint* of judgment in his voice—not bad, by Jeremy standards.

"I think I . . . Yeah, I brought someone back to my hotel room."

"Where did you meet her?"

"Where are you going with this?" I say, but my heart is starting to beat too fast. "I met her at the pub. There's, like, one pub in Gilmouth."

"The pub where you met Lexi?"

"I mean . . . yeah."

Like a gust of wind, it comes over me: I'd had that weird feeling of déjà vu at the pub on that first night, hadn't I? I knew I'd met someone chatting across that bar before. I'd wondered for a split second if it had been Lexi, but then—like I'd told her—I figured it can't have been, because I would've remembered her.

At the time when I sold the boat, Lexi was away, but Penny was working behind the bar at The Anchor. Lexi told me all about how Penny was in those days, how she drank too much, how she always ended up going back with someone.

What if . . . what if that someone had been me?

"Can't you remember her? The woman you slept with?" Jeremy asks, and this time the judgment's definitely there.

And justified, I guess. It's just . . . at that stage of my life . . . I was going out almost every night, drinking, and the women did . . . blur.

"You think I slept with her best friend?" My voice is croaky.

"Worse," Jeremy says, his mouth set in a grim line. "How old is this woman's kid?"

My hand flies to my chest.

"What?"

"How old is she?"

"No, I'm always—I always used protection even when I was a stupid teenager."

I suddenly feel like it's hard to breathe.

"Condoms are only ninety-eight percent effective even if used perfectly," Jeremy says, raising his eyebrows slightly behind his glasses. "And I don't think a drunk teenage boy counts as perfect. I believe the percentage drops to eighty-something in reality."

"Eighty-something?" I'm clutching at my chest, gripping the fabric of my T-shirt.

"Even if you used it perfectly, Ezekiel, ninety-eight percent means that if you have sex one hundred times, two of those times, some sperm—"

"Oh my God."

"So the kid," Jeremy says, infuriatingly calm, "how old is she?"

"She's . . . She's . . ." I can't sort through the fog of my mind. "Four. She's four."

I remember the conversation Lexi and I had on the floor of the houseboat bathroom. How Lexi had said Mae is *four and two months, to be precise, which she always prefers you to be.*

"Four and two months," I say. I feel like my heart's straining to reach my hand, shoving against my ribs. I'm light-headed. Dizzy. This can't be true.

"Four years and two months, plus nine months, that's just shy of five years."

There's no judgment or mockery in Jeremy's face now. He's entirely serious.

"Dad's heart attack was five and a half years ago," he says. "It took about six months to sort all the legal business after that, didn't it? Do you recall when you sold the boat? You got rid of it pretty sharpish, if I remember rightly."

"It was about a week after I turned eighteen," I say hoarsely. I remember because there'd been loads of faff about my age—at seventeen, I was too young to sell it, so I'd had to wait until after my birthday.

"Well, then. The dates add up perfectly."

"No. No. It can't be that."

I stagger toward a tree by the path, needing something to lean on. I rest my back against the trunk, turning away from the sunshine to stare at the cold castle wall.

"You said Lexi's friend pulled her and the child away. You said—"

"I know," I snap, "but it can't be that. It *can't* be that."

Because if I am Mae's father, then Lexi will never, ever forgive me.

Lexi

"TRY THE RED, try the red," Penny says, draping a dress on top of the enormous pile of clothes that I'm clutching in both arms.

"Red makes me look stressed," I tell her.

It's the first day of school. After dropping a very excited Mae at the gate in her adorable new uniform, we fled from the eager-eyed parents we already knew from preschool, all desperate for gossip about my misadventures—*I can't imagine what it was like! That Ezekiel, he's so handsome, isn't he!*—and have come to the high street to find me an outfit for my TV appearance.

I am not the sort of person who has a TV appearance. Or an "outfit," to be honest. I just have clothes, vaguely assembled in a combination that allows me to cover up the maximum number of stains and worn-out bits.

"I'm not sure it's the color palette, Lex. I think it's all the stress that's making you look stressed, probably? Here, take this one as well."

"Is this secretly a workout?" I ask, hefting the clothes into a new position, arm muscles groaning. "Have you actually brought me shopping to try to make me exercise by stealth?"

"You need options!" Penny says.

There's something frenetic about Penny today. She's always been an emotional person, but lately she seems to be swinging from one extreme to the other several times a day. She's not sleeping well—the other night I woke from a nightmare about the rig crumbling away beneath Zeke, and I went downstairs and found Penny crying quietly over a glass of milk in the kitchen. It turns out she'd had a nightmare, too. I know these things will happen to me—I accept that. But why are they happening to her, too? *Maybe it's sympathy pains*, she'd told me, pulling me in for a hug, and I'd held her tightly, wishing I could take away the pain I've caused her.

"I would never wear that," I say, examining the pale pink dress Penny has pulled from a rail and is holding critically at her eye level. "It's not me."

She smiles.

"What?"

"You're totally right, it's not, it's way more me than you," Penny says, shoving it back. "But I feel like two months ago you wouldn't have said that. You'd have just asked me which makes you look best. Now. How about this, then?"

She pulls out a jumpsuit. It's black, structured, with a tuxedo-style front that ties at the waist. It'll suit my curves, which are slowly returning now that I'm back to snacks and square meals, and the sharpness of its lines appeals to me. It's a no-nonsense jumpsuit. Dressed-up, but badass.

"Look at your face," Penny says, beaming. "This is the one."

"It's too expensive," I say, getting close enough to read the label. "I don't want to try it on."

"I'll pay!" Penny says, already walking toward the changing room.

"What? Don't be ridiculous," I say, "you're not buying me a jumpsuit for three hundred quid."

"Why not?"

"I don't know, because you don't *have* three hundred quid to spend on jumpsuits for me?"

"I'd do anything for you," she says, turning so suddenly I almost walk into her. Her expression is oddly fierce. "You know that, right? I know I'm not perfect, but I've only ever wanted you to be happy, and—"

"Penny!"

She's started to cry.

"Oh my God, what's going *on* with you?" I pull her away from the women waiting outside the changing rooms, who are eyeing us with curious interest. "Is something the matter?"

"No, no," she says, wiping her face furiously. "I'm fine! I just want you to be OK. And I'm worried you're . . ." She looks up at me, searching. "You are OK, aren't you, Lexi?"

"Of course," I say. "Of course I am! You know me. Tough as old boots."

"About that man . . ." Her voice drops to a whisper. "About Zeke . . ."

I stiffen, glancing toward the changing rooms. "The queue's gone down," I say, but she catches my arm.

"Did anything happen with you two?"

"Well, we got lost at sea . . ."

"I mean, I know you took him back to the houseboat. Or he took you back to the houseboat, since it was his, or—whatever. But after that first night. You didn't like him like that, did you?"

I flush, ashamed. I don't want to lie. But I desperately don't want to tell Penny that I fell in love with the scumbag who abandoned her, either, and I can see she's got an inkling, and it's frightening her. I *hate* seeing Penny frightened.

"We were mostly just focused on staying alive, Penny. I'm fine, OK?"

"You'd tell me if you weren't?"

I feel a flicker of irritation. Every day I wake up and lurch to grip the sides of my bed, not because I think I'm in danger, but because everything feels wrong: the sea should be moving beneath me. I sometimes remember moments so starkly it's as if I've been transported back to the rig or the boat or the storm. Do I have to tell her that? Shouldn't she just know?

I *am* fine: I'm coping. I'm not lying. But I can feel that Penny is *desperate* for me to get back to normal, and there's only so much I can do to fix myself, especially when I can't tell her that the really broken part of me is my heart.

"I'll try the jumpsuit," I say. "But *I* will pay for it if I want it. OK?"

"OK," she says, with a shaky smile. "But I'm buying you some shoes. You need to stop wearing those grotty black boots, Lex. They look like you dredged them out of the ocean."

"Well," I say, "I kind of did."

Her phone pings, and her eyes widen. "Oh, God!" she says.

"What?"

"Your memorial!"

"My what?"

Now everyone in the changing area is staring at us again. Someone emerges from behind a curtain, and I drag Penny into the empty cubicle, dumping the huge pile of clothes she gave me onto the bench along the back wall.

"Your memorial. It was this policewoman's idea. They said it would help us all move on. So we scheduled it for next week. I don't think anyone canceled it. I've just had an alert about confirming the flowers," she says weakly.

"The flowers for my . . . funeral?"

"Memorial!"

"I actually don't know that that is any less macabre, but thank you," I say, gazing at myself in the mirror.

The lighting in these places is always awful—I don't know why they do that. Don't they want me to feel good in these clothes? But I'm lit by bright yellowish bulbs from right above my head, catching every dip and shadow as I wriggle out of my jeans and T-shirt.

My body looks back at me, soft, hard, strong, weak. Now I don't just see what it ought to be, and what it isn't. I see a body that got me through hell, no matter what shape it is, no matter how much weight sits on my hips. I look at the softness beneath my belly button and place a hand there for a moment, then slide it around to my waist, up to my breast.

"I'm sorry, is talking about your memorial turning you on, or . . ."

I drop my hand. "I'm just looking at myself," I say. "Properly. Which I don't think I have ever done in a changing room before."

Penny smiles slightly, putting her phone down on the bench and sitting beside it.

"I like your face right now," she says. "You're looking at yourself like you're amazing. I'm *always* trying to get you to do that."

She is, this is true. Penny has told me I'm beautiful every day of my life. *Morning, gorgeous!* she'll say when I come down the stairs. *Night, beautiful!* But it never sank in—it always just slid over me, like the words didn't count.

"Out on the water," I say, "it really stopped mattering. All the negative thoughts I have about my body, they just . . . I didn't have *time* for them. They seemed so much less important, and after a few days of genuinely not thinking about myself that way, it's like I got out of the habit."

"I love that. That makes me so happy," Penny says, but her voice is quiet and she's looking down, fiddling with a coat hanger in her lap. "But I . . . I wish you'd tell me more about your time at sea. I just can't imagine it. I hate that you've had this crazy experience and I'm here on the other side of it, with no idea what you've been through. It's like there's a big gap between us all of a sudden. There was never a gap before."

I reach for the jumpsuit, fingering the fabric.

"I think maybe there was, Pen," I say. "Lately."

She looks up, hurt.

"Do you mean that?"

"Not in a bad way, I just think . . . Look at the houseboat, for instance. You would have told me about that, before, but you didn't." I raise a hand when she starts to protest. "Things *have* been changing. I think I've been living in the past a bit. It's like I've been stuck in that first year with Mae, when you really needed me, and she really needed me, and I had . . ." I trail off.

"You had . . . ?"

"A role. Someone to be."

I remember feeling in a weird way that I had been waiting for it. Like when Penny phoned me and choked out the truth about the pregnancy, something fell into place. *Aha*, my brain said. *Here's what you were born to do.*

"Who do you *want* to be, Lexi?" Penny whispers.

I fasten the jumpsuit at the waist, then lift my gaze to the full-length mirror.

The jumpsuit makes me look like myself, but fiercer. Walking through the wind after dropping Mae at school has turned my hair wild—I've stopped wearing it tied back, enjoying how good it feels to have clean hair, and now it tangles and tumbles over the jumpsuit's bold shoulders, giving all its sharp lines an edge of chaos. The woman in the mirror looks as if she's survived storms and heartbreak, but she also looks like she's running the show. She has main-character energy; that's what Zeke would say.

"Her," I say, meeting my own eyes, pointing at my reflection. "I want to be her."

~~~~~

Marissa is driving me to the *Morning Cuppa* studio, but Penny insists on coming along to support me. She seems almost as nervous as I am, fidgeting in the front seat—she always goes up front because of her car sickness. I'm sweating. I can't believe I'm doing this. The money is amazing, but I'm not sure any amount is worth what I'm about to do. Not the television part: I mean seeing Zeke.

"Christ," Marissa says after a long stretch of silent motorway. "Where's Mae when you need someone to chat shit about Peppa Pig for an hour or so?"

"I should have called Zeke," I say, leaning my head against the glass. "I should have called him before now. Seeing him again for the first time like this, it's . . ."

"Cruel?"

I swallow. I *have* been punishing him. I know that, deep down. I wanted him to figure out what he'd done, and I wanted him to feel *awful* for abandoning Mae.

But I also knew that if I spoke to him, I'd break. I've been living in Penny's flat, in Mae's world, and the idea of letting Zeke into my life again even an *inch* felt like such a monumental betrayal. I've been using every ounce of energy not thinking about him.

"What do you mean, it's cruel?" Penny says, voice too high.

"You haven't seen the poor boy at the bar every night, pining," Marissa says, reaching for her sunglasses as we turn westward. Her car is cluttered with unopened mail, empty Coke cans and various spare pairs of glasses, all serving slightly different purposes, all largely indistinguishable to the untrained eye. "He looks worse than he did when he got off that boat."

I press my hands into my stomach and close my eyes. "Don't."

"Why?" Penny says, turning to look at me over her shoulder. "Why is he looking so awful? Do you think he knows about Mae?"

"No," I say, voice strangled, as Marissa says, "No, Penny, I mean because he's madly in love with Lexi."

"Marissa, shut up," I say, glancing at Penny for long enough to catch her shocked expression and then shutting my eyes again, pressing my head to the glass.

She'll find out soon enough, I suppose. We're only on *Morning Cuppa* for a fifteen-minute slot, so I'm hoping there isn't time for us to talk in too much depth about what happened at sea, but there is no way we can discuss that experience without revealing quite how deeply we fell in love.

"She doesn't know?" Marissa says, catching my eye in the mirror. "Lexi."

There is a lot of weary judgment in that *Lexi*.

"Are you serious? Lexi?" Penny is straining around in her seat now, gripping the headrest, staring at me with the exact horrified expression I've been desperate to avoid.

"It doesn't matter if he's—if he thinks . . . It doesn't matter what he feels about me," I say, turning my gaze to the gray town streaking past the car window. All towns look gray to me lately. "He's turned out to be a dickhead. *The* dickhead, the original dickhead, the dickhead we refer to as the standard by which all other dickheads are measured. He's the man who abandoned you, Penny."

She's quiet for too long. Still staring at me.

"Marissa," she says, with a wobble in her voice. "Can we pull over?"

"What, here? Now? Are you going to vomit?" Marissa asks, already checking her mirrors. "Stop turning around, you know that makes it worse."

"Just do it, would you?"

We pull over into a parking space. Penny climbs out of the car and walks away down a suburban street—one of those ones where everyone has extended their houses so much they all look kind of monstrous, growing attic conversions out of the tops of their heads. The cars are shiny and sleek; a woman pulling up weeds in her front garden eyes the staggering Penny with open suspicion.

"What's she . . ." I trail off, watching Penny fold over on herself, covering her face with her hands.

"Hmm," Marissa says from the driver's seat.

"What does that mean?"

"Penny means well, but she doesn't always do the right thing, and I've been wondering for a while if this is one of the times when Penny has been a bit of a coward."

Marissa yanks on the handbrake and checks her watch.

"Go talk to her. You've got three minutes. And, Lex—"

She stops me as I climb out of the rear passenger seat.

"Don't let her make you feel bad. And don't let her squirm out of telling the truth. Penny sucks at owning up to things, and she needs to get better at it."

"She doesn't mean—" I start, but Marissa holds up her hand.

"You coddle her. You know you do. She's an adult. She can cope with a bit of a bollocking when she deserves one. In fact, it might do her some good. We're all dickheads sometimes, Lex, as your mum used to say—even sweet Penny."

I frown as I climb out of the car. Marissa has always been harder on Penny than I have—she's only known Penny as an adult, whereas I saw the bedraggled, sad girl who used to climb our back fence to escape the chaos of her mother's house. The Anchor was Penny's retreat, her safe place; *I'm* that for her, and I never want that to change.

I catch up to her as she leans against the fence outside a house with Grecian-style pillars on its porch. The sun is shining, but weakly, as if someone has watered it down.

"Penny?"

She's sobbing into her hands. I tug at her arm, trying to see her face.

"What's going on?" I ask.

"Do you love him?"

I open my mouth to say what she wants to hear—*No! Of course I don't! How could I possibly love the man who turned his back on you?* But the lie won't come out. I think of him for a second, unable to help myself. I see him tanned and bearded, a breeze lifting his curls, and it winds me; I press the heel of my hand to my chest.

"I haven't wanted to ask," Penny says, her words almost lost in her tears. "But I think I already know the answer."

"Penny, it doesn't matter, it's over now. It's done. I'm sorry that . . . I'm sorry for . . ."

She emerges from behind her hands and looks fiercely at me.

"*You* do not need to be sorry."

I am sorry, though. It feels like such a betrayal to have loved him so deeply. It feels like a betrayal every time I let my guilty mind slide into the sweet, devastating pain of remembering him. And it *definitely* feels like a betrayal every time I think that maybe I don't care, maybe I don't give a damn about the worst thing he could possibly have done, because I love him so much I'd forgive it all.

"I need to tell you something," Penny says, taking a gulping breath.

I glance back toward the car, and then toward the Grecian-pillared house, where someone is peering out of an upstairs window. We are officially making a scene, and we are also approaching the end of the three minutes Marissa gave me.

"Does it need to be now?" I try gently. "Because—"

"Yes," she says, her voice a little firmer.

She pushes off the fence and starts walking again, further away from Marissa's car. I walk along the pavement beside her, glancing at her, trying to read her. Is it about Mae? Or is it Penny? Is she OK? I've been worrying about her not sleeping—was that a sign of something serious? Is she ill?

"When I got pregnant with Mae, I was so ashamed of myself," she says. She's twisting her hands, tugging at her sleeves. "I knew you and your mum would be disappointed in me. She was always telling me off for going home with customers, and you . . . I knew you thought the same."

"I didn't," I protest, though I remember how it felt every time I saw Penny flirting with some cocky, over-aftershaved guy at the bar, how sometimes I wished she'd just be *sensible*.

"I remember you asked me if I knew who the father was," she says. "Not who the father was, but *if I knew*."

I wince. "Sorry. That was totally insensitive."

"And I did know. It was this cute curly-haired eighteen-year-old who I could've sworn was called Zach. He had made it very clear that he only wanted one thing for one night, like he'd spelled it out *so* much, checking in with me all the time that I was cool with it all, and I'd said sure, absolutely, same here."

I actually cannot bear to think about this. The very idea of Penny with Zeke makes me want to claw at my skin or hit something. I look back toward Marissa's car.

"Shall we just—"

She talks over me, determined. "Then when your mum asked how involved I wanted him to be, I felt so panicked. Imagine this stranger coming in and being a *huge* part of your life all of a sudden, Lex," she says, finally looking at me.

Her face is beseeching. I start to feel cold, despite the heat of the sun, despite the nerves that have had me sweating in the back of the car since we set off this morning.

"This stranger who made it so clear he never wanted to speak to you again. I mean, what if he decided to push for joint custody of the baby? It was such a mindfuck, being pregnant when I had *never* expected to have a kid, and there you and your mum were, offering to drop absolutely everything to help, and it felt so nice. You said the baby and I could live with you both. It sounded so amazing. I wanted *us* to be a family, and I didn't want some guy—"

"Penny," I say, pulling her arm to stop her. "What are you telling me?"

She starts to cry again. I step back slightly, and then I remember what Marissa said in the car, and instead of easing off like I usually would, I push.

"Tell me, Penny. Say it."

"I never told him, Lexi," she whispers. "I never told Zeke I was pregnant."

I drop my hand from her arm and reel away. "You—you—" I turn back to her. "Are you fucking joking? Are you *fucking joking*?"

"Don't be angry with me!" she sobs. "I can't stand when you yell at me, Lexi, please don't, please don't be mad."

"You said you told him and he didn't want anything to do with the baby!"

"It was the easiest thing to say!" she cries. "And what did it matter? He didn't want a kid! He *was* a kid! I felt like this was better for everyone, the baby included, and . . ."

"You weren't thinking about Mae," I snarl. I am *hot* with rage. "You were thinking about yourself. You were thinking about avoiding a difficult conversation and getting exactly what you wanted, no matter the consequences for anyone else."

She looks horrified. "Is that what you think of me?" she whispers.

"There have been . . ." I press my hand to my eyes. "How many times have you had the opportunity to tell us the truth? You let us raise Mae thinking her father didn't *want* her, and in reality you never even gave him the chance to."

"You know that's not what she thinks!" Penny says, and there's fire in her now; she straightens her shoulders. "I have *never* let my daughter feel unloved. Don't you dare make me feel like a bad mother."

"I'm—you're—" I break off to let out a growl of emotion, turning back toward the car. "Why would you tell me this *now*? I'm hours away from getting interviewed on the television and—and *seeing* him and . . ."

"That's why, Lex. You had to know. I didn't realize you cared so much about him, or I would have said sooner, but it just seemed like . . ." She sounds so miserable. "It seemed like it was better to stick to the story."

"Better for you."

"Better for *you*. Better for Mae!"

"How? How is this better? No, I don't have time for this," I say, walking away from her.

I scowl at the person in the window of that house, the woman with the limp handful of dandelions in her front garden. I give no shits about causing a scene. I feel like I want to burn something down, let this whole street char and smoke like the oil rig, as if that might help with the roaring emotions tearing through me. Aside from the years of lies, the thing that hurts the most right now is knowing that the agony of the last month has been built on *nothing*. Knowing that Zeke is hurting, too, that I've been hurting him, and he never even did anything wrong.

I yank open the car door, getting into the front seat. Fuck her car sickness. I don't want to have to look at the back of her head right now.

"Drive," I say to Marissa, as Penny climbs in the back.

"Lexi, please," she sobs.

"Just drive."

Marissa pulls out into the traffic. The only thing that will help with this storm in my chest is seeing Zeke. Telling him I love him. I want to run into his arms and bury myself there the way I would when the wind was raging around the boat, when he felt like the only safe place in the world.

I have no idea how the hell I'm going to handle all this. But at least I know where to find him.

Zeke

"YOU SURE ABOUT this?" Jeremy says.

Weirdly, he's the one person I wanted with me today. There's just something so solid about Jeremy. Solid and reliably irritating: he spent the entire journey here telling me what I had better not say on camera, all of which will now definitely end up coming out of my mouth.

"Sure about seeing Lexi, you mean, or going on TV?" I ask, adjusting my hair in the greenroom mirror.

We've been given a few minutes on our own. I was desperate for the hovering makeup artists and production assistants to leave. But now there's no distraction from the pit in my stomach.

"Actually, I meant the outfit," Jeremy says, clapping a hand on my shoulder.

"Did you just make a joke, Jeremy?" I ask, meeting his eyes in the mirror.

He smiles. I smile back. This is all new and kind of nice.

"The outfit is very trendy, I'm sure," Jeremy says. He's only thirty-two. The way he talks, you'd think he was sixty.

I do like the outfit. It's a fairly traditional suit, in navy blue, but oversized, the trousers too long. I'm wearing three silver necklaces over a white tee underneath the jacket, the three necklaces I wore on the night Lexi and I met. The ones that came with us on the houseboat.

"Five minutes!" someone says, poking their head around the door.

People keep doing this—leaning around things to talk to me, as if they can't afford the time to come all the way over. This whole place makes me edgy. I'm waiting to be caught out saying something stupid. I can't even believe I've agreed to this. It's like the opposite of our time alone at sea: here, the whole world will be watching me. I've never felt less comfortable.

"So I don't get to see her first?" I say to the head that's already trying to disappear behind the door again.

"Sorry, no!" she says with a sympathetic grimace. "No time!"

"Hmm," Jeremy says, unimpressed, as she ducks away.

"You smell bullshit?"

"You could put it like that, yes."

I do, too. I glance toward the clock.

"I'm going to see if I can find her," I say, heading for the door and out into the maze of corridors beyond.

"Oh, excuse me, Zeke!" someone calls immediately.

I sidestep down a different route. There're just endless white doors. It reminds me of the rig. Dread rises in my chest.

"Zeke, hi," someone else says, touching my elbow. "We just need you to step back into the greenroom while we wait for go-time? It won't be long now."

"I just need a minute," I say, still walking, leaving their trailing hand behind.

More doors, all closed, all unmarked.

"Where's Lexi's dressing room?" I ask the person tailing me.

"Oh, sorry, I can't—"

"If you don't tell me, I'm going to start opening random doors," I say, taking a left. Am I going in a circle here?

"She's not in her dressing room anymore," the person says. "She's . . ."

I see her. I've stepped into the edge of the studio—I can see the hosts sitting on their strange fake sofa with their cups of tea and their cozy rug, and I can see the shadowy audience curving away from me, and I can see Lexi. The rest fades instantly.

She's on the other side of the studio, in the wings. She hasn't spotted me yet—she's looking out into the audience. She drops her hands to her stomach, smoothing down the fabric of her jumpsuit.

Seeing her reminds me of the moment on the houseboat when it began to rain after all those endless thirsty hours. I've been starving for her, and here she is, looking more beautiful than ever. Her hair is loose and wild, brightened to a new shade of blond, and her wide eyes are lined with thick lashes so that they pop even brighter. I've never seen her all made up like this, and she looks different, but she somehow still looks exactly like the Lexi from the boat, too. My Lexi.

For a second I think about running to her, even as the hosts of *Morning Cuppa* burst into laughter over some news piece about dating apps. I could just storm right in front of them. Reach for her, tell her I promise I never knew about Mae, tell her I'm so sorry and I know I've hurt her, and if I could go back in time and fix it, I would, I'd be there for every step of the last four years and three months of that girl's life, but—

There's a warning hand on my shoulder. Two large security guards in black, with various things hanging off them that, on inspection, are walkie-talkies, but still give off the vague air of potentially being guns.

"You're on in two minutes, Zeke, just hold back!" whispers someone new at my other elbow.

Lexi's seen me now. Her eyes widen slightly. She looks . . . I don't know. It's harder to read her than it should be. We're too far apart. We've so rarely stood at a distance like this, and never with all this noise around us, all these people . . .

"You OK?" says the stranger at my side. She's got headphones half on, one ear in, one ear out, and her smile is too bright. "All good?"

I keep looking at Lexi. I try to tell her without saying it. *I love you. I'm sorry. I love you so much.*

"Now, we've been talking this morning about how tough it can be to date in the modern world," says Delana, co-host of *Morning Cuppa.*

She's in a pink dress and slippers—wearing slippers is a *Morning Cuppa* thing. I think there're some waiting on the stage for me and Lexi. I stare at the tape marking the edges of the fake living room.

"So let's talk about one of the strangest tales of recent times: the adventure dubbed 'the twelve-night stand' by the tabloids. The story of Lexi and Zeke, who had a one-night stand that just didn't end! They spent twelve nights together on the houseboat they went back to after meeting for a drink at the pub and being swept out to sea. Talk about unusual, right? I mean, that's one way to really get to know a guy!"

"Right?" Yusuf says, laughing. "It's unconventional, for sure, but can a bonding experience like this really lead to true love? Should we all be jumping aboard with our crushes, and seeing if we can sail away into the sunset?"

Lexi and I haven't stopped looking at each other. This scene happening between us, it all looks so small. These people don't get it. They weren't there. They think it was a *bonding experience.* They think the boat made us what we are. But *we* did that, and we found each other in *spite* of being lost out there, and suddenly I can't fucking stand it, how they're making this feel like a gimmick when it was the biggest thing that's ever happened to me.

Lexi turns away. "I'm sorry," I watch her say, and then she's pushing between the gaggle of shadowy camera crew and producers.

"Now," Delana says, blinking a little faster—someone's talking in her ear. "We'll be hearing from them very soon, but first, we want to hear from the audience! Would *you* ever live on a houseboat?"

I turn around and do the same as Lexi, shaking off the hands trying to snag at my arms.

"I'm sorry," I tell someone, "but this is just not us."

~~~~~

I find her outside on the lot, the wind blowing in her hair. She's looking out at the traffic—it's noisy here, though you can't hear a single trace of road noise inside the studio. She's braced, standing with her feet planted. I remember she stood that way even before we went to sea. Like she's always been ready for waves underfoot.

"Hi," she says, turning to look at me over her shoulder. "I think we just pissed a lot of people off."

"Well, a lot of people just pissed me off." I walk toward her. It's as if there's something pulling me—I couldn't stay where I was if I tried. "So fair enough, I reckon."

"It's not their fault they don't understand," Lexi says, looking back out at the cars and lorries streaming by. "They're only doing what people do. They just want a good story. It's human nature."

I come to stand beside her, then reach out to take her hand. She grasps mine, and that touch is enough to send sensation surging through me. Too many feelings to name, but I'd call the whole powerful mess of it *love*, I guess: it's too much to be anything else. I just love her. That's all there is.

"Do you know?" she whispers, turning her head to look at me for a split second before glancing back to the road.

My heart hurts. "About Mae?"

I feel her stiffen and I hold her hand tighter.

"I didn't know she even *existed*, Lexi, I—"

"I know." She turns to me properly then, but her eyes are still downcast. "Penny told me on the way here. How did you figure it out?"

"Jeremy did what he does best."

"Be condescending?" Lexi says, then pulls a face at herself. "Sorry, sorry, not my place. I kind of forget I've still not even met him. I feel like I know him just from all our conversations on the boat about your family."

I laugh. "You're not far off. But no, I meant puzzles. He worked it out from the dates, and how you disappeared off with Penny and Mae at the marina." I swallow, sobering. "Did you think I'd lied to you? That I'd known all along and . . ."

"Not really," she whispers, then, "Maybe. Sometimes."

"I wish you'd thought better of me."

"But I didn't know you, that's what I told myself," she says, glancing up for one pained moment. Her eyes are full of tears. "And I knew Penny inside out. At least, I thought I did. Whereas I didn't know who you were in the real world."

I can't stand it any longer—I pull her in to my chest.

"You know me," I say, as she burrows her head into me, the way she has a hundred times before. I close my arms around her. "You think this world's more real? Look at us, we're in a place where people sit around pretending to have breakfast together at four in the afternoon, with a whole audience watching them drink tea. The fruit on that table isn't real. It's polished plastic. I have so much makeup on I can't really raise my eyebrows, Lexi."

I feel her smile as her shoulders lift on a quick gulp for breath.

"Was there *anything* more real than the life we had on the water?" I ask her, pulling back slightly. "It was—it was where I was most . . ." I close my eyes, frustrated with myself.

"It's OK," she whispers into my jacket. "It's where I was most myself. Is that what you mean?"

"Yeah. Exactly. And you cutting me out the way you did . . . It hurt so much because you knew me. Maybe better than anyone ever has. If *you* felt like you never wanted to see me again, then . . ."

"I know," she says, beginning to cry. "I hurt you. I wanted to hurt you. I thought *you'd* hurt the only person in the world who I love the way I love you."

I hold her so tightly I can feel her catching her breath. What I say next, it matters: I have to get it right, and I force myself to wait until the words arrange themselves the way I want them.

"If I'd known Mae was mine, she would have known every day that her dad was there for her. I would never have hurt her, and I never want to hurt her, Lexi. But I do want to know her. And I realize you may not want that. Penny may not want that. And that's going to be complicated."

"Complicated," she whispers into my chest. "We've not really *done* complicated, have we?"

"I mean, I don't think staying alive on the water was uncomplicated . . ."

"It was difficult," she says, finally lifting her face to mine. "But it wasn't complicated. We knew what we had to do."

I tilt my head, brushing her hair back from her face. "OK," I say, smiling down at her. "Well, we're good at difficult."

"We are good at difficult."

"Reckon it's worth giving complicated a go, too?"

"We've had a month off from peril and trauma," Lexi says. "We do probably need a new challenge."

I link my hands at the small of her back and look down into her face. She's more relaxed now, a smile lingering in the corners of her eyes. For a split second I remember how it felt to gaze at her like this on the lifeboat deck, just moments after we were rescued. How absolutely floored I was to get to hold her in my arms when I thought I never would again. It makes me want to keep living like that, keep feeling like that—not the terror but the gratitude. The intensity of this love. I don't want to lose it, not even for a moment.

"I love you," I whisper. "And I don't care how complicated things get. I'm not letting you go."

She smiles. "It doesn't end for us," she whispers back. "Remember? Not ever."

She kisses me, standing on tiptoe to bridge the space between us. I tighten my arms around her and close my eyes as she deepens the kiss, running her hands up my back like she wants me even closer. Somewhere in the back of my mind, I register the quiet click of the fire-exit door behind us, but I'm too lost in her to care.

"Oh, now, hey, would you look at that!" Yusuf says.

We break apart and turn to see him and a scuttling, bent-kneed cameraman coming toward us.

"I think we've walked into the middle of our happily ever after," Yusuf says, beaming. "Isn't that just perfect!"

Lexi

A STRING QUARTET is playing their own version of Taylor Swift's "Sweet Nothing." There are white balloons hanging from the rafters, interspersed with bright blue ones—the color reminds me of a summer sky. And there are giant pictures of me and Zeke hanging like tapestries from the walls.

"So it's not been a totally seamless transition from memorial to welcome home party," Zeke's sister says briskly, casting an eye over the main event space of Lemmington Hall. "And some of these lilies were repurposed from the funeral wreaths we couldn't get a refund on. But I think it's worked out pretty well, considering."

"Looks great to me. I like a lily. Where's Jeremy gone?" I ask.

"He's talking to Paige," Lyra says.

She widens her eyes in a way that manages to capture both the gravity of the situation and her vague dislike of Paige. She's jealous, perhaps. Jeremy has a new aunt—a whole new family, should he want it. Lyra strikes me as a woman who likes things neat, tidy and just so; rogue aunts aren't really her scene, particularly slightly scatty ones with houseboats. I happen to know that right now Lyra and Jeremy aren't speaking to their mum; Zeke calls her every day,

though, and between them all, with time, I'm confident they'll figure it out. Family is always complicated, but ultimately, the Raven-
hills *do* love one another, and lately I've started to think that as long
as you've got that, you have a really good shot at working out the rest.

A harassed-looking event organizer power-walks over with her
clipboard clutched to her chest like a shield. Lyra homes in on her
immediately.

"Cutlery!" she barks, and the woman jumps.

"Christ," Marissa says, appearing at my shoulder as Lyra drags
the event organizer off somewhere. "And I thought *you* were intimidating."

"You should have seen her directing Penny to parallel park in
the space outside when we arrived. Penny literally cried. Still"—I
watch Lyra go—"I think this is Lyra's way of telling Zeke she
missed him. All the funereal flowers, the perfect tablecloths, the
expense . . . it's a big, dysfunctional I-love-you."

"Is he here?" Marissa asks, glancing to the door.

I don't need to look to know he isn't. We've both noticed this: a
sort of instinct for where the other person is in a crowded room.

"He's nervous," I say, checking my phone again. "He went to
take a moment in the garden."

"You want to . . ."

"Yeah," I say, already moving.

Zeke and I have both noticed this as well: the tug that comes
when we're apart, as if whatever tethers us is pulling taut. Since we
joined hands again in that studio lot, we've barely parted. He's
cooked me truffle pasta and spiced jackfruit and every dish he used
to talk about on the water, and I've shown him the little details of
my life as it was before him: the best coffee shop in Gilmouth; my
favorite spot on the beach. It's been almost deliriously lovely, but
not—as suspected—without complication.

Penny is struggling. It's hard to untangle what she wants from all her guilt and shame and people-pleasing, to be honest, but she says she's ready for today, and I am trying to take her word for things instead of thinking I know best. Marissa's right: I do coddle her, and ultimately, that hasn't helped her at all.

I step out into the formal gardens and find Zeke immediately: he's in suit trousers and a silk shirt, hands in his pockets, staring down into the pond at the center of the garden. His curls are neater than they ever were on the boat, and the clothes are new to me, but the line of his neck is so familiar it could be my own. I know that the tilt of his head means he's thinking; I know that the hands in his pockets will be balled into nervous fists.

"Hey," I whisper, coming up behind him.

"Hey."

"OK?"

"Mm. Will be soon."

"She's going to love you," I say quietly, coming to stand beside him at the water's edge. "Even if she doesn't right away."

"I don't want to mess her up," he whispers.

"You think I'd let you anywhere near that girl if I thought you would?" I turn to kiss him on the cheek. "Trust me, even if you can't trust yourself yet."

"Hey, you two," comes a shaky voice from behind us.

We turn in unison. Mae is on Penny's hip, her special-occasion butterfly sandals tapping against Penny's leg as they approach. Mae's eyes turn wide and curious as they land on Zeke.

"Hi," Zeke says, then clears his throat. "Hello."

I keep hold of his hand. I can feel him trembling.

"Are you Lexi's boyfriend?" she asks.

"Yeah," he says, smiling. "That's me."

She inspects him closely. "OK," she says. "That's fine."

Penny manages a smile. "A glowing review, by Mae standards," she says, lowering her daughter to the ground.

For now, this is what we've decided to tell Mae; the rest can come later, when everyone feels a little readier. But even this feels pretty huge.

"You have curly hair," Mae says, staring up at Zeke. "Like me."

I feel the collective intake of breath—me, Penny, Zeke, all at once. I'm sure Mae feels it, too, and I smile to soften the atmosphere, taking her hand.

"Curly hair is the best," I tell her. "I wish mine was curly. You want to try skimming stones? Zeke's really good at it."

He takes my cue, dropping my hand as he crouches down beside her and sifts through the gravel of the path leading to the pond, looking for a flat-enough stone.

"This one's perfect," he says, voice catching slightly as he glances at Mae's profile. "You need one just the right size. Here, do you want to try first?"

I look at Penny. She's watching Zeke and Mae, her face tight and frightened. I feel the knot of anger I've carried this week beginning to loosen, and I reach toward her.

She takes my hand and holds tightly. "I'm sorry," she mouths at me, and I smile at her.

I might not be completely there with forgiving her, but I do understand why she lied. I know she just wanted to protect herself, and protect Mae, and that self-protection is big for Penny. I know these things are never as simple as they seem.

"I love you," I whisper to her, and Zeke and Mae glance up.

I could be talking to any one of them, really. I love them all, and lately, since we got home, I've had an almost compulsive need to say these things out loud. I wonder how long this feeling will last—knowing how lucky I am, and actually *feeling* it, instead of just moving through the days without noticing. I hope I can hold on to it forever.

"Are you the one who sailed away with Lexi?" Mae asks Zeke.

"Yeah, that's me." He skims a stone over the water—it bounces once, twice, three times.

She thinks about this. "Next time," she says, "can you call us to say you're going?"

Penny bursts out in surprised laughter.

Zeke grins. "OK. That's fair." He sobers, looking at her properly now, holding out a stone for her to take. "In future," he says, "I promise we'll always tell you what's going on."

She nods at this, then hurls her stone into the water. It lands with a satisfying *slup* of pond water, and the ripples spread outward, reaching for us, steady and sure.

"This is a welcome home party," Mae says, taking the next stone Zeke offers her and hurling it after the last one. "But this isn't your home. Is it? Do you live in Gilmouth like Mummy and Lexi?"

Zeke glances at me. We've touched on this a little, but we've not discussed what to say to Mae about it, and I feel Penny stiffen.

"I think home isn't really a place for me," he says. "It's people. My people. So I want to be where they are, because then I'm at home."

Mae thinks. "OK. So is Lexi your people?"

"One of them," he says, with a small smile. "Yeah."

"She's mine, too. Her and Mummy and Ryan."

"I know," Zeke says. "That's exactly why I really wanted to bring her back to you."

There's so much emotion in his face when he looks at me. I have to bite my lip to keep from crying.

"I get it," Mae says, with a nod. "What it means. Welcome home." She points to me. "It means you brought home back."

I can't hold it in any longer. I bend to hug her against me, and she leans her head into me with the childlike trust that's always floored me, even when she was the tiniest bundle falling asleep on my chest.

I've seen the wilderness; I've seen an endless sea in a gathering storm; I've nearly died, and I've watched the man I love come close to death, too. But there is no emotion out there as big as the love I have for this little person in my arms. That love—it's what got me home.

TWO YEARS ON

Lexi

"SO, WHAT HAVE you got for me, forager?" he asks, as he reaches to lift her aboard.

"Coriander!" Mae shouts, in the way you might shout *Duck!* or *Open fire!*

"Coriander!" Zeke responds, with similar enthusiasm. "Amazing. Wow. *Lots* of coriander."

His eyes soften as he smiles at me, offering me a hand as I step over heavily from the bank. It's midsummer, and the morning sun is already glancing off the water and catching in Mae's new glasses. Behind me, Ryan and Penny are setting up the chairs on the canal bank; Penny is detailing exactly what was said in her last therapy session, and Ryan is making supportive, Ryan-like *mm* noises, lifting our blue folding chairs one-handed while he eats one of Zeke's special breakfast sandwiches with the other.

As I step aboard, I feel the weightlessness that comes with being on the water. Technically, I still live in the flat two stories down from Penny and Ryan's place in Gilmouth, but I've spent less and less time there over the last year. Zeke used the rest of the money he inherited from his grandfather and the *Morning Cuppa* fee to buy this two-bedroom narrowboat just months after we returned from sea.

It's more than a home to him now: it's also our place of work. *Eugene the Traveling Seagull* can usually be found on a stretch of the Tyne, dishing out a menu built from whatever the local market has on offer. We've made a bit of a name for ourselves, thanks mostly to Zeke's cooking, but also to my Instagram page for the boat. We set out our next week's travel every Sunday on there, so everyone can follow our journey, and we will often find that when we reach our mooring spot there's already a queue waiting. My Instagram feed looks totally different these days: it's filled with latte art, vegetarian food ideas and tips on houseboat life, and it brings me nothing but joy.

"Sit down!" Penny barks at me from the bank. "If you *must* be on the boat, will you *please* sit down?"

I obediently lower myself into one of the striped deck chairs, trying not to laugh. Penny has tackled "working on herself" with such fervor that we've all inevitably been caught up in the process; for the past six months she has been trying to become less co-dependent, which has manifested as her aggressively turning the tables and micromanaging the rest of us. She'll swing back the other way soon, and end up somewhere around healthiness—that seems to be how it goes.

I shade my eyes and watch as Mae unpacks the bag of vegetables from the market for Zeke.

"Celeriac," she says, very seriously, holding it up for him. "I only found one."

"It's a beauty," he says, inspecting it with a level of interest that you might think is to humor his child, but is in fact entirely genuine.

"And eggs," she says, then shrieks as Zeke fumbles the box when she hands it to him. "Dad! Don't break them!"

I smile. Mae is so at home on the boat—she shrugs on her life jacket the way she slips into her favorite *Frozen* rucksack (*Frozen* still hasn't got old. I think every member of our very modern family now knows the words to all the songs). The second bedroom on this narrowboat is hers, and she loves her adventures on the water almost as much as her father loves taking her on them.

"I think we'll have . . . spiced scrambled eggs with fresh tomato and coriander," Zeke says.

"And?" I say. "Tell me you didn't forget."

Mae grins at me and pulls the last item out of her bag. "I didn't forget! Here you go. For the baby," she says, pointing at my swollen belly.

Chocolate digestives. My number one pregnancy craving. I reach for the packet, already salivating, and Zeke laughs. He always comes alive on the water, and I do, too. It took me a little while to overcome the fear—and we are *very* careful with our moorings these days—but over the last two years, I've realized what Zeke's father meant when he described liveaboard life as true freedom. It's nothing like the raw terror of our stint on *The Merry Dormouse*, but it does have some of the simplicity and truth we found in that time. Life on *Eugene* is stripped back to the purest things: good food, fresh air, love.

I lever myself up from my chair, digestive in my mouth, as the first customers begin to arrive on the bank and Zeke ducks into the kitchen, shoving open the hatch with one hand and reaching for his frying pan with the other. Then a heat slides through my belly, a convulsive force like a squeezing fist. Not painful, but strong enough to bring a gasp from me.

"Zeke?" Penny calls from the bank, her eyes on me.

"Yup?" he shouts back.

"Zeke . . ."

Penny points to me as I lean forward against the railing with a low, slow breath.

"I think your next adventure's starting."

Acknowledgments

I owe a *lot* of people a big thank-you for helping me with this book.

Let's start with Tanera, who picked me up and dusted me down every time I stumbled with this story. Thank you for being such a supportive agent, and for your belief in me.

Next, it has to be Paddy, who helped me with so many of the details in this book (if you're writing about the sea, get yourself a friend in the Royal Navy), and who also gave me the courage to start it in the first place. Thank you so much for all your insight and encouragement.

To Erika Melen and Polly Clark, thank you so much for talking houseboats with me; Kate McAllister, thank you for letting me poke around your beautiful one! Mike Green, thank you for answering all sorts of bizarre questions about oil rigs; Neil Petrie, thank you for your help with the lifeboat logistics; Emma Bamford, thank you for giving me so much brilliant insight on life at sea. It goes without saying that any impossible things and unrealistic bits in this book are on me.

To Gilly McAllister, for being the kindest, most generous friend, for your unbelievably lovely endorsement of this story and for telling me not to give up when I sobbed at you on WhatsApp: thank you. Caroline Hulse, Lia Louis, Lucy Clarke, Pooja Menon, Nups Takwale and my family: thank you for listening so patiently and putting up with me being angsty. I promise never to write such a difficult book again. Probably. At least not for a bit.

To Cassie Browne, Cindy Hwang, Emma Capron and Kat Burdon, my brilliant team of editors, thank you so much for getting on board (. . . sorry) with this wild idea, and for all the help you gave me along the way. As always, the book is so much stronger and bolder with your expert advice. I'm grateful to the whole team at Quercus and Berkley for their incredible creativity and enthusiasm, and want to say a particular thank-you to Jon Butler, Ella Patel, Hannah Robinson, Ella Horne, Katy Blott, Charlotte Gill, Khadisha Thomas, Angela Kim, Elizabeth Vinson, Tina Joell, Hannah Engler, Chelsea Pascoe and Lauren Burnstein.

To the incredible readers who share their love of stories both online and offline—thank you for spreading the word about books you adore. It means the world to authors like me, and meeting some of you on book tour has been one of the biggest highlights of my career.

To Sam, the love of my life. We might not be fighting storms together, but we are battling toddler tantrums and childcare crises, and sometimes that can seem like plenty. There is nobody in the world I would rather have by my side through this adventure. Thank you for being my person, always and forever.

And finally, to Bug, and to the little one curled up in my belly as I write this. Thank you for showing me a new, vast, bottomless kind of love. Thank you for teaching me that I can be so much stronger than I ever believed I could. Thank you for every single moment, from the dark times in the middle of the night to the snuffly warm cuddles in the morning. I cannot believe I am lucky enough to be your mama.

Photo © Holly Bobbins

BETH O'LEARY is an internationally bestselling author whose novels have been translated into more than thirty languages. Her debut, *The Flatshare*, sold over a million copies and is now a major TV series. Her subsequent novels *The Switch*, *The Road Trip*, *The No-Show* and *The Wake-Up Call* have all been instant *Sunday Times* bestsellers. Beth writes her books in the English countryside with a very badly behaved golden retriever for company. If she's not at her desk, you'll usually find her curled up somewhere with a book, a cup of tea and several wooly jumpers (whatever the weather).

VISIT BETH O'LEARY ONLINE

BethOLearyAuthor.com
 BethOLearyAuthor
 BethOLearyAuthor

Ready to find
your next great read?

Let us help.

Visit prh.com/nextread

Penguin
Random
House